Newtons Sleep

Faction Paradox

Newton's Sleep

by Daniel O'Mahony

RANDOM
STATIC

First published in New Zealand in 2008 by
Random Static Ltd
PO Box 10104
Wellington 6143

www.randomstatic.net

Cover and title page illustrations by Emma Weakley

Created using X∃TEX and GIMP on Ubuntu linux

National Library of New Zealand Cataloguing-in-Publication Data

O'Mahony, Daniel, 1973-
Newtons sleep / by Daniel O'Mahony.
(Faction Paradox)
ISBN 978-0-473-12498-4
I. Title. II. Series.
823.914—dc 22

Every body perseveres in its state of being at rest or of moving uniformly straight forward, except in so far as it is compelled to change its state by forces impressed.

A change in motion is proportional to the motive force impressed and takes place along the straight line in which that force is impressed.

To any action there is always an opposite and equal reaction; in other words, the action of two bodies upon each other are always equal and always opposite in direction.

Book One: The Rituals of the King

⇛ Chapter 0: *The Waste Book* ⇚

Impelled as though in sympathy with the earth, a spittle's-worth of dark humour slips from between the high branches of the tree into the mild air. So it plunges from its zenith, drawn by its yearning for the honest Lincolnshire lime. Thus does base matter descend, while pure spirit rises to join the light.

This hungry glob does not however find the soil, but impacts instead upon the head of a boy stretched out in quiet contemplation upon the ground at the foot of the tree. So a story is a-borning, one that shall bear repetition until Judgement and yet grow more grand and pregnant with each telling. Like a coin it shall be passed from party to party, its sovereign features slowly obliterated by the erosion of hands, until the markings be smoothed and unrecognised. Thus the fallen matter, which in fact most keenly resembles the manure from which all garden idylls spring, becomes in fiction a happier symbol; how sly that it should be the apple, that sweet fruit of bitter knowledge and exile. But this is not Eden bounded by the Witham, and this boy, this youth, is no Adam. He is a child of nine summers with shite on his brow.

Observe the boy, on his blanket of warm grass, in his cradle of grey tortured tree-roots, in his open-roofed bedchamber of hazy autumnal warmth. Observe his lank limbs, spread careless and empty of purpose. Observe his lolling head, the blond crop of his scalp, the beak'd face, the eyes oscillating palpably below the drooped lids. You might think him idle. You might think him asleep, and he *is* dreaming in his own fashion, but he is not idle. Sloth is not his sin; he has spent his day dialing (it having been determined that he is not fitted as a shepherd, neither as a merchant, and is therefore doomed to be that least practical of animals, an educated man). In his dreams he dials still, smoothing and shaping raw stone with a diamond-sharp blue blade. It is a more precise instrument than he has ever found in his waking life, making for a nicer dial on which ever finer gradients of shadow will reveal the stations of the hour in detail unknown even to the astrologers of Cathay or Ægypt. These are, he contemplates in his dream, the oldest machines to be the work of man; only the heavens themselves turn on a finer and more perfect mechanism. In his dream he builds a great Palace of Time to contain all his dials, a plain wood house of ever-expanding wings and atria. This is Heaven and he will be its architect.

These are not the dreams of an idle child.

But he is a child of man and therefore sinful, and this sin – because he follows the true faith – cannot be wiped clean by the sanctified pisspot-fonts of Rome or all her whorish indulgences. If not sloth, then – what? It is not gluttony, his meat is on the brain not the bone. Lust, then? Lust has its smiling possibilities. These are cold years, but the summers are yet warm enough for the local children to seek out cool and lonely waters. They go in groups to bathe in the ponds or the streams, this lad among them, though he is neither an intrepid boy nor a healthy one and is content only to wade while his half-friends sink naked to swim below the line of the water. Once in jest they caught him and held his head under the surface, untroubled by his thrashing, releasing him at their leisure. His skull swelled when he broke into the free air, while blood and bile dribbled from his nose and mouth; he had swallowed from the stream, and was afflicted for a month by fevers and flux. They had most blasphemously baptised him, but while a-bed he had contemplated the quality of light that penetrated the murk, and found there a riddle that he turned casually in his mind. He will unlock it later; more often his thoughts turned to the bodies of his companions, friends and villains, sons and daughters alike; but this is the innocent curiosity of a child. As an adult he will lust for men – and also for women, but most often for men – but it will be a penitent's flagellant lust, a tamed thing that inspires as much disgust as pleasure. It brings home proper Godly guilt as its harvest. Do not look for lust here; it does not drive him.

Oh, but there is pride.

His sleep and his dreams are those of a woken mind. He merely covers his eyes from the sun, which lies in a warm pane across his face. The sun has been a pitiful thing in these years of his life; there is a cold winter coming in, but there are better days yet to come. He dreams of how he will fill those better days. The shite spatters on his face as though it were a new thought, inspiration from the divine. *I will have a book*, he decides. He can see it already, waiting for him on a trader's stall. A heavy book, with yellowed pages that smell of must and learning, though all those sheets be yet blank. It was once proudly bound, but the stitching has disrepaired in its travels, its spine infested with spiders and small insects just as the spine of man contains his unproven seed. He sees himself, a little older, touching the book, worshipping it, wooing it. Each season it is taken, and each season it returns, and he comes as though a puppy in love to watch it lay upon its stall. How he fears that other hands will spoil her. How he yearns to spill ink on her pages with his thoughts and designs. The stallsman, once suspicious of his attentions, grows to love this gangly moon-struck boy. – You might save enough coin to buy it (says he) – And how long will that take? (replies the boy, now truly a youth).

The book's keeper laughs, then shakes his head sadly, then laughs again and ruffles the youth's bowl of hair. – Maybe one day you could prevail on someone to present it you? (he speculates, correctly as it will transpire) – And will you keep it for me until that day? – (another laugh) I must sell it to who will pay for it. Oh, don't look so glum, boy! There will be other books.

– But I want that one!

One day I will have a waste book of blank leaves that I will decorate.

Beneath the tree, he shakes these thoughts from his head, somehow uncertain in himself that the dream has not already come to pass. In shaking, he feels the patch of foreign skin that now dislodges further and drips across his eye; and for a moment he thinks himself wounded; and for a moment he thinks himself dead.

Lately cannonballs have flown their arcs, leaving the crystal sky unbroken, while on Earth their traces are all too visible: Englishmen reduced to piles of offal and powdered bone; the ruins of fastnesses, once impregnable, now shattered and exposed; the earth ripped asunder and scorched by sizzling violent impacts. The glass dome of the sky is undisturbed, and Heaven has never seemed so far away. So are proved the observations of the Europeans; of Copernicus, Galileo, Brahe, Kepler, and of freshly-dead Cartesius (whose worlds whirl not by the command of the *primum mobile* but on dimly-imagined vortices): the celestial spheres are of a distance only God can conceive. Yet as the divine recedes, it seems also terribly closer. War on Earth presages War in Heaven; the struggle between the holy houses of Christ and their eternal Adversary has erupted among the living. The party of angels is in ascendant, though not yet triumphant. The good old cause has routed the forces of kingly tyranny upon the field, and those Englishmen who despise our Protestant liberties have fallen silent; but they are not yet extirpated, and royal sympathies – so often clothed as though of a part with gentle living and good government – conceal the actions of those true and monstrous traitors who have suckled their love of slavery from the teat of the She-Wolf. All Earthly affairs thus lightly conceal the true conflict that shapes the cosmos, and all occurrences are as portents of the divine, or of the damned.

And does our boy believe this? Perhaps he has not yet thought on it too long nor too hard, but if prevailed upon, and if assured that an honest answer will yield no harsh reward, he might say that he is not yet wise enough to draw a conclusion and that more observation and patient measurement is required. Such equivocation obscures his true conviction about the case of the world: if war be fought in Heaven then Earth be strewn with its portents. He believes *this*: as above, so below.

What to make then of this caul bespeckling his face? He puts his fingers to it and scrapes it away. He holds it on his tips and it has the glistening look of shite, not birdshite as might be expected, but the shite of beasts or men. See him furrow his brow, disgusted as any boy would be when showered with diseased soil; but see that he still does not remove himself, as any boy would, but stays lying in his poise of deceptive contemplation. He does not run to the nearest brook or well. He does not even wipe his hands. That wrinkle he wears grows, with each passing second, less a mask of disgust and more one of perplexion and enquiry. This substance is not wet. It does not have the texture of shite, it is uncommonly smooth. It does not (he sniffs) smell of shite. It does not (he pecks) taste of shite. It is black and viscous, but he knows no earthly substance like this. It is an unknown humour.

He rolls the glob onto his palm and stares, as if wringing further truths from it. They do not come. They –

He no longer has a boy's smooth hands. The skin is tautened and lined with experience, the fingertips sharpened and flattened like a worn nib. They contain old aches and twinges. These hands have been washed clean of ink on more occasions than the numbered days of his span. There is no dirt on his palms, but a puffed satin pillow bearing clean coins, sparkling metal fresh from the mint, bearing the likenesses of monarchs as yet uncrowned, perhaps not yet born.

He holds them out for inspection. *If it please Your Majesty* –

No. He tries to fling them away. He has a boy's hands. He has shite on his palm. There was no pillow, there were no coins, there is no Majesty. He finds himself shivering out of a waking nightmare. Carefully he rolls the unexplained matter into a ball, as he would the skin of a cheese. It sucks to his fingers. There are no more answers to be found here, so he shifts his investigation elsewhere, turning his head upwards towards the source, the high branches above his head.

Caught and held among the tangled limbs is the shape of a man. The boy wonders how he came to be there, for he could have not have climbed so high without setting loose some alarum or motion to stir the boy from his contemplation. Nor has he been resting there since before noon; the shroud of leaves might conceal, but not from this distance, nor a body so large. Besides, there is something about this bodikin that draws the eye, a blankness that cannot be avoided. Well, then, he must have fallen from the sky.

The boy laughs. His laughter is a death-rattle in his gullet, and is not pleasing to the ears of others, who have heard such noises too frequently before and too often in circumstances not conducive to good humour. So he does not laugh among them, and is thought to be a most humourless fellow. He springs from where he lies, for he was always alert, and determines to climb the tree. It is an easy business for him; he is forever scrambling into unlikely places in his investigations. His hands pass lightly over the green mosses of the trunk, across the peeking purples and yellows of wildflowers, around the secret crevices that house teeming colonies – roanokes, jamestowns, whole americas – of a million insects, until he finds a secure handhold. Another follows, a third, a fourth, so he scrambles up the tree by increments until his hands and feet be resting safely on branches and boughs, and he comes at last to his dripping benefactor.

The man in the tree has no face, which is the second of three remarkable attributes to command our lad's attention; first and most terrifying is that he is a black man. And our lad almost plunges from his perch in terror – *the Black Bastard*!

For it is known that the Bastard, though routed and fugitive, is abroad in England. He no longer stands at the head of a troop of Papish Scots, nor a horde of wild Irish – they were smashed by Oliver's army some weeks since – but the Bastard himself escaped the field, his head intact upon his shoulders. He is a supple one; he slithers like a serpent, he dances like a reed, unlike his father who would not bend upon the winds of righteousness and so snapped and lost his head. The Bastard is at large, and though hunted, he has the Knot, that invisible cohort of supporters and sympathisers, to aid him in his flight and his dissemblances. While cool heads advise that he will most likely be making his way to the sea (and thence to exile, to some cave from where he might make pronouncements of blood-curdling impotence), other voices are more strident in their fears. He haunts England like a monster, devouring its bread, leeching its blood. He climbs through windows to pluck juicy babies from their cradles; he erupts from wells and drags honest men down to drown; he lures the unwary maiden with honeyed words that he might despoil her, and if there be no maidens why then he will make do with a pretty boy; he insinuates into churches that he might shit on the lectern and wipe his arse on pages ripped from his grandfather's bible.

These are the words of hot heads, and our young man knows this well. He is not swayed by panic or base gossip, though his heart tolls like a monkish bell in his ribs' cage. The fear that grips him is instead, quite rational. For he is, as best he can be in such provincial circumstances, a well-informed youth. This is not the Bastard. For one thing, the Bastard would be a fool to flee towards the Wash; this Shire is solidly for Parliament; its soil is so sensible of its faith that were he to cross into its borders the very air would cause him to shrivel into stone. For another thing, though called *black*, the Bastard is merely a swarthy man, dark of complexion and thick of hair; were he to be transported to the markets of Africa or Araby, he would seem as pale as any other sun-pinched Scot. Thinks the child then of those merchants of hotter lands; he has never set eyes upon a Negro, but his reason tells him that they cannot be truly black either, not the blackness of coal or pitch or night, any more than he with his pallid pink skin could be called white as snow, or the savage red man of America approaches that ideal colour found in the embers of a spent fire. These are similes and approximations; they do not describe men as they are.

But they describe this man, who is truly black, as of coal, or of pitch, or of night.

And the second miracle: this man has no face; he has a head, but it is entirely without feature. It is a smooth bowl on his shoulders, so perfect that it might be a helmet, but it is not of metal or glass. Those fabrics have the quality of reflection; if it were either, the boy would see the angles of his own face peering back at him, though stretched and distorted as they would be in a puddle. He looks into that face, that no-face, and sees nothing of himself there, and nothing of creation.

The third miracle; this is not a man at all. He is naked, he is spread among the tree with blunt branches punched smoothly through his body as though unbroken; his arms and legs are thrown open, and he is visibly without the privy parts of a man. Yet nor is there that puckered female difference that our boy has sighted while paddling sullenly in Lincoln waters; nor is there any mark left by barbarous surgery. The thighs meet with a smooth and uncomplicated join.

Our boy recalls Christ among the Sadducees, and the unsexed angels of His description. How his heart pounds, and how he regrets the foolish laughter when he first thought this creature might have fallen from the sky. Yet, if this is an angel plung'd to earth, where are his wings? Where his halo? Why has he been so expelled? Is he perhaps a casualty of that great conflict imagined to rage beyond the horizon? If this is an angel and not some eructation from the pit, then how fares the War, for God and Man alike? Wind catches the branches, the leaves rustle, the boy shivers, the green-cast light moves in patterns across the angel's broken body.

It is surely dead. It is impaled. It is burst. It bleeds from every part of its body, its skin – the colour but not the texture of coal – hanging in ripening beads. The boy feels for this dead thing, no matter what its provenance, for it must have been exposed to intolerable pressures in its journey through the voids. He imagines it falling and enduring, sparking like a firework, only to drop hither into this tree and expire unnoticed and unmourned, save only for a child caught beneath its wake.

He puts a hand to its body. He seems to touch empty air; it is not even cold.

He removes his hand and the body comes with it, the blackened skin moulded round his fingers like a glove. It feels not unpleasant; it looks far worse. The boy, briefly careless of his footing, stumbles back, and the body stumbles with him. The fuliginous tide rolls onto his forearm, and advances steadily toward his elbow. He scratches at it, but his blunted nails make no mark on his new second skin. He kicks at the body – still more foolish, his naked toe plunges into the yielding corpse and is swallowed, followed by foot and ankle. He struggles, but it is only panic and it is ineffective; in a few moments the body of the angel has consumed him from tip to toe. It saves his face for last, and only as it swarms across his eyes, his nose, his ears, and into his mouth does he think to scream. It comes out like a squeak on a reed. The angel skin wears him now, smothering him, sinking into his pores, his organs and beyond into his very –

He is not dead. He did not die then, all those summers ago as a boy. Today they call him the Master. He came through draughty Whitehall passages bearing the new coins on a puffed satin pillow for the inspection of His Majesty. All Masters answer to higher powers, and even Kings are commanded by God; he has, after some consideration, grown to accept this as a practical position, though he might grumble sometimes in his cups about that promised republican paradise, now lost to time. If we must have a king, then let it be a reasonable king as His Majesty is, a dull personage who turns his attentions to England and her attendant nations with bored reluctance, not with any kingly passion that turns in time to oppression. Let him be this blunt Orange Duke, this Prince of the Republic. Let him set aside kingly wrath only for those who seek alternative governance out of spite and wickedness; the noisome Papists, the heathen Irish, and that tiny Tory rabble (out of – he sighs – many good Tories who have abided the new *status quo*) who have pitched outright into treasonable Jacobitism. The Master sits in Parliament for Cambridge now –

Do I yet? That will happen, but is it happened yet?

– and still speaks for the good old cause, but accepts that the cause has been transformed by time and new certainties. He sits in a Parliament that has approved and checked the King's powers, thus is the circle squared and old grievances resolved. Royalist and republican, Whig and Tory, now we are all one. Besides, he is older.

But – oh! This king is a tiresome man!

The Master speaks to him of the new œconomicks, of how the wealth of a nation be measured not in the contents of its coffers but in the sum of its productions and the harvest of its trade. The King nods his bullet head and burbles his enthusiasms in his accented English, but he does not *see*; or rather he sees only the profit that might be made out of this new arrangement of affairs. The Master, tempering his frustration, attempts to enlighten; the King wags a finger as though he were still a boy. 'Uh, uh, uh,' says his scolding guttural Dutch mouth. The Master perceives a tree, a proud sapling carefully nurtured in good soil, trimmed, regulated, organised; he sees also that the growth is governed by numbers, buried so far in the infinitesimal that even his calculations cannot tease them free, but he knows that those unguessable numbers must be beautiful. They are the truest of God's works, they speak to his soul of their creator; this is what the tree represents.

Where he sees a tree – where he sees an act of God – this dull king sees firewood, to be sold for a pretty profit.

So it is with the recoinage, when trading throughout the nation shall be suspended. The King was easily persuaded; he sees an opportunity to line his pockets, to suck wealth out of the land and pay for his sports, his revels, and his pursuits. The Master feels faintly excluded from these sodomitical activities; he disapproves, because all carnality invites disapproval, but he aches to know more of them. The rough and boisterous king finds the company of rough and boisterous men pleasing, which has never been the Master's preference. His desire is for the smooth skin, the shy young man or genteel young lady, whose pallid bodies will reflect his nervous enquiries.

Oh, would that I had Sir Xtofer's grace and wit! Would that the Queen still lived! She was graceful, she was air while her oafish husband is of the earth. Yet I could never speak to her without losing my tongue to a Gordian tangle, while that wing'd troglodyte found it so easy to charm her.

The Master explains the significance of each new coin in tedious detail. The King yawns.

He has an odd sensation, as of falling from a great height.

No, the point of the recoinage is not to facilitate the greed of the wealthy (though, he admits to himself, this will certainly be an outcome), but to attain precision. All things must tend towards perfection, and if that cannot be achieved in governance, then let it be sought in other endeavours. Those coins we have passed among ourselves through our lives, whether they be issued for the purposes of a James, a Charles, or an Oliver, have become debased. They are cut. They are shaved. They are reconstituted with impurities. It is intolerable that this state persists. It is motivated by thievery, but it is worse than thievery. The dilution of the coin is a fall away from precision, just as the dilution of the soul with dross renders one more remote from the grace of God. So he says to those who call him unduly harsh. There is a worse crime than stealing bread, and for this they must hang, these wicked counterfeiters of souls.

– I would not care to be a hangman.

Your life will unfold as you see here. The rate of change through time is exponential. There will be no perceptible alteration within your lifetime.

– I will not be a hangman.

You will be a hangman. It is written.

'Master?' The King. His head bobs forward, a mask of genuine concern. He seems unshaven today, though the Master cannot be sure of his impression. The Master touches his temple and winces, feigning pain; he is more profoundly disturbed, the world seeming for a moment to have slipped away and beached him on a foreign shore.

'A – a slight headache,' he protests, affectedly.

The King's fingers percuss on his bristled cheek. 'You think too much.'

Graciously the Master nods, the Master smiles in acknowledgement of the King's trite observation.

The black ghost inside him rises upon his gullet, but will not spew forth; it has made a nest in him. The world slips again, he is tumbling, not through air but through moments of his life. He recalls seeing in a memory a silver-skinned man framed by the moon through his window, naked save for his flat helm and winged sandals; he recalls next that his memory was inflamed and addled by the fumes and retorts of his experiments and he saw nothing more remarkable than trees swaying and scraping on the night-winds. He recalls his industry in the plague years, his *annus mirabilis* that bore fecund innovation from the isolation of his Lincolnshire Ghetto. He remembers composing the *Principia*, and the treatise on *Opticks* (which is not yet written), and his summa vitae *Praxis* (which shall never be completed but will lie stillborn in his fingers on his deathbed). He recalls his struggles with his enemies, those base plagiarists who would claim his rightful and unique insights as their own; he would hang them if he could; he imagines himself in Hell and at their mercy; they have put their hookes into his flesh...

He recalls being born, being thrust out of his mother's body into the fallen world.

I will call this the limit. It is possible to extend earlier, but at this point the gifts of your life become intermingled with those of your mother.

The spirit is with the boy, watching him as he haunts the moments of his life, those few disasters he has already lived, those many triumphs yet to come. It dwells within him as the quietest and most unassuming of guests. It must then be a devil after all, but no – it does not guide him, it simply rides and sees the world through his eyes.

– Sir, am I to be your vessel?

No. I have need of a vessel, but it will not be you. Your journeys will be your own.

– Then what am I?

You are my port.

– Am I a good port?

You are the best-defended port on this world. My enemies cannot touch you. They dare not.

– You imply a purpose sir, and a mission. What then is our enterprise?

I must fulfil the instruction given to me by my creator.

– And what is that instruction?

Destroy the Adversary.

– That is the noblest of causes. How may I aid you?

Live your life, and let me shelter in its shadow.
– I will do my best.
Now wake.

He strikes the earth with a thunder clap, that now he thinks upon it, rumbles not within his skull but in the sky. Grey late summer weather has snuck upon him as he lay beneath the tree. Cracked branches and wood splinters lie arrayed around him, and dislodged yellowing leaves descend like dying moths to festoon his limp body. There is a jolt of impact in his spine; his hands extend upwards, the fingers curved as if to grip on the empty air. He has a certain memory of falling, a-whirling and a-tumbling through the sky, from a bough that could not take his weight; in spite of his aches he is not certain that this was not a dream, but one so vivid that his body now trusts it to be true. He does not recall climbing the tree, nor any reason why he might wish to. He remembers nothing of what he might have found in the high branches, though henceforth he will find that certain dark or bronzed mirrors will have an equivocal magnetism for him, one that attracts in fascination and repels for fear of what might be revealed.

The fields and the villages of this little Earth extend around him. He hears his world, the chattering of birds and the tumbling of water-drops down the streams; he breathes his world, the fresh sheep-dung and the shorn fields and the galvanic sizzle of the storm. He knows on some distant morning he will wake with all faculty for taste and smell gone, worn away like silt upon the shore by nights of strange alchemy. Rain cracks the sky, and our boy, whose life-to-come has been forgotten, laughs heartily and like death as it washes his face. He is not merely cleansed by it, but wiped to a blank. There is so much to achieve. He remembers his dream of the book, with clean pages to be filled and ordered. He imagines God birthing a creation that is both matter and – as the Divine John describes – a word. The book of all things is opened. The Lord takes up His instrument, and moving His bloody and invisible hand, He makes His first mark.

⇒ Chapter 1: *Killer of Sheep* ⇐

It was a bleak January morning, tasting of blood even before the dolorous stroke came down, tasting of the smoke from so many winter fires. The wind howled down from St Giles's Circus into the heart of Westminster, across the Palace of Whitehall towards the Thames. The entire crowd felt it, each and every individual no matter how well-wrapped they were for the day. Afterwards a story was started that the sacrifice had dressed in two shirts that morning, so that he might not be seen shivering on the stage and have his chill mistaken for fear. It may have been true, it might not; it was one of many rumours. It was one of the earliest observations recorded by Nathaniel Silver, who was there in the crowd when the blade fell and history began.

He was distracted by the old wound. It bulged in his skull below his brow, above his eye. It felt as though a fat bulbous spider had crawled into his head, first to lay her eggs there, then to die thrashing. No one around him acknowledged his discomfort; perhaps they mistook it for royalist distress. There were as many mourners here as there were celebrants. When he bowed his head, he was a subject of a kingdom. When he looked up again, he was a citizen of a commonwealth. He felt like neither.

This was true: a low moan rose from the lips of the gathering when the sacrifice's head came away from its body; but it was also true that there were ragged cheers and whistles. The guard pressed tight round the edges of a crowd that jostled them, but the movement was as much revelry as it was anger or despair. The fall of the axe was a symbolic moment for republican and royalist alike, to be picked-over at length in rival accounts. The first duelling apologies would appear in the next few days: the *Eikon Basilike*, said to be from the King's own hand, and the *Eikonoklastes* penned by the Secretary of Foreign Tongues (or 'some Puritan nobody' as the other party had it).

Beyond the war of words there was the ever-growing library of myths and legends about the day, which seemed conceived to bolster the King's case yet in the end were too strange to argue for any cause. A star of ill-omen fell from the sky that night; a whale beached itself at Dover, and thrashed, and died at the moment of the stroke; a raggedy man danced a gleeful jig in the street to celebrate the regicide, and a flock of birds fell upon him to peck the eyes from their sockets and the tongue from his jaw. Nate Silver was not bothered with the truth-hood or falsity of these little pearls of rumour, but observed their effect dispassionately. Whalebones were soon sold as holy relics; any number of disreputable travellers could produce (for a fee) an unlovely stone that had dropped from the heavens; and every blind-mute beggar from Berwick to the Lizard had a tale to tell – or, to be accurate, *mime* – in exchange for pennies.

When that cowled and anonymous fellow who had killed the King displayed his un-crowned head, it was in silence, without the customary denunciation of a traitor. The only words that rose from that stage to address the crowd came, like a Greek oracle, from the lips of the severed head. It was said the executed king held forth on a variety of subjects for half an hour before his eyes rolled back into the sockets and the royal tongue slurred into stillness forever. And that was certainly untrue, Silver noted in his commentary; he'd been there, he would have noticed.

For all his dispassionate poise, Nathaniel Silver was no different from any other Englishman, but he did not care that morning to share his convictions with the mob. As the mood of the crowd surged and turned like a tide, he felt grateful that he had neglected to wear his red-coat. He had no desire to be booed and spat upon by strangers, any more than he wanted to be applauded or kissed. He had not meant to come to Whitehall at all, but fate had made him unwell – his headaches grew harsher than usual in winter, and on the sixth anniversary of his deliverance one had a come upon him violently, as though it were a fresh wound. Fate thus placed him in care in London away from the troop; fate had also cleared his head that morning and replaced the pain with curiosity. He was compelled to attend the execution. It was in God's hands.

Even so, he had no particular desire to see another death, especially one performed so detachedly, like surgery but to an opposite end. He came to walk among the crowd, to gather impressions of the commoners of the new-born weal, to see the people for whom he had fought. Crags of faces peered out from behind bonnets and beneath hats; the young and the elderly both, they all seemed carved from breathing stone. They were waiting for life to be poured into them, to be animated. Oh, there was movement and gossip, and the laughter of children – who alone in the crowd seemed truly free, scampering and playing and japing and forming whorls with the children of strangers until their elders gripped them and shushed them. All adult bodies here twitched, but their souls were held tight in anticipation. They stood spiritually as still as the pikemen and cavalry who guarded their perimeter. Silver felt humbled among them. He felt he should stand out from the crowd, say something, declare himself. He did not – this was not the moment, and he did not wish to be misinterpreted.

In later years, he forgot the faces that he had carefully committed to memory. He did not, however, forget the smell or the crush, the twin and overwhelming pressures of the human flock. They smelled of sweat and dust and blood and fever, mingled with the muscular perfume of horseflesh and the decay of winter vegetables. They pushed around him until he could not breathe, while octopus-armed passers-by pawed and tugged at him; some meant to rob him, he had no doubt, but for the most part it was simply a production of the human entity. Hands reached out to touch unexpectedly across a void. It was, at times, intolerable, and he sometimes wished himself onto the balcony overlooking the stage; then again, quite a dense congregation was gathered there, and would hardly be afforded a happier perspective on this final ritual of the King.

At the appointed hour, Charles Stuart – by the Grace of God King of England, Scotland, and Ireland – was led from the window on his last parade. The crowd sighed, the crowd seethed. There were some cheers but they were soon silenced, perhaps by force, perhaps not. The King came out dressed simply, all in white beneath his hat and robe, so that he appeared as a new Christ on his road to Calvary. Long dark hair fell in curls upon his shoulders, soon to be shorn to republican satisfaction. He took his last mortal steps down to the stage accompanied by a chaplain and retainer, both of whom loomed. He had the saturnine eyes of a hawk, still regarding his subjects as prey; yet hands still clutched for him, to touch his hem as he came by. Silver, perhaps alone in the crowd, was unimpressed. Charles Stuart was, after all, just a man. Silver believed that. He had fought for that. He had killed for that. He had nearly, until the miracle had delivered him, *died* for that.

To put Charles's head on the block now and with such ceremony was to undo the great work of the Republic. It was an acknowledgement of the king's separation from his nation, and thus of his divinity. It was, in a subtle way that Charles himself might not have appreciated, his victory.

The stage was raised above the level of the ground, so the gathered masses had to crane their necks, even the tallest of them. The shortest shuffled or stood on tiptoe; the short-arsed king himself, had he been among the audience, would have been lost behind a tide of hats and helms and plumes. Children were hoisted up above the line of heads, as offerings, or for a better view. The watchers on the balcony leaned gingerly forward, and seemed ready to topple onto the stage so the King might die among a shower of well-wishers. The King, stripped of his robe and hat and medal, pulled on a white cap to make himself holier still. He knelt before the block, as if seeking supplication. Silver found hate difficult to muster, but resentment came easily; his head now throbbed thickly from the blow the King had struck him at Edgehill.

Upon the sacrifice's signal, the blade came down. Blood decorated the front row of the crowd. Then came the moans and the cheers, and when Silver looked again, there was only a stump leaking onto the stage, while the nameless axeman leant down to claim the head and hold it aloft by its hair. There were still gasps and shrieks from the assembly, and – Silver imagined – the strangled sound of a man spending. On the balcony, women turned their heads to look away, and on the ground a swell pressed forward, their handkerchiefs and cloths and sometimes rags extended to catch the blood or mop it from the damp red wood. Silver leaned forward, fascinated now by the aftermath as he had not been by the act.

The Puritans would ban the playhouse. Perhaps they sensed that it was no longer necessary; all theatre had been eclipsed, all stages become scenery, and all scribblers out-penned by the wrights of history.

Silver saw that already Charles was a Martyr King. The King's blood was a holy souvenir. It would be taken away and cherished; it would be scattered like seedlings through the realm. Those dirtied handkerchiefs would not be displayed on a stall or as a relic, and certainly would never be offered for sale – that was their significance. Faustuses and charlatans could construct chimærical whales out of the bones of many dead animals, and any able-bodied vagabond might concoct a fiction about the cruelty of pecking birds, but they would fool only those who wished to be sold a yarn. But these keepers of the royal blood had witnessed a divine Mystery and a divine conspiracy; their lips would wilfully be sealed.

The King is dead – and on the continent, a courtier commences a report with the fateful phrase *Your Majesty*, and is mortified when his teen-aged charge bursts into tears – and remains dead, long live the people! So? The sun will still shine, the crops will still grow. Even as the human sea began to break into their individual beads, the wary pike and horses yielding to let them slink away, Silver stood unmoved on his place. He was staring directly, he realised, at the naked sun, a poor thing these days and obscured by white clouds and black smoke. It was still sharp enough to sting his eyes and leave its impression on the inside of the lids. The sun will rise on his cycle; the seed will grow on hers.

He was not thinking of that yet, he was thinking of the pagan kings founded in England by Brutus in the age before Christ. He had some schooling and a little understanding of the old Roman accounts that described a fearful heathen epoch of blood and sacrifice, an age that extended in the numberless years since the fall. Those pagan lords, though not ordained by any remembered god, were themselves offered as bloody sacrifice at the end of their short reigns. To be elevated was to be condemned, after a certain cycle of years had elapsed, to death in the most barbaric fashion, a means that would in the modern world be granted only to the worst of traitors. Oh, they had power, these kings, and doubtless they abused it as fervently as any Christian monarch, but they must also have swallowed humbly when they came to be elected.

Yet it was their sacrifice that made the earth rich and kept the sun turning in the sky (or as now seemed to be the case, the earth turning in the sky around the sun); and their successor was the same lord of misrule, reborn in a new body with a new face and a new person and sometimes even a new sex. Those days, Silver saw, were gone, but he felt he had seen them re-enacted or evolved on the morning stage.

With his mind's eye he glimpsed a grand design. He was distracted and it was gone, but the memory of it remained.

'Move along now, sir,' said the red-coat, who had put his hand not unkindly on Silver's shoulder, 'there's nothing to see here.'

Silver shook and cleared his head. 'I was thinking.'

The trooper frowned beneath his visor and looked again. 'You're Nate Silver, aren't you?' Silver stared at him blankly. 'Don Taylor's mate? We fought together?'

'I've fought in many battles.'

'We fought for our money when Parliament wouldn't cough up.' The trooper cocked his head towards the bloody remains, still on the stage, soon to be removed and stitched back together for proper burial. 'You ought to be pleased.'

'Yes, I suppose I ought to be.'

Silver left soon after that, with his mind filled with thoughts of pagan kings. They shrieked as the skull-headed druids cut them open still living and scooped out their lights to make a better garrotte; they howled when placed like Guido Fawkes upon a bone-fire; they died worshipped and in agony with painted men and flower-decorated women dancing around them, singing and carousing and celebrating the death of one sun and the birth of another. This was the first of the many observations in his collection, soon joined by the legends of beached whales and fallen stars, and other, more subtle and sophisticated thoughts, as he sought to recreate that perfect vision of the ordering of mankind. But the first was scribbled only idly and on a scrap of paper as he prepared to move out. Having done with it, he put the paper away, then scrabbled to find it mere seconds later, so that he could add, in underlined text, the description:

Observations upon the cycle of the sun in the sky and the seed in the fields; and upon the same cycle as might be reflected in the affairs of kings and of all human polities ancient and modern, in the natural philosophy of the present age, and in the formation of the world that is yet to come.

Within a few days, Nathaniel Silver returned to his troop, and was marched hither and thither around a nation that – though now shorn of its Leviathan – was far from peaceful. Then the other nations were roused in revolt; he was dispatched there also, and conducted himself according to the standards he had set himself long before, which were high but not insurmountable even in trying circumstances. He gathered observations wherever he went, spoke aloud whensoever it was politic, and felt the stirrings of a pearl forming around his grit.

Wherever Silver went he took three things with him. The first was the pain in his head, which waxed and waned like the moon, but even in lulls was tangible by its absence and its promised return. He coped silently.

The second thing was his scrap of paper, which swelled over the years to become a pile of such scraps, then a bundle, and then a book. He spent his free moments adding to the sum of his knowledge or amending earlier reports. He read and re-read each page religiously, like a forgetful man with a scroll he had written to describe unto himself his life; but it was – he insisted to himself – a practical book and not scripture. Much of what he had written in earlier days grew obscure to him, as if blazed onto the page only half-understood, and as well as new observations he revised and clarified and made fresh interpretation.

The third thing Silver could not be parted from was a wooden box he had made himself, small enough to be carried in his hand or concealed in his pocket. This box contained the most precious object in the world, the proof of his deliverance and his miracle.

The ride from London was a short matter of days, but the journey felt longer. A hundred years he had been travelling, or a thousand, since the time this island nation was not yet Protestant, was not yet Christian, was not yet a nation. Only now he was so close to his destination did he begin to feel the slightest impatience. He was carried by cart, having no aptitude for mastering horses, and was met on the twilight road by a mounted party. He peered through the gloom. Civilians. Militia? No. He breathed out, but did not relax.

'Nathaniel Silver!' came a quavering call, in a voice a-feared to be out in these circumstances.

Silver called back: 'Sir Denzil Lynch?'

'The same,' the lead horseman replied and brought his beast alongside the cart so that Silver could grasp his hand in friendship. Sir Denzil's voice had the natural cadences of the mummer's shire, a little sharpened perhaps by learning and cosmopolitan company. He was a vague grey apparition in the gloom, under his cloak and plumed hat, but he was palpably timid. This expedition must have cost him much courage. Silver knew him from his letters and entreaties, but felt he would not find the man for sure until they were safe indoors.

'You are most welcome, Master Silver,' Sir Denzil declaimed from his high horse. 'Shall we' – he coughed, embarrassed – 'giddy up? We're but a short mile from my home.'

Silver nodded, and bade his driver to move them on. Sir Denzil's party rode leisurely before them, but the man himself remained abreast of the cart for a moment so that he could offer a stumbling apology.

'I trust our abrupt appearance didn't disturb you. I couldn't be certain it was you. The others are appearing on the road in their ones and twos and have been for the past week. You do not yet have an army, but by God you have a schoolroom!'

Silver brushed a smattering of insects from his face, where they had been blown by the breeze and the velocity of the cart. 'I don't understand!' he called, over the wind. 'What others?'

'Silverites, sir! Your followers!'

He closed his eyes; spider pain formed in his skull, and remained there even after his lids opened again. 'I have no followers,' he said, cautiously.

'Call them what you will, they have followed the rumours of your coming.'

'Then I may have led them to the gaol or the gallows.'

Sir Denzil laughed then, his first sign of heartiness but somehow not at all reassuring to Nathaniel Silver's ears.

Silver put cold fingers to his temple, but they failed to draw out the sting as he'd hoped. Sir Denzil left him after that to ride with his own men, and he continued the journey south in silence, save for the grinding wheels of the cart over hardened mud. Turning away from the pain, he saw ragged fires through a line of trees, and he imagined ironsides putting torches to thatches and barns to make great conflagrations, cleansing killing blazes. But the cart skirted round the copse, and in place of his morbid imaginings he found an itinerant camp arrayed upon a grey gloomy field like a makeshift freshly-planted New World village, a cluster of adequate tents and tumble-down huts. The fires were lit here, pitiful will-o'-the-wisp things that might have been pissed out, yet he saw an endurance and he heard a community, the chorus of human voices rising sometimes in fear and sometimes in anger but mostly in hope. And some were singing, a medley of plain hymns on one side and foul-mouthed carousing on the other. Silver bowed his head, having no doubt that these were the Silverites of whom Sir Denzil had spoken. They did not hearten him; gazing down on that poor camp merely proved the enormity of the task he had set himself.

They came at last to Sir Denzil's home, deeper in his estates. It was a plain house on the outside, but the interior was richly furnished, speaking more of luxury than piety. Silver warmed himself upon the hearth and wondered again at his host's sympathies, which his letters had always made seem ambivalent and unclear. He must be wary of this bluff knight, who was surely quicker-witted than he appeared. Sir Denzil had hugged him mightily before they came through the door. Be wary then, he amended, but also generous. He owed this man everything.

Servants scurried forth to relieve of him of his belongings, but he kept the case with his manuscript, and his box. He had dreamed lately of crossing London Bridge with them and unexpectedly hurling both into the air, so that they fell into the Thames and were lost forever. He woke from that dream sweating, and had since taken care not to part with book nor box, not even for a moment. He was bustled through into a dining room where a supper was prepared for him; here he got a first proper look at his companion in letters and the man who, to all intents and purposes, was now the lord of Silver's manor.

Sir Denzil was, by Silver's estimation, some twenty years his elder, the taller man here by a good foot, but also heavier. Age and worry – and perhaps good living, though not recent – had put weight on his flesh and his bones, and though balding, he had contrived a neat grey beard and moustache in the old Cavalier style to offset this. He had not seen action, Silver was certain, and envied him. There was a keenness in his eyes that belied the softness of his tongue and the heaviness of his body; not great intelligence, but shrewdness maybe and sadness certainly. Sadness was everywhere; it oppressed England by action or by consequence. Silver wondered how he must seem in Sir Denzil's eyes; like some thin Quaker raven, like some narrow scarecrow in a Puritan's stolen coat.

'Am I really so renowned that there are rumours of my coming? he asked, before he could sit.

'Someone put the rumours about,' Sir Denzil replied cheerfully. 'I can't imagine who. Now sit down and eat, you look starved. I hope' – he added, caution slipping into his voice – 'that you have not chosen to starve yourself? Or have an appetite only for vegetables?'

At table, Nathaniel Silver proved that he had neither. He was desperately hungry.

Sir Denzil said little as his guest ate, but watched him with smiling eyes, as of a boy who has won a prize. There were other eyes too, not in the room, but peering in from the black between two jambs.

'My daughter Alice,' Sir Denzil explained then, casting his head back to call her in: 'This is the gentleman I told you would be coming, Alice. Come and meet him. This is the fam'd Nathaniel Silver who is here to make his experiment on our new lands.'

The eyes blinked and hesitated, but at last she came into the room, like a timid sparrow coaxed into the light by warmth and spots of food. She was still a child, dressed as a child would be, and Silver removed his hat out of politeness; she paused then, seeing the roundheaded trim of his hair, but he smiled and that drew her further forward until she was into the room and then sat upon her father's lap.

Though she had made a pause, it seemed to Silver that she was not afraid of him, but was measuring him and making her own curious observations.

'How old are you, sir?' she asked, in a voice without any trace of her father's yokel imperfections.

'Alice!' Sir Denzil sputtered, but Silver raised an indulgent hand.

'I was born in the year the last king came to the throne,' he told her. 'Older than you,' he clarified.

'I'm older than I look,' she protested. She was a clean-skinned child, save for two blemishes on her right cheek.

'She's seven. Eight soon.' The father ruffled the daughter's hair. 'She's of an age that she won't remember the things we have done.'

'Just the consequences of them,' Silver murmured, but no one had heard him, as he intended.

'She is a spark!' Sir Denzil continued, but Silver was thinking just the opposite. Alice Lynch was not a spark but a deep pool, in which all light was extinguished by emerald coolness. She was lean and wore her hair in long tresses smoothed by careful brushing.

'She is that, sir,' Silver thought it polite to agree.

'And she sings. I will have her sing for us tonight,' Sir Denzil announced. On his lap, unseen, Alice pulled a face. Silver's smile conveyed approval to father and daughter alike.

Her mother was dead, he knew that; in childbirth or soon after, he guessed. A rich farmer, then, and his indulged but troubling child; he knew the type and would cut through them in time, to find the honest people beneath – but wait, Sir Denzil was holding forth again.

'I must admit, Master Silver, that when I first laid eyes on you I was perplexed. From the manner of your writings I imagined you to be an older man than me by far, then when I meet you on the road I find myself greeting a stripling. I would have put your age at no more than a score but now it seems you are half that again. Tell me your secret, sir, so we might both profit from it.'

Silver pursed his lips seriously. 'Alchemy,' he said. Sir Denzil's laughter sounded like a devil's fit. It was going to be a long evening.

Then Alice's tiny voice piped up: 'And are you still a soldier sir?'

A long evening, yes, but perhaps not as long as all that. 'I have given that up,' he said honestly.

Nathaniel Silver was rarely less than honest, if he could help it, and was afflicted by conscience when he could not.

As promised, Alice did sing for Silver that night, accompanying her father on the virginals. She was a poor singer. She told him so, tugging politely at his hem to catch his attention while her father was excusing himself. 'I am very bad,' she told him. He leaned down from his chair, brushed the hair back from her ear, and whispered: 'But I am your father's guest and he loves you, so once you've finished I'm going to sit there and applaud until my hands fall off. Got it?' She got it. She wailed out *It was a Lover and his Lass* in a manner that implied both lover and lass were feral cats. Silver praised her as effusively as he could, and she, his co-conspirator, accepted his words with quiet grace. Truth be told, she was only as bad a singer as Sir Denzil was a player, and Silver spent the recital imagining himself plucking the strings from the instrument one by one with a blunt knife.

In time Alice was sent to bed, and the two men sat by the fire to discuss their serious business. Sir Denzil lit a long pipe of foul-smelling tobacco. Silver declined, not wishing to so pollute his body, but indulged his host. Sir Denzil was implicating him in his vices and habits.

'I hope you know what you're doing,' Silver told him, not unkindly.

'I'm a man of the world, which is more than you are. You fellows will ever need people like me, or must turn to men who are worse by far. I'm not offering patronage and I expect no fealty.'

'That was understood,' Silver agreed. The bluff old man had retreated, the shrewd marketeer was taking over. Silver did not care to speculate too much on the extent to which his host would bend laws for his own enrichment. Smuggling perhaps? Anything worse would prick his conscience.

Sir Denzil's mouth expelled smoke. 'I was never a soldier, but I have done my bit for the war.'

'To the profit of all concerned,' Silver suggested, and Sir Denzil was not offended.

'Indeed, and I see no wrong in that. To make gains for my nation and my family from the miseries of the French or the Dutch or the Spanish is one thing. Then came Parliament's war, and that was another matter. My country ripped itself apart, and only stopped because it was too spent to raise blade or musket again. Only fiends would seek to grow rich from that, and instead I grew poor.'

He placed a familiar hand on Silver's wrist, and leaned forward as if to persuade him with the mere tension of his body. 'I never declared for the King. My neighbours flocked to the royal standard, but I damned both sides equally. That cost me much.'

Silver understood and nodded.

Sir Denzil: 'I meant what I said though, about the will being spent. There will be no more war within England for at least two generations now, I am sure of that. The Scots, perhaps. The Irish for sure, unless Cromwell drowns them all in blood. Foreign wars... well that is the way of things. But Englishman against Englishman? Not in my lifetime, or yours. The Protectorate may endure and the prince will do nothing to dislodge it. Or it may fall and then no hand will be raised to prevent a new King Charles riding to London in triumph.'

'You are sir, I think, more optimistic than I.'

'No, I'm just tired. There will always be hot heads and rabble rousers, but we are wise to them now. We would rather flinch and walk away than declare war on our own lands. This year we have seen how feeble armed revolt has become.' He puffed on his pipe. 'You believe in England's future, Master Silver, and men like you must be nurtured. That's why I'm doing this, so I might leave this life in good conscience.'

Silver saw his other meaning, and leaned back in his chair. 'You think the age of fighting is passed, and I will therefore be overlooked. I fear you are not alert to the state of England, or the curious interpretation of liberty that now prevails. The age of experiments is five years gone; they were tried and they were crushed.'

'Which is why we now have a better opportunity. How many poor nonconformists were tarred with the brush of the Levellers and crushed alongside them? Lilburne rots in gaol now, and no one will mistake your enterprise for his.'

'I heard Lilburne speak, and Winstanley too. I was minded to follow the one or the other.'

'Yet you did not. And Winstanley's problem was more trivial still: he contrived to piss on his neighbours one by one. Here I am your neighbour, and how more cosy can it be than that? Those others who had clout round here foolishly showed their colours, and live now only in expectation of the noose, their lands forfeited and given to us – to *you*, Nate. It is a gift to *you*. *Take* it.'

'I'm still not convinced.'

'Yes, you are. You were when you saw the strangers camped on my land. It daunts you, but you are sworn to it. You would not have come here otherwise.'

'There is the decimation and the militia.'

'The one is paid. The other may be paid-off.'

'The Major-General...'

'Goffe is a pussycat. He would sip milk from my bowl and sit in my pocket if it pleased me.'

'And if I preach blasphemy or sedition?'

'You won't.'

'You would be surprised how easy it has become to preach blasphemy or sedition without meaning to.'

'So long as you are discreet, there's no charge that can be brought against you that I can't make vanish, or reduce to the size of a fleabite. I know you from your letters, Nate; you are a good man put on Earth to do good, and I will protect you. Now let us cut to the heart of your objections.'

Sir Denzil could not have burned fiercer than his fire, but he seemed willing to fill Silver's lungs with his sulphurous personality.

'I don't know if I can do this,' Silver admitted.

Sir Denzil made his dreadful laugh: 'Have faith,' he insisted. It impressed on Silver no confidence whatsoever. Still, the old knight was full of plans that he began to lay out at length through his tobacco haze; it was said that this coated the insides of a human body with the same sooty excrement that caked the walls of a chimney. Silver leaned forward and held his breath and listened.

Tomorrow they would inspect the site and assess the existing buildings, perhaps also meeting the so-called Silverites and arranging the first migration into the experiment; the next day would see the start of construction of the walls, and if enough hands were willing, the first new houses; sundry details extended into the weeks ahead. In the longer term, Sir Denzil would support the colony with a percentage of the output from his estates; they hammered the final details out between them, the exact quantities, the limitations on the period dependent on the weather and the harvest and the size of the commune; also those respects in which Silver was obliged to be Sir Denzil's tenant and those in which he was not; also those circumstances in which Sir Denzil might request farming and labouring assistance from the commune; also the terms of trade and the terms of law; and a hundred hundred ant-sized details. Sir Denzil had it all worked out in his head, and Silver followed closely. He was afraid of finding the item that would prove beyond doubt that he was being cheated, but it did not arise. Instead, he began to see the old knight's purpose, and came to understand the ease with which he wrote off Silver's doubts. It mattered little to him whether the experiment worked or no, but it was a good thing to try and would be his mark left on the world and the legacy to his Alice. Sir Denzil Lynch imagined himself to be damned. Together they were plotting nothing less than his escape from Hell.

That thought kept Nathaniel Silver awake into the night, that and his trepidation about the morning's events. He placed the case containing the book and the box beside his bed, the first time he had not slept with it safely in his arms for many months. He had not described the book to his host. He had mentioned the box and its contents to no one. As he lay on his cot he heard Sir Denzil's rasping snores from an adjacent room, and from the other, the sighing breaths of Alice Lynch.

How had Nathaniel Silver come to have followers? It was true he had spoken more than once in public, and had put his name to pamphlets, slim digests of his latest observations. It was something he imagined all educated men did, and he aspired diligently to that condition. Somewhere in that his name had become currency. It had turned potent enough to draw people from across England to join his experiment. He misliked that. It was a dangerous year to have a celebrated name. Still, their enthusiasm and numbers excited him.

Blasphemously he wondered where it might end. Maybe Jesus of Nazareth had only ever been a man who couldn't keep his mouth shut? Divine, yes, he added to himself in his next breath, there can be no doubting that, yet perhaps his ministry was shaped as much by circumstance as design.

They started arriving from the camp while Sir Denzil was leading him on his first inspection of the land. The old manor, formerly occupied by a single family now fled to exile, could be set aside for those communites who came with large families, and also as the commune's heart, the schola. A recent brick structure of uncertain purpose – possibly a studio of some kind, as the former resident was known for his artistic leanings – would serve as Silver's own quarters. 'A grim Puritan hole,' Sir Denzil observed. 'You could sleep on the floor.' Silver nodded happily, not entirely mocking him. Then there was a barn, which could provide adequate sleeping space for temporary dozens. It was all most promising. As they emerged from the barn, they saw the ragged line of Silverites descending the track from the hillside like an army of the living dead.

There was no shared character to their background, save that most professed Protestantism of some stripe or creed, though Silver detected a certain Catholic reticence here, a Ranterish insolence there, and, in one particular case, a sharp-witted atheist zeal. He threw these observations unspoken onto the wind. Let them all come; like Joseph's coat, let his congregation be of many colours. He would have had Jews, Mohammadans, and Hindoos had such bodies presented themselves. He was surprised at how few were uncomplicated vagabonds, and how many were skilled in trade or craft. They had one thing in common, whether they admitted it or no: they were displaced, they were scarred by eternal war and had turned their back upon it. They would not be his army; the world had enough armies already.

The first man through the as yet intangible gates was lately a cooper, from London, named John Braybon. Silver clapped arms around him and clasped him in welcome. Later he resorted to shaking and kissing hands, or he would have expired from a surfeit of hugging. There were so many faces and so many names coming into his experiment, he despaired of remembering them all. Still, he tried. Here came Donald Bull and Elizabeth Frick and Thomas Wilson with his family and Robert Pettifer and Mister & Mistress Harding and Solomon Devices and Martin Creadle and Incorruptibility Brown and James Kendall and Emily Marner and Noah Gay and Howard & Elizabeth Penswick and Ann Brownlow…

Ann Brownlow was not beautiful as society reckoned beauty, but she turned Silver's head. She was, he would learn, daughter of a Bristol vintner whose family had fractured into five different factions when war came; she believed her brothers all dead, and had lived these last years first in the company of radical women and second in the company of her own disappointment. He saw little of this when they first met, save perhaps a smidgen of the latter. He took her hand, and she forcefully took it back and refused to be kissed. She had unclean strings of dark hair under her bonnet, a plain and horsey nose, a mouth full of outsize teeth, and sensible eyes, brown points in wide all-seeing whites. She was beautiful as Silver reckoned beauty.

Most of the Silverites slept in various rooms of the old house that night, but not Silver himself. He had meant to, but it felt too much like an unexpected temptation. Besides, he had his brick-and-plaster cell to make habitable. He lay on a hard cot with his coat as his pillow and the book and the box at his feet. He didn't sleep, but contemplated the walls, splashed with a little grime here, stains like blood there, and carved with obscure and obscene symbols. It smelled of old paint and old cabbage; he felt as though he had taken up residence in another man's soul, and that this soul was a mean thing bounded in base materials without beauty, without Ann.

The walls began to go up the next day, paid for from Sir Denzil's purse and overseen by Sir Denzil's men. Silver had hoped for a low and friendly barrier, a wood-fencing at first that might be replaced in time by stone; mosses would grow there, children could play on its top, old men could sit in quiet contemplation of the bleak Hampshire landscape, and lovers would meet here under cover of cowls and dusk to make their trysts. The walls of his imagination were dwarfed by the high tight poles of real wood erected round the boundaries of the experiment. He complained – not to Sir Denzil, who had business elsewhere, but to his man Hudd.

'You have enclosed us!' Not so much anger as honest protest. 'They will say I have built a prison.'

'These are dangerous times,' Hudd explained, conveying Sir Denzil's words. He was a blank bald man who left the impression that he would abide all manner of nonsense in pursuit of a quiet life. Ha! The very soul of Oliver's England. 'Sir Denzil wants you to present a formidable face to the world.'

'We present no face whatsoever; this is a mask without holes. It is most uninviting.'

'The time may come when you need stout walls. 'Tis only a precaution.'

'We are not Americans cowering behind blockades for fear of the red men.' He was losing his temper. 'We may have enemies, it is true, but let them come. All are welcome. Let their enmities be turned to friendship by our honest countenance and welcoming walls.'

Hudd shook his heavy head, at once sad and amused. Silver paced for a while to work out his frustration. It would not be healthy to waste anger on anyone save Sir Denzil himself, and Sir Denzil was wisely well away from the scene. Besides, it was at heart a sensible precaution. That precious bloom tolerance grew in unexpected abundance on England's wounded land, but it took only one snip to prune it down or cut off its life at the stem.

But a stockade! – that seemed to invite trouble.

'I liked your idea for a lovers' wall.'

He stopped mid-pace. 'Thank you; perhaps you could persuade your father?' Alice had come down from the house with Hudd, and had spent the morning trotting round the limits of the commune and drawing in its sights with her seldom-blinking eyes. She seemed impressed. It was a rare opportunity for her to play in the mud and slick dirt all over her shoes and skirts. She was not heavy, but she moved heavily, as if mocking her father who did not resemble her in the slightest.

'My father won't change his mind,' she said, not sadly. Her face, no matter the expression it wore, conjured an easy insolence. 'It's like shouting at the rain or hitting a rock.'

'Are you really seven years old, young lady?'

'Nearly eight.'

'Old enough. I could do with your wisdom. Would you care to join my imperial court as counsellor and chamberlain?' He thought he could make her smile but she refused.

'Don't be silly. I'm not wise. I can read and write... a little.'

'But you can't sing?'

'No.'

'Well neither can I. And I could only read and write a little at your age. I had some schooling, but most of the rest I picked up here and there on my travels. We were meant to be soldier-scholars, you see, though I'm not sure that's how it worked out.'

'What do you know?'

'A broad sample of the liberal arts. Some natural philosophy, which intrigues me even as it escapes me. A few words of Latin, picked up like a handful of pebbles from a beach that bounds the horizon. No Greek whatsoever.'

'Will you teach me some of that?

'That's the aim of this experiment, or one of the aims; to be a schola as much as a farm or a home or a new way of life. With your father's permission?'

'He'll give it if I ask. So I'll be a Silverite then?'

'No,' replied Silver, who was coming rapidly to mislike the word. 'You must live with your father, and I doubt he'd give permission otherwise.'

'You'd be surprised,' said Alice as she blinked, at last, like a dead frog restored suddenly to life by lightning.

He moved that evening to nip all talk of *Silveritism* in the bud. He assembled the community, and reminded them that he was neither master nor preacher, that he believed that God alone was the one true authority, and that if the commune were to have a name at all he hoped it would be the Church of Christ Sublime.

'But we like being Silverites!' called Edward Mudge, who had arrived that morning, as they were still coming in their dribs and their drabs. 'They'll call us some name in the end, some slur like *Ranter* or *Digger*, so why not make it one of our own choosing?'

'And what's the alternative?' – that was Ann Brownlow – 'If we're the Church of Christ Sublime then that makes us... what? Christ-ians? That name's already taken.'

He swallowed, and resigned himself to Silverites. He had wanted no kind of name at all, except 'the commune' or 'the experiment', but if it was the will of the majority and of Ann Brownlow, then he had no objection. Ann had expressed herself most forcefully, but with good humour; if it had not been for her, he might have resisted.

On the third day, the Silverites became builders, and set to work on erecting the first houses, the barns, and other structures. It was too late for planting now, and they would survive on Sir Denzil's indulgence and the profits of their labours until the spring – that was the plan, at any rate, and Silver was nervously mindful that such plans could go awry. It was his first real doubt since his confession by Sir Denzil's fire, and that felt an aeon past; in the meantime activity and complications had crowded them from his mind. But though they might have no crop, they had plentiful carpenters and other craftsmen, and the work went quickly.

One of the first structures – both the simplest and the most necessary – went up in a day. It was a small wooden shack with unadorned walls, a high narrow window, and a carpet of dry earth pocked by stones. It was completed as the sun flattened and bled on the horizon, turning the evening sky into a patterned pink curtain of silk. How humble that crude and tiny shack appeared beneath such natural majesty. It was under that sky that Silver gave his sole speech to his Silverites, something he dared do only once for fear of turning into a priest, a king, or a general. And he was none of these; he was a simple man, once a soldier, with an idea.

They expected something from him nonetheless; not instruction but inspiration. He stood between them and the new building with his arms held up and let them settle into hush. They were all there, more than three dozen weary souls now, plus Hudd (who was already on the bottle), plus Alice (who couldn't keep away, the spiritual opposite of her father who had not been seen here since the first morning). They were a rainbow of greys and browns and greens, any gay colours among them long coated over by grime or twilight. They had been gathering food and drink for a celebration that would whet the commune and bring it to life, and somehow an unheard communication had passed among them that this would be the night. Tonight there would be revels and good-natured drunkenness and – he looked hopefully to Ann, who leaned against the grim stockade and chewed on a long stalk of dry grass – love-making. They must be fertile, like the pagans. They were impatient, and for that reason...

'I'll keep this brief', he announced into the hush. 'We are all tired and we would all make the best of this evening while there is still a little light. Nonetheless a few words are called for –'

Heckles of 'hurry up then!' and 'get on with it!' He stopped talking, and found he was enjoying himself. He gave them a great unguarded grin, the first time they had seen a smile from him that was not a timid fieldmouse hiding from an owl.

'Liberty!' he called. 'We have heard so much of this word these last years, and why not? It is a great and powerful sentiment – and yet it is only a sentiment. It is a state of human endeavour that, like all others, is both corruptible and transient. Lately we have seen much of the hardships brought by liberty, and aye, the tyranny of liberty too, because all human action is subject to sin and there is no condition, no matter how beneficent, that cannot be subverted and debased by the lusts and greeds of sinful men. Worse than sinful men are those who would impose a false liberty upon the heads of others for their own profit and claim yet that they are setting us free.'

He paused, he breathed. They were listening. As always when he spoke, he marvelled that people would listen! 'I do not attack liberty itself, but liberty alone is not enough. It requires other qualities to sustain itself. The first and most important of these qualities is love.

'Without love, liberty is nothing. With love, it is everything. Love itself may be subverted, for it is all to easy for a wicked or unloving man to hurt another, claiming in word to be righteous, while yielding in fact to a base unspoken desire in his own soul. That is not love. Love is not constant just as man is not constant. For that reason I do not claim that we are here to build a perfect world, merely a better one in which we grow ever towards that one goal, the single vision of a love so pure that it renders good action from good intentions. Only if we can act with love can we be free.

'There will be fights here, quarrels certainly, worse probably. We will not agree, we will squabble among ourselves, yet look to the example of the loving family who so long as they be not unbalanced by irrevocable selfishnesses and stubbornnesses, will knit always together. In true love all actions are sanctified. The loving man cannot of himself sin. Without love there is nothing but sin. Those of you drawn hither by the expectation of a wicked libertinism that would indulge in self-serving lewdness, rapine, the free handling of knives and firearms, or the triumph of the strong over the weak, had best leave now. It will not happen here. No, wait – where do you all go?!'

There were spots of laughter; none had moved (though there were a handful of absentees in the next few days, who left the commune never to return, and Silver wondered if his words had cut too close).

'So what is sin? I say that sin is thoughts formed and actions performed without love. And what is God? We are told by all Christian parties that God is love. What they have neglected to add' – and he paused now before the blasphemy, though it would come as no shock to anyone present, except perhaps Hudd who looked as though he couldn't care less – 'is that God is nothing but love. God is in all things capable of love, and being loved, so God is everywhere. God is here! By loving – by *living* – we worship Him. By seeking that perfect and unreachable love, we dedicate ourselves to Him. So, do not look here for a church, because we *are* the church.'

They were getting restless. He coughed. 'Nonetheless, there are those of us who would make their prayers outside the glare of nature, and so we have built this retreat, this commune within a commune, this miniature church which is unadorned with any symbol that would separate us from the living reality of love. If I would command one thing of you it would only be this: ask no one what conversations they may have had with God in this praying room. This is the keystone around which all our buildings will rise.'

The stars were slowly becoming visible overhead, and the dimming light made it hard to make out the faces of his audience. They were reduced to a dull grey sameness, stood stock-still contemplating him as the Westminster crowd had once stood before their dying king; no Alice visible, no Ann, no Mudge nor Braybon nor Bull. No one spoke or laughed or cheered or booed. He could not be sure they had heard a word he had said these last five minutes. They were a ragged band, these tiny humans, sheltering behind a spiked wall against the enormity of creation, dwarfed by pinprick lights so infinitely distant...

He shook away that odd thought.

'Now that's enough from me. Go and enjoy yourselves.'

They heard that all right.

Nathaniel Silver was not in a mood for celebration. There was still too much to do and too much to worry about. He spent a few moments trying to catch Ann's eye, but she seemed wilfully ignorant of his attentions. He would be no cheerful spirit here and would only dull the party with his long-winded anxieties. So, after a time, he slipped away; he was after all just an ordinary man of no special import now that the commune was bringing itself to life; he would not be missed.

A lie. He hoped he would be missed.

He walked through a hole in the unfinished and unfriendly stockade and into the darkness. It was a dry night; he knew this land well now, and did not expect to lose his footing. He climbed the hill for some moments, then found a flat and comfortable patch of grass on which to sit and contemplate his work. The walls and buildings of the Church of Christ Sublime were of a piece with the night's darkness, but the lights of the party carried towards him, flickering like a moth caught on a candle. The same thought occurred and recurred; how little we are; how little we will amount to.

He lay with his back to the ground to study the stars instead. He hoped this would be how she found him, if his fantasies were to be fulfilled. – Why Master Silver, you are fled from the party? – Call me Nate. – Very well then, Nate, might I lie beside you for a while and press myself to your heat? – You may do what you will with me. – Do you think I would really be so forward, even in your dreams? You are in love with who I am, Nate, not what you think I might be.

He sensed rather than saw her approach up the hill towards his resting place; she was less sure-footed than him and stumbled and slipped a few times, but kept her silence until she was almost upon him.

'Ann,' he murmured softly.

'No.'

She squealed then, slipping on soft earth. He leapt up, reached out for her hands and more by luck than judgement caught her before she could fall. Her bones strained and popped but he held on and kept her steady; then he hauled her back to her feet.

'You saved me!' she squeaked, as if he had dragged her selflessly from a blazing house. Her gratitude sat unhappily with the sound of her fingerbones crunching in his memory. He sat back down on the earth and heard her settle beside him. Her skin was dimly glowing, that was all he could see of her; that and the white hood she'd worn in the camp. As he watched, she fumbled to remove it, shaking loose invisible long hair that fell across her face and obscured the light.

'You should go back home,' he told her.

He imagined her shrugging. 'Hudd is drunk. He'll sleep it off in your barn and take me back tomorrow.'

'You can stay in the house then, unless your father sends to bring you home.'

'Can I stay with you?'

'No. It's not proper and it's not comfortable.'

'And because you want her to come to you, don't you? Ann Brownlow. I'm prettier than her.'

'That's beside the point.'

'Why do you need a place of your own anyway, if you say you're not special?'

'I need a place to work and think. The others will have houses of their own in time. We've started building them already, you've seen.'

'That's not what I mean, silly. Why are you cutting yourselves from them, if you're just a man?'

Because.

'She loves you, if that'll bring you out.'

'She –?'

'Ann. She just doesn't know it yet.'

'And what makes you such a great judge of character?'

'Because,' Alice trilled.

Silver said nothing, and kept saying nothing until he became afraid that Alice might imagine he'd slipped away. Her breaths were unmistakable, little soothing bursts in the darkness. His were so shallow he need not have been breathing at all.

'I'm writing a book,' he said casually. It was no secret, but he had never spoken of it so easily before.

'I'll read it one day, when I'm good enough. What's it called? And what sort of book is it?'

'*The Cycle of Sun & Seed*. As for it's subject, well... I can never quite decide. It's always something new from day to day. It's my observations of the world, you see, and they're always changing.'

'My father knows printers. It could be published when it's finished.'

'I wouldn't like to put myself in further debt to him, and it's far from finished. It's a… history, I think I've decided, but it's a history of future events that are yet to come.'

There was a thoughtful pause from the night. 'So… kings and queens of the future, when they are crowned, when they die, what battles they fight, that sort of thing? I can't imagine anyone would want to fight a battle after reading your book; they'd know how it would all end and might as well stay in bed.'

'It isn't that simple. Perhaps it's better to call it a book that describes how the future could be, and how we could make it so.'

'Ah,' Alice sighed, 'but that just sounds boring.'

'It probably is. Let's not bother your father's printers with it.'

They waited in the dark as, slowly, the lights from the commune winked out one by one.

'I'd like to live in your world of love,' Alice said.

'It's still a tragic world. There would still be death.'

'She's not coming, is she?'

'No.'

In the lull, the night was filled with noise. It seethed with the presence of the unhuman creatures that were walled outside the commune, the furtive rustling they made across the ground, the hunting swoops from the air. He almost wished that Alice would sing and dispel the hungry silence with the wail of her goat-song. His wound, forgotten in the last days of activity, began to throb again until he felt he was bleeding from the corners of his eyes.

'I almost died,' he confessed, 'in battle. I went to Edgehill with a fervour for war and a child's faith in the rightness of my cause. And I was shot in the head.'

'That would have killed you,' Alice said.

'No. I was thought dead. I had a slow wound of the kind that kills over days and weeks. It robbed me of my strength and my reason for a time, but I survived. I woke again on Christ's Mass Day, when they'd already put me into the earth.' *Don't tell her what it was like. Don't tell her how you had to dig your way out through heavy layers of clay to reach the fresh air, because that would distress her. Don't tell her about the box, because that would confuse her.*

And don't tell her about the light, because that was sacred.

'Is that,' she asked at length, 'why you've done all you've done?' He couldn't see any expression or any gesture she'd made, but she meant the commune, perhaps also the book. He'd had to tell someone; otherwise his whole project felt fraudulent, a deluded man building an edifice on the fact of his survival when so many others had died. He told her *yes*, and he felt her nod in the darkness, her liberated hair tingling on the breeze.

'Then that's good,' she decided.

He held Alice's hand on the way back down into the settlement, afraid that she might slip again and hurt herself, or at least ruin her clothes, but this time she didn't fall. He let her sleep on his cot that night; he himself stayed awake until the morning, afraid of the pain that would well up again when he lay down as if in the grave, and overwhelmed with an exhaustion so immense that it made him too tired to sleep. Hudd would return Alice to Sir Denzil in the morning, but she would be back as an honorary Silverite. He showed her pages from his book before she slept, and because she could make no sense of the words, she held the paper reverently as if it were a holy relic. And once Alice was safely insensible in the arms of dream, he reached for his box and opened his one last secret.

How to explain what he had seen as he died, sweating and convulsing on his bed beyond Edgehill?

I saw Heaven opened unto me, and the new Jerusalem greeting my soul. I appeared to myself as one confounded into the abyss of eternity.

Yes, it had been something like that, but there had been more to the ecstasy and the agony of the sacred than light and sound and fury. There had been presences in the beyond, who took his broken self into the deep where Christ's scalpels and chirurgeons awaited him. He had seen that wretched puppet-thing, himself, spread out on the slabs of the divine abattoir, then slowly rebuilt by their celestial physics, knitting back together all the frayed imperfections of his life, until he was clean and whole again. They had not spoken to him, these mechanicals of body and soul who appeared to him as cowled giants in cloaks of light, but he knew their purpose and he wept tears of joy as they restored him, reborn and ready to be placed back on the Earth.

'But I can hardly tell her that, can I?' he asked the silent egg that nested in his crude box. 'She'd call me mad. And no other soul would be so generous as her. They would have me burned.'

The egg, as always, did nothing but sit in the box, giving off a faint light that suffused the room yet was not harsh enough to wake the sleeping girl. It had been silent and still for twelve years now, ever since that day when he'd climbed from the grave and had been found by the dismayed hospitallers. They'd sworn it had been clutched in his hand so tight that he had left impressions of his fingers on its soft shell, though these had soon rounded back into smoothness. It would not be lost, this egg, nor thrown away, nor stolen. It always came back to him. It was, apart from its glow and its strange substance, quite inert and quite ordinary. It refused all of Silver's efforts to unpick its mystery.

One day – he knew, he hoped, he prayed – it would hatch for him.

Not long after the commune was walled and established, Nathaniel Silver realised that he must kill a sheep.

There were still a few houses to build, though fewer than expected as the trickle of incomers finally dried up, and others chose – often regretfully – to abandon their fresh start and leave. There was bad gossip in the neighbourhood, and stories circulated that the Church of Christ Sublime was a pagan sect whose members cavorted naked, fornicated, and committed upon themselves the most heinous debaucheries imaginable; this prompted a surge of furtive and mostly disappointed enquiries. The early fluctuating population eventually stabilised at somewhere just over four dozen souls, mostly adults. Silver hoped that families would be attracted here, and would be raised here, because he missed the laughter and painless screams of children; but that was an aim in the long-term. The experiment had to live before it could thrive, and in those first months before the deep winter set in, he counted it a modest success.

Their manpower was depleted at the harvest as Sir Denzil called in his debt of hands and bodies to help in his fields. Silver himself – still the only teacher at the schola – remained, but was left idle. Alice was his only devoted pupil. Instructing the Silverites in natural philosophy was another luxury for the long-term. He paraded round the world he had made, and found it quiet and empty; except for the sick and the old and Alice, they were all in the fields. He resolved to find a fresh purpose for himself, and also to break his dependency on the kindness of Sir Denzil Lynch.

So he would be a farmer and a butcher both; he had no experience of either, but he had no doubt it could be learned. He threw himself into mastering the rituals of killing with holy devotion, attending on both Sir Denzil's slaughtermen and those few Silverites who had experience of farming; they dripped their wisdom into his ears. Most of the commune came from towns and had no grasp of country ways; still, so were the first pilgrims to Virginiae, pious urbanites who neglected to put practical tools on their inventory, and in their ignorance, would name a hare as a jackrabbit. Still, at least he had no ocean between his New World and the experience of the Old. Sheep were the most plentiful animal in these parts. He would kill and butcher a sheep, and he would do it alone.

The sheep they brought him was already shaved. Silver, by contrast, had let his hair grow long so that it curled upon his cheek and tickled the nape of his neck. The killing was done in the barn, where they gathered for their first and final meeting, the shorn Roundhead sheep and its courtly Cavalier murderer. The sheep was agitated, already transported a mile to the commune. The stupid animal backed itself into a corner and shat itself in fear. Silver knew the stench from battlefields, the abattoir of men, where offal and entrails were laid on the devil's plate. He had killed men. This should be easy.

He approached the sheep timidly, sat by it, and stroked its naked skin and petted its rough black nose, until it became convinced of his friendly intentions and allowed itself to be led into the centre of the barn, where Silver had placed his hammer, his knives, and his saws.

She. She allowed herself to be led. She was a ewe.

The hammer had a light wood handle that fitted perfectly snug in Silver's fist. The dense black metal head – black as the sheep's own rounded snout and ears and collar – was a weight, and needed a mild effort to lift it. He held it as far above his head as his arm could stretch, judged and tested his arc while the placated victim pushed her nose cautiously into his apron. With his free hand he cradled and pinned the sheep's shivering body. He brought the hammerhead down onto the sheep's skull; it fell in a smooth arc, like the pendulum of a clock compelling all men one second at a time towards the grave.

The blow cracked the sheep's head-bone, but did not stun it; as he had feared, he had not put enough strength behind it, and he paid the price as his maddened hurting victim shrieked and fought to break free. One black leg came up and slashed him across the face. He heard the bone of his nose pop and felt the blood ease from a new laceration on his cheek; his old wound was at least numb today, perhaps satiated by the thought of fresh-spilled blood. He punched back at the sheep, the hammer forgotten in his hand until it connected with the side of the skull. There was a noise like wet earth being crushed in a child's fingers, and when he withdrew his weapon, he found the less blunt end decorated with fur and blood and scraps of bone. The sheep, tired by its exertion, wobbled on its narrow legs and settled down on the floor to rest.

The hammer clattered on the floor; he had not been aware of dropping it. Now, while the ewe was stunned, he would have to slit her throat, bleed her, and allow her heart to stop. He hesitated before touching the knife, paralysed as he had been after Edgehill. When he finally moved his fingers, they touched the boning knife, resisting the lighter blade he'd intended, as if trying to argue against this final killing blow. What persuaded them was the sense that he had already gone too far, and that killing the sheep was the only kindness he could offer her after dashing out her brains.

He found the sharp knife, then the proper place for the incision on the ewe's throat, then made his cut, drawn long and shaking round her neck. The blood fizzled out, much as he expected, splashing his apron and his face. He had not expected God would address him to spare his victim, as he had once instructed Abraham, and his expectations were met: God was silent. The sheep fell into his arms, like a dying soldier, and Silver cradled it as the sheep-blood seeped from the carcass to the floor and the throbbing of the sheep-heart beneath his hands grew fainter until he could no longer feel it, until it was no longer there.

After that he was left with two advantages; the first, that he was too numbed by what he had already done to feel any more remorse; the second, that the sheep was dead and could suffer no more injury. So, as if watching himself through a cold fog, he skinned and gutted and boned the creature, leaving the edible remains. His work was not elegant. It was sheep-meat, that was enough, and he had proved something to himself. After that day he would kill more sheep, but while the Church of Christ Sublime lasted he never again ate cuttings from the bodies of the dead.

In later days, of course, he was obliged to.

He saw Ann Brownlow as he came out of the barn, still thick with the sheep's guts and blood. He moved like a dangling mannequin, swaying on the motion of strings but without feeling in his limbs or his heart or his head. – I must stink, he said to himself as Ann hoisted her skirts and moved swiftly across the mud to join him.

She draped herself across his shoulders; he wasn't sure if she was mocking him. 'Oh, my brave soldier –' she began. He shrugged her away.

He stripped off his bloodied outer clothes and went to a trough to wash away the evidence. The water was freezing and burned his face. Blood dripped in pink puddles around his feet. Finally he felt soaked and shivering, which was an improvement on *nothing*, and went in his bare feet and breeches back to the brick house. He found Alice sat cross-legged like an Oriental sage at the door. She greeted him with one hand raised.

It was hard to close off his heart when Alice spoke to him. Her mix of guile and innocence made her a perfect companion, neither faculty having been corrupted by adult disappointments.

'You won't have to do that again,' she told him.

He said nothing. So she picked herself up, patted the earth from her skirts and said: 'I love you more than she ever will, Nate.' She stood on tip-toe to kiss him on the cheek before she made her way placidly in the direction of the Church's gate; now an aggressive mouth of wooden teeth as per Sir Denzil's fancy.

Ann Brownlow was sitting on Nate's cot when he came inside, with his thickest blanket raised to cover her nakedness. There was little light, so it was impossible to tell if she had been crying, as he first imagined. Still he said nothing, but went to sit beside her, and presently they kissed and committed acts of fornication.

If there is love there is no sin.

Love was his wound and his weakness, he would decide later. It turned his head when it should have been staring straight forward at the dangerous road before him. It distracted his energies when they were most needed elsewhere. He didn't regret it though, not a moment of it.

Before the year was out, he and Ann were married, though not in a way that was marked in any parish record, or in a fashion that would have been recognised by the faiths beyond the commune walls. They were married in the eyes of God and God alone; he and she went to the praying room together, she dressed in a gown of white patches and he in his dusty old trooper's coat, which was as formal an attire as they could muster. They went in at noon and came out as the midwinter evening was drawing in. Whatever vows they made, prayers they offered, and service they concocted went unheard and remained secret.

Alice Lynch sat outside, not listening but occasionally expressing her feelings by making blunt exclamations at passers-by. 'Huh!' she grunted. 'Huh! Huh!' She seemed to be happy, in other ways. She had told her father about *The Cycle of Sun & Seed*, and after a few weeks as a constant irritant at Silver's ear, she had persuaded the author to surrender a portion of his manuscript. He handed it over with reluctance, and Sir Denzil read it with greater reluctance still. 'I know only every third word in this,' he explained patiently when they next met, 'and even then they make no sense to me. But I will make enquiries in London, and if it is sound it will find a publisher.'

Silver had less faith in that proposition, but allowed Sir Denzil to proceed, secretly elated by the possibility. He spent less time in the fields or the schola, which as a result grew neglected, and concentrated his efforts on his revisions and his marriage.

In the end these were just more distractions; already they knew it was a thin harvest, and every meeting with Sir Denzil brought worse news about their prospects for the winter. No one would starve, Silver was sure, if the commune grew no larger, but there would be many miserable, barely-filled bellies. Faced with that prospect, the congregation of the Church of Christ Sublime began to contract for the first time, squeezed thin by hunger and the lure of easier rewards elsewhere.

Silver consoled himself; he had hopes for the new year, he told his wife. The commune would subsist long enough to sow its first harvest; it would begin to wean itself away from Sir Denzil's teat. There would be students at last and families. Perhaps they could tear down those awful walls and raise new ones. It was all a question of endurance. If they could but make it to the spring...

On the first day of January, Robert Pettifer was found moaning outside his house in a mud patch where he must have lain all night, unnoticed. He was dead in all but fact, but not from exposure. When he was carried inside and his muddied clothes taken from him he was found to have blue spots upon his breast. He passed within hours.

Within a week, three other Silverites had fallen ill with the same symptoms and were isolated in their houses. Silver went to them one by one with a soaked handkerchief as his only protection, but he could do nothing for them, and they died as Robert Pettifer had. Similar outbreaks sprung up in the local countryside, and it was no great consolation to Silver that his unloved and unvisited commune had only a tiny number of fatalities. A dozen others fled the visitation; most of them caught the blue death in the outside world and died less than two leagues from the Church's walls.

Ann Brownlow died on the tenth day of January.

She did not wish to be buried, claiming a fear of tight spaces, so they burned her instead in a ceremony outside the praying room.

Alice Lynch sang for her – an ugly, discordant wail as the body vanished into flames and ash.

Alice scratched at the door to Silver's brick home, mewling like a housecat to be let inside. He couldn't make out her words through the door, but the sound still distressed him, so he wrapped the blanket round his head to muffle them. She loved him, so she must stay outside and not touch him. He had inspected his skin every day for the past two weeks searching for some hint of disease or corruption and there was none; he was as pasty and healthy as ever, in body if not in mind. So he himself must be the source of the contamination, a carrier not of plague but Death itself.

He had confessed to Alice in the praying room and she'd said he was mad.

'God is not punishing you,' she had insisted. 'My father says so. He says this is not judgement for what we've done wrong but a test so that we might do right.'

'I denied sin,' he'd snapped back, too harshly he judged for she'd looked stung. 'The imperfections of the mind are visited on the body.'

'Why would *she* die because of something you did?'

'Because I loved her, and there is nothing that could have hurt me more.'

'If that's how God likes to act then I'd rather spit in His eye and run off with the Devil. Get up, Nate' – he'd been slumped in the corner on his haunches, curled up like a child as yet unborn – 'they need you outside. They look to you.'

'They should not. I am no leader.'

'They look to you for *love*!' Alice had stamped her tiny foot and bounced against the walls, a little fury. He'd stared at her through eyes skinned and raw, all fluid wrung from them, until she had calmed herself and knelt beside him. Their eyes were level, hers narrower than he had ever seen them before and wet for the first time since Ann had died. 'I love you Nate; since you came to my father's house I loved you. I am not her, but I can stay with you and keep you warm and help you heal.'

She'd taken his hand in hers – his were small for a grown man, but hers were more delicate, so he'd felt like a giant in her grip – and leaned in close to kiss him on the lips.

He had screamed in her face. 'Christ, no! You are not even a woman!'

'I will be.'

'You are a child! You are only eight –'

(quiet) 'Almost nine.'

'You are only eight. Don't presume because you have a little learning to have shucked off a child's foolishness! If you want to live to be a woman, you will not touch me! You would better kill me and cut up my body and bury it at some crossroads so my spirit will forever be lost! You must go and live very far away from me, Alice Lynch.'

There had been dark stains below her eyes. 'I love you. I don't mean to take her place.'

'Get out!' he'd howled. 'Get out! Get out!'

She had already fled.

He'd left soon after, and those few remaining Silverites who were at liberty and not working on Sir Denzil's winter projects had stared at him as he'd trudged back to his bed, or they'd forced themselves not to stare or meet his eye. They had all heard some of the least silent prayers to be made in their makeshift chapel. He would not be able to look on them again. Better to die, damn himself to the wood of suicides where he might at least hear Ann Brownlow's brittle yelps of torment carried to him on evil winds from some other cellblock in Hell.

Alice had returned, as he'd been afraid she would. He'd barricaded his door and refused to let her in. She'd stayed outside, wailing herself hoarse, and that state persisted until the sun went down. Then she either gave up and left, or fell silent but remained huddled at his door. He knew Alice; he knew which was the more likely; but at least he heard nothing more and was able to drift into a restless sleep. Unconsciousness preserved his pain as if in ice; it would thaw again when he woke. There was a timeless moment of oblivion.

He decided, while sleeping, what he had to do.

He woke purposefully and thought it morning, the dim brown light filtering in through the windows and the gaps in the walls. He had worked to scrub away the stains and etchings on the plasterwork, but the light, faint though it was, seemed to reveal them again and starker still as if all his efforts had been unmade. Alice was probably still asleep on his threshold, under the protection of some two-headed pagan deity. He shook the sleep out of his bones, then climbed onto the cot to peer through the openings. Still it was night.

No matter, he would make only a little noise, and not enough to disturb the sleeping commune. His bags and belongings were stacked with military discipline on the floor; he fished among them and found the hammer, its head cleaned since the last slaughter. He was naked and his body was blessed with only sparse patches of hair, so he felt exposed to the night-frost, but the unnatural light took its edge away.

The little wood box he had made thirteen years earlier was sitting on the table in plain sight. No thief – if any were so foolish as to think the Church worth robbing – would have thought it valuable or even intriguing. The light lay heavily round the box, as though shining from within. He opened the lid, and was unsurprised to find that the glow did indeed emanate forth from this little sun, his miracle. He tipped the box and let the egg roll onto the table, caring not if it be broken because he knew it would never hatch. He would make sure of that.

Whatever power had brought him back from the darkness, it was not for the betterment of the world, but some cruel mischief. The Greek gods were said to play tricks on mortals. Perhaps then it was not Christ but his parody Apollo who had gifted him this new sun? Better to smash it now and end the game.

He brought the hammer up then swung it down.

Gentle hands caught his arm mid-arc and arrested the blow.

~ *No* ~

Those hands relieved him of the hammer. They were not mortal hands but those of giants, three clawed tapering fingers on this one, tight in a ribbed leather gauntlet. The leather, like their skins, was blanched white. He knew these hands.

~ *You cannot destroy this* ~ *You will only exhaust yourself* ~

The hands of angels placed the hammer on the table. Only then did they release his arm to allow it to drop mildly back to his side. They were the same colour as the egg, the same luminous white. There were three of them and they towered, higher than he could have imagined possible in his low-roof'd little house. They wore columns of white light for robes and shapeless hoods over their heads, eyes invisible behind black slits in the glow. They were Christ's chirurgeons and messengers. He dropped to his knees.

~ *You have not seen us* ~ said one angel, not the closest one who had relieved him of the hammer; their soft voices were reasonable, like the babble of a summer stream or the rhythm of rain on a window pane ~ *We are not here* ~

'You are angels,' he whispered.

~ *We are pilots* ~

There were three of them. They were still. They flickered suddenly and danced round the room, rearranging themselves in new positions that seemed to Silver's eyes more relaxed, though who could tell with angels? One seemed to sit on his bed. He was sure this was the one who had saved him from folly.

~ Forgive our confusion ~ The egg, as you call it, is compensating for our opposed velocities and translating ~ You understand our words? ~

Of course, they spoke in the language of Enoch, which was the tongue of all of Heaven and Earth before Babel. 'I hear you,' he told them.

~ Good ~ The egg is a construct downloaded in the form of a linear continuity stroke access point from this instantaneous event window and extends in both space-time directions during your lifetime ~ As you understand this already, it will save us some very long and tedious explanations ~

'I hear you,' he repeated blandly. And he did, as he saw them, but he doubted that he would be able to touch them. They were made of light, and who can catch the light? They shifted again, skittling around the room with the egg as the axis on which they turned. One had manifested behind him, and he could feel it with senses that he had not been aware he had. It was not moving, but it was there.

They had a scent, these angels. Sometimes they smelled of alchemical stinks, like gunpowder and yet not; but mostly they smelled of nothing, a holy absence that sucked all other odours from the room.

'You brought me back from the brink of death,' he told them. They said nothing. Now he was bolder and looked closer and saw that the line of their robes was not constant; the lights trembled and broke in places revealing the plain wall of the house through their transparent bodies. 'You gave me more life and I failed to make anything of it. Are you come now to kill me? I would welcome that.'

~ We would not harm you if it can be helped ~ We have observed you and would learn more of you ~ We would offer you a compromise or a bargain ~

They danced around the room again. The angel with the hammer was back on the bed where it did not sit so much as balance. It was the angel with the hammer, Silver was certain, because it had the hammer back in its clawed glove. Then instantly the weapon was gone and back on the table as if thrown invisibly and so lightly that it made neither sound nor damage. The angel of the hammer spoke.

~ The fact that the egg exists is proof of the opening of negotiations ~ Should they fail, it will continue to exist but remain inert ~ Should they fail, then of course we would be forced to resort to other measures ~ You can see how failure would benefit neither of us ~

~ The question is ~ What can we offer you, Nathaniel Silver? ~ What do you want? ~

Hope beat in place of his heart. He leapt to his feet. 'I want her back! You rescued *me* from the grave so it must be within your power. If you be angels or Christ's pilots or what-you-will, I want Ann Brownlow alive and healthy and by my side, and a long and happy life for both of us. Even if you be devils I would have that from you.'

~ We are no devils ~ began the angel of the hammer, but another raised its claw in a smooth gesture, and Silver imagined (if the temperaments of angels could be so interpreted) it had silenced its comrade. They paused, then they spoke as one:

~ We will not do this ~ What do you want, Nathaniel Silver? ~ What is your purpose? ~

Some minutes passed before he could clear his throat and speak again. He bowed his head. 'I pretend to be a natural philosopher. I would understand the world so that we might better it.'

~ We can help you with this ~ but he hardly heard them.

They parted for him as he went to sit on the bed, carrying the egg pressed to his chest.

The light it radiated was white, white as Christ's pilots; it was only the wooden veil of the box that had made it appear brown.

'What do you want in return?' he asked.

~ *At the end of your life, we will take your ~ your pardon, there is no term for this you would know ~ your... life-gifts? ~*

He sighed and laid back on the bed. He had expected this. 'You mean my soul? You are devils after all? Don't you know I am already damned to eternal torment?'

~ *Call it your soul ~ We are no devils and we will not torment you ~*

'No? I don't believe you.'

~ *We want to study you ~ We would return with you to Civitas Solis so we could learn from you ~ We would understand you so that we might better you ~*

~ *Use your wits and reason, Nate ~ You believe you have rung up a debt with devils already ~ Nothing you can agree with us would make it worse for you ~ You would be declining the benefit of our deal for nothing ~*

'There is nothing you can give me that is worth the weight of my soul.'

~ *You are wrong ~ If you accept then the egg will instruct you ~ It is ~ in a manner of speaking ~ our life-gifts and the equal of what we would take from you ~ We are projections of its presence, just as you, Nathaniel Silver, are the sum of your life-gifts ~*

He should have felt astonishment when he heard that, but he was already blasé in the presence of deities and miracles. Still, his mouth widened a little. 'You would grant me your own souls?'

~ *There is nothing else on this planet in this time-frame that would be more useful to your enterprise ~ This is the stone that all philosophers seek ~*

He was tempted, yet simultaneously wary. 'Could it, through my actions and experiments, do harm?'

~ *A greater quantity could, but this is stable ~ It was designed to be causally-neutral at this mass ~*

'I don't understand.'

~ *Just don't eat it ~ It's not a real egg ~*

They flickered again and then there was only one; it reared forward and gibbered into his face:

~ *Suburate vantimax lyacal lyacal marfgalineaux dorat shupanis ~*

He gasped. They were three again and passive.

~ *Apologies, we are trying to stabilise synchronisation ~ Manifestation at this level should generate visible anomalies, and the strain of causal dampening is immense ~ We must maintain our invisibility from the higher powers of the Spiral Politic ~*

'I don't understand half of what you say,' he remarked.

~ *You will ~ At the end of your life ~ If you agree to our terms ~*

His tongue moved to speak, but he stilled it, rose from the bed, and looked around him. This whole scene had the content but not the quality of a dream. It could not be a dream, because he felt so comfortable with it, he neglected it as he did the material world – all the familiar objects and items that he used or ignored because they were so familiar that they had become invisible. Yet now he found that familiarity in the presence of three vast angels on pillars of roaring white fire, who had repaired him from death but now came by night to haggle terms with him like any merchant in a market, like fishmongers. And he lay casually before them, with barely a thought of wonder and worship. He felt deadened in the presence of miracles.

He felt deadened in the presence of life, a life these pilots had restored to him.

He knew, as he realised this, what his answer must be.

~ *Well?* ~

The following morning he found Alice crouched up against his door, wrapped in blankets so long that they had gone three times round her but still trailed in the wet mud. It had been raining last night – he hadn't noticed; fierce winter rains that turned the commune's floor to warm sludge and steaming muck. Alice might have been asleep or dead; he put a hand to her face and found her skin still warm. His touch, though light, disturbed her and she murmured. His fingers left a wet black mark on her cheek.

'You should come in out of the cold,' he said, and then: 'I'm sorry. I shouldn't have shouted at you.' But she was struggling out of her sleep and didn't seem to hear him. Sticky eyes peered up at him, weighing him.

'You look like I feel,' she said.

'I've been awake most of the night. I've been working.' She was looking at his hands and his smudged inky fingers, so she needed no more explanation. 'Alice, do you forgive me?'

She smiled slowly and lazily. 'I would forgive you anything.'

He helped her to her feet. 'You must report something to Sir Denzil for me,' he said casually. '*The Cycle of Sun & Seed* is not ready, we must put off publication for a few weeks while I make revisions.' Then, because he couldn't help himself, because it was flowing out of him: 'There are so many revisions; so many of my observations were incomplete or misunderstood. I feel like I have begun all over again.'

He had; that was true. He laughed for the first time since Ann had died; it was the sound of fresh knowledge and new insights spilling out of his mouth. Alice was hugging him now; she peered past him into the brick house. 'Nate,' she said, 'I see a light. You have left a candle burning.'

'No,' he told her. 'I have not.'

After that night he did not neglect the commune, but even as he carried out a day's work his attentions were half-turned elsewhere. By night he sat and listened to the whispering of the egg, which no longer blazed so bright as when in the presence of angels, but reflected the darker glow of his corrupted human soul, just as the moon casts a lesser beam than the sun. He questioned it and it answered, and occasionally volunteered knowledge, in the voice of Christ's pilots. He wondered if others would hear this voice, or if it were planted precisely in his ear so that it might not be overheard. Sir Denzil pressed him for the revisions, and he delivered a fresh manuscript that, while much improved, he was not yet happy with. The world was a globe, this work a faint scratch on its surface.

But the commune was diminished, by attrition as much by any single disaster. When the spring came there were too few hands to make a planting worthwhile, and Silver reluctantly asked that they join Sir Denzil's workers on his lands instead. For many this was both an insult and a break with the ideals of the commune; they complained to Silver that they had not abandoned their old lives and servitudes just to end up as tenants of yet another petty moneyed monarch. He couldn't answer them, so they left, a small exodus but enough to doom the experiment. They were too few now, he realised, for the commune to support itself; barely a dozen men and women remained, and no one came to replenish the numbers that were lost. No more rumours of orgies circled in the local taverns, only rumours of depression and failure and near-starvation.

Silver pushed all these thoughts to the back of his mind. He did not think to ask the egg for a solution to his problems; its realm was knowledge, not mundane practicalities. The Church of Christ Sublime that had once resembled a small village now became a ghost town, haunted not by the dead but by the failure of the living. Ann's ashes were buried in a bed of earth; wildflowers grew there in spring, but no other seeds would grow within their limits. This was, Silver had learned by measures, poor land. He started writing by day as often as by night, venturing out mainly to teach Alice, who still attended her lessons and was the Church's sole triumph.

The end was not far off – he could no longer deny that – but there was still hope.

One day in May a rider came through the gates on a black horse, dismounted outside the old manor house, and bellowed at the few Silverites who were not working Sir Denzil's acres. It was raining hard and he had to shout above the rain: 'Nathaniel Silver! I know this to be his house! Send him out to me!'

Alice teetered on a chair to see him through the window and the rain. 'A tall man,' she described. 'He has a black coat that makes him look fat, but he isn't if you look closely. He has a beard and looks fierce; he has a hat with a black plume, and I can't see any more of his face. He has a satchel with a seal that I can't make out. Oh, and he has a sword.'

Silver got to his feet. 'Stay here,' he instructed Alice, but she trotted out at his heels.

He left the schola and moved meekly across the sodden field, sucking up mud and rainwater through the holes in his boots, to address the stranger. 'Sir, I am Nathaniel Silver –' and then he stopped.

The newcomer, in fact no stranger at all, vaulted across a puddle, slammed Silver bodily against the nearest wall, squeezed the breath from him and kissed him on both cheeks. Once the scrape of his assailant's greyed beard was out of his face, Silver was finally able to gasp. 'Honest Don Taylor,' he declared weakly.

'Nate, you have not changed a jot,' Taylor boomed. He was still a reverberant man; he might have been an actor in another age.

'Neither have you,' Silver coughed, still choking, but the English Scot shook his head. 'You have *not* changed Nate. How do you do it? Do you bathe in the blood of virgins? Here is one now, I see.' The hat and its plume rolled from his head into his hand and he made an exaggerated bow, dropping on one knee in front of a startled Alice. She was still aghast at what she had seen as an attack on her teacher; she began, within seconds, to cry uncontrollably. She was after all only a child.

'Alice, this is my friend and comrade-in arms, Donald Taylor. We were soldiers. Don, this is my friend's daughter, this is Alice Lynch.'

'Sir Denzil's girl? Ah, she has my sympathies. Have a flower, child, and dry those eyes. I'm not here to frighten children, that's just a sad consequence.' He still had the scars, Silver noticed. They had not faded with time, and he had become a gaunt man in the lean years after the Revolution. He could see how Alice might have grounds to be afraid.

He also saw Don Taylor's bag, and decided that he too had grounds to be afraid.

Silver took her aside and said, quietly: 'Go and find someone who will cook and get them to make up a meal for my friend. I'll fast tonight to make up the difference, but make sure there is meat. This man is a carnivore.'

Once Alice left them, Silver invited Taylor into the schola, out of the rain. The newcomer dumped his cloak and bags and sword in the corner, and took a place on a plain wood bench that, coincidentally, had been Alice's perch that morning before he had ridden in to disrupt her lesson.

'So,' Silver began, 'you escaped the army in the end?'

'In a manner of speaking. You seem to have made a more complete evacuation, though. This place, Nate... well, we all knew you had it in you. How goes it?'

'As well as can be expected.' That was hardly a lie, and he feared his drab demeanour and pasty skin had already betrayed the condition of his enterprise. 'No, it goes badly. It will be a miracle if we make it to the autumn.'

Don Taylor nodded his head and dislodged raindrops from the brim of his hat. He removed it then, and tossed it into the corner with the other wet things. Just as casually he said, 'I feel that way sometimes about the Republic. Just between you and me.'

'Don, why have you come here? It must be for some purpose.'

'There is a purpose, but you are not it. I am required to carry intelligences to Portsmouth. I had learned you were close – your name is being heard in London gossip – and, since I was passing...' He threw his arms out wide and left the words unspoken.

'I wish you had not found me like this, but remembered me from happier times.'

'Those were *happier* times? You misremember, old friend. Those were bloody awful times. We are all better off out of it.'

The bench was damp, but Silver, who had been hovering like a crow spying its prey, sat beside him. He could feel the damp of Taylor's costume and the warmth of his body; they were crushed together as they had been on old campaigns. 'Don, are you truly out of it? I saw your bags.'

'They carry my intelligences.'

'I saw the seal. You are about the business of the Protector.'

Taylor shook his head – more fine and second-hand rain – and raised a finger to his lips, then spoke softly: 'I am on England's Service. They are two separate things, though at present converged. Indeed, General Warts-and-All mistrusts us. There has always been something of Roman magic about our rites.'

'I have not heard of this.'

'It is Gloriana's secret order, first entrusted to Walsingham and Dee.' Silver must still have looked a blank, as Taylor sighed and clarified: 'The unholy game, Nate. The dirty business of *espion*-age.'

'If it's such a secret, why tell me?'

'Would you believe I am trying to persuade you to our order, or *turn you* as we say in tradecraft? No, I see you do not. You are too honest, Nate, you are the only man in England who is not in another's pocket. There isn't a royalist anywhere who isn't tied up with the Knot, while Warts-and-All has his agents in the post office. There is a man called Morland who reads the correspondence, and a man named Milton who reads all the pamphlets – or has them read to him at any rate.'

'Read to him? Why?'

'He is blind. Like all Godly sorts he is familiar with the sin of Onan. Still, if it keeps him busy all the better. It leaves him no time to write his bloody awful poetry. I maintain a loyalty to the old ideals of the Service, but the game is played by mundanites and mediocrities now, and will be for fifty years to come.'

'You're right Don, I wouldn't care to be part of such a world.'

'Good. There are other worlds and colleges, equally invisible but far more honest.'

'You were the honest one. You kept us all on straight and narrow.'

'Nate, Nate, Nate, men tell me there has never been a soldier born who would not slit his own grandmother's throat for a penny to buy a pretty trinket to tease up a whore's skirts, and when they tell me that do you know what I say to them?'

'No, Don, I do not.'

'I say to them – Sirrah, if that be true, then my friend Nathaniel Silver was never born but placed clean on the earth by God, like Adam but not so foolish this time.'

To that Silver would have replied: 'I have been exceedingly foolish' – but at that moment Alice brought in a jug of wine, the last left in the commune, and food soon followed her. They distracted Don; he swallowed the offerings like a wolf, while Silver sat and watched him patiently and ignored the tight cramps in his stomach that were almost as acute as the cramps in his skull.

'Now,' Don Taylor resumed, after he had proved his satisfaction with a healthy belch, 'I need to talk to you about this *book*. I must present you with two urgent matters and criticisms –'

Silver's brow furrowed and he gestured to interrupt him. 'What book, Don?'

'*The Cycle of Sun & Seed*. It is your book, is it not? Don't tell me I have ridden two days out of my way only to find that it is the work of some upstart who has stolen your name?'

'It is true I have written a book of that title, but it is not yet published. The matter is in Sir Denzil's hands.'

'It is published a month back in London and already much talked about, though that is perhaps not a healthy state of affairs in this day and age.'

Bewildered, Silver looked to Alice, who mirrored his confusion and shrugged and flapped her arms.

'I will have words with your father about this,' he said, using soft and rounded words to make clear that she would bear no blame. She nodded; the heavy-lidded child was back again, those resentments he had seen stored up in her breast until the commune had offered her a release.

'All this is by the by; the book is yours, there is no doubt about that. And this is the problem. Not for me, Nate! Sit yourself down again, I have read part of it and much enjoyed what I saw. But I am not your only reader, and there are some who claim it teeters on the verge of blasphemy.'

He tried to speak, but Don Taylor silenced him with a raised finger. 'Furthermore, parties of all colours are finding much to mislike in its politics and philosophy. They see a book that despairs of all authority, and so they see an attack on themselves.'

This time he was allowed to protest himself: 'I do not endorse any side in any conflict. There are lessons to be drawn from what I say, but not singular ones that a zealot might latch onto and say *this book is mine and speaks to me alone*. I follow no doctrine but my own and the Lord's!' He had become heated as he rambled through his defence.

'Calm yourself! These are not my accusations, but if you refuse the creed of any party then they will assume you are against them. They are little fortresses with their gates snapped shut. You have done something that is either brave or foolhardy or perhaps both. With luck, your accusers may only carp and feel you too provincial to bother with, but I worried for you and came to warn you.'

Quieter now, he asked: 'What then is to be done?'

'I don't know, because I don't know what will come to pass.'

'I will be true to myself, come what may.'

'You will, I have no doubt of that, and this brings me to my second criticism of your book, Nate, which is of your methods.'

'My methods?'

'Indeed. I am no pure natural philosopher, but I mix with them in my line of work. You are not trained to it, as they are in those great priest-factories of Cambridge and Oxford. There is much you do not know; your approach lacks the authority of your insight, and so undermines it. You sit and observe the world and think you can wring meaning for it through contemplation.'

'It worked for Aristotle.'

'It worked for many dead Greeks, and we have lived with the consequences of that. Our static sciences are built upon two thousand year old errors. There are new ways of doing things; an age of experimentation and measurement is upon us. In your book you rely too much on the eye' – and here he tapped his own face beneath his one good eye – 'and too little on the hands.'

'You cannot say I do not experiment. My experiment is all around you.'

Donald Taylor's sombre wink said more to him then than any word could. The silence lingered until Taylor, his face grown ruddy and robust, stuck out his wet tongue to lick his lips. 'I've drunk you dry, have I not?'

'You have. It's no hardship.'

'I worry for my horse now. I'm afraid your people will have eaten it.'

Taylor's whole body rippled on the bench to make himself more comfortable. 'I'll be a month in Portsmouth, six weeks at worst. After that I'll come back here. I can recommend you to some experimenters. They could do with your wisdom, and you with their experience. How does that sound?'

Nathaniel Silver made a smile to humour his old friend – 'That sounds fine, Don. It sounds fine.' – and knew with some certainty that by the time Taylor quit Portsmouth the Church of Christ Sublime would be gone, driven into the earth and forgotten as if washed away by the rain.

The killing blow came quicker than expected, mere days after Don Taylor had departed. Silver was awoken by a violent hammering on his door; he snapped out of his sleep, which had been brief and shallow after an evening's instruction by egg-light. *They have come for me at last*, he thought, as he pulled on a robe and gazed out through the slit of the window at an azure sky still mottled with stars. The egg was well-hidden; they would not get that. He went slowly to the door, keen to give away no hint of panic or hurry.

It was not the militia, it was Sir Denzil's man Hudd, with a lantern. Behind him, the gates to the experiment swung ajar and clattering on the breeze, and beyond that, on the track leading to the road was a cart laden with a few meagre sacks and boxes. It had a look of flight to it, and Hudd himself was sweating and unkempt.

'Sir Denzil has been arrested,' he declared.

Silver's face creased. 'On what charge?' His mind whirled with possibilities; so many things were now outlawed in the free Republic, but he came ever to the three cardinal sins: treason, blasphemy, and sedition.

'Forgery,' Hudd spat, literally spat, a wad of black muck onto the ground at Silver's feet. 'Debasing coins.'

Silver shook his head in bewilderment. 'I knew nothing of this,' he exclaimed.

'You're the only man in three counties who didn't,' Hudd gruffed. 'He is no longer in the general's good books. The militia have taken all his accomplices and most of his household servants.'

Silver tugged the robe tighter; it was too baggy for him by far, inherited from a fat Silverite long since gone or dead. 'Send Alice to us. We can shelter her. I have a friend who has friends, perhaps he can pull the general's strings?'

But Hudd was shaking his head, a lumbering motion for a man with no visible neck. 'Too late for that.' He beckoned, and swinging his lamp before him, crossed to the cart with Silver in his wake. They found Alice lying there asleep on the soft sacks; in her long shawl and hood she looked like just another bundle on a pile of rags.

'They'll question her if they get her.'

'She's a child,' Silver protested, his voice thin and stripped of conviction.

'That's why they'll question her. Kids you see, they break easy. They'd break her to break him, you know they would.'

'Where will you take her?'

'First to Salisbury. From there to London, to stay with her mum's brother. I reckon they'll write this off as a local matter, not worth the bother of bringing her all the way back. Her dad's finished though. Poor thing.' Silver wasn't sure if he meant the man or the girl; the man he knew would not go easily to punishment. He had tried to crawl from the pit of Hell, and now all the devils had come to pull him back down.

'It will be easier for him to know that she is safe and well,' Silver mused.

Hudd snorted. 'Doubt he could care less about her. Men like him shouldn't have kids.'

Silver reached out with careful hands to slip back Alice's cowl and stroke her hair. He was not careful enough, and she jolted back to life beneath his touch. She saw him swaying over her, and saying nothing, stretched out skinny arms to encircle his neck and pull herself up into his embrace. He stood stooped like that for a while, letting her hold him, until twinges bit at the base of his spine and he had to let her down. He saw her face again, for the last time, and she was crying.

Those eyes, ever shadowed by the hood of her lids, were now wide open but still unreadable.

'I want to stay with you,' she told him, but he shook his head. 'I love you,' she added, and still he shook his head.

'You can't stay here. We've lost all our protection.'

'Don't leave me, Nate. Don't abandon me.'

'You have to leave,' he echoed, sad and insistent, 'but I'd never abandon you. God is everywhere, remember, and He is love. No matter where you go you will be here in my heart.'

She sniffed then. She had never been sentimental.

And you, Nathaniel Silver, have been far too sentimental. If you live through the next few days, that will have to change.

He had to let her go. He bade them both good fortune, then stood at the gates watching as the cart receded northwards up the track. The militia might catch them on the road. They might get lost on the way to London. Hudd might get drunk and betray her or forget her. They might be ambushed and robbed. Any number of calamities might befall them once they were out of his sight, but he put all such thoughts from his mind. She was gone, and the only hope he had left in the world was that she was now safely beyond his baleful influence.

There were seven other Silverites still living in the commune. Every single one of them was woken by the commotion, and had come out of their houses in time to see Nathaniel Silver – not their leader or their shepherd but an ordinary man like any one of them – tread broken and defeated back through the gates of the world he'd made for them. He had cursed them. He tried to look at their faces, but saw only smudges of pink, instantly forgotten. He saw what the King must have seen on his final walk to the axeman's block, parading forth not with dignity or according to any ritual, but simply dazed, helpless, and frightened by the crowd that damned him and prayed for him in equal measure.

Silver stood before them and gave them one final piece of advice; and for once it was a practical suggestion. 'Run,' he said.

Then he went into the praying room and knelt, listening as the last of his followers gathered up their possessions and fled the camp. He could hear the sound of marching boots in the distance, drawing ever nearer. He could hear the bolts on the cells drawing close on the career and the life of Sir Denzil Lynch. He could hear Alice muttering in her sleep as she made her escape. He could hear the promises of angels. He could hear the steady beat of his own heart. He listened to all this and waited and waited and waited until at last they came for him.

= Chapter 2: *Mistress Behn's Holiday* =

Proud ALBION, you spurned all suitors,
'til fateful vessels brought you Brutus,
washed upon your shores untold,
to end that idyll, the Age of Gold.
'Gainst Trojan majesty, the giant Gog
and his brother, called Magog,
did tumpty tumpty tumpty tum
something tumpty tumpty – *ballocks*! I almost had something there. Starts well but turns rapidly to doggerel.

She hated ships. Bloody *hated* them. Not the ships as much as the journey, and not the journey out so much as the voyage home. There were always drizzling clouds waiting for her, and worse than a spot of rain, there was disappointment or humiliation or worse –

There was also the sickness. Today her stomach was wambling ceaselessly, as usual, but the sea was completely flat from horizon to horizon. Not a wave could be seen there, just a solid clean sheet of blue, a little darker than the sky. There was no land visible in any direction, except over her head, as the clusters of stars had merged together to form new and unexplored continents. She searched and found her patron and protector, the constellation of Virgo, reclining demurely on a verdant lawn with her legs chastely crooked and her head turned away from Earth and the follies of mortal men. The goddess smiled down on her shipbound mortal aspect, who curtsied back to her from the deck.

Her return from Surinam had been a journey like this, full of sickness and calm seas with no land in sight from one end of the sky to the other, though at least then there'd been motion and precious cargo. She had borne back Indian feathers and butterflies from the New World, plus prosaic reports on Governor Willoughby's philanderings, plus a new name. Now she had only her failure in Antwerp, and nothing to look forward to but potential penury, but this couldn't be the Mare Germanicum, could it? They couldn't have become bogged down so far from land or sight of any ship in such a narrow sea? It was more like they had become becalmed in the Sargasso, doomed to die of thirst and starvation under the American sun. Perhaps through ill luck or magic they'd navigated into the great pangaean ocean that encircled the flat world in the Golden Age, before the Earth diminished into a sphere.

Ah, this had to be a dream then. There was no magic in the world any more, except in memories of childhood or in dreams. It would explain the green skies and the stillness and the youthful triteness of her poetry.

It was a shame the world was no longer flat. She amused herself imagining righteous pilgrims packing themselves into boats and setting off to the New World, only to topple off the edge and plunge screaming into the abyss of stars. She laughed and almost threw up. Still, at least they were despatched to another continent where they could do no harm, except to the poor red savages, once proud but now oppressed by breeches, drink, and Christian blather. A shame – she could think of no happier an afterlife for a Puritan than the insides of a wild man's belly.

The sea was unmoved by her good humour.

It was funny that she should dream herself back to the worst of her disasters, as she slunk to a home that might have burned to the ground, to masters who had forgotten her and were embarrassed by her intelligences, to debt and the purgatory of Clink Street. Her reports were ignored. When some months later the Dutch fleet sailed up the Medway and snatched the *Royal Charles*, she might almost have danced about her cell in delight. I told you so! I told you so! I told you so!

She was dancing now in her dream. Men and rats were staring at her, seeming faintly ashamed. It upset her stomach, so she calmed down, leaned herself on the wooden rail and waited impotently for a wind to puff the sails and her skirts alike.

She felt a disturbance behind her, but it was just a man come up on deck. He was a Florentine merchant with whom she had exchanged a few words earlier on the journey; she had the sense that underneath their daytime disguises they were both about the same business. He was an ugly man with a face like a ruined abbey; only a few white hairs hung wispily from the back of his head, and without being fat he was huge and solid. The last time they had spoken, he had held forth about the beauty and history of his home city, and she had nodded politely and immediately forgotten all but a few bits of local colour that might one day serve as a decoration for scenes in her drama or her prose.

Aphra Behn liked to show to men exactly the sort of woman they expected to see. In courtly circles, she was an aristocrat; in the theatre, a solid wordsmith and the equal of any male; among the rabble, an honest working girl made good. It was all too easy for her to be the sort of woman that ugly old men desired.

'I have something to show you,' he enthused, ignoring the light green pallor of her cheeks. 'You'll recall I mentioned a present for King Charles, and you were most excited?' – in fact she had delicately covered her yawns with her hand, which he had mistaken for coquetry – 'I have it here for your inspection.'

From his case, which he placed at his feet and took a little effort to open, he produced a heavy bronzed cylinder, decorated with tiny dials along its length and lenses of differing size at either end. She knew what this was, but smiled politely nonetheless as she waited for the explanation.

'This is the latest of its kind, and will far surpass any found in London. Have you ever had a chance to use a telescope with your own eyes?'

She had, many times. 'No, I would be most honoured.'

He leaned forward to adjust its dials. 'Then see, you merely stroke it thus and it extends to a considerable length and girth.'

Oh, 'tis going to be like that, is it? What a tedious man. 'Sir, I am amazed!'

'Now support its head with your right hand and put the slender end to the other, thus. You have it, madame. I will adjust the magnification. Just gasp when the view comes clear.' Not that there would be a view, just the blue emptiness circling the whole world. She considered turning the telescope upwards to inspect the viridian heavens. She wondered idly what species of heathen lived there. Eyeless angels? Huge-toed, one-legged men? Cannibals with no heads but mouths in their stomachs? Dronish bee-men, parading around a marvellous bee-woman Queen?

'This is miraculous!' she said dryly as a distant blue blur crystallised into an indistinguishable blue sharpness. 'His Majesty is such a scopophile, he will be beside himself with joy.'

The Florentine was close behind her, hot breath against her neck, hands trembling and willing to touch. 'I had wondered,' he said at length, 'on the whereabouts of Mister Behn?'

'Him? Oh, he is in Arcadia. Two years gone.'

'You have my condolences.'

'Well, one grieves and moves on. He left great debts, of course.'

'Debts?'

'Indeed. I fear they will remain unpaid on my landing in London, and then who knows what might happen to me?' She sighed. As expected, he moved to steady her, confident hands on her shoulders, then on her waist, then crooked round her breast, and then – ah ha! – creeping downwards to where her lap would lie if she were seated. She sighed again, making it seem happier this time. Better to be banged-up below decks than banged-up in Clink. His fingers tightened on her womanhood through the lines of cloth, bought from Flanders merchants from the Service's depthless purse before she had learned that it was not, in fact, as depthless as she imagined.

The Florentine was exactly the sort of mortal man she had found attractive when she had still been young. Her sleeping self, a-bed in Paris some sixteen years later, rolled in her slumber and prepared to argue – but then she stopped and gasped. She had spied something in her dreaming that she had forgotten in the waking world.

She was so surprised she almost dropped the telescope, and the Florentine released his grip on her delicate parts immediately and made to catch it – it was more delicate still. She steadied herself.

'I didn't presume –' he began.

'The hell with that – what am I looking at now?'

He leant over the prow in the direction of her gaze, no doubt creasing his lids and shielding his brow from the sun with the flat of his hand. He wouldn't be able to see it, she realised. This vision was for her eyes only. 'What do you see?' he asked.

She saw a vast green pillar rising out of the waters, decorated with carvings, statues, and strange flowers along its length, and topped with an emerald dome, greater in size and majesty by far than the basilica of Saint Peter in Rome. *I have seen this before,* she thought suddenly. It felt at once like a Catholic place, yet not; it was a building that could only have been born out of a baroque imagination, sixteen hundred years old, steeped in ancient ceremonies and traditions, burnished by pomp and power. Yet she had no doubt that the prayers conducted beneath its canopy were wholly un-Christian, dedicated to the pagan immortals who once walked the Earth until desert-dwelling Jehovah had swept them away. And as she stared at it through her narrow lens, she was sure that the swinish heathen priests were staring back not just at her but at all creation from their all-seeing domain, their Aleph.

'I see a tall pillar, floating on the sea,' she babbled out an inadequate description.

'Ah! It is a *fata morgana,*' the Florentine non-explained, and satisfied with that non-explanation he rested both hands on her buttocks and stroked playfully.

'Y'what?'

'A derangement of the opticks. When sailors see it, they imagine it to be narrow castles with thin spires and battlements, but it is only the vision of their own ships reflected back to them on the air. It is usually,' he continued brightly, 'a sign of uncouth weather. There'll be a storm soon.'

'Good,' she decided, 'I can't wait to get moving.'

But she kept scanning the ocean-top with her telescope, even as the visionary temple vanished into the first haze of rain, searching in vain for a sight of *her,* for a glimpse of fiery immortal hair or glowing immortal skin. Even later, as the Florentine pinned her heavily to his comfortable berth, she was still desperately scouring the sea of her memory. Then the storm exploded and dashed the ship onto rocks, and the Florentine's telescope was forgotten in the evacuation and sank to the bottom of the sea to delight the mermaids, and she woke up and found herself in –

Now.

There was a candle lit in her room, and through the window came the night-time sounds of Paris, the city that never slept and was buggered if it was going to let her get any rest either... and the curv'd ache was back in her spine and her limbs, so she knew she must be properly and disappointingly awake.

George had lit the candle, and was creeping around her room picking his clothes from the floor. The light exposed his yellow nakedness to her: hairless chest, skinny buttocks mottled with the spots of a youth and the lacerations of a cadet, a drooping unexcited cock. Very disappointing. She wondered at how quickly her tastes had turned from ugly men twenty years her senior to pretty young boys who would still have been in the cradle when she'd returned from Antwerp, and unborn when she'd been in Surinam.

'George,' she whispered; he looked back guiltily, holding a bundled shirt and breeches to his chest with one hand, the candle in the other.

'I have to go,' he blurted. 'They'll kick me out of the academy if I'm not there in the morning.'

'Not yet. Don't leave me alone in a city full of tempting Frenchmen...'

She rolled onto her back beneath the sheet, letting it ride back like a streamer as she turned, so that her bosom and stomach and thigh were slowly and tantalisingly exposed to him. He leaned across her and his hardening penis touched and drew a thin sticky trail up her flank, but he moved only to put down the candle by her side and peck her cheek.

'I'll come back to you as soon as I can,' he promised, his free hand then tickling down her neck and forearm and onto her breast. 'You are my goddess, how could I not?' Then he ran for the door, still nude and aroused and skinny, trailing ribbons and bits of uniform behind him. He was off back to his martial studies, all those leering old chevaliers just yearning to introduce him to the twin disciplines of sodomy and masturbation. She slicked her fingers on his cooling ejaculate, spreading it along the length of her thigh.

'Fuck!'

She threw off the sheet, folded her arms, and crossed her legs in petulance and disappointment. All men let her down in the end, that was a condition of time, of course, but also of their sex. Most were born slaves, in their minds if not in fact. The best of them would still shine through even if literally enslaved, as she had seen in the American colonies. The African Negroes on the plantations had still been tall defiant men, smouldering and metallic-black, as if fired in the furnace of the sun. They were better men by far than the pallid colonial runts who professed to own them – that was the base injustice of slavery. She had realised this most potently when she'd come upon one Oroonoko,

once a proud prince among his people,
now chain'd in body yet not in mind.
He caught his spy and found me kind
With Afrique tongue he drew me hither

I flowed across that mighty river – *Christ*! What a way to dignify a quick fumble and fuck under a bush in Surinam. That had been a long time ago; lot of water had passed under that bridge, and she was a (much) better poet nowadays, but hc was still one of the few men she remembered with fondness. He had been her dark young gentleman, her muse, and had set her on the path she'd followed ever since.

– He was your muse, and you used him and promised him a lease of freedom you couldn't deliver.

Warm and unsatisfying air caressed her body; it would still be an hour or so before dawn, hardly worth drifting back to sleep and into odd dreams. She reached for the other ingenious young gentleman who shared her bedroom, in word if not in flesh – the much-thumbed copy of Tom Creech's *Lucretius, the Epicurean Philosopher* that she'd blurbed last year. She opened it to a favourite passage, rested on the crook of her leg so she could turn the pages with her left hand, leaving the right free to exercise itself.

– As men ever use women for their pleasure and profit, so I am content to use men in return to serve my own desires.

The following day Aphra Behn had an appointment with *le Pouvoir*. They hadn't given her a time or a location, but so long as she remained in Paris, *le Pouvoir* would find her. She suspected that so long as she remained in France, or even in Europe, they would track her down and deliver her at exactly the time they required. Such was the extent of their reach.

That was fine by her; she wouldn't need to worry about the time, but could browse in Paris at her leisure. Let them do all the legwork if it made them feel important...

Where to go though? The bookstalls beckoned; over here they had something called *magasines* instead of newspapers or pamphlets, and little bands of cruel and satirical drawings that would never catch the imagination of the provincial English. Perhaps the theatre; she was always on the lookout for promising new material that wasn't nailed down, or just an Italianate clown comedy to tickle her fancy. Or there were the caffés, or the churches...

The French churches appealed to her. They touched her spiritual being in a way that English churches did not; they were decorated and opulent, not simply to indulge in worldly riches but reflecting the immaterial wealth of their faith. She could not – *would* not – buy into that faith, as a matter of course, but even so the gold-draped jewel-crusted mysteries of stern French Catholicism turned her soul into living song. By contrast the English churches had all the mystery of a simple man squatting in a ditch to piss. Not their fault of course, they had a hundred years and fifty of vandalism and theft to contend with, but the bleak greys and blacks and whites that had survived to become the Church of England no longer moved her, if they ever had. Aphra Behn preferred the Latin murmur of the Eucharist to the hectoring hellfire bark of the Protestant preacher.

Not today, perhaps. She was about to meet *le Pouvoir*, and they were more formidable by far than the Christian God.

Or she could just perambulate about Paris, trusting that Gallic insouciance would allow a woman to make her own explorations without the benefit of a companion or chaperone. She would have to hobble as her legs felt especially crooked today, but she still refused to use a stick. No one was going to call Aphra Behn a cripple or a sot!

She admitted this very reluctantly – because they *were* after all French, and therefore the second most disreputable people on Earth after the joyless colonials of America – but the French were far better suited to authority and statecraft than the English, who seemed to have backed timidly into their global estate. It was only a pity that their capital was such a slum, especially compared with the magnificent new architecture at Versailles. Paris could do with a Great Fire of its own, demolishing the narrow wooden streets and higgledy-piggledy buildings to make room for a new and monumental city of towers and boulevards, better fitted to an imperial imagination. There would be no surrender in France to the petty fogs thrown up by small-minded planners and bureau-crats as there had been – and still were – in London. Wren, a man of stature and vision, was said to have wept when his Great Design for Saint Paul's was rejected; *too Popish*, they said, *where is the nave for the procession?* they said, *the time it will take is an impediment to worship*, they said, and the King had heeded their complaints. Let them try that on all-powerful Louis here, and see how far it would get them!

Like London, like any city, Paris had an individual scent. A city's effluence revealed the eating habits of its citizens, and so offered an insight into their tastes and practices; that might be valuable information in the right hands. She imagined an expert with a nose trained fine enough to tell the subtle distinctions between the different bouquets of shit; he might make an amusing character on stage. No, too trivial. For the moment though she was thinking of a lasting work that might recommend her reputation to posterity. Not drama or poetry perhaps, but a narrative in prose and at length. With the right subject –

'Mistress Behn! Aphra!'

Fuck, is that Samuel Morland?!

She was passing a printer's with galleys pegged out on lines like washing left to dry in the sun, and suddenly there he was further down the street, a reedy streak of piss in black, pushing his way through the passers-by towards her. It is Sir Sam! Fuck!

She swung round and pushed her face close to the nearest pages, incoherent French type focusing and unfocusing before her eyes as through a flawed lens. Pretend you haven't seen him! Don't make eye-contact! God's tits, he's still coming!

Run! Into the crowd!

Fuck! Fuck! Fuck! Fuck! Fuck!

He was hollering her name from a distance, and she trotted away on her dumpy aching legs, knowing that his long strides would soon catch her unless she could shake him off. As if sensing her distress, every door in every wall in Paris opened up to flood the already-squeezed alleyways with the human carnival. Bland faces stared at her and careless bodies contrived to block her way. She wished she had a stick after all. Out of my way you bloody baboons, can you not see I am a cripple?!

'Aphra! Wait!'

Sir Sam was still hot on her heels. Damn the man, what could he want? Was it just coincidence that put him in her path? Maybe he'd just want a friendly chat or a stroke of her pussy, and she was damned if she'd let him have either. Or maybe he was about the Service's business, or *le Pouvoir*'s...

Oh fuck, what if he's my contact in *le Pouvoir*? He was said to be a favourite of the French court, in spite of all his shortcomings...

No, not Sam. They would know about all his disasters. They'd know about the fiasco at Salomon's House, and how he'd disgraced himself. Master or no, they wouldn't let such a fool and a turncoat anywhere near the levers of power. She thrust herself into a fissure between two houses and squeezed her way through to another street, scraping pitch and dirt onto her skirts as she went. She burst out into the fresh air and right into Sir Samuel's waiting embrace.

'Why it is you!' he exclaimed, ignoring or perhaps oblivious to her face of dismay and contempt. The hunt only stirred the blood of men such as him, if the ground was dry and the prey slow and easy. 'Mistress Behn, the celebrated she-spy. It's been far too long since we last spoke.'

Aye, since Carola died, and you rolled over readily into the bed of the first whore who would have you. Who just happened to be Aphra Behn, but so what? For *me* it was grief.

'I must walk, Sam,' she insisted, stumbling away on feet now sore and wracked with the pains brought on by her twisting treacherous bones. 'I have a lot of ground to cover.'

'Then let me walk with you,' he said, hoving unhurriedly alongside her like a black pirate frigate preparing a boarding party. His hand went down her back to pat her bum. She felt her face burn red with so many resentments and frustrations. But keep yourself cool, Aphra, if he is *le Pouvoir* then he's the last man you want to cross.

'You look tired, Aphra. You should rest.'

'Perhaps,' she said on reflection, 'we can stop for a drink. Catch up with old times.'

She found she was still able to smile into that face, now much older than she remembered. Sir Samuel Morland, Cromwell's chief spy and Charles's Master of Mechanicks, lately visiting engineer to the Court of Versailles. Sir Sam, the tutor, postmaster, and turncoat, who bent whichever way the wind was blowing. Sam Morland, poor dead Carola's callous husband...

He was dressed all in black, in a cape and shirt and puffed breeches that would have been the height of fashion in London, but here in the dandy's capital made him appear as stolid and unexciting as a provincial schoolmaster with straw sticking out of his boots. Age had not been kind to him, and he had always been a pinched and sour-looking fellow. Like the Florentine he was an ugly old man now...

She prayed God he would not steer her into his bed again, or into a storm...

He guided her to a seat outside a nearby caffé, under the row of hanging hats left there by Parisian gallants as they fermented their plots and drank their filthy brew within. Like the unenlightened English, the tiny-minded French barred women from their coffee-houses for fear that womanly magics would somehow disrupt the potent masculine energies within.

She was still wheezing from the effort of her escape attempt. 'Not coffee,' she insisted. 'It is abominable. And not tea either, they don't have the first idea about tea over here. I'll have red wine or a pot of beer and damn what the quacks say.'

Sir Samuel obliged, disappearing for a moment – she considered legging it in the other direction, and only stayed seated for fear that she might drop dead otherwise – and returning with a bottle. He poured them out two equal measures. 'Shall we make a toast?' he asked.

'Carola,' she proposed.

'Carola,' he concurred, and if her suggestion stung him it did not show on his face, the bastard.

'You're still loyal to Her Majesty,' he suggested, as she took her first sip. 'Still drinking that filthy Iberian beverage,' he clarified.

'I like the taste, that's all. As I grow older, I must admit I find it sour and take it sweetened with a little milk or butter.'

'You Tories,' he said, and swallowed, 'you are all Catholics, sweetened with a little milk or butter.'

'We are of the King's party, but Charles is no Catholic.'

'You think not? His brother is. And he must convert eventually. I have seen the secret treaties, I know this to be so.'

She knew how to field this. 'He will not convert. The moment Louis has what he wants, the flow of French coin into Charles's pockets will dry up; then he'll have to go to Parliament to pay for his races and his wars. And how do you think that hive of villains will treat him after what he did to them last time? If he'd lately declared for Rome too...' She left the implication hanging and unspoken. Civil War renewed.

'Agreed. Rowley is subtler than the rest of them. Out of a family of fools, he is not a fool.'

'Sam, you speak treason.'

'Aphra, since you were born there hasn't been an Englishman who hasn't, at one time or another, held views that might be called treasonable. We must learn to compromise.'

Like you did, when you ran snivelling to the court in exile the moment you fell out of Cromwell's good graces? I may find his ideas repulsive, but the man himself was great and deserving of respect.

'I don't want to talk about this.'

'But Aphra, the crunch will come one day, and soon. *Le Roi Soleil* grows impatient. In the end Rowley will have to go to Parliament for funds, and like it or not he will have to hang your precious Duke out to dry. The King will bend, Parliament will have their exclusion, and the Americans will have a city to rename.'

'Sam!'

'*New Monmouth* has a nice ring to it, don't you agree? York will probably be given some governorship. Give him a chance to boss some long-faced Protestants around, eh?'

Exasperated now – 'Sam, let us not talk politics.'

'I don't talk politics, but as we are on Service we must be aware of the way the scales tip.'

I am on Service, Sam, but *you* are not. She didn't say that, though. She had some inkling of his game now. She was disappointed that it wasn't a ride he wanted. Their feet lay side-by-side below the table, and Sam made no effort to tease her legs apart or let his hands wander; if he'd been a better fisherman he might have done.

Still, best to deflect him into a new topic: 'So, what have you been up to? I hear you were building a water engine for *le Soleil.*' She'd also heard it hadn't worked, and he'd been expelled from court for a time, pursued by the braying laughter of the King's ridicule. Not that he'd admit it.

'I decided not. It would have been a demotion of my proper talents. I have a greater project on my tables by far.'

'Tell me, Sam.' It wouldn't be anything important, she guessed, and she would only have to flutter her eyelids to get him to let her in on a great secret. Men like Morland needed to be visible, no matter how trivial their endeavours.

'Oh, it is not something I am at liberty to talk about.' Flutter, flutter. 'But I can hardly refuse Aphra Behn! I am designing a new engine for the exploration and conquest of Selene, so it might be added to French territories.'

God almighty, the man was mad. 'That sounds most intriguing.'

'We may yet be the first, especially since many earlier voyages have been discredited as frivolous fancies. The Chevalier de Cyrano, for example...'

'His method of transportation would hardly be suitable for conquest, but pray go on sir...'

'The Society of Jesus sent an expedition to the Orient two years since to ascertain the veracity of Domingo Gonsales' account – you will recall he claimed to have been carried to the moon by migrating geese – but they are yet to report. And the Franciscans are breeding, from the preserved seed of one of their number, flying children who could make landfall on one of the habitable regions. I am determined that the flag of France will beat them to it.'

She could not longer resist it. 'You men! You want the moon on a stick.'

Not realising he was being mocked, Sir Sam ploughed on. She could see the line of the bottle steadily descending, and she herself had barely sunk a mouthful. 'My engine is the most practical proposition. It is all a question of applying the right *thrust* in the right place.'

'You are moon-crazy, Sam. I can't imagine why anyone would want to go to there. We have our own vast globe to explore and despoil.'

'Such cynicism, Aphra; you have become old.'

'Nonsense. I was always like this. I live in cynical times, Sam.'

He gave her a cunning smile. Full of wine now, the old fox was preparing to resume his attack. 'What does bring you to Paris, Aphra? I'm right that it's Service business.'

So he was fishing, nothing more. He was a beached fish himself, struggling to survive on dry land, desperate to get back into the sea. She almost felt sorry for him. 'It's Service business, and therefore not yours.'

'Whose business is it, Aphra? Who's running the circus these days? It's not like the old times when we had the Cabal. At least we could narrow it down to one of five men with Rowley's ear. I miss our cabal too, our old friendships.'

'You were never part of *my* cabal, Sam. That was Carola, and she is dead.'

He winced then. It was affected. She knew all the actor's tricks. 'I can hazard who pulls your strings. It's Sunderland isn't it? Oh, I see I have pricked you! Sunderland, eh? Well the Service is in good hands. He's a man after my own heart.'

Indeed, he was a man of no honest convictions, who would jump into bed with whichever faction served his interests best. 'You might be twins,' she commented lightly.

'But I see wider designs still; why else send you to Paris?'

He was rambling drunkenly now, and she felt compelled to release a little knowledge just to shut him up. Christ, he could be standing on the table with his arse out in a minute, or bellowing to the crowd that she was an assassin sent to kill *le Soleil*. If anything would stir the blasé French mob, that would. 'I have a letter to deliver, and I know nothing more than that.'

By now the afternoon sun was beating down on them; Sir Sam was well protected by the brim of his hat, though he must have baked inside that dark costume like a potato in its skin. But Aphra felt the heat worse, she was sure; it had made her flustered and unguarded. Sam's vile wine was clinging to the inside of her stomach like a sheen of sick. She cocked her head and vomited a small ball of it onto the cobbles, among the horse dung. *There! He won't want to put anything in that mouth now, will he?*

'The sun,' she explained. She swilled some more wine to wash her palate. 'Where did the romance go, Sam? They send me back and forth delivering correspondence that I never read and might be trivial beyond measure. When I was young there was a gallant prince in exile, a dark enemy at home, a secret order I swore myself to. What is there now?'

'You have your other outlet for romance. Your scribblings. You wrote for bread –'

'– and now I am ashamed to owne it, Sam. I want to have done something good and lasting with my life. What happened to it all?'

'Tempus fugit.'

'We were cursed when time entered the world.' The bottle was almost empty, so she slugged it back and let the dregs drip moistly onto her lips. 'Do you still like me, Sam? I have a room a little way from here.' Actually it was bloody miles, but she doubted he'd want to walk that far.

'You're old, Aphra,' Sir Samuel Morland told her wistfully, 'and you were never that pretty.'

He had to duck then. The bottle bounced off the wall and shattered among the shit and vomit on the street, a fine carpet for a stinking city. Aphra Behn felt the wine stewing inside her and began to plot a play that would last. It was to be all about the folly of reasonable and rational men, those foolish tinkerers in mechanicks who thought they had forged keys to unlock men's souls. So you want to go to the moon? Well then, I will have a great emperor descend from Selene to mock your worldly follies and conceits. I will turn you into greedy and foolish alchemists and make sport with you all, and I care not if I am remembered for it. All pages are burned by history, all inscriptions fade, and all finery turns to dust. *Time* does this.

This is the Dark Age.

She soon calmed down, and began to feel better disposed towards Sir Sam, who had at least stood her a drink and was a familiar face from home. It wasn't his fault that he preferred skinny titless women, and it wasn't as though she were looking for anything more generous than a clinch or a kiss. A few years back, after a decade of widowhood, she imagined that she might find herself a husband some day; maybe not that elusive mischief *love*, but some steady presence to share her life, who would be content to let her run round with her plays and schemes and handsome young men. Most of her relationships had been with libertines who balked at even that little surrender of their person to another, even in exchange for all her rights and properties.

Still she slunk back to her rooms feeling a little merry to begin with, but strewing that happiness like petals as she went, so by the time she was 'home' she was thoroughly miserable. She trudged to her door and up the narrow wood steps, only to find shabby female bodies obstructing the way to her room and her bed.

There were two, both more slender than her and taller. Both had puffed white hair, like pastries; one had thick muscular arms, the other had bared nipples, nut-brown and nut-textured; and both women wore ivory vizards, chinless so she could see their thin and spotted lips. One tossed a pile of coins, leisurely, on her palm. Tired and in no mood for conversation, Aphra tried to brush past them and was blocked.

'Look at this spoiled meat,' one muttered in elegant-accented French, 'muscling in on our patch. Name your principals, madame.'

'Out of the way please,' she said, straining for politeness and finding herself unwittingly speaking English.

'Hah! She's a fuckoff, come over here to steal our jobs and our men.'

'I may be English, but my French is perfectly good, and I am no harlot.'

'We know a harlot when we see one, don't we Jeanette?'

Jeanette smiled cruelly below her line of ivory. 'The English would call us *punks*, would they not? Who pimps your purse, madame punk?'

Aphra had finally squeezed through a gap, braving their tickling fingers around her neck and waist. She was almost to her door when one called in clear plain English. 'It isn't the Earl of Sunderland. We know that now.'

Aphra stopped mid-tread.

'Do you know his name? No, you don't. Names don't matter for the likes of us, do they, Madame Astraea?'

She turned to stare down at them, wordlessly. They beckoned to her as one and spoke as one: '*Le Pouvoir* persuades. *Le Pouvoir* protects. *Le Pouvoir* punishes. You will come with us, please.'

Oh Christ, not now, not when I have a splitting headache and so much dead wine in my guts. One word out of place and they'll slit me and gut my lights and dunk me in the Seine.

'*Le Pouvoir* is polite,' she said, through painfully gritted teeth, holding out both hands so they could lead her away. She was no longer Aphra Behn, the punk and poetesse, but fearless, immortal Astraea who was more than a match for *le Pouvoir*'s furies.

She just wished she felt more like Astraea and less like fearful, mortal Aphra.

There was a carriage waiting outside that hadn't been there a minute earlier when she'd arrived home. It was varnished a dense black that made it seem almost invisible in these streets, hidden in the overhanging shadows of the surrounding *maisons*. There was no livery and she saw no coachman (or, she supposed, coachwoman) as the two harlots escorted her smoothly into the cab as though she were a noblewoman and they her faithful retainers. They had pistols concealed in their skirts or their bags, she had no doubt of that. She sank into the luxurious upholstered seat, and smiled politely across the gap at the two blank-faced agents of *le Pouvoir*.

'Madame Astraea –'

She risked a moment of defiance, raising a finger to her mouth to silence the woman. 'Just *Astraea*.'

'Very well then, *Astraea*, but do not interrupt again, or Jeanette will be forced to snap the little finger on your left hand.'

'I'd like that,' Jeanette told her, with her visible lips forming something like a smile, but broken. 'And Sandrine will enjoy watching.'

Sandrine found a stick beneath her seat and rapped on the ceiling with it; the carriage lurched forward, pushing Astraea back into the deceptive cushions. The stick had a grey metal fist for a head, clenched – when it came to symbolism, *le Pouvoir* were nasty, brutish, and to the point. She said nothing for fear of her fingers.

'Now you will be blindfolded.' Sandrine produced a white bandage from her bag, and Astraea offered no resistance as it was wrapped round her eyes. It saved her having to look into the masked eyes of the furies and so imagine the casual cruelties they must have learned to rise so high in their masters' hierarchy. As she was bound, Jeanette leaned closed and whispered into her ear: 'When we arrive at your destination, you will be searched by men. We would like you to know these men are the worst scum in France, murderers and rapists reprieved from the gallows or the military prisons for *le Pouvoir*'s purposes. Should we for a moment imagine that you have betrayed *le Pouvoir* your body will be forfeited to them. Do you understand?'

'Perfectly,' she replied, smooth and confident. Another good thing about the blindfold – they wouldn't see her fear.

'Good, then *le Pouvoir* will guarantee your health and liberty; all will be well.'

The rest of the journey passed without incident, except for the smooth sensation of a glove – Jeanette's, she presumed – stroking her little finger, up and down, down and up. The coach clattered through the tight streets of the city – Astraea doubted they would go further, not even to Versailles – and paused frequently for jams, still patches of boredom punctuated by the hoots and complaints of pedestrians. Their foolish voices made her feel a lot better.

When they halted, Astraea allowed herself to be taken down from the coach, into a building, and then on an expedition through a maze of interior tunnels. She was searched by silent and scentless fingers, but by now she was confident enough to sense the mummery going on round her. She knew these tricks from the theatre, and felt at once both an affinity with the devious masters of *le Pouvoir* and a complicit party in their deception. This was a dance or a ceremony as impressive, in its own way, as any Catholic magic. They found the letter among her effects, but thrust it back into her hands once they were done. Then, finally, the hands of *le Pouvoir* guided her into a comfortable chair and stripped away the blindfold. She was thrust back into the light, which radiated brighter than she had remembered and left her blinking in the inner sanctum.

It was rather less impressive than she'd imagined. The dust was everywhere, underfoot, on the walls and furnishings, crumbling almost as she watched from naked wood beams and rotting old tapestries. As well as dust, there was everywhere light, a least a hundred candles on every available surface, raised on stands, and hanging on chains from the ceiling. There were no windows, no openings. They were deep within the heart of the fastness, deep inside and possibly down. And by the far wall, covered in sheets to catch both the dust and the eye, were three regular shapes, twice the height of a tall man, with sharp corners poking at the fall of the cloth.

Astraea felt quite lightheaded in this hollow but airless hall.

In the centre of the room, between her and the concealed objects, a man sat at table eating. He appeared, if Astraea was any judge, to be partway through a light supper; fish, she guessed, or a white meat in sauce, with vegetables and slices of fruit on a side plate. He ignored her, and continued to work his way through his meal, chewing slowly and using his cutlery diligently as if he had only recently learned how they should properly be held. This man had egg-white skin, rouged around the cheeks and painted with uglifying spots. He had a livid red wig in the French courtly style that ran halfway down his back, but he was otherwise dressed in off-white, slightly dusty fabric that in its mock-shabbiness was more elegant than Sir Samuel Morland could have imagined.

This man's servants too failed to look at her, though in their case it was harder as their eyes were pointed straight at her. There were two flanking him, both maids, both tall and naked except for their caps and knee-length socks. And there were more at her back; Astraea turned to look over her shoulder to find Jeanette and Sandrine, dressed as before but now armed with flintlocks. One shot only, but then they would only need one shot, if she tried anything. Which, she decided at length, she wouldn't.

Astraea's host kept on working his way through that fish (or chicken). She filled the dead time with idle speculation about the other women present. What were their names? How could they stand the cold? Were they even French, or perhaps recruited from some obscure portion of the Amazon? She allowed herself to be impressed but not intimidated. Gradually she allowed herself to become bored. She had imagined worse than this *pantomime*. She turned the undelivered letter in her idle hands.

Eventually her host finished and made an extravagant belch, an extravagant fart, an extravagant dabbing of the mouth with a handkerchief that he found after a long search through his pockets. Finally he pushed the plate away, so it fell from the table and struck the floor with a crash; then he kicked out the leg of the table so it followed and broke into five pieces. The rounded tabletop rolled on its edge for a moment before settling down. The maids hurried forward to clean up the wreckage, removing it – and themselves – silently through the only visible door.

Her host showed her yellowed, browned teeth – an imperfection that was surely not affected – and regarded her as a hungry man would regard a succulent sweetmeat.

'You were born Aphra Johnson,' he told her, 'in the English county of Kent, some forty-two years and six months ago. You have claimed aristocratic descent, but in fact your father was a barber-surgeon. Twenty years ago, you were married, briefly, to a German or Dutch merchant named Johann or Joachim Behn, though there is no sur-viving record either of the marriage or his death. You work for an organisation that calls itself the Service, and have done, in one way or another, for the past thirty years. Your number within the Service is 160, and your nom-de-guerre is Astraea. You have writ-ten a number of plays and other works distinguished only by the fact that their author – unlike all other practitioners of your trade – has a *cunt*. This is all that we need to know about you.'

She gave him her most disarming smile. 'Charmed. And you must be the esteemed representative of *le Pouvoir*.'

He snorted. '*Le Pouvoir, c'est moi!*' Then he was all dirty-toothed smiles again. 'You may call me Monsieur Pantaloon.'

'Charmed,' she repeated dryly. 'This letter is for you, I think.'

Sandrine plucked it from her lap and delivered it to M. Pantaloon. He held it between his thumbs, sniffed the paper suspiciously and did not make to break the seal.

'For me, yes, but from whom? Sunderland is the hand, almost certainly, but not I think the author.'

'I don't know who –'

'Did you fart, madame? Your pardon, you emitted a noise from some orifice or another. It is insolent to speculate on the affairs of your superiors.'

In spite of the guns at her back – or perhaps the sensation that there was now only one still at her back as Sandrine had removed herself to M. Pantaloon's side – Astraea felt a surge of cocky confidence. For all its menaces, this was the game of espionage as she'd hoped she might play it. 'I have nothing but admiration for my superiors and yours, sirrah, but I do not care for the insolence of servants. If le Soleil knew what sort of man was acting in his authority –'

At a gesture from M. Pantaloon, she was seized from behind, the vicious vice of Jeanette's elbow hooked tight round her neck. She couldn't breathe; her hands snatched pathetically at the air.

'Louis is nothing! There is only le Pouvoir! Enough!'

The pressure was gone, and she fell forward from her chair choking and gasping like poor pathetic Aphra, not defiant and radiant as Astraea should be. Her windpipe felt crushed, but worse, it fell dry as though she were drowning in desert air. She coughed up imaginary sand. M. Pantaloon rose and paced round her in an orbit, his precise tread leaving a circle of delicious marks in the dust.

'You English have become the little Arab boy who finds a jar in the sands and breaks it open expecting treasures or precious oils, only to release a howling demon with many eyes and hungry teeth to eat you up. You made of yourself, however briefly, l'etat raté. Your revolution may have failed, but you have let an evil precedent into the world. How long before such incontinence spreads to France? It may take a hundred years, but it will come eventually. It will overwhelm le Pouvoir, and then who will secure for the people their rights and freedoms? There will be only the tyranny of the mob.'

'A hun'ed years...' she gagged, '...'s a long time.' She thought of protesting her life-long devotion to Royalism and Toryism, but he would find some way to twist this to her disadvantage.

'On the contrary, it is all too short. Le Pouvoir has been forced to contemplate the futures and consider how they might be shaped. In time, we will have to adapt and become not an organisation but a form of knowledge, a set of ideas that can be passed from mouth-to-ear or hand-to-hand. We must float across oceans like seeds and settle in the New World. Le Pouvoir must migrate.'

Astraea felt better now, and had climbed back into her chair. 'Then you will no longer be French,' she replied.

'La France is a mayfly! Le Pouvoir is eternal!'

'Aren't you going to read your letter? It might need a reply.'

M. Pantaloon still held her letter in his exquisitely-gloved grip, but seemed taken aback by her suggestion. He held it up again as if it were a handful of seaweed or a dead bird. Then his lips rode back to reveal those teeth again, and the blood-starved gums in which they were set. He mock-bowed to her, and retreated from the room. Sandrine and Jeanette fell into line behind him, closing the door and leaving Astraea alone with the candles and the mute oblongs against the wall.

She felt perplexed, but quickly adjusted to the realisation that this was another piece of *le Pouvoir*'s tradecraft, perhaps the lull between acts. She swivelled round on her arse to look at the back wall, suddenly afraid that there might be a restless audience there, chattering, whoring, or sucking oranges, waiting for the action to resume. She was, of course, alone.

Astraea stood and walked the length of the room, slipping cautiously between the candles, which burned furiously hot in such quantities. She went to the door, opened it, found a pistol in her face, closed it again gently. So she was to be kept in here. *Le Pouvoir* did nothing without purpose, even if it was her Masters in the Service who would be left to decode it from the details of her reports. Even that long rant about the coming century seemed designed to send a message. A change of American policy, she thought, or perhaps hints of the discovery of even Newer Worlds, like the fabled *Terre Australe.*

Or maybe it meant nothing at all, and was just a distraction, so that the finest minds in Service might lose themselves in ever more devious layers of interpretation...

There were times when Aphra Behn had to admit to herself she wasn't cut out for Service life. It was only her day job. Really, she was a playwright.

She found her way round to the back of the hall, where the tempting shapes were still buried under their covers. Too tempting. She tugged on the edge of the sheets. They slid away smoothly, revealing three tall mirrors in plain wooden stands. Three Astraeas stared back at her from a surface that might have been darkened glass, or thin black metal. She had realised that she would appear tired, and perhaps also a little frightened, but not so harassed, nor worn so thin (not literally, of course, there were still the chubby rolls of flesh around her neck and her hips). The mirrors, she guessed, were destined for the ice cream gallery at Versailles, or maybe its shadow built in the secret warren inside the walls of the new palace. Even spear-carriers had to make themselves presentable backstage before being thrown into the public eye.

Candles on stands both side of her rustled on no detectable breeze and snuffed themselves out.

She turned and found it was a plague of darkness and every flame in the room had succumbed, dying with insect-trails of black smoke rising from their spent wicks. The hall became a lot larger and colder, full of ever-deeper shadows and pervaded with the meaty scent of the beasts from whose fats the candles had been rendered. This was a good trick *le Pouvoir* were pulling on her. The Duke's would pay good money for an effect like this.

Still, she backed slowly to her chair, in case there was more to it than just smoke and mirrors.

There was still a mild light in the hall as the last candle went out, reflected in the triptych glasses. No, not reflected, it was on the glaze itself, and there was more than light, there were images as if projected on a camera obscura. She whirled round looking for a concealed mechanism, but it was well-hidden in the dark.

Right, this is beginning to look a lot like witchcraft...

There must *be a trick to it!*

The best part of the trick was that each mirror showed a different picture. She could see each clearly, the lustre of the glass and the smoky darkness of the room sharpening her senses. In the central frame she saw a city much like the Paris of her idle morning's imaginings; the old brick buildings torn down and recast in marble, filled with wide white avenues, arches, and spires into the sky, and towers seeming fused together from a thousand panes of glass. The human ants were dwarfed in this metropolis of white stone monuments; trees and animals were nowhere to be seen, but the people surged around in hasty mobs. Their supine smallness disturbed her a little, and the more she looked, the blanched triumphant architecture seemed less like majesty than leprous sickness. The men of this city carried swollen sacs of flesh on their necks and had no eyes, their ghost sockets hollowed out by surgery. They climbed and descended staircases joylessly like trudging Calvinists, while arrayed on all the walls were banners celebrating their wealth and freedom, and great murals in which naked men and women swived freely and bathed in luxury. This was a stagnant and interminable vision, but it was at least unthreatening.

The second possibility – Astraea was sure now she was looking into glasses of future-time, the imaginings and projections of *le Pouvoir* as they pondered the outcomes of history – was far more terrible. Here, in the mirror on the right, there was no city, but an enormous foundry where men and women lived in narrow breeding cages built into metal walls, or among the fabric of the ruling machines. There was no longer a sky here, it was blotted by the grey pollution of the world-factory. Those persons not harnessed to the machines or confined in cages were regimented in deep and narrow trenches cut sheer into the Earth. They were literal regiments, a new model army in uniforms and banners decorated with the recurring symbol of six crowns. There were no longer pictures of carefree copulation on the wall, but images of their enemies gagged and leashed and hooded, tortured, raped, and killed. The numb eyes of the indentured soldiers described an eternal struggle against an implacable Adversary that could be held at bay only by the constant sacrifice of fresh bodies and fresh blood. Was this the future that *le Pouvoir* wanted? It depended, Astraea reasoned, on who flew the flag of the six crowns. If it was *le Pouvoir*, then this would be their paradise; if not, then this was an abominable tyranny they must destroy. Her eyes left this mirror just as a black sun rose over the Earth, impaled and caged by metal spikes and what looked like settlements. Perhaps Sir Sam Morland's moon-engine had drifted to the wrong sphere…

The vision in the mirror on the left was by far the strangest, the reflection of a dream rather than anything conceivable or solid. Here was an idyll, a sunless world with iron skies patrolled by stained-glass birds, above a glistening landscape of crystal trees and pillars of solid light. Men and women strolled here, sometimes clothed, sometimes naked, sometimes in machine-like cages of hissing steam, sometimes in bodies that rippled into new shapes with each step, yet never hurried or distressed. Such calm and contentment commanded the scene, Astraea knew she was looking at a world lost.

As one, all three mirrors shimmered and changed, all three revealing a new image, a glimpse into a world almost like the infinitesimal universes revealed by the glare of microscopes. Like those freshly-discovered atomies, its worlds were populated by micrographian insects, with grey skins and segmented bodies and mandibles. They dropped lightly through the vasty black air on buds of water or some other grey liquid, sucking out fluid through tube-like mouths and excreting it through what Astraea had assumed were eyes. It came out as clouds of powder, each mote finer and tinier than the most powerful microscope could uncover, the same shimmering fabric as this trio of magic mirrors. She *understood* this, as if it were written for her. These sights were more than vision; they had a sentiment to reveal or a compulsion that invaded and shaped her thoughts. She was seeing a flat world that the mirrors promised to make solid. She looked again – the insects sat at the prow of cylindrical boats, which carried unimaginably tiny figures – people, angels, monsters – on the vortices between spheres. Their cargoes seemed happy and mindless, but the insects themselves sat vigil on the surface of the mirror, keenly probing for the slightest twitch and tremble in their world, for the ripple that might overturn their craft and pitch all into the black waters beneath the glass –

Astraea flinched and looked away. When she looked back there were more visions, flickering rapidly over the glaze in mosaic fragments and impressions: a city with a vast crater burned into its face, the pit left by a dead cancer; golden vessels like screwthreads floating in a black sea pocked with lights; faceless shock-troops in leather armour charging, with fragile wire-metal banners sprouting from their heads; a dusky maiden moving frightfully through a library of identical, black-spined books; they whirled too quickly, these *fata morgana*, and they made her seasick on dry land.

Astraea stood and the floor lurched like a wave beneath her feet. She closed her eyes to block out the future. When she opened them again, the windows had calmed down to show a single image, the same in each glass, but this was no reflection. It was the same stately slender woman, still young, with long red hair cascading down her naked yet somehow sexless body to preserve her modesty; her hands held out, palms displayed, as if knowing she was watched, as if drawing Astraea towards her... and she *did* take a step forward, and *did* put her hand to the glass, which neither yielded nor wobbled.

The nymph opened her eyes and they were black from lid to lid, swirling and molten.

Astraea's legs – so strained today – finally give way.

Then she was brought round by the gentle splash of warm water across her body and onto her face; and then it was the rank smell of the stream that jolted her completely back to consciousness. The candles had been relit, and the sheets restored over the mirrors. Light glistened off the stream of M. Pantaloon's piss. He shook the last few drops from the end of his penis, then slipped it back into his tights.

It took a moment for her to think of an appropriate comment. Ah, there it was. 'You are aware that our two countries are supposed to be allies.'

'England will forever be the junior partner. Be grateful I did nothing worse than piss on your ugly face while you slept.'

'I can't go home like this,' she protested.

'Sandrine! Jeanette! Make sure she is bathed and freshly costumed before you take her home. Well, Madame Behn, you have seen our secret here. Tell your Service *yes* – *le Pouvoir* has the windows of divination that no other nation will ever have. Tell them they are well-defended. There is no earthly agency that can take them from us'

Astraea sat up and flapped haplessly to shake the thickest droplets of piss from her skin. Some splashes landed on *le Pouvoir*'s furies and she felt rather better about herself after that.

'I had a letter,' she said, as she stood. 'They will expect a reply.'

M. Pantaloon span on his heels, her letter in his hands. He folded it rapidly then ripped it apart, tossing the pieces into the air, where they floated pathetically for a moment before dropping to the floor.

'*Le Pouvoir* is generous,' he declared. 'We have our windows and they cannot be duplicated. Your request is granted and will be delivered to your lodgings tonight. Tell your catchers they may have their rat.'

It was all she could think about on the journey back to her room. No one had told her there would be Ratcatchers. There were *never* Ratcatchers on her missions, not even to Antwerp when their invaluable assistance had been palpable by its absence. If it had been the daytime and had she been spared Sandrine's bluff, she might have spent the trip back staring out the window looking for them. Not that she expected them to parade around in Paris in their waistcoats and hoods, that would have been ostentatious, but she could look on the coiled, burly men she saw and speculate that they might be on England's Service.

The blind ride home was, in the end, much less fraught than the ride out. She was simply too tired to be intimidated, and she sensed that the furies who guarded her were wearier still. *Le Pouvoir* was only as powerful as the people they employed, and so long as they still came in vulnerable and exhaustible human bodies, then it would never live up to its fierce reputation. She spent the journey half-sleeping, with her head pressed into the upholstery and bouncing painfully whenever the wheels of the coach hit a cobble or a pothole. Eventually it reached her door, and her keepers couldn't wait to strip her out of her blindfold and show her out into the street so they could make their way in the direction of their own beds.

She was just grateful to be back; she stumbled up the stairs, stepping this time over a genuine harlot who lay sprawled drunk and drowsy at the bottom, clearly not successful enough to afford a room. Aphra Behn – no longer pretending at Astraea – felt a twinge of some long-buried sentiment as she got halfway up the stairs, turned back and pushed a small coin into the child's unresisting hand. If it would keep her from the whorehouse or the prison for one night, it might have done some good.

Then back up the stairs again, hobbling on her crooked legs; finally, Aphra Behn made it back to the safety of her bed only to find there was a man already in it.

He had been left there trussed and gagged, a look of naked terror in his eyes. They bulged wider as he saw Aphra, and she went stumbling to free him. He seemed familiar – a youngish man, no longer a youth but still her junior, and fair-faced (though currently contorted by mortal fear). Her numbed fingers picked helplessly at the expert knots that bound his wrists behind his back, but found no purchase. She paused then, watching herself through a haze of exhaustion, finding this to be an odd way to end an odd day.

'I wouldn't touch him,' came a sardonic voice in English; a Yorkshire accent, but muffled. She hardly needed to turn to know she would find him hooded and wearing a tanned and neatly-tailored manskin uniform. He and his troop had come very quietly up the stairs behind her, the furtive tread of the exterminator in pursuit of his verminous prey. She doubted that they would have left coins for the half-dead whore in the doorway.

'Who is this?' she asked.

'One of the most dangerous men in the world. We'll keep him here under guard tonight and get him aboard ship tomorrow.'

She stared at her captive, ignoring the desperate pleas of his eyes, seeing only the hateful ropes that held him tight. She thought of him aboard ship, being dragged across unfriendly waters to a fate she couldn't even contemplate. *They've made you a slaver.*

The Service and le Pouvoir *alike – they've turned you into everything you always hated.*

She turned to face the Ratcatcher-Serjeant, summoning up as much anger as she could from the depths of her half-slumbering soul. 'So where the fuck am I going to sleep tonight?!'

And that was how Aphra Behn came to spend the last night of her trip to Paris squatting in a chilly doorway snuggling against the warm body of a blissfully unconscious prostitute, sharing a tatty blanket and a hard pillow from her room. In spite of circumstances, she found it very easy to get to sleep.

And just before she slipped away, it occurred to Aphra that she *did* remember the trussed, frightened man that *le Pouvoir* had left for her. He had been at Salomon's House... twelve years past... he'd been with Aphra the last time she'd seen *her*...

And soon she was away in a shallow sleep, dreaming of nymphs and old idylls.

⇒ Chapter 3: *The Family of Eyes* ⇐

Mistress Piper had only one dream, and it had come true on the day she was married. It was this: she wanted a house, a respectable little building, neither too large nor too small. It would be far enough outside a great city that she wouldn't have to suffer the busy-ness of metropolitan life, yet still within easy reach so that she could – when the whirl took her – dive into its streets and sample its excitements and heady pleasures.

In this house she would have a respectable husband with a respectable trade. He would work hard and humbly at his appointed vocation, which would earn him no honours in court or society, nor make him rich, nor rob her of the pleasures of his company. They would be comfortably-off and never troubled by worries over money. Their concerns would be domestic and prosaic; their arguments would be reasonable, and never loud enough to shake the walls or alert the neighbours to the petty storms of their private world.

Outside the house there would be a garden, which her husband would cultivate for vegetables and she would tend for beauty. There would be bright green trees in the summer garden, and proud naked brown barks in the winter. They would live among modest folk like themselves, half of the city and half of the country, with wholesome ambitions but a repertoire of interesting stories. No one who lived in England today could not have some choice anecdote about their lives during the interregnum. There had been privation for all, no matter what their politics. And yes, that was another thing: politics would not intrude on this cosy dream; all voices would ever turn to flightier topics.

She imagined, but did not dream, that some day the house would fill with new voices. Babes would add to the burden of her happiness, and her husband's. Children would not divide them, as they did some families. A grown son would provide for them, a grown daughter delight them and most pleasurably break their hearts when she found her own beau, and both between them would illuminate their old age and speed them contentedly to Arcadia.

There had been only one minor blemish when her wishes had come true, and it was that she did not love her husband, while her husband, in his turn, did not love her. What surprised her was how little difference this made. She'd fretted over it for a time, but decided that they were better off without love, which would complicate their plain relationship. Far better to have a shared life founded on the rocks of quiet respect and occasional affection than the quicksands of momentary passion. It was babyish to think otherwise.

Their union still had magic, of a kind. Their wedding day had come barely two years after Charles, a prince no longer, rode into London on the hopes and relief of his subjects. Some blood was spilled, but moderately and within the letter of the law, so old wounds were not reopened. The riven land began to mend, and bitter enmities melted like the snows in spring; it was not simply kingship that had been restored, but the very soul of England. Charles was the panacea the nation craved. He laid hands on the sick and they were cured, on the lame and they were made whole. He brought more than just an end to war – he brought peace. It was called a new Golden Age. So it was with Thomas Piper and his young bride.

She had been fifteen, and he almost three times her senior, the ranks of her contemporaries having been drastically thinned. He was a glove-maker by trade, and a most successful one, with a little house waiting for her in the parish of Hornsey St Mary to the north of London. It still bore the marks of his long widowhood, but nothing that couldn't be erased. She, by contrast, was a virgin who first broke her maiden's blood in the honeymoon bed, and who had not lived in a time when the banners of King and Parliament hadn't been set against one another. So there was a fusion of two opposites: the man and the wife, the old and the young, innocence and experience, tradition and modernity. Their carnal rutting was just that, unblessed by love or children, but still sanctified by God and His church.

Thomas Piper was a-bed now. His wife, still young, did not dare join him or touch him.

She had not dreamed hard enough.

He called his wife's name weakly – his first wife's name, for he was addled.

'I'm here,' she responded, but he may not have heard. His voice was chipped and parched for lack of water, and bile had risen to clog his throat. Hers was simply weak. She lay in the cold arms of the bedroom door in her wonderful little house, and wept. Her limbs were all bone now; all the food she could spare she fed to him, cut into the finest chunks so he might swallow them.

She no longer trusted herself to hold a knife. This morning she put the blade across her finger and drew an even wound that washed across the last, browning vegetables. She doubted he would taste it, and who knows, perhaps a drop of her blood would make him stronger.

No. No, she knew it would not.

Through her shuttered windows, she could see it was night. She found the cold black oblivion preferable to the sticky heat of the day, when the sickly smell of blooming summer flowers was all that covered the stench of nearby decay and the carnal stink of the bonfires in the street. Sometimes she heard low moans, and distant tolls of despair, and they were just about tolerable in darkness, when the eye of God was turned from the Earth; by day it was unbearable. The sun still rose and shone on the rotting world.

'Thomas,' she whispered, 'you must be brave for me. I have food to prepare and will return soon.' She hoped that she didn't lie.

She found the strength in her legs to rise and stumble to the stair-head, not so much walking as throwing herself against the closest wall and bouncing, pushing herself along.

She stumbled more than once, grabbing for any handhold she could with fingers that trembled incessantly. If it were just a walk along the landing to the kitchen then all would be well; if they'd had a more modest home, with only one storey then all would have been well; but there were the stairs. They were a dozen and three steps – she had counted them up-and-down in rhymes of happier days – easy to descend, hard to climb. If she went down now, then her Thomas could die alone, thinking himself unloved...

But there was no alternative.

She sat and bumped herself down the stairs on her backside, like a child; there was a little pain and a lot of scuffing to her skirts, but that hardly mattered now. Bump-bump-bump. She lost control of her speed, twisted sideways, and began to roll uncontrollably the rest of the way. A wood post slapped an ache into her forehead, and loose nails ripped at both her clothes and her skin as she came tumbling down. She landed with bruises all over her body. Severed hands swayed ghoulishly above her head, reaching leisurely for her...

No, they were just gloves, just empty gloves hung unfinished on a line. She wept.

A little further... just a short way to the door. She crawled now, pulling herself painfully along the ground with her forearms. And there was the door, black and un-yielding. It would be barred. It might even be nailed now, but she didn't need to escape, just to reach it, a little further, a little further...

Finally, panting and retching, she was there. She pulled her eye up to the knot in the wood, the spy-hole she had found last summer, no wider than a man's thumb. There was a little light outside. There would be a guard. There *should* be a guard. She prayed he had not already fled. She made to control her breathing, to control the strum of her heart, to control the force and timbre of her voice.

She called: 'Is anyone out there?'

Nothing. Nothing. Please God I have not dragged myself to die on my own threshold.

'Mistress Piper, you must not come out.'

Relief washed over her; her eyes were stinging again; she clapped hands over nose and mouth to stifle the sound of hope. Then: 'Is that Harry? Harry Fletcher, are you our watchman?'

'For tonight, Mistress. All the others are gone.'

'Fled?'

'Or dead.' She could not tell his mood through the door; there were just the words, blunted by thick English wood. Was he here from duty or fear or despair? Did it matter? She pushed her mouth as close to the knot as she could manage.

'Harry, we are near starved to death! They promised they would leave us food, but have not.'

'They're all dead. There's nothing to bring and no one left to carry it.'

'There's you, Harry.'

'I dare not.'

'Harry!' she pleaded – let me not lose my voice now, let me seem calm and reasonable, or he will surely step away from the door and all hope will be gone – 'Harry. We are not ill. We are only starved. There is a mark on our door and the Angel has passed over us.'

'I dare not break the quarantine. Forgive me, Mistress Piper, but I'm scared. I couldn't bear it, not the rashes and the swellings and the horrid lumps on my body. And there is *nothing* left to bring!'

'Then let us out. Enough time must have passed.'

'Forty days and forty nights! And, no, they are not yet done!'

'Forty days – in God's name, Harry! We are not fasting in the wilderness, we are plain and simple folk! And we are *not* diseased!'

'Then where is your husband?'

'He is a-bed –'

'Ah!'

'– from hunger!' She lied, oh how easily the lies came now. 'He is otherwise healthy.'

'There are no signs on his body?'

'There are not.'

'He breathes freely and does not cough up the blood or the choler?'

'He does not.'

She thought she almost had him then; he was on the very brink, but then he fell silent. She made one more gasp: 'We would be grateful, Harry. You could take anything from the house you wanted, if you just give us back our lives!'

Still silence from Harry, but then: 'May God have mercy on your souls,' and then footsteps retreating from the door, through her garden to the gate and the green way beyond. She didn't hear if he stopped there, as she was already screaming, her face buried in the wood of the door and stroking so that her flesh was scraped with pitch and impaled with tiny splinters. She howled herself out, her lungs and guts and stomach, her name and her life, until there was nothing left of her but a wet and whimpering thing huddled by the door and waiting to die.

God have mercy on our souls.

She woke from this monstrous dream at last, wondering how she could have come to fall asleep on her own porch. It was spring again, and the sky was warm and cloudless. From the garden she could hear the songs sung by the eldest of her grandchildren, and wondered when it was they had come to stay. Thomas must hear this, she must fetch him from his bed; so much older than her and yet still so vital. There was no love, but there was bounty, and they had endured...

She rolled onto her back; the emptiness in her belly was a painful spiked stone.

She thought she heard her husband whispering her given name, but the bedroom was too far away for such a tiny sound to carry. She hoped, for the first time, that he had already died.

She heard the door opening, distantly, and felt it banging on some impediment. There was also a flat pain against her leg, but it quickly ended.

'Harry... I knew... Harry...' she murmured.

Strong arms were lifting her. Oh Lord, is this what it is to be raised into Heaven? And angelic voices:

– Yes, of course I can manage, you retarded little shit. Get her something to eat. Then see what's keeping Mother. (There was a reply; she didn't fully hear it.) – It's not pulling rank, Amphigorey. It's called *experience*. What did you ever do with your old life but lounge around in your pants eating pot noodles?! Yeah, and fuck you too!

Gentle fingertips, running through her hair and teasing the curls. 'Poor girl. You look like you could murder a pot noodle.'

Her head swayed as they carried her into the parlour and laid her down in Thomas's armchair, a so much more comfortable place to die. The hands that held her now patted her face; they were gloved, warm and dry, and this was the most pleasant thing Mistress Piper had felt in a long time. Something pressed to her lips, a narrow opening like a bottle but with a strange smooth texture. There was water there; she sipped. Oh, yes.

She drank greedily until she began to choke, and let a small river's-worth of fluid out of mouth, down her chin, and onto her breast. There were more footfalls, another person entering the room.

'Marvellous, she's wet herself. Is this really the best we can do?' That was a man.

Closer and sharper, the voice of the hands with the water, a woman: 'She's suffering.' 'We're all suffering.'

She heard the woman's tongue click, as if about to make some sharp retort that never came. Instead she said, 'Give us that here. Let's get something in her belly. Not *that* way, you filthy sod.'

They passed objects into her hands, that she didn't need eyes to identify. Warm bread, freshly-baked; thin slivers of cooked meat; apples; oh! and an orange. She ignored all social niceties and gorged herself, ripping each fresh item with her teeth, bolting it down. She bit into her mouth as she chewed, and swallowed blood, and didn't care.

'She'll sick it up in a minute,' warned the man, but in fact she did not.

Soon, she felt strong enough to open her eyes and risk dispelling this dream of rescue. By then the woman had stepped away from her, while the man had gone – she gathered from a few overheard whispers – to attend their mother. The woman was moving round the parlour to light candles. She was taller than Mistress Piper, and dressed in a cobalt blue gown in a continental style that Thomas would never have allowed his wife to wear out. She had the most alarming deformed head that Mistress Piper had ever seen.

No, there was suddenly a little more candlelight and this benevolent burglar turned, and it was just an alarming deformed mask.

There was a commotion in the hallway; the man returning and with company. He was not nearly as tall as his companion, but also dressed in fine and outlandish fashions that would perhaps have been more sedate in a racier continental city than this plain parlour in fusty old England. The third party, whom he ushered ahead of him, was more conservative in her costume, choosing a simple Quakerish black, but then again she was their mother and much older. She walked slowly with the aid of two sticks, that wobbled tautly beneath her immense weight. There would be harsh marks in the Norwich carpet, Mistress Piper thought idly, that would never be erased.

Walking ahead of them all was the fourth intruder, a small cat, still kittenish, mainly white but with calico patches and a most winsome countenance. Among the new-comers, it alone showed a naked face. The man and his mother both wore versions of the same masks, white and ridged like the skulls of demons described in Genesis, the Lilithim. They were alarming at first sight until she began to see the purpose of them, the semblance they bore to the leather snouts worn by physicians that she had seen abroad before her confinement.

'You are a doctor?' she asked, still wet-jawed and trembling.

'No,' said the man, and simultaneously the woman said, 'I am.' The fat old woman chuckled but said nothing.

Their plague-heads had no effect on their voices, which escaped cleanly through the many breaks and holes in the bone. She still could not see their eyes. She started to wonder if this woman calling herself a doctor was a joke, but decided not to. The world had moved beyond jokes; it was as bad as she feared, and all capable hands of both genders were being called upon to hold back the triumph of death.

Their corpulent mother finished her slow tread into the room and settled down on the couch, which sagged under her bulk. The cat, who had spent its first moments in the room sniffing around the legs of the tables, trotted to the old woman's feet and reached up for her knees. The mother scratched at it idly, on the patterned M of its forehead, and it purred. There were so many simple things in the world that Mistress Piper had forgotten these last days.

The younger woman stepped forward. 'Who else is here? Alive or dead?'

'My husband Thomas, in his bed.' She pointed to the ceiling.

'Dead or alive?'

She closed her eyes for a moment's pause, then replied: 'He was alive when last I saw him.'

'Can you show me? If you're still too weak, I can find my own way.'

'No,' Mistress Piper replied, pushing herself up against the arms of the cacquetoire. She was still weak and still sore and still bloodied, but these strange Doctor Beaks had given her food, and better than food, hope. 'What sort of hostess would leave a guest to find their own way?'

It was still difficult, and the woman-physician stretched out a solid hand to pull her to her feet, then put her arm round her waist to support her. Mistress Piper could only manage a graceful nod to the two strangers she left behind. They were followed out by the cat, who started to delight in picking at the shreds of her hem. When they reached Thomas's door, the she-doctor bade her sit down to rest while she went inside. 'The damage has been done already, but there's no point in taking any risks, especially if it's pneumonic,' she explained, and Mistress Piper nodded politely as if she understood.

She sat outside while the doctor went about her business. Her husband's coarse and audible breaths gradually grew softer and easier, and still a little hope flared in her heart. The strangers' cat continued to play at her ragged skirts for a while, then made an attempt to blunt its claws on her legs, then trotted off happily into the night-shadows. Its mewls spiked the silence and made it friendly.

The woman reappeared, pulling the door gently to as she came.

'We'll talk about your husband later, but now I need to see you. Is there another room where I can examine you?' Mistress Piper felt herself nod numbly. 'Please show me, we may not have much time.'

'Is it *new monick* then?' she asked, as she stood.

The heavy skull-mask shook from side to side. 'No, septicaemic. It's a wonder he's lived this long.'

Just then the cat returned from the shadows with a dead rat in its mouth, which it presented bleeding and twitching at their feet. The woman-physician clapped. 'Good girl!' she announced, and was thus distracted from seeing Mistress Piper's expression as the last flicker of hope was snuffed in her heart.

There was a room they had set aside as a nursery, that would now never be used for that purpose. Thomas, like any husband, collected things here. She remembered how she would complain to him about what he called his *paraphernalia* and she called his *clutter*. Oh Christ –

She watched the physician place each item of her clothes in a shining black sack, along with the body of the rat her cat had killed. 'These will have to be burned,' she explained, casually, or callously. 'I'll see what I can do about your cuts and bruises, but obviously my main worry is if you're infected or not. Even if you are we can nip it in the bud. We got here as quickly as we could.'

'Where are you from, then?' Mistress Piper was curled on the dusty old daybed with her arms and legs folded against the cold. She could not look at this woman, she could not, she could not...

'Venice. Not originally but... no, Venice is simpler.'

'Ah.' They probably had women-physicks and all kinds of wonders in Venice. She had never left England. She doubted now that she would. She wanted to bury herself beneath its soil and be forgotten. 'Is this the end of the world?'

'Yes,' said the doctor, blithely. Finally she raised her hands to lift the mask from her head and Mistress Piper flinched, suddenly frightened of the hidden face – but it proved quite ordinary. She was perhaps ten years her senior, a raven-haired woman with an olive pallor to her face and a sharpness around the eyes that whispered of an Oriental ancestor in distant generations. The Venetians had gone to Cathay, hadn't they? 'It's always the end of the world for someone. But not for you, I hope.'

'How bad is it, then?'

'The plague killed a thousand people today, in London alone.'

There was nothing more that Mistress Piper could say, and she allowed the Venetian woman to examine her, to prod her and poke her with needles, caress her throat and inspect the pits of her arms and legs for buboes.

'When this is done,' she said, absently, mid-examination, 'we will have to introduce you to the family. I'm Cousin Hateman, and downstairs there's Cousin Amphigorey – he'll want to fuck you, but I wouldn't recommend it – and Mother Sphinx. She doesn't say much these days, Mother Sphinx doesn't, but we love her anyway. There is also Cousin Suppression, who you haven't met – he's back at our shrine. The cat's just called Faction Cat.'

'Oh.'

'I think it's a cute name for a cat. Not really a name but, y'know, cute.'

'Are you really from Venice?'

Cousin Hateman looked down at some measurement she'd taken on one of her re-markable medical instruments. Then up again, 'I was born in the Benign Union of Daoust, which is further from here than Venice in so many ways.'

'In the East?'

'If you like.'

'Thomas is going to die, isn't he?'

'Yes.' Hateman fished around in her bag and produced two shrivelled white pips, which she dropped into Mistress Piper's palm. Then she poured a measure of water from a bottle into a cup and offered it to her. 'These will help you sleep, and I think you should sleep now.'

'Can I sleep in the room with Thomas?'

'No, that would be a very bad idea.' Cousin Hateman put hands over her face, as if wishing she hadn't removed her plague-mask. 'We're not here to cure anyone, and even if we were, your husband is too far gone. I've given him something so he won't feel the pain and to ease his breathing. Come on, dry your eyes and swallow the pills. That's the best you can do for yourself.' And she started to dab Mistress Piper's face with a flat of Bible-soft paper until her charge turned her head away.

'I want to see him again before he goes.'

'All right,' said the Venetian, after a time, 'but don't touch.'

Cousin Hateman walked her to the door of the bedroom and stood with her awhile, staring at the darkness between the jamb, and the shallow half-imagined movement there.

'Why do you do this?' she heard herself say, tinily and faraway. 'If you won't cure plague, why bother to help me? Why not leave me to die and be happy?'

'Because we're here for you,' Cousin Hateman told her. 'Just you and no one else. We need you, Mistress Piper. The *loa* need you and they brought us to your door.'

She washed down the sugary pips, and they knocked her out until the morning. Cousins Hateman and Amphigorey helped her make the daybed comfortable in the nursery, as the magic of the pips spread round her body, making her limbs sluggish, her head soft, and her whole body leaden. Under his mask, Cousin Amphigorey was a callow youth with a small effort of a beard. He looked up from patting cushions to inspect her in her nightgown.

'Wanna fuck?' he asked, eyes hopeful.

'No,' she said dreamily. The pips made her feel exceptionally comfortable, but unsuggestible.

Mother Sphinx did not come to the nursery, but stayed downstairs; from the look of her, the strain of making the ascent might have killed her. The family retreated outside, leaving her to sleep. She lay on her side under three blankets but still shivering, and listening to the crackle of the bonfire in her garden, scorching her lawn and her flowers, destroying her clothes and her rats – then she was gone.

She woke fuzzy-headed, as her bladder emptied itself in a thin hot trickle onto her legs. She was still too drugged to move much, or care much, and simply rolled onto the damp patch. The two cousins, skull-headed again, were standing over her, but it was difficult to tell if they saw her awake. They stood facing each other and chanting a litany of what might have been Italian words, or obscenities, or something entirely other. They had drawn symbols on her wall, so it was magic they used on her. The practice of medicine, Mister Piper had once assured her, had all the hallmarks of witchery and devil-worship. – *I do not say that they are the same, but their territories overlap. They poke around for signs in your entrails, the both of them, and it's as easy for a physick to bring death as to restore life.*

Mister Piper's wife dreamed she was lying in a bed of black and undulant serpents. They writhed under her body, their slimy skins wetting her where they touched. Their flat, curious heads rose up on narrow necks to peer at her face and her fingers and her shadow and her soul. She felt herself sinking into them, a hundred deep layers of hungry snakes. A vicious red beak came down to peck them away, and the frightened reptile heads ducked back down below the line of her body.

The proud cockerel fluttered his wings and strutted back and forth on her chest, her sentry.

'What are these?' she asked.

– *Oh sweet wife, these are the things your doctors have let loose on you. They are the* loa.

'And what are *you*? You sound like my husband.'

– *Why I am Mistress Thomas Piper and all her dreams! I am the house and the marriage you live in and the children you would have and the grandchildren they would have for you. I am the Golden Age of England. I am, in my own way, a* loa, *and I will protect you from these interlopers who would ride you in my stead.*

'What are *loa*?'

It was her waking lips that spoke; she was on her side again and cramped, one arm bloodless and limp under her own dead weight. She'd wrapped the sheets tight around her body, with her rolling and night terrors. Through bleary eyes she saw the two cousins sitting together at the foot of her daybed; they had discarded their masks again, and were sprawled on the floor like children playing in the mud. That brought a wry smile to her lips, recalling the happier moments of her own girlhood not so long ago.

Neither had heard her, they were lost in their own conversation. She could see Amphigorey's sleep-starved face, and the back of Hateman's head with her once-neat hair trailing loose and tired strands.

'I prefer Venice, better than England,' Amphigorey was saying. He made a vague gesture with his fists.

'It's not so bad here. Why, what don't you like about it?'

'It's so *wet*.'

'Hah bloody hah. At least we're doing something useful. Sitting round watching out to make sure nothing happens for the next eighty-seven years just isn't what I was told to expect when I joined up – what?' Amphigorey was nudging her with his eyes. Hateman looked over her shoulder and saw Mistress Piper was awake. Half-rising, half-crawling, she pulled herself alongside the bed and reached out with a hand, ungloved now and soft, to stroke her hair.

'Oh, little sister,' she murmured gently, 'what's wrong?'

Mistress Piper felt her weak tongue moving, the same question as before: 'What are *loa*?'

The Cousins exchanged glances, then Hateman smiled warmly and explained. 'The *loa* are spirits. They look over and protect us. Sometimes we ask favours of them, and other times we let them ride us.'

'Why?'

'Because they're spirits and have no bodies of their own, because they like to see the solid world through the eyes of solid people, like you and me...'

'...and Cousin Amphigorey?'

'Yes, even Cousin Amphigorey. The *loa* can't be picky – there are so few of us left these days.'

'So, my dream is right. You are witches, and you consort with ghosts and worship evil spirits.'

'No,' Hateman said smoothly and sighed, and Mistress Piper knew she was about to hear a rehearsed answer to a question that the cousins had been expecting and dreading since they arrived. 'Our order worships nothing. We're not witches and the *loa* aren't evil. They're like... like the Saints of the calendar. In a way they *are* the Saints.'

'Then you are a Catholic order? From Venice, which is a Catholic city?'

Amphigorey rolled his eyes. 'Nice going boobs, you've just made us out to be the one thing they hate worse than witches round here.'

'I hate no one,' Mistress Piper insisted, struggling and failing to sit up. 'Not even witches.'

Hateman settled her down and stroked her face and her forehead, which suddenly seemed sticky and wet. 'We aren't Catholics either. Venice is full of spirits, some friendly, some not. We forget that other parts of the world aren't like that yet.'

'Spirits of the dead?'

'Sometimes, and sometimes of the living, and sometimes of the not-yet-born.'

'One day, I'll go to Venice.'

Hateman pursed her lips, not quite unsmiling, but still concerned. 'You're burning up, you know? I hope it's just a fever, or just stress, but you'll be in bed for a few more days yet.'

'Smashing,' murmured Amphigorey.

'And Thomas?'

'I've sat with him, when he's been awake. He says he loves you.'

'He says he loves me and calls me Kate, does he not?'

'Yes.'

'So he's dead then?' A pause. 'Tell me! He's dead, isn't he?!'

'Yes.'

She felt her lips curl bitterly, but the rest of her body was paralysed and gave off no hint of grief. Hateman's arms curled round her shoulders, but the doctor touched a cold fleshy thing – not Mistress Piper, who felt nothing. 'I'm so sorry, can I – ?'

'Give me more of those sweet pips. Let me sleep.'

The next few days blurred for her, lost in sleep. She no longer dreamed, and as far as she could tell, the order did not stand at her bedside every night to summon their Saints. That work, as she understood it, had been achieved. She would wake during the day and know at once the time by the quality of light: a hard square of it across her face and it was morning, a melancholy yellow suffusing the room and it was later, dimming red and it was evening. Sometimes she woke alone, but usually one cousin or the other was there, and they would feed her a little, and help her on and off the pot when she needed it (which was less than she expected). She allowed Cousin Hateman to wash her face, but resisted any other attempt to clean her sheets or her body.

'This won't help you get any better,' Hateman said, and Mistress Piper saw her brittle defiant smile reflected on the woman-doctor's brown irises.

They took Thomas's body while she slept and delivered it to a plague pit. They consecrated him, according to the rituals of their order, before he was buried. She imagined Hateman insisting on this; Amphigorey standing awkwardly at the grave – not comfortable, but not insensitive enough to try to disrupt the moment with his own selfishness; the gross Mother Sphinx watching and wheezing from a nearby seat.

Sometimes she dreamed of the cockerel with Thomas's voice, snatching at licking snakes. Sometimes Faction Cat climbed into her bed and tried, unsuccessfully, to shove her out. Sometimes she wondered if she were wise to let this odd family of doctors have the run of her house. Mostly, she lay on the bed and festered.

There would come a time when she would have to get up, and that time came when she was startled out of her sleep by a violent rasping from downstairs, followed by a tremor that passed through the floor and the bed to jostle her bones. She thought it must be the trumpets of judgement, except that it was so harsh and discordant and mechanical.

It forced her out of bed, onto legs that trembled from their lack of use. Her arms looked the same, just bone decorated with a paper-thin and blanched-white layer of skin. There was a mirror somewhere here and she spent some time looking for it, perhaps grateful to have a distraction from the noise that had now abated downstairs. The face that stared back, when she found the glass, was no longer one she recognised. It looked more like one of the skulls of the family, with flesh and hair still to be boiled off and eyes and tongue still in their rightful sockets, yet unmistakably a death's-head.

But you're not dead are you? You've come through the plague and triumphed over death.

It was hard to see it that way.

Raised voices filtered up through the floor. The family were arguing among themselves. She made for the stairs to eavesdrop better; Faction Cat was already there in the best place, with her nose pointed curiously through a break in the banister. Mistress Piper sat beside her.

Cousin Hateman's voice carried the loudest: '– how dare you come here now and tell us what to do! The Empire abandoned us months ago! We had no direction and no replies to our communications – of course we were going to have to take matters into our own hands!'

Now came a voice she didn't know. Mother Sphinx? It didn't seem likely. 'The Venice mission was meant to be a passive observation. Ensure the next hundred years go smoothly and pave the way for the Gregorian Compact. That was the extent of your responsibility.'

'Oh right, yeah, we wait for the Godparents to show up and hold their coats while they strut around being impressive. But it's *not* going smoothly, is it. We have a real anomaly on our hands and the *loa* are going out of their heads. The Great Houses –'

'– wouldn't dare subvert a world like this and a time like this unless things were desperate for them. And they're not desperate, are they?! They're wiping us out across the board, whole colonies and long-term projects ripped out of history as if they'd never been there. We need to retrench and wait for this wave to pass. After that –'

'And what if there isn't an *after that*, eh? This could help us turn the tide.'

Silence then from the unfamiliar voice. Then: 'It may. It may not. As it happens, we've decided to let you run this course. But you're on your own with this – we're too tied up with our Dunkirks across the Spiral Politic. It's bad enough I had to travel here –'

'Does this make any sense to you, little cat?' Mistress Piper asked. Faction Cat shook her head.

She pulled herself back to her feet, and considered drifting back to bed, but she was no longer tired and when she turned the first thing she saw was the door to her husband's room, now closed. She shuddered at that omen and crept downstairs instead.

'I've read your reports and I don't see what the widow here has to offer you.'

Amphigorey answered this time: 'If you've read the reports you'll know we've narrowed it down to two options. No one else comes close – it's either her or the boy.'

They were bickering in her parlour, and didn't see her as she approached. Hateman and Amphigorey were both standing, the youth still and composed, the woman agitated. Mother Sphinx seemed to be sitting asleep on the couch, with her head bowed and her hands folded on her huge belly. The newcomer was by far the shortest person in the room, not even five-foot tall, white-haired but still vividly young and sharp-featured. It had been impossible to tell from the voice whether it came from a man or a woman, and on sight, Mistress Piper found the identification harder still. The newcomer was dressed in what seemed to be light black leather armour with odd whorls and crests, and a distinct curved spine decorated with spikes so it seemed to be of a kind with the masks they wore for their rites. Like many a veteran of the last decades, the newcomer was mutilated and had lost an arm.

More likely a man then, but still it was impossible to say for certain.

Despite the harsh words, he or she seemed quite calm and dignified.

'Why not the boy then? He seems more suitable.'

'Too suitable,' Amphigorey replied – Mistress Piper had never seen him so collected. 'He's already aware there must be great powers out there, and he's working on ways to contact them.'

'Then he seems ideal for your purposes.'

Cousin Hateman stepped forward. 'He's too self-interested, Father-Mother. He'd make a poor recruit.'

'You're still young, Cousin. The self-interested are the easiest to twist and deceive. The Godmothers could make mincemeat of him.'

'Well, we don't have the Godmothers with us, you've just told us that. We couldn't cope with a loose cannon.'

'You lot seem so willing to take risks about –'

She or he was silenced by a hard rapping of a stick upon the floor. It was Mother Sphinx, doing more damage to the Norwich carpet with the tip of one of her crutches. Slowly and painfully she pulled herself up the spine of the staff, and craned her skull-face to point at the Father-Mother. She alone remained masked here, and Mistress Piper suddenly understood the purpose of the masks: not to protect but to terrify.

'Father-Mother Olympia, you hold your tongue and listen,' growled Mother Sphinx. The cat, whom Mistress Piper had left lounging at the top of the stairs, came bounding down the steps, into the parlour, and onto the warm spot on the couch that the Mother had just vacated.

Olympia, though taken aback, stared her down. 'You have wisdom to bring to the table, Mother?'

A buzz like a swarm of bees in high summer rose from the Mother's huge gullet. 'Mother Sphinx were older than you and wiser than you before the Faction come for her. She don't sit in the barbershop of shadow but she knows the voice of the *loa*. She knows a mambo when she sees one and she knows a bokor when she sees one, and that boy – he's a *bad* bokor!'

And Father-Mother Olympia was trembling visibly before this obese apparition. 'But... the girl...'

'Come the day, she make good mambo. So says Mother Sphinx.'

Breathing out so heavily she might have emitted smoke from the sockets of her mask, Mother Sphinx deflated back down, narrowly missing the cat's head, and resumed her old pose. Mistress Piper leaned further forward, and suddenly Olympia – as if looking for a distraction after Mother Sphinx's declaration – leapt to the door and seized her by the hair, dragging her through into the parlour. She found a sudden cold pricking on her throat, the sharp point of a pin or a knife, though one that must have been held in an invisible hand.

'Father-Mother!' Hateman warned, and – closer to them both – Amphigorey twitch-ed, caught between two equal impulses, but didn't quite move.

'*This* is your mambo?' Olympia queried. Mistress Piper gurgled and tried not to move. And then –

Why shouldn't I move? This is my house! If there are loa *here then they've been my* loa *for three long years. And Father-Mother Olympia is an uninvited stranger.*

She twisted round to look the intruder square in the eyes. Behind her, she saw their two shadows squashed together. She suddenly saw how simple it would be to take her shade out of that violent embrace. She raised her hands slowly to her throat, and they moved through empty air, though the cold of the blade was still pressed on the soft skin.

Without moving her body, she contorted like a serpent, and on the wall the two shadows fluttered apart. She saw Olympia's clearly, holding a narrow line suggestive of a sword or long dagger, in the shadow hand of a shadow arm that was missing from his-her worldly body.

'Did you see her coming, Father-Mother?' Hateman said softly. 'Because I didn't.'

The shadow-Olympia thrust the shadow-blade into a shadow-sheath.

'That's an easy enough trick,' Olympia said brusquely, but the tone of voice was quietened. 'Mistress Piper? I'd like to talk to you outside.'

She looked to Cousin Hateman, to get her nod before she agreed. Then she let the Father-Mother lead her to her own door, and as they left the parlour Mother Sphinx began to cackle throatily in her sleep.

It was warm enough that night for her to walk out in her nightgown, and the garden and road beyond were faintly illuminated by the candles in the parlour window. There was no sign of Harry Fletcher, who she presumed fled or fallen to the plague. If there was the sign of the cross or the warning bill still on her door then it was invisible in the night. She had not thought about the outside world much since the doctors arrived, but she'd imagined that it would be desolate and strewn with the bodies of the dead. It might well have been – it was too dark to tell – but the overall sense she got was one of nocturnal tranquillity. The world might have been emptied of souls.

'If I understand correctly, from what I heard,' she said coldly, 'you are superior to the cousins and to Mother Sphinx in your order, and you've been sent to assess their progress. They saved my life.'

'Well, hooray for them.'

'Don't make light of it! Not if you want to set foot in my house again.'

'I'll be leaving shortly anyway,' the Father-Mother said, but he-she seemed cowed in voice if not in words. 'So this is Hornsey St Mary? It's very... natural, isn't it?'

'How so?'

'Green. Everything covered in bushes and trees and grass. I was never that keen on nature. You know, I can remember a time when this'll be covered in concrete.'

'You talk nonsense, sir, or madam, or...'

'Both. I was a woman once, and if the Grandfather grants it, I will be again. Bloody Morlock!'

'You still talk nonsense.' Mistress Piper sighed and breathed. Fresh air, how long since she had taken a taste of air that hadn't smelled of the mouldering insides of her house and marriage? 'But yes, it's very beautiful here. The road takes the traveller out of London and into the lushest countryside. Thomas and I, we called it the green way.'

She had to admit there were no greens visible tonight. The leaves on trees and bushes were rendered black against a velvet blue sky. The sun couldn't be far from coming up, she decided, or going down. In any case, Olympia didn't seem to be listening.

'Back home we've got a very promising young cousin from this part of the world, place-wise anyway – one of Mathara's protégés. I can't say I thought much of him when I first saw him.' Olympia stopped, and put his-her good hand on Mistress Piper's shoulder. 'All that I'm saying is that I've been known to be wrong – and I shouldn't have insulted you in your home.'

'To tell you the truth, sir and madam, I don't feel that it's my home any more.'

'You don't, eh?' Olympia whistled, a nightbird calling.

'It's changed, since your order came calling – longer, since the plague. I don't think I could live there any more, not once Mother Sphinx and her children leave. I would rather see it burned.' At that, Olympia's shrill piercing note broke up into laughter. 'Is there something wrong, er, Father-Mother?'

'You poor thing,' the Father-Mother replied, 'you still don't understand. They don't want to leave you here once you're better. They want to recruit you.'

'Recruit?'

'To our... our order, you call it. That's as good a word as any other.'

'But... I... I don't share your faith!'

'You wouldn't need to. The Faction isn't a religion, not in the sense you understand.'

'Then what is it? I don't understand.'

Olympia had paced away from her until he-she was a part of the darkness, but now the Father-Mother turned and his-her eyes glinted and his-her good arm was held out wide, preaching. 'If there were ever any gods it would be necessary to abolish them. The Faction was dedicated to bringing energy to an exhausted world, the oldest world. We profaned everything they held sacred and raised all their devils. The Faction was misrule. It was meant to shock. The biggest shock of all was when the order started to admit people like me – and you.'

'English folk?'

'Human folk.' Olympia laughed. 'Don't think of it as an order. It's a carnival and we are the flesh and the bone. It was.'

'Then what is it now?' Mistress Piper insisted

'A shadow of its former self. We're at war and we're losing.'

These words were meant to discourage Mistress Piper, but somehow they didn't work. 'With what nation...?' No, that was wrong. These people, their order, was on a different scale to anything she had experienced before. 'With what power?'

Olympia was silent, so Mistress Piper surmised, 'It was this power that you provoked, wasn't it? The oldest world? You pushed it too far?'

The Father-Mother shook his-her head. 'The Faction was never that much of a threat to them. No, they encountered another enemy entirely, and they had to develop what you might call a new model army to fight it. But now their new military is destroying us just because it's convenient.'

'So you need numbers for your cause? Recruits?'

Olympia snorted. 'Not from here. We're far from the front. They have something quieter in mind for you.'

Mistress Piper preened herself and folded her arms. 'What makes you think that I would want to join your order?'

The Father-Mother paused before replying, regarding the widow as if in judgement. Mistress Piper realised she must look a poor prospect for the order, starved and shivering in the night of a dead world. She *resented* that impression, but Olympia was talking again: 'How did you feel when you pushed my shadow back, in your parlour?'

'I don't know. I felt, I suppose, a sort of strength.'

'And a thrill? A little rush of excitement?'

She was nodding, enthusiastically in the dark. 'Yes, exactly that. I could not be so indelicate as to describe the feelings it recalled to me.'

'Ah, well it's made you eloquent, that's good, and confident, that's good too. We need that.' Then Olympia sucked air: 'And damned, of course, damned beyond redemption.'

That gave Mistress Piper pause. It was as if Olympia knew her soul, but was that so surprising? Their shadows had been locked together, and perhaps that had laid Mistress Piper's feelings bare. She had felt a damnable and unholy power, because these *loa* couldn't be God's creatures, and the strength she found in herself was surely nothing but a little magic, a taint on her soul. And yet –

'I would spit in God's eye,' she said firmly. 'How worse can Hell be than what He has already visited on us on Earth? I'll join your order, if you'll have me, and if you advise it.'

Olympia was still laughing. 'No, no, I don't advise it – I don't think you have it in you. And anyway, we're on the point of a total wipeout. The Faction's finished. The moment this arm grows back, I'm out of there.'

Treachery and murder! You left me on my deathbed to dabble with these loa, *and now you side with them against me. You mean to kill me!*

'You can't fool me. You're not my husband. And yes, I mean to kill you.'

I never claimed to be him. I am Mistress Thomas Piper, I am you, and I cannot be killed.

'No, but you can be sacrificed, and I will have a new life and a new name.'

She knew she was dreaming. Her sleeping body was on the daybed in the nursery, finally to be dedicated to a newborn, though not a child. She knew that Cousins Hateman and Amphigorey were standing over her, chanting the names and rites of the *loa*. She knew that Mother Sphinx had made the long trek up the stairs to be here in her room, chanting with them. She felt them anoint her forehead and palms and feet with their order's ointments, and drip the seeds of time into her mouth.

Spiritus vobiscum. *The* loa *be with you.*

In her dream, the rooster still strutted on the bed of serpents, but its beak no longer pecked but protested. Her dream-body knelt on the bed with the spotless white bowl to her left and her knife of clean steel on the right. She could feel the slick skins of the serpent-*loa* rippling against her naked soul. The rooster cawed helplessly and smashed them down with its wings; but she wasn't distracted.

'I call upon the protection of the *loa*,' she said, as she picked up the knife. 'By this act I strip away all that was Mistress Thomas Piper. By this act I set my unnamed soul free on the winds of time.'

She reached for the bird and found its sharpened beak in her fingers, drawing blood. She endured the bite and snatched at it again, quicker this time, grabbing its legs. She dangled it upside down over the bowl, its head bobbing furious and impotent.

'I offer myself to the *loa*. I offer them a share of my body so that they might ride me through the solid world that lives in time. I make this offer freely, and in the certain faith that the *loa* will be generous. This is how I sign the compact.'

She slashed the knife in a swift line across the cockerel's throat. Its blood splattered out, across her face, her arms, her chest, her stomach, and her legs. In her dreams, she felt washed clean by it.

'This is the *loa*'s meat, this is the *loa*'s drink,' she pronounced, as the blood began to flow again, dripping from the stump of the neck into the bowl until it was full. Serpent heads began to cluster round the rim to satisfy their thirst. She hacked the rooster's body into chunks, dropped them into the bowl, and watched the *loa* surge turn into a frenzy. None of them went for the severed cock's head that had fallen between the supplicant's legs. Its eye still twitched; it looked as though it was winking at her.

'By this act I am unnamed.' She wiped the blade clean on the rags of her old clothes. 'By this act I choose the name I will be called by my brothers and my sisters in the *loa*, by my cousins and my mothers and my fathers, by my godfathers and my godmothers, and by the Grandfather who isn't and never was and never will be. I choose the third of the names offered to me, as the name the *loa* will call me.'

And she felt her undreaming body in the solid world being lifted upright from the bed by her new cousins. Then she felt the weight on her shoulders as the skull that had been chosen for her was lowered over her head. The inside smelled of mothballs and burned meat and the hot savannahs of distant worlds, distant times. She could hear the voices of her cousins through the bone, welcoming her.

Little Sister Greenaway? they said. *Little Sister, we are Faction Paradox.*

And now, so are you.

Book Two: At Salomon's House

⇒ Chapter 4: *Annus Mirabilis* ⇐

Blood. It always came back to blood, the most vital and copious of the humours. It seeped from his mouth, from his nostrils, and from the corners of his eyes. There the fluid pooled and hardened, so that his lids became gummed and he could barely see. They had given him a wet rag to wash it away, but he no longer had the strength to lift it. The blood smelled of his own rank insides, the pollution killing his body. It was sweet though, much sweeter than that other portent, the now excruciating pain under his temple.

He lay on a slab below an oblong of light, the little window that allowed in fresh air and swollen insects. His legs had been strapped to stop him from lashing out. Colourless shapeless forms moved round him, perhaps tending to him yet never touching. The voice of the chirurgeon made no words he could hear; it was a wolf growl. He felt abandoned, on Earth and in Heaven.

He had been the last left at the Church of Christ Sublime. They had taken days longer to come for him than he'd expected, to the point that he had almost blissfully starved. The other Silverites had scattered like the Jews after Masada, but they had no ancient faith to sustain them. He'd had no doubt his name would be, in time, forgotten. Even his captors hadn't thought him a great threat, more of a hundredfold nuisance. No capital charges had been brought against him. He'd been taken to Winchester Assizes, where an impassive, stone-faced, blind judge had named him guilty and condemned him to gaol in the space of a single breath. They had already taken the egg, and Christ's pilots no longer spoke to him.

And perhaps that isn't a bad thing? A navigator can only guide you so far. Eventually you must loosen your dependency on the voices of angels and find your own.

The thoughts that occupied him in prison were dark in the main, dark as the walls. He had lost track of how long he had been kept here, of when – or if – he might be released. He'd been accumulating debts and deeper incarceration just by crouching on the pallet in his cell. Sometimes they'd taken him away and tried to break him. The night-voices had whispered that Cromwell was heard dead, but it hardly mattered whose coin the gaolers were taking. When he wasn't beaten, the pressure in his head had grown worse, and he'd been twice dragged before baffled physicks who did him no good.

Sometimes, the gaolers smuggled in women, but he'd refused them, knowing that it would give him no satisfaction and only add more pennies to his slate. He no longer felt any physical desire, hadn't done since Ann had died and he had foolishly wished himself into Hell. His one distraction had been imagining what he might do if he were free again; incarceration in a stone room had made the outside world seem infinitely pliable and suggestible to new methods and philosophies. The political solutions he had sought were a mistake – whatever their faults and merits, they were bound to be crushed by thoughtless leviathans. Politics was ever the domain of man, but science was the realm of God. It was the secure fulcrum that could turn the world.

In the night, he'd dreamed of a golden net, lonesome sparks leaping across the darkness to form ever tighter connections and lines of communication. He'd imagined he could touch it. He'd reached for it.

He'd fallen frothing on the dirt-tracked floor, and his cellmates had withdrawn in panic.

Then they'd brought him to the slab, and laid him out expectant of his death. His skull pounded, an eggshell breaking open from the inside. The sawbones, muttering to himself and with black thread dangling from his lips, put a cold metal tip on the bone above the epicentre of the pain. There was a light tap –

– and the pain exploded out of his head –

– then his temple felt wet and wounded again, as it had done at Edgehill. The chirurgeon's apprentices were at his arms, struggling to stop him raising worried fingers to his head to probe the gap. And silhouetted against the window, their master held up some small bauble and whistled in amazement.

The same grey metal bauble, cleaned of blood and bile, sat unremarkably on a cushion a year later, at the centre of a gathering in a summer garden, held up for the attention of the new king. 'And you mean to say,' Charles asked dryly, 'that this was cut from the head of a living man? We're not sure we believe you, Master Gentle.'

The chirurgeon, now cleaner and better-dressed and lit by perfect evening sunlight, nodded humbly and kept his eyes averted. Though he tried to appear neat, his efforts were defeated by the patched stubble on his chin, curious for a barber. 'That is Your Majesty's prerogative, but you may have my word and that of a half dozen witnesses, my apprentices and loyal men alike.'

'And this is the fellow? Bid him step forward,' the King announced. 'What is your name, sir?'

He took a single clumsy step, wary of the armed footmen and yeomen arrayed around him on the edges of the lawn. He spoke, but even he didn't hear the name from his lips.

'What's that? Speak up, sir, and find your voice.'

'Nathaniel Silver, Your Majesty,' he replied.

The King clapped. He saw no slight. His face was too restless, too eagerly puppyish to find any offence in Silver's awkward gait. He was dressed in silk finery, yet wore it casually, without any of the mock humility of his father. He did not stand, as his father had on the stage, but lolled easily in his outdoor throne. He had the thin makings of a moustache, but his rich brown mane was a wig. He was a taller man by far than his dead father, and Silver could immediately see why the old Charles was called a cuckold and this new one a bastard. No, he was his father's son, but the old man was well-hidden in the fresh young face.

'May we see the scar?' Silver brushed back his hair, and leant to offer his scalp for inspection. The King tutted impatiently and beckoned for a flunkey who rushed to him with a magnifying glass. 'This is remarkable, sir! To have healed so cleanly and quickly...' The King waved the glassman away, and Silver took the cue to stand out of his stoop. He wondered idly if he should mention where he had last seen Charles's father, but dismissed the thought. The royalist retribution had so far been more restrained than many feared, but such comment would hardly be tactful.

Instead he said: 'I have survived the wound twice now, Your Majesty; once when the ball was shot into my head, and again when it was cut out of me.'

'Yes, you were shot at Edgehill, were you not? When, from the look of you, you must have been about ten years old. Which cause did you fight with, Master Silver?'

'Parliament's,' he replied, wondering if the King's unmoved soulless smile was a good thing or no.

'Might we assume that your experience of the mercies of the Protectorate have persuaded you against their cause?'

'I'm afraid not, Your Majesty.' Then, before he could stop himself: 'Please understand that I mean Your Majesty's person no harm, nor do I challenge your authority. That time is past, and will not come again while I live. But I believe what I must, and I don't believe the late example of republican tyranny invalidates all republican sentiment.'

'Nor do the mistakes of a king argue against monarchy. Quite the opposite, in fact,' Charles quipped back merrily. 'Ah, but we see you are an honest opponent. There is a story they tell about an old Carpathian *voivode* who bade two monks tell him the state of his principality – one lied and told him he was well-loved, the other spoke only the brutal truth – and at the end of it he rewarded one, and had the other tortured and killed. Which do you think he allowed to live, Master Silver?'

Silver thought on this, under the King's cruel and amused stare, then said: 'I don't believe I could answer the question, Your Majesty. There are a dozen subtle reasons that might have turned the case.'

The King stopped smiling for the first time since Silver had been brought before him. 'We have been told we must be a subtler man than our... predecessor. We have lived among the common people, and would have them believe we understand them the better for it. We'll see how far that takes us. And you sir, you are free now under the provisions of the restored governance. What will you make of your life?' He was smiling again and Silver felt shrived.

'I have an interest in natural inquiry. I will dedicate my life to that.'

This pleased the King, who clapped again. 'Capital, sir! We have a common interest. If it will keep you out of mischief, we'll arrange for a small stipend to promote your work. Only a *small* one, mark you, don't get your hopes up. One last thing, *this* –' To the palpable horror of half the court, he reached out and plucked the clean old musketball from its pillow. '*This* is remarkable. May we keep it?'

'I believe,' Silver replied, breathing out heavily, 'that it was Your Majesty's property to begin with.'

His first few weeks out of captivity were aimless; he had nowhere to go, and the prison years had ground purpose out of him. His head had never felt so clear or so peaceful, but the insistent pain was replaced by a numb and lazy void. The world had changed utterly while he'd been out of it, and now he scrabbled to find a handhold on its smooth surface. The King's stipend (and it was, indeed, pitifully small) paid for lodgings in London, but it had never been the friendliest city in his estimation, and he began to yearn to return to Hampshire to find if he had any friends or followers left, or Worcester where he might still have family.

No, they were the past. He had to find his way into the future.

Barely a week after he was summoned before the King, he found that he still had one ally alive in the world, and he doubted that the two events were unconnected. Donald Taylor's letter was carried from Dover, where – reading between the lines – he was evidently tied up in business to do with the return of the royal court from exile. Nevertheless, a week after the letter, Taylor presented himself at Silver's door. He had changed little in the intervening years. His good eye flicked up and down Silver's circumstances.

'By Christ, Nate,' he exclaimed as Silver took unsteady steps towards him, to take his hand, to hug him, 'what have they done to you?!'

'They would have done worse if they'd cared about me or my crimes,' Silver said, trying to wave away his friend's concern as a trifling embarrassment. It was hard. He was adapting only gradually to the weight and pressure of the real world. It was a matter of relearning those things he had forgotten, remembering how to move smoothly and how to live in the light.

Taylor didn't weep – he was a tough-minded fellow – but took them on a tour of the nearest pubs and whorehouses at his own expense. Tracking through muddy streets and narrow alleys they must have looked like fearsome monsters, as the wounded of all wars were wont to, but in the packed, crowded Southwark dives, Silver no longer felt so unique nor so alone. He heard in the boisterous rowdy chatter a faint echo of the warm community he'd hoped to build on Sir Denzil's estates. The Restoration had brought England back to life out of its death-like austerity; there would be revels and carnival for a while, but they would not last. Sir Denzil was dead, Don told him. He had been spared the hell of prison; he had been hanged.

Nate Silver didn't love the first woman he slept with since Ann had died, but even without love it didn't feel like a sin. She was a young woman, but knew how gently a veteran should be treated, and smiled rather than leered as they coupled. She wouldn't kiss him, as was a whore's prerogative. No love, not even real friendship, but she was company, and that was love of a sort, he thought as he fell asleep.

'Have you thought any more about the offer I made you?' Taylor asked the next morning as they broke their fast. 'I heard what you said to the King, and it's a promising sign that you still have lights in your body. He'll favour the Invisible College with his patronage soon enough, and I could get you in.'

'I don't speak their language, Don,' Silver replied.

'Maybe not in through the front doors, but I can put you in their way. *Sun & Seed* did you as much good as harm. The name Nathaniel Silver will be remembered after four years.'

Silver didn't reply; he was filling his face, not greedily, but with the hurry of a man who was afraid he might be eating a last meal. Taylor had known, he was sure, about his incarceration, perhaps even instrumental in striking down charges of blasphemy or sedition. There was only so much he could accept.

'I should make my own way,' he suggested, but Taylor shook his head slowly.

'This isn't a world where a man can be alone. I don't believe there is such a world, and even if there were, I wouldn't leave you there.'

That seemed to settle it, so the following week they travelled to Holborn to see a man cut up a dog.

The stalls of the theatre – so-called, though they struck Silver more as the gallery overlooking a tribunal – were plain wood, scrubbed white, and patchy where blood and offal had splattered from past operations. Taylor led Silver to a seat in the corner, a high vantage point looking down on the circular pit where the vivisection would take place. 'This isn't the best or most comfortable post,' he explained, as Silver brushed crumbs of dust and snuff tobacco from the bench, 'but it does afford the best view if you want to see into the guts of the subject. And trust me, you do.'

The lecture was free, and conducted in both Latin and English by the *Artium Magister*, a confident and handsome man who appeared far too young to be a professor of the college, though Taylor assured Silver this was the case. The animal was a mongrel bought from a street merchant, and treated well so that it would be in the best of health for the procedure. The *magister* explained in both tongues what he intended to prove this evening, the explanation in Latin seeming to Silver's untutored ears more precise and compact. English seemed an unwieldy language by comparison, but he followed the gist. The dog would be lightly sedated, not rendered completely unconscious, because the object of the lecture was to keep it alive. It was to be sliced open so its inner parts might be surgically removed.

'Thus,' declaimed the lecturer, in English, 'we will demonstrate the fallacy of Galen's physick. For we cannot live, he says, without the *eucrasia* of all four humours, including the black bile of *melancholy* formed in the spleen. I hope to display to you at the end of the evening on the one hand a fit and healthy beast, bounding and woofing round these stalls' – and there was polite laughter at this – 'and on the other, the spleen of said beast in a preserving jar.'

More laughter. Silver whispered into Taylor's ear, 'Is this not a little cruel?' but his companion shushed him.

The *magister* washed his hands in a bowl of scented leaves 'for luck' before beginning his procedure. The first incision sent a spurt of blood across the auditorium, decorating some over-eager students in the front row, and turning the lecturer's gown scarlet. Silver had been given paper and a wadd marker to make notes, but he was out of practice at writing. The fingers that once diligently recorded every phenomenon that occurred to him now clawed helplessly round the wood stick, and Taylor had to reach over and guide his hands for him. He found it easier not to write, but to make diagrams of what he saw, trusting the details to memory. The *magister* slipped unconsciously into nothing but Latin occasionally, and had to check himself. As the layers of dog were sliced and its innermost components opened up to the light, he took both pains and delight in pointing out each raw red part of its body, each one still functioning perfectly.

When they came to remove the spleen, disaster struck. The dog, which had lain breathing peacefully on its hard bed while the professor poked around in its guts, suddenly thrashed and frothed from its eyes. It tried to howl, but its mouth had been muzzled shut. It shook violently for an instant, then sank unmoving back onto the slab. The *magister* paused over it, licking his lips, before turning to the audience.

'Gentlemen, I fear the dog is dead. So this week Galen has the upper hand. I'll best him another day.' And there was more of the same laughter, a little jollier this time. Silver spotted bottles being passed around the student's stalls, from hand to hand at surreptitious knee-level. It was an odd world, this. He already felt a part of it, absorbed by it, contaminated by it.

The death of the dog was only the second most remarkable incident of the evening. The greater came later, as Silver and Taylor emerged from the college and strolled down into Holborn. The light was fading into the west already, and this was not a part of London he knew well, but Taylor seemed familiar enough with the terrain and Silver was content to follow his lead. Like all of London's satellites, its thoroughfares were heaving even as the night descended. There were harlots and inns a-plenty on its streets, and Silver was beginning to understand Taylor's limitless taste for both, but this was also England's escritoire, where many of her books were published. *The Cycle of Sun & Seed* had been printed here, Taylor explained, all without Silver's knowledge. He wondered how many copies had been made, if any still existed, if he had taught or misled anyone with his example.

'What did you think of the experiment?' Taylor asked. He had pointed out the lights of a nearby tavern that he knew well, and they were making for it at a slow walking pace.

'As I remarked, Don, a little cruel.'

''Twas an accident the dog died. I have seen it done many times before. You may find yourself with the knife in your hand at some point. You can't hope to peel back the layers of the world if you won't get your hands a little bloodied, or suffer a little pain.'

'I doubt I'd be the one suffering the pain. I see times when it may be necessary, but even so, we would not do this to a living man.'

Taylor stopped him in the street. 'Living men are treated with less dignity everywhere, and you know it because you were one. I heard about that bullet taken from your head.' Silver nodded, conceding the point. 'That turned you from a poor bloody soldier who might as well have died in a ditch into a miracle presented to princes –'

'But still a *subject*, Don, nothing like a living man at all.'

Donald Taylor wasn't listening. He had cocked his head towards a commotion on the street. It shoved the crowds aside, including one woman who went shrieking into the mud. It saw Silver through mad eyes and lunged for him. It was a portly man, red-faced and dressed in a coat, shirt, and breeches that might once have been fine. He was hatless and wigless, and his thinning hair rippled in a dozen directions as he stumbled against Silver and pushed him into the wall.

'You are Nathaniel Silver!' he raved. 'Don't deny it, sirrah! You have haunted me!'

In the corner of his eye, Silver saw Taylor draw a dagger from his glove, but shooed him back. Having seized his prey, the madman had begun to weep, and pressed his damp face into Silver's breast. He was a pitiful thing, filled not with hate as Silver first feared but rage. 'I don't know you, sir...'

The fat man broke into wracking sobs. 'That is the worst cruelty! You have destroyed my life and never knew it. Take it! Take the abominable thing back, you damn'd wight, so I may drown myself in the Thames and never hear its damn'd voice again.' And he shoved a soft object against Silver's stomach, turned, and ploughed back into the crowd, fleeing from Silver's life as abruptly and violently as he had appeared.

'What in the name of buggery was that all about?' Taylor stared curiously after the madman's escape, and stowed his blade before anyone else could get close enough to see. Only now did Silver think to look down at what had been thrust into his hands, not willing to believe from just the touch or texture. Discreetly, it did not glow, but it couldn't completely hide its shine. It was as smooth and beautiful as he remembered it, and it whispered in his head, in the tone of angels ~ *I will ever return to you* ~

'What's that?' Don asked curiously, as Silver stowed the egg in a tear in the line of his coat. Its anxious weight would hang there, preying on his mind, until he got it back to his lodgings in Southwark the following morning. Only then would he feel elated to be given back his burden.

'It's a sign,' he said simply and truthfully, 'that you've put me on the right path. It's an instruction.'

'To get your hands bloodied?'

'To experiment,' he replied, and said nothing more about it, but went with Taylor to the favoured tavern where he drank enough to forget the dying twitches of a murdered dog, and the madness placed by angels into a blameless man's mind.

∞

He had begun to wonder how the egg worked.

There would have been a time when he could have dismissed the question – it was simply God's mystery – but his new grounding in science showed this up as an inadequate explanation. The natural world clearly abided by rules, which were obscure to man but must surely have been put in place by divine will. It was conceivable to Silver that God could create exceptions to His laws – such were miracles and the workings of grace; but the solid, unspontaneous egg was neither. Further, it was provided not by Christ Himself but His pilots, who could not be so easily excepted. Were they not themselves a form of mechanism, devices for communicating between the divine and the mundane? It seemed likely that the egg was governed by rules of its own that could be discovered by the correct method, and by definition that method could not be completely beyond the reach of man, of Silver himself.

He worried this line of thought might be blasphemous, so he consulted the egg directly, the first question he had asked of it since it had been returned to him. To his surprise, it encouraged him to experiment further, talking blandly about how it might be dissected and remodelled. It didn't fear human blades.

Emboldened, he asked the question he had been dreading: 'The man who brought you back to me – what did you do to him?'

~ *After you were removed to gaol, the egg passed to this man in exchange for tokens of wealth and status in a mercantile economy* ~ *We made reasonable arguments to him* ~ *He was unpersuaded* ~

'So? What did you do?'

~ *We showed him the true cost of his wealth* ~ *This destroyed him* ~

'You drove him mad. I would not have wished you to do that.'

~ *We only showed him the connections of the world, as we will show you* ~

'And will you also drive me mad?'

~ *We will make you sane* ~

Silver put the egg on the table, took up one of his several knives, and began to make incisions.

The surface of the egg yielded easily. There was no hatchling within; it was the same substance and constituency all the way through. The wounds he made healed quickly; indeed, he found he was able to take out chunks, then reattach them seamlessly into the whole. The egg's reassuring voice guided him every step of the way. If only the dog of Holborn had had this power! – to calmly guide the chirurgeon's hand, and describe in English (imperfectly squeezed from its canine mouth) the exact workings of its own body.

Hours of experiment stretched into days then into weeks. The egg seemed almost divinely malleable, like the clay from which God had first made the Earth and Adam alike. Maybe it was the very same substance? With the application of heat it could be melted out of shape, beaten, stretched, and reformed. One morning he was able to turn it into a perfect cube; another day he rolled it into a cylinder that extended almost the length of his room (which was not long); then he was able to spread it thin across his floor, so that it had barely any detectable thickness but covered the floorboards, the bed, and halfway up the walls – and he had to climb on a stool to avoid being swamped by it. He tried every test he could imagine, and when he could think of nothing more, it offered its own suggestions. As winter drew in, he found he could rely on it for warmth and light, spending much needed coin elsewhere. He held down a number of temporary jobs in the Borough, which he pursued thoroughly but without enthusiasm, and always rushed home as soon as he could to continue his enquiries.

Don Taylor, to his credit, didn't ask about the egg after the night in Holborn, and in fact began to fade out of Silver's life. He had his own activities in the Service, after all, and seemed content that Silver had righted himself after his years in prison. He found time to introduce Silver to a couple of dabblers on the fringes of the Invisible College, who were university-educated and made him feel an ignoramus without meaning it. He did not feel drawn into their cold and lightless world, but they offered him sound advice and suggested experiments that he could repeat, mainly in optics and motion. More of Taylor's contacts lived further afield, but Don provided him with letters of introduction, and he soon had a lively correspondence going with learned men who were not afraid of amateur interest. Occasionally, very occasionally, he would surprise them, though he kept most of the egg's observations to himself. It said things that might have upset them, and the last thing he wanted was to drive them away. At their urging, he began to learn more about mathematicks and al-gibra, and the egg helped him with translations and obscurities.

He studied medicine but from books, not bodies. That would come, but, please God, not yet!

After a time in Southwark, he relocated to Holborn, a simple enough move as he had accumulated virtually nothing in personal property other than a small library of philosophical texts in English. At Holborn, he was disappointed to learn that the excitable young lecturer he'd seen a year before had left the college to take up a new post in Oxford. That was a blow – he would have made an interesting addition to Silver's growing list of correspondents. He found new work, enjoyed a two-and-a-half-week romance with his landlord's daughter, continued writing his letters and conducting his experiments. The next year, in high summer, his friends in the College burbled happily about gaining royal patronage for their Empire of Learning. They were ecstatic; he felt their delight as though seen on the surface of a mirror. The first few months of activity among the new Royal Society were a lean time for Silver, but he dedicated himself to solitary work; then the fashion passed, and he was soon in rapt communication with many of its fellows, and laymen, and also philosophers of the Service who mistrusted this new body.

Don Taylor was one of those sceptical presences-by-mail. He wrote to Silver from a variety of odd European addresses and beyond, including Flanders, where he claimed to be on an expedition to track down a race of malevolent blue-skinned fairies. The Royal Society, he wrote bitterly, had disenchanted the alchemist's art, and he would have nothing to do with it. Silver ruefully realised he knew this type, the guarded minds of the old philosophers for whom knowledge was to be hoarded rather than shared, a secret badge for the elect.

A final letter from Don Taylor came from New Amsterdam, where the old soldier was on Service. He was heading into South America on a new endeavour that he refused to describe, claiming only that Silver wouldn't believe him. Reading the letter for the first time, Silver was struck with a calm certainty that Taylor was now dead. He asked the egg, which replied ~ *He is no longer in this world* ~ and thereafter fell silent.

Silver took to his bed for the rest of the afternoon, not sleeping, not thinking, only studying his blotched ceiling and contemplating a future that seemed to be filled with nothing more than days like this for the rest of his life.

The following morning, Nathaniel Silver heard the first reports of plague in London.

The egg instructed him, and he wept to learn it.

~ *To repeat* ~ *Instructions to best avoid contracting plague* ~ *Instructions for treatment of plague in case of infection* ~ *We cannot allow you to administer mass treatments, as this will create ontological uncertainty and alert the great powers to our existence* ~ *First method* –

'Enough!' he almost screamed. 'I would that you had told me this ten years past when my Ann might have been treated! The numbers you describe – I could have saved the Church! Whole lives would have turned out differently.'

~ *You make your own mistakes* ~

'I was ignorant!'

~ *You make your own mistakes, but you have our sympathy* ~

He could no longer bear to listen to it, and went instead to the window, where he was no better comforted by the screams of the desperate and the dying. He thought it, but did not say it: *Your Christ has made a Hell of Earth.* The robes and hood he had stolen sat on the table by the egg waiting for him, the snout of the mask filled with scented herbs that the egg had informed him would be entirely useless against this outbreak. Only Silver now knew enough to walk among the sick and the dead without fear of infection, and he was cursed to remain silent.

The end of the world served his purpose in two ways. It granted him a distraction – as the capital emptied of souls, there were fewer eyes that might latch onto his activities, and even if they did, the doctor's costume lent him anonymity and authority. More importantly, the sweep of death through the city left him with a hundred opportunities a day to extend his researches into the field of anatomy. The work itself was hard, but the circumstances made it all too easy for him to remove human bodies from abandoned houses, from the mud of the streets, from the very heaps on the plague carts. As the visitation intensified, the niceties of burial were denied to the swell of victims, and Silver consoled himself with the thought that his holy investigations would dignify their souls and turn their bodies to Christ's purpose.

He found an empty house just inside the Moorgate with a cool, brick-walled, and spacious cellar. The residents, long since vanished, had buried wine, cheeses, and a small quantity of gold here, but only shallow in their haste to escape. The wine and cheese became his companions in the long evenings he spent there; he left the gold, which was in any case worthless. He set up his equipment here in this chilly cavity under London, some of it improvised, much looted from an apothecary (despite the egg's instruction, he had no way of manufacturing jars and instruments to the specifications his work demanded). Silver spent his days cutting up bodies, in an underworld lit by harsh lanterns, and his nights carrying those same lamps through the dying city, shunning the living and seeking out the dead. It was a bleak task that grew no easier. The bodies yielded their secrets, with the egg describing and guiding him through his discoveries; it ridiculed the little physick he'd learned from Galen and Aristotle, and instead taught him to see what he might with his own eyes.

His enquiries were general most days; other times he focused on the transmission of the plague itself, wondering if there weren't some way round the angels' restrictions. To go against their desire was inconceivable, but if he could find a new method entirely of his own devising – well then, they could hardly command him against it. He accumulated bodies and body-parts, caring not for how they might be disposed of in later days, because he could no longer imagine any kind of future, in spite of what the egg told him.

He had neglected Christ in favour of His pilots, and at his lowest ebb he found time to make direct prayers to the Lord. He came away reassured. Christ did not speak to him – it would be foolish to expect otherwise – but He was there, nestling naked and obsidian in Silver's soul. Silver took up his knife again.

Some days, as he wheeled his human cargo through the tight streets of the city, he imagined he was being followed. The wood buildings swelled and creaked around him, putting paranoias into his head. He had grown too accustomed to working undisturbed, so was taken by surprise when finally caught.

He had a child's body laid out and stripped on one of the tables, and spent an hour prising flesh away from her cheek so that he might make a better study of her teeth and gums. This was old work, done almost for the sake of practice, and he did not need the egg so it was fortuitously concealed in a box in the far corner. Its glow was hidden when the intruder came, stepping faintly but not quite faint enough. Silver put down his blade, unhooked the lantern from its post, and turned to the stairs. Let this not be the owners or the watch, please let it be some cutthroat or hobbledehoy who might fear me and my cellar of corpses.

A lad crouched there, a gaunt starveling who tried hard not to flinch when the light hit his face. Silver's heart beat again – it was just some stray – and he moved forward to scare him off. But the boy didn't react as Silver expected. He stayed crouched – not from fear, but with a subtle defiance. He was shirtless and shoeless, and his body looked coiled, wiry, and healthy. There were no marks of plague on him that Silver could see; that was the first thing he'd looked for.

The boy extended an arm easily, pointing beyond Silver to his surgeries.

'She were a skinny bitch, weren't she?'

Silver's voice echoed in the leather bowl of his mask: 'You should not be here.'

The boy's hands rippled. How old was he? Ten years? Younger? 'Is good mate. I know what you're up to. Been watching you, I have. Even come down here when you been out picking your precious flowers.'

'You must leave. You are in danger of contracting plague.'

'And you ain't, eh?'

'I have precautions and protections.'

The boy-child reached for something at his neck. Silver raised the lamp to get a better look. 'Funny thing that, 'cos so have I. Look here' – he held out a thick leather twine, on which had been strung a hollow metal disc carved with crude symbols, the bleached skull of a mouse, and a soapstone carved into the shape of a howling face – 'these all work so far.'

'That is superstition –'

'More 'n that. You read a lot, don't you? So do I, but different books, like. The boils and the bleeding won't cost me my soul 'cos it's already someone else's property like. I sold it see, to a pretty lady, and now you want to know what I sold it for?'

'No. Go back to your home boy –'

'Oh, doctor high, doctor mighty, I will do that sure as you take your hood off and let me see your eyes.'

Casually, Silver removed his hat and stripped back the hood to give the child what he wanted.

'They are dead,' said the boy, grinning merrily, 'my mother and father and sister all. Dead or dying back in the old pit. I sat and watched them for a while, but I got bored and thirsty, so I left 'em. Straight out the window. Don't look back. That's how you lose 'em, looking back, eh?'

Fleet-footed, the youth wove through the gap between Silver and the wall and darted across to the tables. He stood over the dead child, morbidly fascinated by her face, then sank his fingers into the neat wound that Silver had made around her mouth, to stroke her smooth white teeth. 'I am much possessed by death, sir. I would sit at the right hand of a master magician, if you'll have me.'

'I am Nathaniel Silver. I'm a surgeon and a philosopher, not a magician.'

'No, you're not, with your cave and your robe, your mysteries and your books, you're no Merlin at all.' The child cackled, and began to anoint the girl's forehead with the drying juices from her own mouth. 'Look here, you can't do this on your own. I've seen you struggle. You'll go mad without help.'

'Perhaps. What's your name, boy?'

The waif bowed extravagantly. 'Nick, sir. Nicholas Plainsong, at your service.'

For all his faults (and they were legion), Nick Plainsong was a hard worker and a good servant, and took their duties as seriously as did Silver himself. In other ways he was a nuisance, wringing the bleakest and cruellest humour from his surroundings; this was only natural, Silver presumed, but it made him feel a grey and humourless streak of piss by contrast. The apprentice even contrived to be shorter than the master, who was hardly a tall man himself, so that when they walked together at night Silver seemed to take long strides while Plainsong ambled unhurried and pocket-fisted beside him.

After a while, hearing the lad call him a magician ceased to be an irritation.

Silver shared all his knowledge and experiments with his protégé, but kept the existence of the egg from him. It mattered little in the next year, as he spent his time repeating old work in order to educate Nick. So he found himself become a teacher after all. He gave the boy instruction in how best to avoid and treat plague, but Plainsong refused to throw away his charms, though he seemed in no other way foolish or simple. In the nightlands beyond the walls of their cellar, the plague surged and worsened, and some nights they found no one living at all in London, but the winter and New Year brought a slackening in the number of new victims. By the spring, the tide of refugees had turned back in towards London, and the pool of bodies contracted accordingly. Silver, though acclimatised to his work, found the dwindling opportunities both a frustration and a relief. Plainsong suggested they turn their attentions to churchyards and fresh graves; Silver gave him a withering glance.

There was the ever-present danger that the family whose cellar they had appropriated might return, but by the end of summer this seemed less likely. Still, Silver decided it was prudent to end the experiments in anatomy and move on. They had buried most of their subject's remains wherever they could, in consecrated ground when they could manage it. The remaining organs they burned in the garden on their final night, while Plainsong, drunk on what was left of their looted wine, danced and hollered round the flames. Silver himself warmed his hands, because he felt chill despite the evening's heat. He saw a heart in the fire, the flames licking round it but leaving it untouched.

Christ give me a sign tonight that I am acting to your design.

As they walked away from the house, Plainsong pulled out a small heavy pouch, and tossed it casually into Silver's palm. He opened it curiously and started. 'By Christ, Nick, this is thievery!'

'They ain't coming back for it, are they? And we need to eat. We need somewhere to sleep and some way to carry on your work, and we need gold for all that. You know I'm not greedy.'

Silver nodded, knowing this at least was true. 'The King once paid me to do this. He said it was a stipend, but I only ever saw the one payment.'

'There you go, treat this as monies owed. Question is, what do we do now?'

'There are many more fields to explore than anatomy, Nick.'

'Yeah, but no,' Nick exclaimed and stopped them dead in the street. 'Where are we going with this? What's our purpose? 'Cos we can't go on aimlessly to doomsday, can we?'

'We can and will,' Silver assured him. 'Our purpose is to understand God's creation a little better so we might alter it more to His liking. When we die, our works will live on, to be used or discarded by other hands. These experiments are our children.'

Plainsong snorted. 'Seems to me,' he opined, 'we've been doing too much understanding, and there are better ways of 'aving kids. God's body, Nate! Where's our ambition?!'

'My ambition is to serve Christ – to be His hands. You might think different, and that's your business, not mine.'

Nick sighed, as if he had been expecting an answer like this. He plucked the pouch back from Silver and stowed it safe, his lips puckering wearily. ''Ere's tonight's ambition. We go down Cheapside, wash off the corpse-smell, get a jar or two or three, beer or some of that Dutch juniper muck. There'll be sweet girls down there, an' I've almost forgotten what warm meat feels like.'

'How did you get to be so worldly, young man?'

'Dunno. Just lucky, I reckon.'

Plainsong was right. It would be good to surrender his purpose for a few days. The end of the world was over – he no longer had to shoulder that burden – and the prospect reminded him of his carousing with Don Taylor, six years past. Where had that time gone? He saw his reflection in a puddle, and wondered at how little he had changed outwardly, while inside he felt more worn and lined than ever.

Nick Plainsong was a good companion in merry-making; Silver felt comfortable being the mild, sober half of the partnership, sitting quietly in the shadow of Nick's raucous antics. They trawled round half a dozen public houses beyond midnight. It astonished Silver that his accomplice could drink and abuse himself so without seeming to incur any damage – he was as bright on early Sunday morning as he had been at the start of Saturday's evening. 'Is another trick the Devil taught me,' he explained, tapping his nose. 'Works best on the Sabbath, when I can suck up all the fucking holiness.'

He was tolerant of Plainsong's comfortable blasphemies.

Finally Nick determined to find them beds for the night and bodies to join them. Silver found he was not bothered by the prospect of company, and sat himself at the door of the tavern, exulting in air that was neither too hot nor too warm, and in a black sky licked with red and orange flame and salmon-pink plumes of smoke. There were yells from the direction of the river, and retorts. London was ever an unsleeping city.

'Nate!' Nick hollered. 'Over here, Nate! There are some ladies who need some real magic in their lives! They got husbands need turning to toads!'

'That'd be an improvement!' a woman screeched, and there was laughter. Silver turned part-reluctantly from the door, and picked his way into the yellow-lit body of the building, past drunks and gamblers, to join Nick at his table. The boy already had more than enough company, three women lured there by the flash of his gold more than the flash of his smile. Two sat either side of him, cuddling him; a third was perched with her back to Silver.

'He don't look like no magician,' said the largest, loudest of Plainsong's catches, who had one fat hand on the boy's shoulder and another in his breeches. ''E's a Puritan and we charge 'em double.'

'I'm not a Puritan,' Silver said softly, 'and I'm not a magician.'

'So which of 'em do you like, Nate?' Plainsong said, leaning forward to bang on the table. 'I can't take all of 'em on single-handed.' He reached across the table to tug at the sleeve of the meekest harlot, who sat hunched and tired at Silver's side. She alone wasn't hiding behind a vizard. At the boy's insistent prodding, she loosened her décolletage; a hard shy breath lifted her nipples out into the light.

'Come on Nate, she likes you, at least kiss the girl,' Nick urged.

Silver raised a hand, but to her face rather than her body. He drew the hair back from her eyes, which darted downwards timidly. Her forehead, her whole face, was powdered white, so she seemed as pale as a lifeless body on a slab, but she was warm, warm and somehow familiar. She saw it too, and made the recognition first, and her eyes turned wet with delight and disappointment.

Nick groaned with boredom, despite the attention of the two livelier whores; outside there was a retort like a volley of cannon, which they later learned was a blackpowder warehouse gone up in flame; Nathaniel Silver heard only her voice, and it broke his heart.

'I thought you were dead, Nate,' she said, as he brushed her cheek, first with his fingers, then his handkerchief, to find the spots he remembered under the make-up. 'Like my father. You've not changed. Funny seeing you like this.'

'Alice,' he said at last. She nodded bluntly and crossed her arms to cover herself.

Christ give me a sign tonight.

═ Chapter 5: *The Third Day* ═

'Congratulations on the success of your *Forc'd Marriage*.'

Aphra Behn hadn't expected company, not when the city was practically besieged by snow. It formed in cakes against her windows; she could hear it accumulating in feather-soft falls on her roof; it turned the January sky a bleak grey, and made a little night of the afternoon. Still, the obscure weather meant there was already a fire laid and ready to roar when her guest arrived unannounced, and there was hot tea in the pot. Sally, the maid, poured it with trembling hands, then retreated to warm herself at the hearth, leaving her mistress and this unwelcome intruder at table. Twin plumes rose from the cooling surfaces of the tea; Aphra waited patiently for her friend to drink first, and while she waited she beamed delight.

There was no doubt about it, Carola Harsnett was the most beautiful woman in this world, even swaddled as she was in winter costume so thick and layered that it quite concealed her lovely shape.

Carola *Morland*, Aphra corrected herself.

Eventually Carola drank, and Aphra reached for her own cup, to draw its much-needed heat into her hands and her mouth and her stomach. They exchanged the usual niceties and gossips – and Aphra felt the warmth spreading through her body and loosening her tongue – until the talk turned to the subject of her play.

'I've been deservedly rewarded,' she said. 'I held out my hands and caught the sun, the moon, and the stars – all silver.'

'So you've come into riches at last?'

'For a few days. It runs out all too rapidly, I find.'

'Then you must write another. I hear the first one was very good.'

'I will if the King's or the Duke's will take it. I need the money, and the bread.' A sense of disappointment crept slowly upon her, and she added, quizzically: 'You've not seen it, then?'

'I have a husband now,' Carola remarked. 'He keeps me busy. I'll come to the next one. Aphra, you must do another! We all know you have it in you. Do it for Killigrew, and show the scoffers you didn't just ride Mistress Davenant's skirts and purse-strings.'

'They say that about me?'

'It's better than what they say about the actresses.'

Carola's acquisitive eyes flickered round Aphra's once-modest parlour, settling on the more ostentatious signs of her new-found new-lost wealth. Aphra hoped she wouldn't find anything too gaudily French nor austerely Dutch, nor pry too deeply into the unrepaired conditions of her leaner years – the fraying rugs and curtains, the firewood furniture, the naked blankness of walls where pregnant and decorous art had once hung. But Carola's face was solemn and seemed swollen by the fire. This scene had all the melancholy of a parting, not a meeting.

Then: 'Do you think you'll ever go back to the old business?'

'God's hooks!' Aphra swore. 'I hope not!'

'I meant to the Service of the nation.'

'That's what I thought you meant. No, I think not. I'm no longer recommended to Lord Arlington, so the issue should hardly arise.'

It took Carola a moment to respond. She touched her teacup with her fingertips, pushing it further along the tabletop until she could hardly reach it. 'It might be that… that it is my Sam who would ask something of you.'

Ah, here was the nub of their business! Aphra looked into the eyes of her old friend and confidant, and found her own disappointment reflected back at her.

'Do they still trust your Sam with anything more difficult than lamplighting?'

'Sir Sam isn't answerable to Arlington. Indeed, they've long been rivals. He knows you, and he knows you'd *enjoy* being back in Service.'

Aphra might have shot a bolt of all her fury into Carola's beautiful face. She hesitated out of courtesy, because it was Sam Morland who was to blame here, putting his words into his wife's pretty mouth; and because it could have ruined their friendship; and because Carola's leg stretched out at that moment beneath the table so that her toes stroked the side of Aphra's foot, before curling round her ankle to nuzzle.

'Oh,' Aphra said.

'I would find it hard,' she continued, after a moment's pause during which Carola's stockinged foot stroked the back of her calf expertly, 'to leave London.'

'Not even for a week?' Carola's firelit eyes glistened. Her foot found a gap in Aphra's skirts, a little patch of bare skin exposed to the cold and to the caress of her narrow, rounded toe.

Aphra took up her cup again and played with it, a prop. 'A week? Maybe. I couldn't leave England.'

'Oh, you can stay in the country. We'd want you to stay in the country.'

There was still a little tea in the cup: black, cold, and stagnant, with shredded leaves clustered at the bottom in matted clumps. *If I were a wise woman I could read them, but no one has ever accused me of* that. Carola's toes stroked her skin as sensuously as a hand or a tongue. *Oh Christ, I would that she'd take off her stockings so I could feel flesh against flesh.*

'It would be good to get out of the Smoke,' she proposed, keeping her voice even.

'It could be the adventure you always wanted,' Carola assured her, and then she leaned back in her chair – the better to send her foot climbing Aphra's leg, up to her knee. 'You'd be more than a courier or a lamplighter. There may even be a little peril.'

'And you, Carola, would you be...?'

'I'm married now. My adventures are over,' Carola replied, and her foot slid elegantly up the meagre length of Aphra's thigh, into the warmth, a crooked-toe away from contact.

Aphra heard a tiny question escape from her mouth. 'Would it please you?'

Carola flicked with her toe. Aphra slammed her cup down hard on the tabletop, striking out any other noise that she might or might not have made. She lurched backwards in her chair and stood clumsily, while Carola's feet slipped intangibly away from her, no doubt to rest daintily and unmoving by the legs of her chair. 'I'd...' she gasped, 'I'd need to see a letter of instruction before I could accept.'

Carola leaned forward, resting her chin on a bridge made by her interlaced fingers. 'Sir Sam has provided me with such a letter,' she said briskly.

'And where is it?'

She twinkled. 'It is concealed somewhere on my person.'

'Right, then!' Aphra clapped her palms efficiently. 'Sally, Lady Morland and myself must discuss matters of the utmost secrecy, so we'll retire to the bedroom and are not to be disturbed.'

The fat-faced maid looked up from the flames and rolled her eyes.

There was no fire in the bedroom, so they had to make their own warmth, especially once Aphra had unwrapped Carola from her clothes. The letter of instruction she discarded on the floor, in the grey-blue gloom. Snow still shivered out of the clouds and gathered in heavy drifts at the window, rationing the light into the room. She could still see enough to admire Carola's naked beauty, but felt cloaked in comfortable shadow as she allowed herself to be undressed; she was always more comfortable showing flesh in front of men than women.

It occurred to her that they might go outside like this – if the world were only suddenly emptied of prying eyes – to fuck in thick white drifts that would burn their skins. Instead, they had to make do with the hot cavities under Aphra's bedclothes, with the sheets pulled heavily over them, and their coats and clothes piled up further to make a heap under which their contrasting bodies could sweat and couple subtly. They were so different: Carola's complexion fair and Aphra's dark; Carola slender, Aphra plump; Carola's temper sweet and Aphra's sour; Carola – both in body and society – high where Aphra was *not*. They were so similar: Carola's slick and sticky hands wrapped round

Aphra's face; the flesh of both bodies felt equally numb and equally thrilling under Aphra's touch; Carola's light breasts and shallow nipples still filled her mouth.

Eventually they just lay together – Aphra on her back with her thigh open to the cool damp air, Carola a mild weight across her, with her head resting against Aphra's ear – with their hands clasped on either side at the edges of the pillows.

'I hate you, you know,' Aphra told her, but her tone was dreamy. Carola licked her earlobe with the tip of her dry tongue.

'For manipulating you?' she teased. 'That takes two.'

'Yes, but you did this for him, not for us.' She could see the empty hairless bowl of Carola's armpit and tickled it, setting the other woman giggling.

'He doesn't know,' Carola replied easily, once the laughter subsided. 'Besides, if he'd come to you himself and said – *If you'll go to Cambridgeshire as my eyes and ears, then I'll give you a good hard shag, promise!* – you'd've laughed in his face.' She mimicked her husband's wheedling tones exactly, and that set them both laughing again for another minute.

Eventually Aphra breathed hard, and felt herself sag back into the surface of the mattress; an old one, too lumpy, poorly-stuffed and much-abused. 'So it's to be Cambridge, then?'

'It's all in the letter. Which is here somewhere. Don't let Sally put in on the fire by mistake.'

'Oh, but Cambridge!' she protested. 'Sam knows my heart lies in Oxford! Please don't send me out to the fens or that chilly city. It's barely civilised there, and the bog-people will eat me!'

'The fens are drained, and if a bogwoman eats you I'll be jealous. And it must be Cambridge, I'm afraid. 'Tis where Salomon's House is, and I doubt he'll relocate on the say-so of a passing spy. *Why sir, can we not hold our convention in Oxford where the climate is fairer and I have good credit in many shops?*'

'You've read my instructions, then?' Carola let her hand dip down to Aphra's stomach, teasing the crack where their two bodies touched, but Aphra was content just to lie and think. 'Salomon's House. Should I know of it?'

'It's just a name. It means something to the magicians and villains and alchemists who'll be meeting there. The house is out on the Gogs, a little way beyond Cambridge. Salomon is the master of the estate. Not his real name, of course, but you know how these dabblers like their dressing-up and their codes and cyphers, don't you my Astraea?'

Aphra laughed. 'It sounds not very different to the Royal Society, or even the Service.'

In fact it sounded not at all dissimilar to *half* the Service, the half to which she was not privy; the half of fakery, magic, and science. She had glimpsed its agents occasionally in Whitehall, on the way to their rites in their hoods and gowns with mock-nooses slung round their necks, with designs of cups, swords, wands, or pentacles sown in gold-thread onto their foreheads. *The Masters of Blood and Venom didn't have time for the likes of us, the everyday agents who have both feet firmly on the common ground.*

Of course, under the hood they were the very same men who commanded her to Antwerp or the Americas on mundane business, but inside the hood they became transformed.

I can't say that I would be unhappy to peek under the edge of that little world.

'My Sam says this is different. This gathering is distracting from their proper duties many members of those more *respectable* institutions.'

'So, let me see.' Aphra shifted comfortably, allowing Carola's tireless fingers a little further down her body. 'Either it is some wicked republican plot to undo the Restoration using dark but probably nonexistent spirits –'

'The new fellow has a history of republican sentiment, so Sam has heard.'

'– or more likely, your Sam is simply peeved that he hasn't been invited to this gathering of England's finest. What new fellow?'

'Sam doesn't know. That's why he wants you to go to Salomon's House – to find out! He calls himself *the Magus*, he's appeared out of nowhere and won over half his peers with new insights and methods. The convention is on his behalf.'

Aphra sighed, and as she sighed she put her own fingers to Carola's mouth, which wetted and widened. 'For an adventure, this sounds dry as dust. Your husband is being nosy, and I'd rather stay a-bed with you for the next week and just pretend I went to Cambridge.'

'He 'inks the Magus 's dang'ous,' Carola replied, muffled as her tongue lapped at Aphra's fingertips. She squeezed them out again smoothly. 'Besides, he'll know when I don't come back tonight.'

And having said that, Carola slid easily back under the covers, taking her head down past Aphra's breast and stomach until she was level with the top of her thighs, where, presently, she began to draw her tongue in languorous circles. It had become too hot suddenly under the covers, so she threw them back, revealing her naked trunk to the welcome bite of winter.

The air above the covers was still an empty death-like blue, still wreathed by falling snow and creaking boards. The window was plastered almost completely white, and the light cast uncanny shadows. So it was, that for a moment in her ecstasy, Aphra Behn imagined she saw another woman standing at the foot of her bed and reaching towards her. This woman was tall and lean, with hair falling in neat tresses around her shoulders; the colour was impossible to tell in the dim, but Aphra remembered her from dreams, and knew it was the rich red of silk and cardinals' gowns. And she knew also that while Carola Morland was the most beautiful woman in this world, there were other worlds whose women were more beautiful still, even when swaddled in shadow and memory.

The snow flattened itself on another glass, barely a week later, as the stagecoach carried Aphra Behn the final few miles towards Cambridge, the *Rose*, and her warm bed for the night. The next morning, she would be up early for the carriage into the Downs, to Salomon's House.

Sir Samuel had spared every expense for her journey. His letter of instruction hadn't made clear that her name in the Service was still blackened by Antwerp and her reputation as a spendthrift. The carriage was draughty, and let in all the January chills; it was old, and shook like a storm-toss'd ship whenever it struck a pothole or got bogged in mud; the driver was surly, and the company had been poor. Indeed, for the past hour she had been alone with only her thoughts, her letter, and her books, and these were an improvement on the coughing, scratching, shuffling, leering specimens of humanity she'd had to endure beforehand. She pulled her cloak tighter around her, and dug deeper into M. Pascal's *Pensées*.

She was to attend the gathering as a guest, and not disguised as a servant or – and she was certain this thought must have crossed Sir Samuel's grubby little mind – one of the

Cambridge ladies who would be shipped out in files like slaves on a chain as entertainment for Salomon's household. Morland had concocted an adequate cover story. His agents had intercepted an invitation sent months earlier to the Americas and meant for an Englishman called Babbage, who had gone native as an Indian *shaman* and now took to calling himself Three Hunting Spiders, or something equally ridiculous. Astraea – with her comfortable American experience – would go in his place as his agent, claiming he was too infirm or drug-addled to travel. It wasn't quite the adventure she had been promised back when she'd been pinned between Carola and her mattress. She couldn't imagine duller and less dangerous company than philosophers and scientians. They could do nothing but think – they were almost as bad as Puritans!

She tried to imagine what the Magus might be like from the scant descriptions she'd been given, but it seemed he was known largely through correspondence and had been little seen. Her mental doodlings were quickly rubbed out by a new figure, the shape of the woman crooked over her bed as she climaxed. She might only have been a delusion, but Aphra wished she could slip easily into that beautiful madness again. She gazed expectantly out of the window, hoping to catch a flash of red hair fluttering on the winter breeze among the snow.

Aphra was a child again. In antic Jerusalem –

The coach ground to a halt – not merely a sluggish pause but an actual stop – in the middle of the white expanse of countryside, still a few miles short of Cambridge and nowhere near any buildings she could see, let alone a coaching inn. She rapped impatiently on the ceiling. 'Fuck's sake,' she yelled to the driver. 'I'm freezing my arse off in here.'

There was shouting outside. Shortly, she heard snow crunch underfoot as someone – the guard, she presumed – climbed down and walked away. *If he's just going for a slash then I'm going to –* No. There were more words, heated at first, then huddled and warmer. Astraea seethed with impatience. She waved M. Pascal around the cab in her hand, no longer content to read.

Then there were more footsteps, followed by a face at her window, followed by the snout of a pistol.

'Stand and deliver!' came from the mouth, followed by a joyous crow of 'Oh, but I was born to say that! Should be on the stage, me.' The carriage door swung open; the pistol remained, pointed unwavering at her heart. She put her book down slowly and made a stout, discreet rap on the roof, met with utter silence from the driver...

Don't panic. You've faced worse than this.

The bidstand hauled himself through the door, slammed it after him, and sank his body into the seat opposite her. He was still a youth, perhaps a little more than half Astraea's age; a narrow boy with a narrow face, not unattractive but scrawny and cruel-featured. He licked his lips as he got his first proper eyeful of her, and she sensed an act – though not one that departed much from the youth's general temperament, she felt. He had unkempt straw-coloured hair that made her think of the occasional schoolboy she'd tutored in her lean years. She could imagine herself combing it straight for him. He put his hands on his lap, but still held the pistol tumescent.

What a crude boy. She smiled courteously. No point in showing him fear.

'I have a little jewellery and less money,' she said bluntly. 'Which I offer in exchange for safe passage to Cambridge.' *And once there I'll make sure they hunt you down and hang you, you runty little weasel...*

The bidstand laughed, more of a waterpipe-gurgle. 'We're not going to Cambridge,' he said, and as he spoke the coach lurched, and began to roll forward down the road again. Astraea hammered on the roof and called for the driver, then for the guard, but neither responded.

She turned back to her abductor, who showed her a raw red mouth full of chipped teeth. 'Is it usual,' she asked, 'for a highwayman to allow himself to be driven away, leaving his horse and accomplices on the roadside?'

'I've neither. It's only a short way from Salomon's House, and I enjoy a brisk walk of an evening. Don't call the guard again, or I'll gag you. They don't pay these poor bastards enough. They're easily persuaded to take a short detour 'cross country.'

She was showing fear now, in spite of herself. Here was no simple robbery – she could cope with that – but an ambush. 'So...' she said, 'you're taking me to Salomon's House?' *And nowhere else, please God, please don't bury me in the bogs, please let me live, I will do anything...*

'Might be, might not. You should've seen us when I heard this famous spy come up from London was a lady, I near creamed myself. I'll let you go if you show us your tits.'

Really? 'Really?'

'Nah, I just thought you might be a bloke passing, you're chunky enough. But I got something to prove, and what will the Magus do if I don't bring you fresh and intact? He'll punish us wicked, that's what he'll do.'

He was a Londoner, she could hear it in his voice now. 'The Magus expects me, then?'

'Lady, *everyone* knows you're coming. You're the worst-kept secret in England. You gotta name?'

'Astraea,' she replied, automatically. He spat, not at her, at her book.

'Plainsong. And that's my *real* name,' he told her. 'See, I'm not afraid of you. I'm the Magus's oldest and most trustworthy confidant. And who'll say different now?'

After that, the rough and shambling journey to Salomon's House was in some ways easier and in another much harder. It was easier because Plainsong had dispersed most of her fears; he was only a lackey, and that diminished the potency of his threat considerably; anywise, he was only taking her where by-the-by she had intended to go. Even so, there was something about him that kept her deeply alert. It was in his poise, the tautness of his face and the squint around his eyes – he was full of dark resentments. When he smiled, it was with a mirthless twist of the lips.

By journey's end, the winter sun was fast fading, but she got a glimpse of a high wall in the coachman's light, and beyond that a brooding manor, half-relieved, half-smothered in snow. This was the last she saw, as Plainsong – without warning – sprang forward and pulled a hood over her head, tightening it sharp around her neck before she could react. He bundled her brutally outside, where she slipped and made helpless impact with wet and yielding earth, a graceless thud followed by more as he hurled her belongings out beside her. The next she heard, though muffled by the hood, was Plainsong's voice at her ear, telling her to stand, while the cold metal tip of his pistol poked her backside.

It couldn't be loaded! What fool would trust a man like Plainsong with a loaded gun?! No matter, the threat was still there. She rose shakily, and at his prodding, began to march into the invisible estate.

They were outside long enough for her hands to turn blue and the pull round her neck to chafe. Then she found herself pushed through a door, and there was a mild commotion, disturbed chatter that she couldn't quite hear, but only from a couple of voices. Plainsong growled at her to keep moving, so she did, through more doors and cramped passages. This must be a servant's entrance, she imagined; underheated but still bound inside four walls, and an improvement on the winter outside.

They climbed two flights of stairs and through more corridors before finally she was ordered to stop and sit. Plainsong pulled her arms behind her and tied her. He touched her wrists with warm fingers, not as rough and crude as she expected, but still handling her as though she were an object, something easily kept or easily broken. Then he was gone.

'Couldn't you at least take this fucking bag off my head?' she yelled at last, but if he heard, if he were even still there, he made no reply. And she was left alone in the tightest of her prisons, in darkness with nothing but her thoughts for company.

Chief among them this: *If I ever see Sir Sam Morland again, I'm going to kill him.*

How many hours passed after that, she couldn't tell. She worked herself into a frenzy of anxiety that exhausted her, so that in spite of her difficult breathing and cramped posture, she eventually slumped into a light sleep. Eventually she was woken by an easing of her breath, first as gentle hands unfastened the clasp at her throat, then by the cool and fresh air washing over her face as the bag was slipped upward and away from her. She coughed and a gobful of spittle spluttered out of her mouth.

'Tha – thank you,' she gasped, looking up into a space barely brighter than the inside of the hood. She was being kept in a tight and dusty room, some attic she guessed, windowless and with only a flickering candle for light; that and the faint lustrous skin of her rescuer.

'Christ.' Astraea let the word out along with the breath from her lungs, but it wasn't Christ. It had none of His phoney humility and pasty grace. It was a creature of far more vivid magics, and Aphra Behn, whose business nowadays was words, found that she simply had nothing to say. Instead she worshipped with her eyes, trying not to blink or look away for fear that she might dismiss this vision, as she had done unwittingly in her bedroom. Red-haired, exquisitely beautiful, raw and natural, it was the nymph who had visited her as a child, who now stood swaying in front of her, with Plainsong's hood still caught on her fingers.

She was studying Astraea intently, as if learning this new adult face that she could barely have seen before. Her skin no longer glowed as Aphra remembered it from her girlhood, but there was a little light from somewhere, possibly in the fabric of her costume which rippled raw red on her. It was as if she were wearing a living creature, turned inside out. Symbols glistened inside its translucent cloth, obscuring a body that might otherwise have seemed naked beneath the lean fabric.

The nymph herself seemed *insubstantial.* She melted suddenly in front of Astraea's eyes, and the hood fluttered through her fingers as though they were empty air. Aphra panicked, and for the first time fought the tension in her wrists, struggling to break free. A ghostly hand reached for her face, made contact, was briefly thrillingly like the touch of real flesh on flesh. Then, her mouth forming unspoken words, the illusion slipped away into shadow.

Astraea, left alone, spent some minutes screaming her heart out.

Then she went limp and hoarse, but her screams hadn't gone unnoticed. She heard footsteps pounding outside, then a door was flung open – a square of light opening in the wall and scarring her eyes. A woman – plainly dressed but clearly no servant, pretty and marked with pretty scars – stomped into the room with Plainsong close at her heels;

he was waist-naked and playing unconcerned with an apple. She, by contrast, took one look at the prisoner, threw up her arms in amazement, and stormed out, leaving the door gaping and Aphra staring tired and bewildered after her. Plainsong remained, leaning back against a far wall and working on the apple with a knife, coring it, skinning it.

'Where is your Magus?' Astraea heard her tired mouth ask, but the boy barely looked at her.

Presently there were more heavy footfalls outside, and yet more bodies piled into the room – the woman again, liveried footmen, then a stranger pair by far.

The first looked like a Quaker, or maybe a plain Dutch vintner; he was quite a handsome fellow, more so than Plainsong, yet almost saintly in his humble garb, where the youth was naked and devilish. He was perhaps Astraea's age, thirty years old, give or take. Untidy brown hair, worn shoulder length, spilled out from his hat, and he had a small moustache and sharp beard in the pre-war style. He twitched, only seeming meek and innocuous; there was something harder in his eyes. This man, whatever else he might be, was no fool. His eyes rolled when he saw Plainsong's prisoner; he turned witheringly to the boy and marched him out of the room. Harsh words followed, drifting in through the open doorway, but Astraea was distracted from them by the second newcomer.

This fellow was indeterminately old. He might be an ancient man moving with vigour, or a youth feigning decrepitude. He hobbled into the room with the aid of a carved magician's staff, his body hidden by stinking grey robes, his head by a leather hood and half-mask, his lower-face smeared with mud and filth and straggling beard-hair. He had a mouth full of perfect young-man teeth, cage for a shrivelled old-man tongue. He made straight for her, pawing first her face then her neck with a smooth but sticky hand. Over her shoulder the woman hovered nervously, and Astraea willed her desperately to intervene. The shambling magician drew a wand from his belt of dangling charms, and prodded it painfully into her breast. His breath smelled foul and chemical. He spat out horrid heathen gibberish.

'I'm not afraid of you.' Her voice crawled but still she made it sound defiant. 'I am on His Majesty's Service. There are a dozen Ratcatchers at my command ready to strike, and when they do –' She left the threat hanging, but the disgusting creature only gurgled and prodded some more. *Maybe I should have made it two dozen? Three?*

His hand went again to her bosom, but this time his crude voice formed English words, and over his shoulder the woman's blemished face turned away, as if afraid to listen. 'So this is Morland's dupe. Shall we tell her what we do to spies in Salomon's House? Shall we tell her how we bleed her, how we smear her in dung, how we remove her breasts and privates and keep them in bottles? Shall we tell her why she will beg for these mercies? Shall we tell her what we do first to her soul?'

'Her soul's her own. You aren't going to harm her. No one here will, not any more.'

The Quaker had slipped back into the room unnoticed while the madman ranted. His voice wasn't strong, but it was melodious and it carried round the room. The woman sighed, and ran a relieved hand through her hair, then slid across the room to stand at his side. Astraea, though worn and drowsy, recognised something there, like love, but not quite…

The ragged man was less happy. He turned away from his prisoner, hunching so that by the time he faced the newcomer he was bent almost doubled. His wand stabbed the empty air between them. 'She is a spy, Magus,' he groaned. 'She comes to steal our secrets.'

Quaker-Boy shook his head. 'I have no secrets. This convention is open to anyone who wants to be here, including her, and she's as much my guest as yours. I'm sorry,' he said – addressing Astraea at last, and she lolled her head to one side to get a better look at him – 'Master Plainsong has stepped over his limits, and I apologise. I hope he hasn't hurt you too badly.'

She managed a shake of her head, but faced with a little kindness, she felt desperate at last, hungry, thirsty, tired, and – above all – wishing she were back in her own little bed in London, with Carola or no. But already the Magus was at her side, working to free her from her bonds. His hands were clumsy – they shook, though only she was close enough to tell – and fumbled with the knot. The blemished woman joined them, and helped Astraea to stand once she was free.

The magician was still growling, but curtly nodded his head. 'Very well, but *you* must find her rooms and food, and we must talk to her before she can leave that we might better understand her ways.'

'Thank you, Salomon,' the younger man replied. He was smiling sadly, the line of his mouth just visible above Aphra's face.

Salomon and his party were already quitting the room, and the two women followed. Aphra found she could barely walk after her ordeal, but though each step was a strain, she still turned back at the door to look on the young, strange, forlorn, prosaic figure of the Magus as he was left alone in her prison. He was holding the back of her chair carefully, as if afraid he might break it.

It seemed to her that he was crying.

⇒ Chapter 6: *Love in Many Masks* ⇐

The theatre at Salomon's House was as large as the one he remembered from Holborn, but cleaner and lighter. A window gazed south across the downs, or would have done if thick curtains hadn't been drawn to block out the cold. He had contemplated conducting experiments into the preservative properties of snow as part of the convention, but Salomon had counselled him otherwise, muttering darkly about Lord St Albans and bad precedents.

The centre of the theatre, in the pit surrounded by stalls, was a circular dais. Here the Magus would stand and address his peers for the first time, men of letters finally translated into flesh. He would lecture here, demonstrate on this stage, conduct experiments, and beg for questions. He prowled the circumference nervously, feeling himself trapped in an endless prison from which there was no escape; a panoptic space in which every eye would be on him and every nervous pause or fault would be subject to the cruel and unsympathetic attention of his critics. There would be no relief overhead; the ceiling was a glass dome, so that God Himself could look down on them and judge. Today it was quiet, the benches empty.

From outside the theatre, he could hear the hubbub of more new arrivals as Salomon's House filled up on the eve of the convention.

Best go and greet them, yes? It's what Salomon would want, and Nick, and Alice...

Silver jumped off the dais, then trotted up the sharp steps to the doors. M. Valentine, the French representative, was lurking just outside, but that wasn't unexpected; he'd been trying to ambush the Magus since he'd arrived. Not Silver himself, but *the Magus*, this fictional creation that he and Nick had concocted between them in the past four years.

Silver wondered how many of the conventioneers had come expecting a monster, only to find an unprepossessing disappointment. He'd tried growing a beard and moustache for devilish effect, but they were puny, lacking the Satanic majesty Nick had hoped for. He found himself patting his beard now with his fingertips, self-consciously. M. Valentine squirmed as he saw him – fear or obsequy, it was hard to tell.

'Ah,' squeaked the Frenchman, 'I hoped we might have words before tomorrow's events. There are private matters we might discuss to our mutual benefit.' He was a large man, much taller than Silver, with a head so high you might imagine that dark wig topped with patches of snow. Unlike many of the others who had arrived these last days, Valentine was not ostentatious, but dressed in sober black, as did Silver – so stood side-by-side they might appear to be irregular twins. He was clean-shaven, and appeared, as Nick Plainsong put it, 'straighter than straight'. So many here were willing to dress up in the most ludicrous costumes to create an affect of power. By contrast, M. Valentine's aspect was contrived to make him seem *harmless*.

'Of course,' Silver said leisurely, 'but I'm just going to the –'

'I will walk with you then, M. Magus.'

'Of course.' And they went off together, Silver moving unhurried through the passages and galleries with Valentine insinuating himself through the air at his back, bowing – almost stooping – to talk into the Magus's ear.

'My associates and I see much potential in you that cannot be tapped on these shores. The English are, forgive me, such a provincial race. It is not that they mistrust *scientia*, more that they simply cannot conceive the uses to which it might be put. On this island, you will ever be a maker of toys and magical trinkets.' Silver listened, but his eyes were directed elsewhere, remembering the faces he passed, and gazing on the opulence of the furnishings and decoration. By contrast with the privations of the war years, such easy and ostentatious wealth felt to him faintly obscene.

'Are you offering the Magus a business proposition?' That was Nick Plainsong, who had slipped half-noticed alongside them, and now interjected into the space between their bodies. Valentine halted.

'We hope he would consider a future with us –'

Plainsong raised a hand, flat palm held out to silence the Frenchman. He looked to Silver for approval, and seeing a nod, replied: 'The Magus does not serve any individual nor any nation. He works for God, for the benefit of the whole world, and not any favoured part of it.'

Was Valentine offended? His face was bland and clean. 'I do not represent France in this matter –'

'The Magus will not work for any private company or party, for the same reasons.'

Valentine rolled his head back to inspect the decorated ceiling, all the while clucking sweetly as if amused by some invisible joke. Then he shrugged easily, and held out his card caught between two delicate fingers. 'We understand, but circumstances change. Should the Magus wish to reconsider, *le Pouvoir* bears no grudges.' Silver took the card, thanked him, and sighed generously once the Frenchman had beaten his retreat.

Nick rounded on him: 'Bloody hell, Nate! That was the biggest, richest power in the world, and you've just told 'em to go fuck themselves. I really fancy Paris of a winter. Bit of sun, money, power, influence, the King's ear, the pick of the virgins if you can find any! It'd be, you know, comfortable,' and he mock-shivered.

Nick hadn't changed much in the last four years. He was a little less sleek now, a little heavier, but on the whole, the passing of time only served to make him ever more like Nick Plainsong. He was dressed a pinch more finely than his Magus – a pinch more comfortable and a pinch more colourful – but not so much as to distract the eye, or persuade an innocent party that he might be Silver's principal. Though truth be told, he was as much Silver's agent now as his assistant; he had learned feral ambition on the rough streets of London, a drive that Silver knew he himself lacked.

'I won't live in a prison, Nick,' he said sternly, 'no matter how pretty.'

'You're happy enough with prisons of your own making. 'Sides, you might be back behind bars for real if the Service get their way.'

'We've talked about this. They're sending a spy to the convention? So? Let him come.'

'They're dangerous. I spoke to Salomon, and he said...'

Silver kept his voice low: 'Salomon has his own secrets to guard, but that's his business, not mine. *And I'm not sure I trust you with Salomon; he is the sort of magician you were looking for when you came burrowing into my cellar – all chants and smokes and wicked incantations to dark powers – and I would not have him lead you astray.*

'Magus –'

'I know you're just trying to protect me, but I don't need protection. Not today.'

'Yes Magus,' Nick replied, through gritted teeth. He was a handsome boy, but he could seem wilfully ugly sometimes. Still, that seemed to be an end to the matter, and they continued in silence to the balcony overlooking the main hall, where the assorted philosophers, thinkers, tinkerers, idealists, engineers, fraudsters, and charlatans of England (and beyond) were gathering. Salomon would be down there – the tall handsome young man dressing up in squalid rags, stoop'd and making a more formidable magician than Silver could ever manage. The new arrivals were his guests as much as Silver's, drawn hither by a year's worth of organising, cajoling, and impressing on his part. The Magus was merely a mayfly attraction in Salomon's raree show.

Silver was more than slightly nervous of Salomon, and chose not to descend immediately. He spotted Alice Lynch at the balcony window, staring out intently at everything and nothing in the white world beyond the walls. He made for her softly, wondering how close he could get before she was distracted from her trance –

Plainsong leaped in ahead of him and slapped her playfully across the rump. She started, but spared only a second to glower at the boy before turning back to the window. She hadn't lost any of her inky seriousness in the decade Silver had missed, nor in the half-decade since he had saved her from whoring herself in Cheapside taverns. If anything, she'd become more intense and murkier.

Silver drew alongside her, so they stood together like two awkward wood pins, tilting into each other's light but not touching. 'What are you looking for?' he asked. She pointed.

The window commanded a view of the grounds of Salomon's House, mostly lathered in snow that still fell in wind-skewed blasts. The drive to the north road had been thoroughly swept and salted, so that the carriages could come and go, depositing their odd occupants on Salomon's doorstep. One of the oddest was perched right below the line of the window – the carriage itself was unmarked and unremarkable, but the driver was something else. Above his coats and furs, and under the tied hat that bobbed and shook but would not be dislodged by the winds, was a mask of bleak ivory. Smooth in places and jagged elsewhere, it had the hint of an authentic skull, but not from any healthy animal, nor from any that Silver knew. Even the great elephant skulls he had inspected in his work didn't have the broad flat majesty of this beast.

It must be Biblical, he thought, the skull of a giant or a behemoth.

Plainsong leaned also at the balcony beside them, and now clapped his hands and whistled. 'Oh ho! This looks to be evil shit!'

'What are they?' Silver asked. 'Where are they from?'

'They're a foreign party who petitioned Salomon for admission, Nate,' Alice informed him blandly; she alone would not call him Magus, and he blessed her for it. She checked her papers: 'The Faction of Paradoxes.'

'Bit of a mouthful, that.' Plainsong grinned and winked across the gap at Alice.

She did not dignify him with even a glance, so he bowed theatrically and backed away. Silver watched him go, sliding down the curling banister to crash the party below. Once he was satisfied they were alone, Silver looked back to the coachman, who was pulling away from the door towards the stables.

'By Christ,' he mused. 'What have I unleashed here?'

Alice finally smiled at him, and made her face pretty. Her blemishes creased when she smiled now, and were more vivid than they had ever been when she was a child. He had often wondered – but never asked – what she had done after she fled her father's arrest, how she had come to fall so far that she had nothing to sell but her body, and how many times she'd surrendered to that cruel trap of poverty before he'd blundered back into her life with his little celebrity and larger bag of gold. 'We should go down and greet them. Show your face. Mingle. You don't want them to think you aloof or frighted, do you?'

He shook his head, and let her lead him to the staircase.

'I'm sorry about Master Plainsong,' he said. 'He'll learn.'

'He's at that age,' Alice replied, 'and no, he won't.'

It wasn't that Alice and Nick hated each other, though they did. It was that they hated each other as a brother and sister would hate one another, the evil sentiment complicated by blood and similarity. They were certainly contrasts. Nick, his assistant, was expansive and loud. She, his secretary, was demur and misliked being touched. Nick had turned him into a monster, while she was there to remind him that he was not so. She had on a plain grey gown with tight sleeves and a high clasping collar; it concealed her completely below the neck, though she wore her hair free in dense chestnut ringlets. She took him down the stairs, and every step was a blow in his chest, his stomach, and his loins.

Christ, Nate, she was seven years old when you first met her!

True, but that was the better part of two decades gone.

As they descended, they heard the doorman bellow: 'Representing the ELEVEN-DAY EMPIRE – COUSIN HATEMAN of FACTION PARADOX!'

Another skull-headed personage had stepped into the hall, this one a handsome woman judging from her dress and jewels, the olive smoothness of her naked shoulders and barely-concealed legs, the daintiness of her tread, and the curve of her hips. Even so, the lecherous old wizards who filled the hall were none too quick to be attracted by her exotic sex, recoiling as they were from the bleached bone of her face that was – if anything – uglier and more brutal than that of her driver.

Salomon, though, was striding towards her as best he could for a man feigning a crouch. He fast-hobbled using his stick, the end still browned and bloodied from the unfortunate footman who, that morning, had made a mistake of calling him *Doctor Bendo* aloud. Salomon took the game of secret names very seriously. As he greeted the newcomer, Silver slipped alongside him.

Cousin Hateman held out a jar with a grizzled grey homunculus squashed inside it, quite dead and blank-eyed, yet somehow still seeming to nudge and prod at the glass. 'Please accept the gift of this petrified monkey foetus on behalf of my principal, Mother Sphinx, and the founder of our order, Grandfather Paradox.'

Salomon plucked the unborn monkey hungrily from her hands, his eyes glistening and tongue licking as though he was about to swallow it, but instead he palmed it off onto a servant. Silver decided to chime in: 'Where exactly is the Eleven-Day Empire, cousin?'

Hateman's skull surrendered nothing. 'It's not a place, sir. It's an aspiration.'

'This is our beloved friend and Magus,' Salomon growled, and the creature called Hateman curtsied and took his hand. Her skin was warm. He had expected a grave-cold thing. She turned back to her host.

'Sir, might we have your permission to raise a shrine in our rooms for the duration of our stay?'

Salomon clucked and spouted more of his nonsense words. *Enochian*, he claimed, though Silver knew better. 'Of course, of course, let me show you the way...' and his arm was round the cousin's waist, pulling her away toward the staircase. Silver smiled softly as both disguises disappeared into the crowd.

'Don't fancy his chances with her, I don't,' Plainsong whispered into his ear. He had a bad habit of creeping. Silver had the odd sensation that everyone present was looking at him, and he felt a powerful urge to hide himself. Better still, he wanted to shout, to yell with all the force of his lungs. *I'm a fake and a fraud. I'm no Magus, and all my insights are gleaned from between the teeth of angels. God creates while I but copy!*

Alice and Nick regarded him, both fondly in their own manners. His further thoughts were half-obliterated by another thunderclap from the liveried servant at the door.

'From TRINITY COLLEGE, CAMBRIDGE – JEOVA UNUS SANCTUS!'

Silver looked over his shoulder, then to his two young confidants, the only people he truly trusted here (and, in Nick's case, only a little). 'You'll have to excuse me,' he apologised, 'this is a man I must meet.'

Of all Silver's many correspondents, the man who called himself Jeova was the strangest and the strongest. It was only in the last two years, once Silver was well-established as the Magus, that they had come into contact. He cherished the letters he received, even the early ones when the mathematician's wariness and collegiate pride were spelled out in brusque, suspicious sentences. Later, as the younger man found no threat in Silver's enquiries, the letters grew voluminous and dense, the words cramped but well-spaced and blotched from hurry. *Jeova* they were signed, always *Jeova*. Even outside Salomon's convention he guarded his true name with the abiding secrecy of an old magician. He held some post at the university that he would not describe, and claimed an aversion to travel – and Silver was grateful that Salomon's House was so well-placed for Cambridge, so that he might lure the fellow here and get a measure of the man in his flesh.

He found a man some twenty years his junior coming haltingly into the hall, perhaps prowling, perhaps stepping into a world he found alien. He had less delicate features than Silver expected; Silver had imagined a pasty, baby-faced scholar but this man had a heavy jaw and stern profile with knotted eyebrows. He had a silvery blond wig on his head and was hatless, but was otherwise dressed as unremarkably as Silver himself. As the Magus hoved across the floor to meet him, Jeova looked upon him and nodded firmly, as if knowing exactly whom he was about to see. As it turned out, the nod was a spasm of a kind to which he was prone, and he had not recognised Silver at all.

Silver greeted him in Salomon's absence, and offered to show him direct to the rooms that had been set aside for him. It would have been easier – and perhaps politer – to hold their inaugural conversation in the hall, where both men could mix freely with their peers, but Silver was possessed of a jealousy and wanted Jeova to himself. The man's insights were unparalleled. Silver could not believe that he didn't have an angel's egg of his own, yet a man capable of such thought unaided would be more miraculous than all of Heaven's works combined.

But the miracle was taciturn, and said little as they wove through the hall and into the passages of Salomon's House. He reminded Silver of Nick Plainsong most of all, and then only of Plainsong when the boy was in his moods. It wasn't until they were in the humble quarters – though Jeova's eyes flickered approvingly as they stepped inside, his university situation could barely be less comfortable – that Silver heard more than the odd word or grunt from those pursed lips.

'I have a gift,' he said, stumbling on his tongue as he had on his feet, 'meant for Doctor Bendo.'

Not Salomon, eh? 'We'll hunt him down presently. Right now he has other matters on his hands. When you see him you must call him by his –'

Jeova had slipped a leather wallet from his jacket and now unwrapped it, holding out a tattered sheaf of browned papers, torn and scratched, divorced from all but the crudest of bindings. The title leaf was half-ripped away, but the first two lines were legible.

Obſervations vpon the cycle of the ſun in the ſky and the ſeed in the fields

Silver felt himself pause, knowing what he was seeing but unable to react or speak or move.

'This may be the only extant copy,' Jeova said plainly. 'I have found no other in my researches.'

'May I?' Silver took the book from Jeova's unresisting hand, and the damp-rippled paper felt like heresy on his skin. 'I have never seen this, it was published without my knowledge. I know not what liberties were taken with the text.'

He could not, now that he had it, bring himself to read more than he had already seen. He stood frozen like this while Jeova eased clumsily past him to the bed, to test the mattress with his hands. After a time, he took the book back, and replaced it in the wallet for Salomon's inspection. He seemed unmoved by Silver's silence, perhaps even a little amused.

'You have read it?' Silver asked, eventually.

'I have.'

'I would appreciate your thoughts, sir.'

Jeova lowered himself onto the bed and stretched back on his elbows, the first hint of the smooth and languid mind in those cramped limbs and trunk. 'It is a juvenile and untutored work. There are insights and crucial observations scattered hither and yon, as wildflowers may be found on the most inhospitable outcrops. If there was an argument, I fear it was so garbled that I failed to find it. You snatch at divinities in the clouds, sir, thinking not of the steps upon which you must stand to reach them.'

Silver had thought he could take the harshest criticism from this man and found that he was wrong; the words were like ash in his ears. But Jeova continued: 'You should not have rushed to publish, though I see 'twas not your intent. Yet among the muddle I sensed a mind rapt in delight, which is to be encouraged in an unschooled fellow such as yourself. And by your letters and this convention I find that you have the greatest of all intellectual gifts, namely the capacity for improvement.'

Silver made slow repetitive bobs of his head. 'You think I journey in the right direction?'

'Indeed I do, though perhaps with unnecessary digressions out of the way. I would strive to clean the dross from your mind as well as your soul. Perhaps then you might become an unparalleled man.'

'Then I thank you, sir, though I fear I will ever disappoint you.'

Jeova turned those unfriendly lips into their opposite, a rare and warm smile, and he patted a space down on the bed beside him so that Silver might sit. 'This convention, I would that it had a more classical name. The word is a trifle.'

'I seek to frame learning in good English, sir. Latin is beyond me; it is a language of the dead.'

'Ah,' Jeova sat sharp upright, his eyes twinkling, 'but this makes it a tongue that cuts across all boundaries, therefore perfect for communication between, let us say, Italians and Poles who might otherwise have nothing else in common. Thus we avoid the confusion of nations.'

'Don't you think, sir, that a language might create its own nation? One from which I am excluded?'

'Perhaps. You could always learn.'

'I have no talent for it.'

'That is indeed a problem.'

Silver looked on Jeova's sly, inscrutable face and saw not just the man of learning and insight he had expected, but something altogether greater. They were kin, like twins though born from separate wombs in separate years. The eyes in Jeova's sockets were *his* eyes, windows into the same soul where the same lights and shadows moved. In personality Jeova seemed a much different man, with other tempers and drives, but those were matters of the body, governed by their varied humours. No, it was as if they were halves of the same being. Apart they slept; united they... they could...

'We might change the world,' Silver said softly.

'Indeed we might,' Jeova agreed, though perhaps he was thinking of another thing. A strand of hair had fallen across Silver's forehead, and the scholar raised a thumb to flick it back into place.

Silver stepped off the mattress and stood to petition his guest, who suddenly looked crushed and longing perched on the edge of the bed, like a lonely child, like a wilting flower. 'You understand the nature of my work here; that it is open and will be shared; that I have no secrets.'

'That was made clear in the invitation,' Jeova opined dryly, the humour that had once settled there now scattering.

'I have one secret, sir, that I have shared with no one, not with my friends or my associates or any of my correspondents. I would be honoured to share it with you.'

Jeova nodded curtly, and Silver – his hand pausing only once and briefly – reached inside his coat to find the bundle he had concealed there, against his heart. He rested it on his palm, unwilling even now to let it go, and pulled back the wrapping until the glow of the egg was revealed to light the room. Silver looked to Jeova, but found a man neither impressed nor awed. He was flat-faced.

'What is this?' he said eventually, without sentiment.

'This is the philosopher's stone,' Silver told him, and watched a little smile crease on the corner of the man's lips. Disappointed, he began to describe how he had come by the egg, how Christ's pilots had appeared to him, the insights it had given him –

Jeova cut across him. 'You would be better off without it. Throw it away.'

'It speaks to me in the voice of angels,' Silver protested.

'It echoes your own voice, nothing more. Learning is not given by divine revelation, Master Silver – if it ever were, those days are gone. Today it is application, measurement, and repetition. The philosopher's stone must be striven for, it does not simply land by chance in the lap of the alchemist. Throw it away!'

'It has shown me –'

Jeova was shaking and almost stood, but checked himself. 'Trickery! You are blinded by false light, like Licetus with his Bologna stone, or that Hamburger who last year found illumination in his own distilled piss.' The hardness held in Jeova's eyes for a moment, then smoothed and softened. 'Sir, I do not say this to attack you. This... fraudulent stone... is a crutch, and I would liberate you. It does not give you insight. You merely hear your own thoughts and see your own brilliance reflected by it.'

'I disagree. Must you take this from me?'

'One must not be confounded by one's own eyes. Come, put it away and let us talk by God's honest sunlight.'

Silver did as he was told, putting the egg back into his coat along with his rejection. He did not allow himself to become truculent, but pushed his bad humour back down into the darkest part of his soul and engaged with Jeova. They turned to matters of pure learning and practical application, and he was soon able to forget, as the language of numbers and the description of methods drowned out that broken little voice of disappointment. The afternoon sun dipped below the horizon and still they talked, lighting candles close by the bed that revealed their faces and nothing more in the darkness. Jeova tested him – and he parried as best he could – but in time he also found himself testing back, probing the limits of the mathematician's knowledge, the nimbleness of his reasoning, and the sharpness of his wits. Once, for a moment, he almost thought he had the fellow confounded.

They might have talked forever, but were interrupted by an insistent hammering on the door, then Alice's voice yelling not for the Magus but for Nate. Silver sprang to his feet and went to let her in. She had sounded distressed, and in the waxy light of the candles she seemed livid.

'Oh Nate, thank Christ!'

'Please don't use that name in vain,' Jeova murmured from the back of the darkness.

But Alice ploughed on: 'It's Nick Plainsong. You won't believe what he's gone and done now!'

What Nick had gone and done now was stage a single-handed ambush of the Service's spy on the road from London. He'd succeeded, though not exactly *admirably*, and had brought the fellow back to Salomon's House at gunpoint. Silver made his excuses to Jeova, and allowed Alice to lead him up into the attic that Nick had converted into a makeshift cell. His anger mounted with every step, not just because Nick had ignored his wishes, but with a burning personal fury. *No one should be imprisoned for my sake — that is abominable!*

There was also the matter of Jeova, of the conversation left disrupted and unfinished, so many precious thoughts stillborn. He had the sense that once he had left Jeova's room there would be no going back — a chance had been laid before him, but he had not taken it and it would not be proffered again. He tried not to let momentary frustration guide him, but when he got a hold of Nick, he bawled the boy out with a ferocity than he hadn't intended, a tirade he would at length regret. Plainsong absorbed the flood of righteous anger, seeming neither upset nor contrite. He wore a cool and baleful mouth; there were teeth in it, but it was not a smile.

Silver was surprised to find that the spy was a woman, a short and chubby creature who looked bedraggled by snow, exhaustion, and cramp from being tied in a chair. He would make copious apologies in time, but he doubted she would be in the mood for them now; she had that air of oppression he had seen before only in men who had spent long months in prison. *And that is on your conscience, Nate, when it ought by rights to be on some other, on Nick...*

I am the Magus. It is done in my name.

He found himself alone in the attic, a roof-space devoted to nothing but the storing of old boxes. Time and decay worked rapidly in these abandoned places; he could smell the crumbling of wooden boards and the flaking of brick, while the mummified remains of insects dusted his soles and his coat. It was a lower but more spacious cell than he remembered. Sure he couldn't be overheard, he let out a demon that hollered and dashed the spy's chair into firewood against the wall.

Composing himself, Silver brushed the cobwebs and grime from his shoulders and went back down to find Jeova. There was still a light visible under the door, and he knocked softly to no answer. It wasn't locked, so calling the pseudonym gently, he pushed inside and found his correspondent still there but otherwise engrossed in a new companion. Jeova was sprawled on the bed, while a half-naked youth straddled his midriff. The mathematician's eyes were fixed unwaveringly on the boy's face while his scholarly hands questioned the hard-muscled chest, the flat board of his stomach, then lower.

Silver watched, frozen. Jeova made a slow lizard-blink and would have turned if his lover hadn't hurriedly leant to kiss him on the mouth and pull his wig playfully down across his eyes. The bare-chested young man then turned and raised a warning finger to his lips, gesturing to his Magus to close the door. Silver, whose memory had emptied itself with embarrassment, recognised Nick Plainsong at last. He pulled the door back into its jamb. He paced away, feeling thoroughly defeated. What little he felt he had was now knocked from him by this final confusion, this betrayal... no, it wasn't betrayal, it was pure theft, the prize of reason snatched away by passion... He reeled in the corridor, grasped for a wall, and found it too smooth to prevent him dropping to his knees.

He imagined he had gone through every subtle combination of humour that the human body could manage, to the point where he could no longer feel anything. What turned and twisted inside him now was formless chaos. *I can't do this tomorrow, I can't...*

Alice found him there, his hand pressed desperately to the wall as though it were his only anchor in the solid world. She gathered him up before anyone else could see them, and helped him back to his quarters.

She laid him out on his bed, took his hat from him, and hooked it on the back of his door. Even that would have seemed an effort to him. She shut out the light from the corridor and lit a solitary candle. It was the only heat in the room, but he did not feel January cold, as Alice must have done. He yawned, a vast eruption that nearly snapped off his jaw.

'Alice?' he said kindly, not wishing to seem too frail. 'You found somewhere to put the spy?'

'Her name's Astraea. She's asleep now in my bed.'

'There's barely room for you in that cupboard.'

'I'll lie elsewhere. We must be rested for the morning.'

Alice took up her candle and pressed against him, pushing him down into the mattress, so there was no gap between the front of her body and his. He gasped, suddenly uncomfortable and suddenly excited. 'Alice...' She put her hand on his lips; her face, in skipping yellow light, was revealed in all its haggard weariness, anxiety, and resolve. He would wish later that it was this look that excited him, but the truth was that he had stirred for her minutes before, when she touched him, when she led him back here.

'You never did abandon me, Nate,' she told him, as she stroked first his chest, then his face, then – through the cloth of his breeches – his cock, 'and I won't abandon you now.'

'Alice, I am a quarter-century older than you!'

'So! No one knows that. Not even Nick knows that. Nate,' she finished, her lips trembling as if they resisted the task of making words, 'between you and me, there is no sin. There can't be.' Then she put her mouth to his to stop him talking, and his lips met hers without reluctance.

When she pulled away a string of his spit came with her, on her tongue.

She put the candle down to undress him, struggling with his numb limbs and fiddly buttons, and forever casting her eyes upwards to make sure that she had not scared him or angered him. Only once he was completely naked – still pressed down on the bed – did she try to kiss him again or touch his body. Her hands were panicked and rushing; they found his erection too quickly, and he spent heavy white gobs across her fingers and the front of her dress. So he found strength to intervene, and took her wrist to guide one set of fingers around his bony body. Her other hand dripped cooling semen onto the candle-flame, which sizzled into extinction.

She was shyer than Ann, and would not undress herself until they were in darkness. Her touch didn't remind him of Ann's, as he thought it might have done, and as she nuzzled her mouth to his face, his chest, and his flank, he realised he could no longer remember what Ann looked like or smelled like or felt like. Alice was the overwhelming presence on top of him, the grey glimmer of her night-time skin half visible, its touch succulent but its warmth nourishing. He grew bolder in the dark and hoped not to disappoint her, but she was ever quiet, not crying out as they coupled, but only breathing harshly to a frantic rhythm.

'Nate,' she said afterwards, while his anointed cock shrivelled and squeezed out of her body. 'I do love you. I couldn't say it, but I do.'

She sounded frightened. He stroked her face, her stomach, and her arse, wishing that she were happier. He had found nothing but joy when their bodies met. 'You didn't need to say it aloud,' he explained. 'I knew it, always.'

She seemed contented by that, made a simpering mewl, and pressed close against him, her breasts snuggling his side; her thigh crooked over his flank; her hand pressed down on his chest so tight and hot that he expected by the morning it would have left a mark. But it did not.

⇒ Chapter 7: *Mumbo Jumbo* ⇐

Little Sister Greenaway paused at the Magus's door, pressed her hand gently to its wood, and listened to what it had to tell her. It was the skill she had learned best in her year's-worth of instruction with Faction Paradox – befriending the spirits of buildings. Cousin Hateman speculated that it must be because she'd invested so many of her dreams and fancies in the structure of Thomas Piper's old house outside London. That was long gone, of course, but it was there that she'd discovered the art of communicating with the walls, the doors, the bricks and mortar; of gaining a house's trust and persuading it to spill its secrets. All architecture had its own ghosts, tiny imagos like *loa* but not *loa*.

She had yet to commune with a *loa*, or find one to ride her. She had tried – the Grand-father knew she had tried! – but they resisted her blandishments and advances. Even in her drugged trances, at the height of Faction rituals, they had only swirled around her, grey as the sea, saying nothing. So disappointing.

She whispered to the door and it told her about the still, sleeping contents of the interior. Nathaniel Silver lay uneasily abed, though his doubts and guilts and anxieties about the morning had been tamed and muted by Alice's love. The little sister smiled grimly to herself and moved on, still not quite believing that Silver could be the fearful power her cousins imagined.

She tried her trick at another door: here, the boy Plainsong and his lover Jeova were abed but not sleeping. The room was swelling with their sweat and carnal energies. She heard Plainsong quite audibly, without the benefits of Paradox magics, though Jeova was as quiet as a dormouse. Nevertheless, he was there, allowing the boy to slake his lusts, perhaps absorbing some confidence from his lover's cocksure manner. Little Sister Greenaway, who might have been primly shocked at such goings-on when she had been plain young Mistress Piper, just hoped it was distracting Plainsong from his customary treachery. No, the room whispered sadly, he is planning some mischief or other, to be put into action once his seed is spilled.

She let them get on with it, and set out through Salomon's House in search of the room set aside for Cousin Hateman. No one saw her or challenged her as she moved through the house. She kept in the shadows, letting them render her mute and invisible to the occasional footmen, servants, or revelling alchemists she passed in the passage. Shade-magic was another discipline that had come easily to her in the plague year of her instruction. She could make her silhouette twist and turn and dance with more elegance and greater precision than any of her tutors (save perhaps Mother Sphinx, whose shadow barely seemed to be there half the time and seemed infinitely more active than her slothful physical body). Nevertheless, she was still a little sister, still in her period of probation after five long years. If they succeeded this week then she would be *cousin* at last, have her own *sombras que corta*, a weapon uniquely fitted to her shadow-hand...

In her flesh hand she carried the dolly, which was a third discipline she had mastered.

Faction Paradox's room was lightless when she arrived, the bed and other furniture undisturbed, the fireplace empty of everything except flecks of old ash. It wasn't quite deserted. Cousin Suppression was sitting in a corner reading a paper-bound book by a portable light powered by *electricks*. She knew Suppression the least well of her cousins, save that his name was well-fitted, as he kept his thoughts and character largely concealed behind a taciturn, almost shy countenance. He rarely spoke to her, and when he did speak he didn't look at her, not out of arrogance but almost the opposite, a kind of reverence. Then again, he did this with the other cousins too; only Mother Sphinx had his full attention, and their conversations were hushed or private.

One thing they all knew about Suppression; he was an inveterate reader. He had a stack of long prose romances called *The Homeworld Chronicles*, which – she had learned – were sentimental works put out by the Great Houses to propagate slanders and malicious falsehoods about their enemies, the Faction among them. The Homeworld itself – that monstrous power that put whole worlds to the sword – was shown to be a haven of civilisation and liberty, ever-threatened by the swarming, slavering hordes of Faction Paradox and the rest. Suppression would sit in the corner reading through them, occasionally looking up to shout out 'Lies!' or 'Hacks!' before returning his eyes patiently to the page. Cousin Amphigorey had once confided in Greenaway his suspicion that Suppression had been one of the Homeworld's tame authors, until the guilt of it had become too much to bear and driven him into the arms of the Faction. Then again, Amphigorey had confided a lot of things in her that had turned out not to be true, the size of his penis for one.

They feared the Homeworld, all her cousins. The Homeworld would kill them all, if they couldn't find some weapon that would give them a decisive edge. And they had found Nate Silver, who seemed to be less like a weapon to Greenaway's eyes than any other thing on Earth.

Suppression looked up as she approached, smiled wanly, but said nothing. He had her mask, and as she placed it over her head, Greenaway was remembered of the claustrophobic freedom that she had not enjoyed for many months now.

There was another door, one that Greenaway instinctively knew couldn't be read. Suppression, a gentleman in spite of his lumpen stolidity, opened it and allowed her to pass through first. So she returned to the shrine she had last seen over four years previously, when it had been built into the wall of an abandoned old stables on the road to Islington. That the shrine had relocated itself was no longer a surprise; her sigh was simply one of recognition, of coming home and finding herself among family.

Here was the altar and the blind stone windows she had spent so much time dusting (until it had been pointed out to her that dust simply didn't accumulate in the shrine as it would in the solid world), though where before they had been mossed and petrified, now they seemed alive. The altar was flecked with glistening points like stars, and all surfaces hummed with the long wordless chant of the *loa*. The architecture of the shrine was a mystery to her; it would never respond simply to her caresses, as stone or brick buildings would. It was not a building at all, she thought sometimes, but a womb, or maybe a world in its own right. This was a between-place, not a place itself. *Of course it could move.*

The family was waiting for her: Cousin Hateman, distractedly removing her spectacles before donning her mask; Cousin Amphigorey, leaning up against the very pillar where they'd first drunkenly kissed during their ill-advised affair; Mother Sphinx, reclining on her wheeled-chair that prowled round the edges of the shrine under its own ticking volition; and even Faction Cat, who was still as perky and kittenish as she had been four years ago, without a hint of grey in her fur or girth round her belly. She had not aged at all.

The last time they had been together, Mother Sphinx had told her. 'While you're out in the solid world, Little Sister, we get eaten up by the *loa*. We sleep in their bellies and don't grow old.' She had thought this a fancy, a turn of phrase, until now.

Greenaway nodded, putting her fist up to the mouth of her mask. She had seen her family only irregularly in the last four years, usually only one and usually Hateman, whom – it had soon become clear to her – was Sphinx's trusted cousin among cousins. And while they slept, she had kept up her vigil over Silver and his growing band of followers, one slow day at a time, until she had almost forgotten her superiors in the order.

With her free hand, she tickled Faction Cat's chin and listened to her purr merge into the thrum of the *loa*. She could never forget the *loa*…

She held up the dolly, built up over the years from his body, his hair, his spit, his blood, his dried shit, his flaked skin, his spunk, and his tears. She'd found a way to collect them all. 'Nathaniel Silver,' she proclaimed, before describing her evening's rites, and what she'd learned from the Magus's room. She could imagine the smiles under their bone hoods, perhaps pride, perhaps condescension. She still felt provincial among these proud cosmopolitan Venetians. They humoured her, but in their hearts felt the solid and spirit worlds were too deep and too complex for her to comprehend.

Hateman, who could be the most patronising of them all, put a reassuring hand on her little sister's shoulder. Greenaway regarded it through neutral eyes, not sure how she felt.

'Tomorrow's when it happens,' the older woman said – was she still older, after resting so long outside time? 'The *loa* swirl round him like the winds round the calm centre of a hurricane. Tomorrow's when the storms break.'

'What will happen?' she asked. 'Will he be hurt?'

Hateman shook her bone-head, not a *no*, just non-committal. 'We don't know.'

Mother Sphinx raised her hands, palms the size of Greenaway's naked face, and brought them together in a thunderclap. 'Powers coming,' she declared. 'Powers and *les mystères*, they coming too. We may be dead tomorrow.' Greenaway felt her heart tremble, a little reflection of the great fear that Mother Sphinx must feel, but the mother was laughing: 'Mother Sphinx thinks that every night. Sun goes down, remind us all of death, of the bargain we all made.'

'I didn't,' Amphigorey muttered, but he was just being bitter. She hadn't imagined he could still be upset after four years, but then it hadn't been four years. Not for him.

Hateman took the offering from Greenaway's hands. 'A biodata dolly. How cute.'

'What will you do with it?' Greenaway asked. 'I still think we could bargain with him. He's a good man, he wouldn't turn us down without good reason.'

Hateman nodded. 'Alice could take the offer to him. She can be very persuasive.'

'She has a very persuasive cunt.'

That was Amphigorey, who was still bristling from the failures of old romance. Greenaway regarded his contempt – for him still fresh – from a distance of years. 'Alice won't be there tomorrow,' she said firmly. 'He's asked her to go into the city for the week. He doesn't like her involved with his work like this. He never has. He still thinks of her as this little spark he first saw on her father's knee. Innocent.'

'He's 'fraid for her,' Sphinx boomed evenly, driving her chair alongside Hateman so she could take the dolly from her protégé's hands. 'He knows he got power, he just don't know what. Nor do we. Grandfather himself wouldn't know. Mother Sphinx makes no deals till she knows what she's buying.'

'That's why we need the dolly,' Hateman continued. 'We have the rest of the night to summon and bind the *loa*, around Silver. Mother Sphinx tells us there are powers and mysteries at work here, so we need to lock them out. We need to build a wall of *loa* round Nathaniel Silver's biodata so thick that you couldn't ram a timeship through it. No one is going to take this opportunity away from us. Not the Great Houses, not their enemy, no one.'

'Houses coming,' Mother Sphinx said; and for a moment there was no sound in the shrine, except the low groan of the *loa* in the walls. Then Mother Sphinx repeated: '*Great* Houses coming. Tomorrow, maybe? Day after, maybe? Mother Sphinx feels it.'

Then there was more silence, this time interrupted by Amphigorey, a faint whimpering noise that chilled Greenaway to the core and put a little pity for him back into her heart. 'Oh fuck,' he said quietly. 'We're all dead.'

Hateman was brisk and practical as ever. 'We need to get started,' she said.

⇒ Chapter 8: *Ghosts of Fleas* ⇐

The Service spy – Astraea as she styled herself – was a slug-abed. She deserved her rest, but it began to irritate Silver that she didn't stir; not after he had knocked (three times), entered her room with a heavy tray of clanking cutlery and dishes, set it beside her bed (so the steamy aroma of the stew and fresh-baked bread might tempt her awake), coughed, stood helpless, tramped round the room, prodded, and finally given up and gone to stand at the window. Alice had not been in his bed this morning, and there was a shallow dent on the mattress where she had lain in the night. Silver resented this usurper who lingered indolently under a mound of sheets with her drool soaking the pillow, while Alice was up early and active.

He breathed out, the air abandoning his body as cool white steam. It was this noise that seemed to wake Astraea. He heard her tiny voice, still new to him, laced with sleepy insolence: 'Oh, it's you.'

'I brought you some food,' he said, without turning. 'From Salomon's kitchens. You must thank Salomon for his hospitality, by-the-by.'

'He's the mad fellow, right? Stoops? Leers? Looks like he hasn't bathed in a hundred years?'

'That's him.' He hid his smile from her as he turned. The she-spy was sat up in bed, her hair undone, her eyes still wary and haggard from her ordeal, but her skin marked a ruddy red that had not been apparent the night before. She was no ravishing beauty, being too thick around the lips and jowls, with a strong nose, a heavy arched brow, and an inclination to scowl. She had on a man's white shirt beneath the sheets. Her toes had crept out at the bottom of the bed, dainty pink things prickling out of her flat feet and stubby ankles.

More clothes had been left for her on a chair in the corner. Servants' clothes, male clothing, left – he suspected – to make her feel uncomfortable, because Salomon did have a few girls on staff, mainly in the kitchens. Astraea's own belongings had been left in the snow by Plainsong, and she'd have to wait for a thaw to recover them.

Her voice crack'd. 'May I have something to drink?'

'There's water in the jug.'

'Water? Fuck that shit! Beer or burnt wine!'

He shrugged helplessly. 'Whisky?' She nodded. 'Whisky,' he said. He fetched some.

How is it that I've become attendant on someone who, all voices assure me, wishes me ill?

When he returned, she was up and prodding at the ashes that filled the fireplace. She had dragged half the sheets with her, curled round her ankles, but was naked from the waist down and shivering. Silver, confronted by the sight of her fleshy buttocks, felt first a wave of embarrassment, then arousal, then a further and deeper wave of shame. Astraea noticed him and straightened to snatch the bottle. She knocked back a mouthful before he could say a word.

She must have noticed the stilted, sightless face he was pulling, because she began to play to it. She slumped onto the edge of the mattress, with the bottle in one hand and her eyes fixed on him – his crotch, not his face. Her legs were crooked open, but she kept her ankles crossed. This was a taunt, not an invitation. He refused to close his eyes or look away.

'You must be cold,' he observed.

She rubbed her arms theatrically. 'You look like a rabbit. You smell like a rabbit. You're a funny sort of Magus.'

'Yes, I suppose I am, Astraea, and you're a funny sort of goddess.' He turned away – but carefully, keeping his head still focused on her blueing body, as if daring her not to shiver. She tore wordlessly at the bread, and began to drop chunks into the stew. Her mouth was an unpretended starving thing. She began to shovel stew away and winced as it burned her.

'I need this,' she said, when her face was full – the closest to thanks he would get from her. 'Why are you still here?'

'This is my assistant's room. I'm sending her to Cambridge and have to collect her things.'

The spy shrugged. *Be my guest.* Silver felt released from the terrible enticing sight of her body and went to find Alice's trunk. 'I'm sure Alice would have leant you a change of clothes, but –'

She cut across him. 'I saw her last night, yes? She's a skinny thing, and whatever else I may be I'm hardly that.'

'If you say so.' She was a heavy woman, if not precisely fat; with shallow bumps of flesh round her neck and stomach. He did not usually find such women attractive. He looked back to her and saw her cramming pitifully, her borrowed shirt spattered with stew dripping from her careless spoon and mouth.

'Once she's gone,' Astraea ate and spoke at the same time, 'how many women will there be in this house? And I mean *guests*, not just servants or sluts. I'd be surprised if there is even one.'

'There's you.'

She took another slug of whisky. 'I am on Service, sir, you would do well to remember that. I am here to run you to ground, Master Magus.'

He shrugged. 'I am no Magus, madam. If you want such a man go to see Doctor Bendo, *Salomon* as is. Under the mask of his title he'll fondle and abuse you, then sell you some potion that'll do naught for you but upset your bowels. I owe him much, but I am not his sort of man. My name is Nathaniel Silver, you may have that for nothing.'

Men such as Salomon believed in the power of names – and it was true that by revealing himself to this agent of the Service he had given her power over him. But if England's power was turned on him, there was little he could do to stop it, whether he was anonymous or no.

'Now, sir,' she snarled, and then she was crying. 'I would have an apology for how I have been treated!'

He stared at her. She put her fists over her eyes to block out the sight of him and he knew the tears weren't feigned. The sardonic mask of Astraea had slipped and her true and nameless self was naked to him. Between sobs she spat: 'Or is this another part of the sport with your bidstand? You are the good man and he the wicked? Such games are old!'

'No, no, this isn't a game. Nick thought you meant to harm me, but he should not have acted as he did. And he is wicked, I acknowledge that and I'll send him to you later to owne it. He won't be contrite, but you seem a formidable woman, Astraea, and you'll drive him to shame.' He did not try to touch her or comfort her, that would only make things worse. He passed her his handkerchief.

'I am your prisoner,' she blurted. He tried to protest; he had not realised it until now.

'Salomon's prisoner,' he clarified. 'I don't care for gaols, but this is a more comfortable cell than any I've known, and look outside – it's still snowing. I'll help you escape when it thaws.'

She came slowly out of her mood, but no longer seemed willing or able to talk. He brought her the clothes that had been left for her and made promises she would be well-treated and allowed to roam freely. She pulled the sheet down to cover her legs, and that simple gesture put into Silver's mind a clear and sudden premonition: they were going to be lovers, he could see them copulating in some bed at some indeterminate point in their future. He saw the same realisation in Astraea's eyes, coming to her as reflection rather than revelation.

He did not want her; she was not pleasing to him in appearance or character; she was not Alice; he did not love her; his callous penis stiffened for her.

She smeared away her last tears and asked him to leave. Perhaps she feared rape, perhaps she just wanted to dress, but he acceded, hefting Alice's trunk before him. As he left, he began to consider what he would to say to the gathering of greybeards and dusty philosophers in the evening. He no longer dreaded or doubted his own abilities, but Astraea and Jeova had each set him unexpected challenges.

He thought also of Cousin Hateman, and remembered that there would be at least one woman at the lecture. It wasn't that he had forgotten her when talking to Astraea, merely that he hadn't thought of her as a woman, any more than her driver was a man. The Paradox folk were rawheaded things, skinless and sexless.

Then to Alice and sweet parting. The convention would be done in a week, and he could rejoin her in Cambridge and they could face the unwritten future together – but how that week would drag! He was full of lusts, but kept them concealed from her, roused as they'd been by another woman's shyness. He did not touch her with his hands when they met; he longed to part her legs and fuck her monkeyishly on the balcony, to a chorus of timid squeaks from the assembled celibates; he pecked her daintily on the cheek.

Christ, I would flee Salomon's House with her if I could. She is a temptation.

She looked tired; still pretty – she could never be anything other than pretty – but with sore patches of blood on her eyeballs, and greyed skin, as if she had not slept that night. He hoped it was not regret that had kept her awake. They said nothing about their lovemaking, but instead she launched – in a wistful voice full of the night's aches – into a description of a future she imagined for them both. Her dreams were surprisingly domestic and stable. Heaven to her was a cottage with four narrow walls without but infinitely large within, filled with many rooms and – though she did not say it aloud, he heard it in the undercurrent of her words – children. He marvelled at how little he understood of her inner life, and only once she was gone did he realise that it was so potent to her because she knew she could never have it, not with Silver, not with the Magus.

When it was time for her to leave, she would not have him come with her to the door. She kissed him and told him how much she loved him, whispered it as if she were a Catholic in confessional. Then, with a shy backwards glance, she turned a corner and was gone. He stood for a while before realising that sending her away was a dreadful mistake, worse than anything else he had ever done in his life, and ran after her – but she had been too quick for him. The passage round the corner was empty, and after that there were any numbers of paths she could take to beat him to the doors, to the cart, to Cambridge.

She had not changed her mind. She was wiser than him.

He started when Nick Plainsong, who had sidled up behind him unnoticed, tapped him on the shoulder.

'She's buggered off then?'

Silver glowered at him. 'I asked her to leave. I should have sent you away too.'

'Oh, but you need me, boss. Alice was ever the ornamental third of the partnership. Good at that, she is.'

'At least she never resorted to kidnap and violence on my behalf. I would have you apologise to Astraea.'

'Yeah, I heard you seen her. What'd she do to turn you round? She cry out a well for you?'

'She was upset, yes.'

'It's always tears that get you.'

'Whether she was upset or not, you still owe her a sincere apology, Nick.'

'Oh, I can do that, Magus. I do *sincere* better than anyone.' He trotted on his way, but turned before he disappeared completely, made a false and mocking bow, and called: 'Nate! Remember this! You could have trusted me. Whatever else I may have been, I was loyal.'

Then he was gone. Whether he apologised to the woman or not, Silver couldn't say for sure, though he heard later that she'd received him but listened silently from behind a flat and ugly face, frozen like a statue's or an ice-thickened corpse into an expression of disdain. And had she been genuine with her tears that morning? He wasn't sure. That afternoon he saw her – resplendent in borrowed serving clothes – carousing with some of the younger guests and students, while shamelessly milking them with caresses and kisses, sly cuddles and peeking nipples. That scene put doubts into him. She was perhaps that legendary reptile that blended its skin to fit its surroundings, at the cost of confusing itself and forgetting its true hue.

He would learn how genuine she could be.

Silver slept a little before the lecture, and dreamed of Alice spread naked and pallid and quite dead on a table before him, with her hair combed into a yew-coloured crown around her head, and her stomach cut open carefully like a vast and erotic iris. Her vital parts were arrayed around her in trays of holy silver, purifying them. In front of an audience of darkness, he took each one in hands smothered by tight pink gloves – that might have been fashioned from the guts of some poor beast – and replaced each delicately in its proper place inside her neat wound, sewing and suturing the pipes where he could. Then once she was filled again and her wound sewn up, he put a mouth full of angel-light to her lips and breathed life into her. He was woken by the servants knocking.

The stalls of the theatre were already filling when he arrived, but the numbers were thinner than he'd expected; an illusion, he imagined, fostered by the size of this room and his sunken viewpoint within it. Salomon held the stage with his preliminary introductions. The madman looked most formidable today, dressed in silks and gold cloth that spoke of his wealth in the way the rags did not. The wizard's barks and jokes distracted the audience as Silver came down to the stage.

His gaze went round the room, searching first for Astraea, though he couldn't find her and suspected she was too low or too careless or too drunk to bother. He found Jeova, who was descending in stilted, irregular steps to a well-considered vantage point in the middle row. Nick, if he was present, had expertly concealed himself from Silver's eye. The Magus gave polite nods to those faces he didn't know but had noticed his attention. Then his eye flitted to the consternation as Cousin Hateman graced the hall with her eloquent shape and horrible vizard. More of her Faction followed, with their own skulls that were as unique to them as a naked face; a man close behind her, then a cluster of three bodies including the coachman. The others both seemed to be women, one slight and girlish, the other obese and infirm and steadying herself with sticks and the support of her assistants. This one – he assumed it must be the order's Mother – need not have bothered with a mask; like M. Valentine, her puissance was vivid and needed no exaggeration. It took her some moments to reach the bench at the bottom of the steps, where her helpers had cleared a space for her to sit and exhale mightily. None of them removed their heads. Silver wondered if they would be able to see and hear through the gaps in the bone.

The stir caused by the Faction of Paradoxes didn't last. It rippled round the edges of the room, then broke like a mild wave on a shore. There were a few other strange masks and odd costumes in the crowd.

Nathaniel Silver no longer felt a part of this gathering; he was as much an outsider as Astraea would be. It was this realisation that conjured the cloud of sympathy for the spy that Nick had so easily dismissed; but he *was* more like her than he was like Jeova. It was not that he felt *special* (though he had been marked out by angels), nor *better* (though doubtless there were frauds and mediocrities here present), merely separate. Even the younger men, the students still unshaped, were part of a world that was not his. They were priests and he was only a supplicant, and had come upon their work from the wrong path. Their learning was built on the years since antiquity, formed like rings in a tree trunk, or layers of heaped sand washed upon a riverbank. Their knowledge was thought to be imperfect; in Greece and Ægypt it had not been so, but those sacked glories had been preserved only in pieces and on the edges of the world by Christian monks and Muslim scholars. These men who had come to see him had dim faces turned towards the past, seeking to recreate old worlds.

Silver's untutored art was turned otherwise. He doubted in Golden Ages. What was learned now was new, or if not new then improving. It should not be trapped by adherence to the likes of Galen, who was not merely imperfectly understood but himself imperfect. The role of *scientia* was not to remake the old but to create the new. And if that meant wresting the art away from priests, so be it.

He found M. Valentine's eyes on him, smiling silently as if Silver's thoughts were written visible on his face. The French were – or claimed to be – princes of modernity. They must know this too. He felt a sudden affinity with this agent of *le Pouvoir*, and its touch was like the skin of a dead man on a slab.

There was an expectant silence; he realised Salomon had announced him, and was now hobbling off the stage. He did not stop to acknowledge his protégé, but Silver planted a solid hand on the man's falsely-hunched shoulder. 'Thank you,' he mouthed, but the magician only mumbled a reply and went chuckling to a cushioned chair that had been set aside for him. Silver mounted the stage.

All those dead faces, all those dead masks, stared back at him.

'Gentlemen!' he said confidently, and in his confidence let the silence roll on for many seconds without feeling it uncomfortable. He had found a natural standing point on the dais well away from Cousin Hateman and her ranks, but his head kept swinging back to regard those unnerving ivoried growths.

'You have all travelled here – some of you across great distances, over seas and oceans – to hear the Magus talk, to see the Magus demonstrate, to learn from the Magus, and to correct the Magus in his many errors. This last I know some of you are looking forward to most of all!' And there was laughter; not much, but enough to hearten him. He smiled, as that lecturer had done over the unfortunate body of his dog in Gresham College, ten years gone. *I could be in Cambridge now, abed at the Rose with Alice across me and touching me and kissing me and sharing my pleasure.*

His voice carried well in this perfectly-shaped room, and he silenced the last echoes of laughter with a curt exclamation. 'I am not the Magus. I was unschooled. I have no Latin, no Greek. I did not trouble myself with the prospect of a universal education until I was become a man, and it was already too late, for if a man is like a pot formed in the heat of a kiln, I was already shaped and cooled. I was a soldier. After I soldiered, I wrote a book that was never meant to be published, yet was, and I suffered for its mistakes. Since then I have dabbled in your art, and was given the disguise of Magus, though I did not want it. Today I wear no disguise. Today I go among you bare-faced. My name is Nathaniel Silver.

'Everything I have done,' he told a crowd now silenced, silenced utterly, 'was not my doing. I have only ever been the hands and the eyes of the power that chose me. I was not enlightened, as many true saints and many frauds have claimed to be enlightened. I was not myself made divine. Instead, I believe it is my purpose to enlighten the world and to make *it* divine. You have all come here to listen to me and learn from me, and yet here I am with nothing to say and nothing to teach you. You may, however, correct my mistakes. I'm always open to that.'

There were murmurs of dissension and disappointment in the stalls, yet they were held by him.

'This convention needs no Magus. It is itself the Magus. What I have to say to you is not as important as the way I say it. Here are the magic words that can tame the chaos of change, turn inexorable destinies, and reshape the solid world: *communication, discourse, transparency*. I see masks here today;' – a glance at the Faction – 'I do not myself care for masks, but that is by-the-by. What is important to me is that *scientia* herself should be unmasked. Our arts have for so long been hoarded and occluded. We pull truths like precious Roman treasures from the Earth, but they do not grow more valuable through being secreted away in chests, or ciphered in books that can be read by no other eye than that which coded it, or buried in the rites and sacraments of institutions that were old when our grandfathers were suckled.

'What I mean to propose tonight is a globe of learning, a great sphere of shared knowledge encompassing the whole Earth. In the Invisible College, in the Royal Society, we have the makings of such a thing, but they are for their own reasons exclusive, and they are also fragile. We have today a king who delights in science, but we will not always have such a king. Two decades gone we saw the word *Royal* and its connotations erased as though it had never been – and if an order be overturned once, then as experimenters, we know it can surely happen again. We cannot depend on the patronage of good governance and the honest paymaster if there is yet bad governance and the dishonest paymaster; nor can we exclude the world, and treat it only as a subject to be mastered by chants and ciphers.'

He had to pause now to breathe, which he had barely troubled to do as the words came out. It was a natural break, the end to the rhetoric. Around him the theatre was twilit; if the eye of God was on him through the glass roof of the ceiling then His eyes were stygian and impassive. The doors swished back and forth silently as servants brought in yet more candles to line the walls, stairs, and stall-fronts. A chamber that once smelled of sawdust and old blood was now perfumed by molten wax. Silver realised he had been sweating from the combined intensity of so many little lights. His audience was lost in grey gloom, but they were listening, even if only charitably. And now was his last chance to remain silent, and leave unspoken words that could never be unsaid.

He tried to find Jeova in the half-dark, but the faces were now indistinguishable. He was losing focus. *No going back, you've resolved yourself to this.* He cleared his throat and found the words: 'I have been a hypocrite these past days, speaking of dispelling our mysteries and enchantments as if I had no secrets of my own. That was not true. I have one. No longer.'

There he was! – Jeova, bristling in the gloom, unreadable but profoundly attentive.

Silver reached into his coat and took out the bundle he always kept there, and this time there was no pause. It came out smoothly, and he put it on the table. Would anyone be able to see in this darkness? It might have been a rock for all they knew. He opened the cloth, suddenly afraid that that was all it would be, that by doing this he had betrayed the trust of angels and they would punish him by turning the egg to hardened dung. No – its light shone forth.

More, it coruscated. It filled the theatre as though it were day. Silver was shocked by its intensity and stepped back, half-blind. Around the room, the most interested gazes were caught unawares, and he saw them – through eyes overlaid by a blotched purple after-burn – squinting or raising palms to shield their faces.

'This was given to me. I call it the Philosopher's Stone, though in truth I know not what it is, except that it has been my guide through our arts. See, I am no master, I still sit at another's feet to learn. It is, I believe, a machine of sorts, but one assembled and set working by the hands of angels, and fuelled by the fires of Heaven. I've had it all my life' – not quite true, but it felt like no lie – 'and have explored but a fraction of its potential. So, I will demonstrate it tonight, and afterwards, I will give it to you so that it may instruct you, *all* of you, all of *us*.'

He raised the egg on cupped palms; it was still no larger than a swan egg, so some in the crowd would be seeing its shape only now. Once it was high enough in the air, he removed his hands and let it float – a freshly-learned action – still sending out its beacon-light. Half his audience were muttering in their clusters. The skull-heads conferred among themselves, their faces colliding comically as they tried in vain to whisper in one another's ears. Yet there were intolerant eyes on him now, not least Salomon, who lounged with his chin resting on his fist, feigning uninterest. That was only to be expected. The men gathered here knew how easy it was to fool the unsuspecting eye. He would call some of them up on the stage soon and prove it was no trick. He reached up and tapped the undercurve of the egg with light fingers, so it bounced like a bladder of air. He realised he was grinning, innocent and healthy, like an unwearied child. He commanded his egg to grow and it did, bloating outwards, ever-rising to fill the void-space over his head. It was another moon, another sun, it was beautiful.

'I would hear the voice of the angels,' he told it. 'Will you speak to us?'

He could hear impressed sighs from even the most chapped lips and senile mouths. Enlarged, he could see whorls and creases on the surface of the egg. The machinery must lie in those barely-visible fault-lines, chasms vast but infinitely small, laden with the engines of God. Light, not candle-yellow but lightning-blue, fizzed along their geology. He asked the question again, silently and only with the movement of his mouth. There was a hard upward surge of light, striking towards the canopy of Heaven –

– it cut shear through the roof, which exploded into fragments so fine that they rained down on the hall as glass dust. Silver felt it as a gentle breeze on his face and hands, then a light itching as a hundred tiny edges brushed his skin, too small yet to draw blood –

– there were screams, he saw the flash of toppled candles and the scent of dry burning wood, he felt a wave of distress and heard the first tumble of bodies escaping the room –

– and there were angels on the stage with him. Just two this time, on their fierce columns of light and silence. Their coming sucked the heat from the theatre and created a wind that extinguished candles, ruffled beards and skirts, and tugged away wigs. In his row the impeccable M. Valentine scrabbled to remove the dark fronds that had fallen over his eyes. Those conventioneers with weak guts who had made for the exit now stopped mid-flight, their jaws dropping, their crotches dampening, their eyes bulging, their panicked babble stilled in the presence of Christ's pilots.

Silver could no longer address the crowd; it would be impertinent while the angels surveyed him through the slits of their hoods. He dropped to his knees, his hands clasped over his heart.

'I...' He stopped himself and began again: 'I had not expected you would come in person.'

The angels flickered, their light-bodies bouncing against each other in conference. Then they stabilised. One seemed to cock its head at the other. It spoke.

~ *Kill him* ~ it said.

Silver heard himself reply: 'What did you just say?' and thought it the stupidest thing he had ever said in his life, which was now finally and divinely ended. He could not retreat, he could not stand; the will of Heaven bore down on him, gliding stately over the dais with a killing hand outstretched. This took a bleak second, in which he had time to wonder if anyone else had heard the executioner's command, if any of his audience were still alive, or if they had died and petrified where they stood under the glare of holy fire.

The angel's searing hand, a blank curve of light, made contact with his forehead and he screamed. In the blistering moment of pain he suddenly realised what was happening and felt, with certainty, that this was wrong; that his life, though they had once saved it, was *not* theirs to take; that he should have stood and protested, no matter how futile or blasphemous it might seem; that he would at least know their reasons for so abruptly striking him down –

Too late now.

'No,' someone said. He knew the voice, but could not name it. All the names were going from him, burned out of his head by the angel's annihilating hand. There was agony, not just where he was touched but riddling his flesh and his bones and his soul. How could merciful Christ's messengers deal out such agony?!

Then, *No!* came again, a scream, and it was hurtling towards him 'cross the room, swinging a staff and knocking flailing bodies aside in its fury. A staff? – Salomon? – no, it was too narrow and splintered into points at one end. Ah, a candle-stand! Silver was almost serene now in the grip of the angel's excruciation. He could make out nothing much beyond his pain, except this wild bone-headed charge.

It was the slightest of the Paradox folk in a tattered dress, the hem ripped away to reveal skinny legs, flapping underskirts, and naked feet. He worried – blandly in his pain – that she would get splinters on her soles, or rip her skin on a nail or loose board. The unchanging mask had an expression that she was showing for him, for him alone – rage. She pounced onto the dais and in the same action drove her makeshift spear through the light-body of the exterminating angel, like a stone breaking the surface of a pool. The spear turned into a crease of angel-light, and flickered through the Paradox girl's hands and body, causing her pain, causing her scream to leap from a pitch of fury to one of hurt.

And Nate Silver decided that he hated this pilot thing and snatched his head out of its grasp. It had burned him; he expected his skin to come away on the creature's hand like raw bread-stuff, but it didn't. The pain stopped immediately. He fell backwards onto his arse. Above him, the impaled angel whirled and flexed, trying to expel the metal from its belly and throw off the woman who still clung there, screaming and desperate. Its hood slipped and flickered and Silver saw its true angel-face revealed, a pestilent grey sac of feelers and bulges and clustered eyes, the face of an insect, the face of a monstrous flea.

The angel made a final triumphal twist and tossed the shaft free. The woman, still howling, still masked, went curling through the air and impacted with the gross and aroused surface of the egg, which flared deeper white and swallowed her up completely, seamless and whole. The spear, supported by nothing, clattered to the floor.

The flea-angels loomed again. Silver pulled himself to his feet and glanced round, but found only glare and the occasional dark smudge of a body fleeing the room. He had no doubt that there had been an exodus as he knelt dying. The egglight had become a dazzle and it had a noise now, a shrill tinnitus howl that might be the poor woman's soul, damn'd and screaming in eternity for her transgression against God. Silver, who had spent years forgetting the arts of hatred, now felt that patience unravelling.

'Why?!' he screamed at them.

~ *We made a deal, and you cheated us* ~

He wanted to scream *That is a lie!* but he was certain his lungs would betray him. He could not fight nor reason with his sponsors; he could not flee, he knew how they moved; but then they were distracted. Behind them, three smears were resolving themselves into silhouettes, clean patches of black amidst the hateful white, each one with jagged and swollen heads, each one with a sword drawn and slowly waking to life.

Swords? How had they got swords in here? Salomon would not have allowed it.

Then came a fourth shadow, superbly fat and waddling, with barbed shadow-sticks in both hands. It spoke in a voice like a stew of many tongues and regions, that turned her words into a throaty brutal poetry. 'You two have declared war on Faction Paradox. That thing over there, walks about like a man but ain't no man' – her sticks gestured, and Silver knew her insult was thrown at him – 'he belongs to us now. We bound his spirit with the *loa*, so you declare war on the *loa*, on Time herself. You're made by dead magic, you're dead things, and you've taken our beautiful baby girl from us. But Mother Sphinx, she's a forgivin' soul, everyone says so. If you *undeclare* your war, she might let you walk away.'

'They killed Greenaway!' one shadow protested, one of the males.

'Hush,' was all the Mother Sphinx silhouette would say, a syllable spiked with bitterness and regret.

The angels said nothing, but splintered into shapes of vicious jagged light. Silver saw the Faction trio raise their swords. He knew he should escape now while he had the chance, out of the light, into the dark and the cold, into the world without angels, into Cambridge, to Alice –

He had a sudden pang of real fear, his first since the angel had touched his skin. Alice. He could not leave her alone. She would think she'd lost him again. She would think he'd abandoned her.

Mother Sphinx commanded her family: 'Hateman, Amphigorey, you stand and fight. Suppression, you get hold of Mister Silver and don't let him wriggle. And Mother Sphinx?' – and the bark turned to a bellow – 'She's gonna bring the *loa* down on these skinny ghosts to eat them up and shit out their souls!'

She brought the hams of her arms down in a flourish, and a wave of shadow slammed into the room; a physical violent darkness that had mouths, that screamed, that was hungry; a shadow quilt of a thousand patches of darkness that shook the walls and splintered the wood stage and set more glasspieces tumbling. It gave Silver a moment's grace, and he ducked and rolled off the stage before Suppression could reach him. He heard the cousin's briefly confounded breaths and sensed a swordless hand prodding the empty air he'd just escaped, but there was no respite. He began to crawl; keep moving, keep running, don't stop till you reach Cambridge, a mile or more through the snow and the night…

Any noise he made while creeping was drowned by the shrieks of angels and shades and the palpable presence of their *loa*. The only light in the room was from the engorged, pregnant egg, still swirling in mid air above the dais, but it failed to illuminate. Assaulted by darkness, the halo of blue fire sputtered and sparked like a galvanic discharge. The egg contracted violently back to its natural size, then plummeted, bounced off the stage and came to rest on the floor no more than six feet from where he crouched. Silver, who was straining to hear the prowl of Suppression's steps above the crashes of shadow-combat, scrabbled through towards it, picking up splinters and glass fragments on his raw palm as he went.

He almost reached it. He was an inch away. His fingers went for it. It was snatched away from above, and as it went he heard something that he had not imagined possible: the death-song of angels as the blades and spirits of Mother Sphinx and her cousins shredded their souls. The egg still lived and burned with subtle light; it was not sustained by angels then, but an angel-machine set in motion by their hands. Silver craned upwards to find the face of the thief.

'She *were* a skinny bitch, weren't she?' said Nick Plainsong.

Silver offered him his hand. The fear was rising again; with the angels downed the Faction would turn their attentions again to him. 'You said' – his voice came out weak and wounded – 'you were loyal.'

'Yeah,' he agreed. 'I *was* loyal, Nate. *Was*.'

He hid the egg in some pocket that immediately occluded its light and plunged the room back into darkness. Then he turned and ran.

'He's moving!' he heard a man – Suppression? – shout. Nick's fleet steps were joined by the sound of pursuit, and crashes in the dark as they careered into invisible stalls, smashed benches, and clattered candelabra. Silver got to his feet and backed away into the dark. He was almost relieved to see Nick go and take the egg with him. It took temptation and responsibility out of his hands.

The main doors were flung open to allow fresh waxlight into the edges of the hall. It framed the lumpy, haggard shadows of Faction Paradox, and others – low and cautious bodies that had hid during the fight; perhaps one was Nick Plainsong. He always knew when to freeze, how not to be noticed. In spite of his betrayal, Silver wished him well. Now, if he could just get away to Cambridge, to Alice –

It was Salomon at the door, Salomon with a retinue of his servants, Salomon who had shed his feigned stoop and some of his robes in order to inspect the wreckage of his theatre. He barked to his men, in a voice that no longer gibbered or retched or deceived: 'Find Silver! Find him or find his body and bring him to me!' They had pistols these men, all of them. Why would they have pistols?

Salomon turned to address the shadows: 'Everyone here is to be detained for questioning by order of the Service of the King! Alice Lynch and Nicholas Plainsong will present themselves immediately to my men and it will be well for them. The order known as Faction Paradox is to put down its weapons and accompany my men. You would be wise to come quietly! This has turned into a fucking fiasco and I am not pleased!'

So, here was the last and least hurtful of the day's many betrayals. Salomon's ulterior purposes washed over him like a soothing and familiar stream; the deceptions of one half-trusted and little-liked ally were nothing compared to the treachery of friends and Heaven. Silver did not stop to present himself to the Servicemen that came hunting, like Suppression but louder and heavier. He slipped through the gloom to the curtains, to the window.

The landscape beyond the house was inhospitable and uninviting, with a bleak grey skin of snow spread across the hills towards the city. Nathaniel Silver slipped out silently into its blank embrace.

⇒ Chapter 9: *Ich Dien* ⇐

She had been played for a fool, but she didn't yet realise how badly. She had suspected Sir Sam of self-serving, of using her for his own purposes, but she wouldn't learn till later how deep his perfidy ran, or how clumsily he had made her his weapon. It would come as a humiliation, but then, he would go on to do worse and more grievous things, and she would dedicate her impassive resolve to snubbing him for those. She would still let him into her bed, when Carola died, and as they tumbled he would whisper into her ear: 'You've always been a bloody awful spy, Astraea. You should stick to what you're good at.' He would say it to turn her blushed and angry, and she would rise to take his bait, but only because it was true.

At the time, she had thought she'd been doing rather well for herself. Salomon's House was a prison, but hardly the most arduous in her experience. Indeed, it was given over to luxuries that she stroked and coveted with unsmiling eyes. She had strange young men – not all of them coarse or ugly – come up willing to whisper the most outrageous secrets in her ear out of the vain hope that she'd let them whisper it again between her legs. She'd debriefed the notorious Magus in person, squeezed every drop of information out of him, and all the while let him believe that she was a hurt thing. *Because of course you were entirely in control of your circumstances and weren't afeared or ready to cling to even the wariest kindness –*

Pah.

There was some talk about a lecture, but she wouldn't be needed there. It couldn't further her investigations, which were into the physical affairs of the world, not those of cloudcuckooland. It would be in Latin and fly over her head. It would be deathly dull and she would better spend her energies carousing and patting down her unwary fellow guests for secrets and gossip. True, little of them had much to say about the Magus beyond their opinions of his impenetrable teachings. Some regarded him unkindly or as an upstart, and an unexpected sympathy for the man grew in her breast. Nevertheless, she had no interest in hearing him talk, and by the time her admirers began to filter away to the lecture hall, she was already in a stupor disturbed only later by distant gnatbite retorts and crashes.

A commotion breezed into the antechamber where she lay. She fell out of blissfully bodiless sleep and into a head that ached, a world that wobbled, and a light unpleasantly hot on her eyeballs. She blinked rapidly. Half her face was patterned and sore from impressing against a coarse wool pillow. From the edge of the room came hushed, urgent exchanges in French, but she would have struggled to understand English at that moment. By the time she had found the strength to look, the interlopers were already hurrying away – an elegantly tall man in black, and his servant. She let them go, blearily. It was none of her business.

She patted her thighs and breasts until she was sure that they hadn't been interfered with while she slept, then – reassured – rolled onto her back. Her stomach was sticky-wet and her shirt-front stained dark and red. Christ! I have been murdered! She shoved her fingers against the numb wound, and found wet lumps on the curve of her belly. She pulled them out: blackberries, out of season, squashed pathetically where she lay. Relieved, she popped one in her mouth, but the taste had been squeezed out with the juice.

Her hat was on the daybed at her side, the one item of her own clothing that she'd been able to salvage from kidnap. It was bashed and sat upon, its proud pheasant feather crest snapped and wilting. She put it on anyway, stood, staggered to the nearest mirror, and regretted it; her skin was so sallow and flabby and pale. There was a hugger-mugger chorus from a nearby hall, and shrill words that plucked the tender strings in her head. Remembering that she had a duty to attend to, she slouched out in search of the fuss.

She found a passage full of babbling scholars and wizards, pressed together by great and burly servants who might have silenced them all with a roar. Astraea imagined the walls tightening slowly to press all these fellows until the concentrated juices of their brains squeezed out through the floorboards, succulent but filled with curds and fatty bits. Most seemed cowed, but one was protesting to the closest servant in the strongest terms. She sidled nearer to listen; this one was too old to be a student, but still young, with ash-blond hair that might have suited a more handsome face and a less lank body.

'I must know how long we are to be kept here,' he insisted, shrill-voiced but truly angry. 'I have duties and responsibilities at Trinity and as the holder of Henry Lucas's chair. They cannot be discharged while I stand freezing in a corridor.'

He glanced uninterestedly at Astraea, who dropped her stealthy gait for a nonchalant swagger, though this made her feel seasick on her own legs. His attention was caught by her unseasonable blackberry wound and she took advantage: 'Wha's goin' on?'

I think you meant to sound a little more authoritative and a pinch more sober, Mistress Behn. He glared at her, as did the servant, who – now she was close enough to see – had a flintlock at his belt. She thought of the little runt Plainsong, who had put his hands so easily on such a weapon. She repeated her question, but bolder, and then: 'How was the Magus's lecture?'

'Travesty, madam!' The Trinity man barked, and wrung his hands. 'He spent five minutes insulting us, then he burned down the hall!'

A weak voice from in the huddle: 'There were spirits! I saw spirits!'

Her contact swung round to admonish him: 'You old fool! There were no spirits. It was trickery!'

'I saw spirits,' came the insistent reply. 'He opened a window on Heaven and it was besieged by darkness.' This time the younger man didn't respond, but flared his nostrils and folded his arms, making his displeasure plain. The servant's hands rose in a gentle pattern to mollify him.

'We only need ask you a few questions about the Magus, then you'll be free to leave – a matter of hours, once this chaos has cleared.'

But Astraea felt she had had no adequate answer, and was about to ask again when the ceiling thumped and rumbled from an impact on an upper floor, and then the far doors swung wildly open to allow Salomon to parade into the room with an armed retinue. More guns, why where there so many guns? And Salomon, whom she had thought infirm and wretched, was now lithe with young eyes full of anger. They scanned the crowd. 'Valentine! Where is the Frenchman?!' he bellowed.

Astraea raised a limp hand. 'I overheard Frenchmen leaving, not five minutes ago.'

Salomon threw his arms up in despair. He barked to his underlings: 'Catch them before they leave the stables. Barricade them if you must. If they get to him first we've lost him.' Liveried bodies piled out at his command while others piled into the room to replace them, and deliver gasped reports.

'Silver was seen climbing from a window. Another man pursued him, we know not who.'

'Then break out the kennels. He can't get far on a night like this. What about Faction Paradox?'

'They've retreated up to the first floor.'

'Good, block the stairs. We have them cornered at least. How many?'

'Four. One was said killed at the lecture.'

'Eaten,' a tiny voice piped up from the crowd. 'She was eaten by Heaven.'

Astraea looked over the scene with uncomprehending eyes. Events had run away from her, as had Nathaniel Silver. It seemed a good time to withdraw, find some bottles that were yet filled, and empty them at her leisure. But Salomon had been allowed a breath between reports and now pounced at her, a chipped and dirty fingernail stabbing at her tits. 'This one is also to be put under arrest!'

Immediately the servant at her side took her arms and held them fast. She protested indignantly, and heard her voice come out like a squealing pig. 'Sir, I am not your enemy!'

'No, but you're a bloody nuisance, and I would know what part Sam Morland played in today's disaster. Serjeant, put her somewhere secure. If she protests, smear her with grease and throw her to the dogs. She's not that important.'

Then she was bundled away in the servant's tight arms. She didn't struggle, but he copped a feel anyway, the bastard. She didn't protest; unlike Plainsong, this fellow was stolidly agreeable, or at least quiet, and any fear she may have felt was smothered by her sore head and the soured taste of beer in her belly. She let herself be slammed through many doors, out of the opulent front of Salomon's House and into its narrow and underlit backstairs where the walls were as spartan as a barracks. When it was clear she wouldn't fight, the man loosened his hold and let her walk sullenly in front of him. His pistol was still slung away and she was glad of that.

'I'd have you know,' she said at length, when she was sure it would not lead to an immediate greasing, 'that I am an agent of the Service and here on business of the Crown.'

'That's an interesting coincidence,' replied the serjeant, 'but we all know you're Morland's dupe.'

'Sir Samuel is a man of importance in the Service and the nation.'

'Sir Samuel is a worm we spat out and now means to wriggle his way back in through you. Now, Doctor Bendo, he's a man of importance. Did you not know? He is one of the Five Masters, and this is a Service house!'

'That is not true,' she retorted, but as she spoke she knew that it was. Then: 'How much damage have I done?'

'Oh, there was sabotage, but it wasn't your doing. Silver got wind he was being set up and legged it. No, it was Faction Paradox did the worst. Did you see them? Did you see their heads? Curious freaks.'

She had not seen them and would have said so, but the serjeant caught her arm again and halted her. The pistol came up from his belt and pointed at the dark well of the corridor ahead of them. 'Who's there?' he called, and with his free hand he pushed Astraea back into a shallow niche on the wall. She peered out, seeing no one, hearing nothing. A pack of dogs bayed purposefully to break the silence, but their hungry barks were distant and muffled.

Her guard stepped forward, the gun raised. They had reached a tight junction, where three passages met a flight of steps into the cellars. 'I am on the Service of the King' he called. 'Stand and declare yourself, or I'll shoot.' Whatever shadow he addressed did not respond, and though Astraea squinted, she found nothing substantial.

The gun retorted. Astraea dropped instinctively into a chimp-crouch with her hands pressed over her ears. The belch of guns fired in anger raised old memories. She found she was smiling ferociously, displaying clenched teeth to danger. The serjeant, meanwhile, had taken perplexed steps forward, the now useless pistol still held ahead of him like a magic charm in the hands of a superstitious hag.

He was scanning the ground where he thought a body should have fallen, his tentative motion suggesting confusion, perhaps doubt.

His attacker came from nowhere, with her flat palm jutting out to touch the man's face. He fell back with a growth of blood and bone budding where his nose had once been. The intruder swung, arms turning like hammers to break his stomach, his chest, then up again and down, pounding him on the back. The serjeant fell, not stunned, but filling his mouth with tortured gasps. His assailant stepped over him and vanished into nothing.

Astraea scrabbled forward to check her sentry, who was still warm and breathing, though not easily. This was good; she would have no murders pricking her inwit. The hairs on the sides of her neck tickled readily, as if she had a lover there blowing on them, but it was just a mild disturbance on the air as the apparition solidified again, and beckoned her.

She was as beautiful as ever. There was blood and mucus still dripping from her outstretched palm, from where she had struck her victim's face. The hand was still part faded and the fluids dribbled through it, displacing along the line of half-formed bone to splatter on the floor. Aphra knew she was being summoned. She resisted.

'I swore myself to the Service,' she declared boldly, but hoped that every ounce of regret in her heart was echoed in her tone. 'I have to stay here. My... my superiors require it.'

'Aphra,' came the reply in a voice that she thrilled to remember, 'you swore yourself to me first, and I'm a higher power.'

She closed her eyes and remembered. That was true.

'You must help me, Aphra,' the nymph continued, in the darkness behind her eyes. It was not a light voice, nor a hurried one, nor one given much to humour. It was, if anything, a little sad. It was not an English voice, there was something about the way the words turned on her tongue that in Aphra's ears felt not *wrong* but *unsimple*. It was not a human voice.

It reminded Aphra of the smell of cocoa and heady American weed in boiling water, transubstantiating to steam; of the fingertips of her favourite lovers describing the small of her naked back; of the sunshafts through the trees in wild Kent when she had been a girl and first met this nymph.

'Larissa,' she named her.

The nymph nodded once, accepting the name. She still wore her tight red suit of translucent skin and seething machinery. Aphra stood for her.

'How can I help you?' That was both an offer and a confused question.

Larissa's spirit phased in and out of the shadows, one moment solid, the next almost gone with the grey detail of walls apparent through her face and her hands. 'I can't stabilise here. I'm in the midst of a forest and all the trees are toppling around me. He is too well-protected now – but we have only two chances, and I won't squander this one.'

'Who...? I don't understand.'

Larissa touched Aphra's lips and put a galvanic shock in her. 'You don't need to. Just get close to the anomaly and I can surge through your gifts to him. I can move you as near to him as I dare.'

Aphra couldn't protest, but let the nymph take her hands. It was a surprise to find she had warm and humanish skin, when Aphra had expected a dank liquid touch or an ungraspable body of cloud. They had touched before, but Aphra had forgotten. It felt sacrilegious, but she wanted to be fucked by this creature, to be drenched in her lusts and juices and brought to a crescendo of pleasure by her; to let the nymph immolate her skin and bone with sacred fire. Gods and demi-gods destroyed mortals with their love, and Aphra yearned to be destroyed.

But Larissa only pulled her chastely close, and even then the churning apparatus sewn around her suit kept their bodies from contact. 'This may distress you,' the nymph warned, 'but it won't hurt.' Her costume writhed and clicked, the death-stutter of a beetle on its back and –

– she was briefly nowhere no time breathing nothing with no stomach to lurch no eyes to see no mouth to scream –

– and Larissa released her hands and let her fall retching onto the ground, which wetted her and burnt with its unexpected cold. And the little candlelight had gone and the tightness of the walls had swept away, replaced by vast openness and slicing winds. If she hadn't already been sobered by her march through Salomon's corridors, the scalding frost would have done it; as it was, it just slammed through her clothes and chipped at her exposed hands and face. Her head reeled still – dizziness now, not hangover – and when she looked she found the oppressive shape of Salomon's House behind her, while around her were shallow hills of blank snow glowing into the distance.

Larissa paced away from her, seeming not to notice the cold – but then she was not completely there. Her feet left unremarkable grooves in the snow that lingered as she faded. Her arm came up to point. 'There,' she accused. Aphra, forcing herself to stare into the wind and follow her line, saw a man's shadow detach itself from the house's bulk and run. 'Is that him?' she screamed, over the winds. But the nymph had gone.

I would not have done this for Sam, nor for Rowley, not even for Carola or Oroonoko.

She pulled herself to her feet and slapped life back into her shivering sodden arms and thighs. They would ache tomorrow. They were aching already. *Sod it!* – she charged her quarry, pumping fierce warmth into her limbs. She whooped like a red American, and knew he wouldn't hear her in the wind. This was adventure after all, and if it be unpleasant and painful today, she would dine on the telling of it tomorrow.

The silhouette noticed her at last and stopped in its tracks, now veering sideways down the hill to dodge her. Lights were shone from the wall he had slipped past. 'There!' came a cry from the house. 'We have him!'

Those lights fell across him and revealed Nathaniel Silver. It didn't surprise her.

Damn, but he could move on those legs!

She plunged downhill after him. A faint commotion rose behind her but she outpaced it; Silver's escape was already lost to them, but not to her. The blank of his back was picked out against sullen white snowfields. There were flakes on the air, but they were not thick and easily pushed from her eyes. She skidded in the wet drifts but kept after him. His hat blew off and skimmed over her head like a flat stone on water. Hers had gone long before, its pathetic feather lost now forever in some Cambridge half-bog.

She kept pace with him, compelled by the downdrag of her own body. She was not given to exertion, and felt all the heaviness of her legs as they pounded down the hill. A stitch opened next to her stomach and her breath tasted of blood and iron. Silver darted and weaved; he threw himself against a line of darkness, and she would have lost him then if there weren't suddenly more light cast downhill and spreading long shadows ahead of them. She looked back and saw the bobbing bright eyes of a dozen lamps. She lost her footing in the snow, fell arse over tit, tumbled into a freezing drift, and rolled the rest of the way down.

Hah! How marvellous if she were to turn into a snowball and crush Silver with her immensity!

No, she came to a halt in a crumple, now as damp as she would have been if she'd dropped into a river. The lights at the top of the hill had scattered as the party had lost sight of their prey and prepared to unleash their dogs on his scent. She heard the familiar hungry growl of the hounds. She had not lost Silver; she looked up and found him still some feet from her. He was paused in his flight, his eyes staring at her in certain recognition, his arm twitching as if not quite ready to reach out to lift her, yet not quite prepared to abandon her.

She robbed him of the choice by pulling herself up and plunging at him. He turned and ran again, across flat ground this time, to the line of trees along the hip-shaped depression at the base of the hill. But he was close enough now, and had little chance of shaking her off. Branches scraped and bashed at her, roots and bushes snatched at her feet, but Silver was no more nimble-footed than she, and the wounds she acquired were robbed of their sting by the cold. A low bow smashed her across the temple and put a sick pain into the base of her trunk. She laughed giddily in the rare air.

She skidded again, but this time turned it into a dive, flinging herself forward and barrelling into Silver's back. It brought him down, heavily, into the mud and wet.

Panting triumphantly, she whispered her nymph's name.

Larissa though was already there. In the lightless woods, her suit glowed and revealed the scene. Silver was battered, scratched and bleeding in a dozen places, but weeping from defeat not pain. Aphra stood shakily and held out her arms, offering the body as a gift. The nymph's head, framed by red hair whose colour was palpable by the light of her costume, nodded in acceptance. She wrenched Silver up by his shoulders and slammed him against the closest trunk.

'Who is he?' she asked, surprising Aphra.

'You don't know him? I had thought... no matter. His name is Nathaniel Silver. He is a man of science, so I'm told. I, ahem' – and she found herself blushing, though she doubted he'd see in the dark – 'I missed the lecture. I was taken with a sudden sickness.'

Silver was not looking to her. His eyes, trapped and terrified, were on this apparition that held him, and scoured his face with an unrelenting gaze. 'Madam, I...' Her free hand clamped his mouth, squeezing it tight in a whitened knuckle as if she were afraid of what might escape from it.

'Yes, he's the anomaly,' Larissa said, and her hand came away – leaving the philosopher's jaw flapping – and went to her belt. It came up again with a nice and wicked stiletto in it, nine inches long and so fine that it might have quivered on the wind (though it did not). It gleamed with unnatural light. She pointed it to the pinned man's chest, above his heart.

'Christ, no!' Silver protested. 'I beg you!'

And Aphra, struck by guilt, stepped forward: 'Larissa, I won't have this.'

The nymph's head turned to her. Thinking back on it later, Aphra would have described it as *a mask of hate*, and indeed it was, but that seemed an inadequate clutch of words. Such a phrase suggested scowls, reddened flesh, bared teeth, a devilish distortion of the visage, but there were none of those things here. Hatred, on Larissa's unhuman face, was blank. It yielded nothing, no soul and no sentiment, just the drive to destroy.

'*Larissa!*' Aphra hissed, but the needle was already wrenched back to strike.

Yet Larissa held back.

She pressed her face close again to Silver's, peering into his eyes, and seeming less certain with each tick of her pupils. The needle drooped slowly in her hand. She pulled Silver snivelling from the tree and shoved him away. Hate was gone from her face, now there was dismay and panic, almost defeat.

'It isn't there,' she declared to Aphra. 'He *is* the anomaly but *it* isn't there! It *isn't* there!'

The needle was back in her belt; she held two empty hands out to Aphra, plaintively. Her eyes were pleading, as Silver's had been but a moment before. 'Help me!' But as Aphra reached for her she faded again, the trees behind her rising and hardening to drown out her form, and this time she didn't return.

Aphra stood there, frozen both in posture and from the cold. Silver fell back against the same old tree gasping and clutching his throat. The aroused yelps of the hunting dogs carried to them from beyond the edge of the wood, where the lantern-lights also danced and skittered, coming ever closer. Aphra regarded them for only a moment, made the decision inside herself, and looked away to address Silver.

'Run,' she told him.

'What?'

'Run! I'll distract them as I can. Christ, I am on the verge of changing my mind every second you stand there gawping! Run! Fucking run!'

She thought for a moment that he'd thank her and give her one of those insufferable holy smiles that seemed to come upon him naturally, but it was too grim a moment for that. His head twitched, all the thanks she wanted or deserved, then he turned heel and plunged away into the trees.

She took the opposite track, charging back towards the house, waving her arms over her head, hollering to distract the lights, and hoping her hot scent would bring down the dogs. She broke the line of trees, then first skidded and second flattened herself into a puddle of mud-slicked snow. When she pulled herself up the dogs were on her, vicious jaws snapping at her face and hands, stinking warm dog-breath and dog-drool sloshing her face, claws on her body as they leapt on her to paw her stomach and her thighs. Let them still be leashed, for Christ's sake!

Their handlers were close behind with lanterns, and called back the hounds when they saw what they'd caught. Aphra, remembering the best mad-eyed stare she'd ever seen on stage, reproduced it now and yelled at them. 'I saw him! The Magus! But he got away!' She pointed wildly toward a path that Silver hadn't taken, and the strange thing was that they believed her.

They also laughed at her, as she picked herself out of the mud. They were laughing still when she was marched back into the warm precincts of Salomon's House, accompanied by Service Ratcatchers who would have to explain to Salomon, to Doctor Bendo, that their quarry still eluded them. The greybearded guise was pacing furiously in the front hall below the balcony and it seemed his evening was full of similar bad news. The other party he had sought, Faction Paradox, had apparently vanished without trace from the room in which they'd been thought cornered. The Service's sole triumph of the night was kneeling by the fire with his hands clapped behind his head and the pistols of three hooded Ratcatchers aimed at his back. It was Nick Plainsong, who seemed defeated yet curiously happy, gazing into the flames with a madman's fascination.

Yet Bendo was delighted to see Astraea as she returned to his house; later she discovered that he believed she'd overcome his serjeant by her own sleight, and this agility and initiative had impressed something in his warped heart. He had to salvage something from this disaster, even if it was only a small thing, and it turned out to be her. All she could see, on the day, was a man standing between her and the fire.

'Oh,' he corrected her, 'but that will give you chilblains. This will warm you better' – and a Ratcatcher-Serjeant with a blooded rag tied round his nose loomed ahead of her and emptied a pail of warm soapy water over her head, to the general amusement of all. Even Plainsong was laughing. She let them have this victory. She still had her secret nymph – who would one day come back to her – and she had Nathaniel Silver, who even now fled further from the Service's clutches, living proof of her one small act of treachery.

She would see him again, but not for twelve years, when he would be dumped trussed and gagged onto her bed in Paris.

⇒ Chapter 10: *Behemoth and Leviathan* ⇐

As a child, Little Sister Greenaway had once thrown herself into a river. She'd been left to her own company and devices, a little girl burning with a little girl's energy. The river was not far from the house where she'd grown up. She'd already paddled there, and knew its depths and its dangers. It flowed in a gully by what she remembered as a sheer cliff, but was more like a narrow incline of a few feet. She'd taken a run to its very edge and let herself spring, and – for a moment – fly, and then plunge, and then collide with the dirt-slicked current with both legs frantically kicking, then submerge down into the deep where the hot summer sun was only a smear on the film of the sky. She'd been in the air for seconds, nothing more, but for those seconds she'd felt completely free of all earthly forces.

She hadn't imagined it was possible to fall any further.

Yet now she was falling forever, and this time she was shorn away from the Earth entirely, absorbed into some other demesne. When she'd sat on the bench at Salomon's House, she'd overheard whispers describing Silver's sacred light as the fires of Heaven, while others muttered grim intimations about the radiance of fallen angels. Falling, she found herself unconcerned by acts of naming or description; there was only the sheer exhilaration of the moment. She plunged infinitely, and imagined herself dropping between the spheres, compelled by no force but her own. There was no final resting point, and she found she had time to turn and twist and change her shape like a swimmer. The void-winds lashed around her, though she knew that in some way they were no true part of this unworld but made real only by her own thoughts. She imagined herself sparking from the red hot speed of her plummet. She imagined observers on Earth with powerful lenses picking out a falling star that dropped out of the sky in a straight line of velocity, spying it was a woman, then opening their dials for a closer inspection. She was become a miracle.

She forgot how she had come to be here, forgot Silver, forgot the Faction, forgot everything but the delights of falling. She was in an egg of perfect light, and all she could see beyond herself was her own shadow, extending from her at all angles and stretched so thin as to appear nothing but a line or a rope. There was as much darkness here as light, they seemed interchangeable.

But no, she wasn't alone - angel-plumes streaked past her. There were two, accelerating upwards like the streamers of the rockets on Guy Fawkes's Night, carrying burdens to explode in the solid world, there to consume Nate Silver –

Burn him in a tub of tar
Burn him like a blazing star
Burn his body from his head
Then we'll say ol' Pope is dead
Hip hip hoorah!

The flight of angels put thought and memory back into her, filling her with shame and remorse. She had failed them both – Mother Sphinx and the Magus alike – by dying this way. It had been foolish, charging the stage like that, but then he had been dying, he was dead already in the world outside the egg, and all those years dogging his footsteps and prying for Faction Paradox were wasted; and she would never be a proper cousin with a shadowblade in her hand or *loa* on her shoulders.

She remembered her little house and dreams lost.

She span in freefall. The ascendants were already too accelerated to be caught but they'd left an arc like a fault on the surface of the world. She saw now that it was not simply infinite or curved like the inside of an egg, but sheer like a channel cut into the earth. She altered the direction of her plunge, finding a new down, and dropped instead towards the wall and the angels' origin.

With nothing she could measure it against, their fastness might have been pinprick small or wider than an ocean. It had no depth or dimension. She descended to it, thinking it ominously a web and herself a sweet insect, but it was too late now. Hers had been the hands that cleaned away the cobwebs and interred the worn-out husks of flies in her house; she could hear the screams they made as the spiders consumed them; this place seemed to be made of old memories.

It would explain why the angels' home seemed so familiar.

By the time she reached it, the structure had resolved itself into a comfortable yet disconcerting shape. She stepped through the door into the parlour of Thomas Piper's old house in Hornsey, over four years gone from her now but unchanged to her eyes, except that she was now a different creature. No, she went to find a mirror – Dutch glass, therefore cruel and exacting – and the old young Mrs Thomas Piper was there in it, prettily untouched by famine, pestilence, and death. As she moved, the unflattering image changed her, making her the Faction's little sister in a hood of bone; then a small child again in a ruined summer dress, with slicked mudwater up and down her legs; then older and naked as she had been on her wedding night, waiting to be blooded. She found she liked Little Sister Greenaway the best and fixed herself as that. Around her the walls rippled as though built of water.

There was a stub in her hand, as if she had caught on something as she'd fallen, but she was distracted by a movement at the window. She whirled, but the frame was empty, peaceably washing back and forth like a lapping tide. Nonetheless, she heard scratching at the walls, skittering and malevolent laughter. Disturbed, she went to the stairs, and climbed to find her husband's old door. On her way, she touched the walls to read them, but they were cold and yielded only a tingling pleasure on her fingertips. It was not like finding a building at all, but a body, living flesh. She could smell blood and sweat and spent semen, and thought for a moment that she might be trapped in the dolly she had made of Nathaniel Silver.

She went into Thomas Piper's bedroom, where he had died, and found a monster curled on the bed. She screamed. It screamed back at her.

It was an angel, or at the least one of those creatures that Silver had named angels. Greenaway and her cousins had seen through their veils of light, finding not cherubs nor the earnest stiff-limbed men of church art. These angels had the heads of insects, magnified to repulsive size. They had cramped, helmet-smooth faces pocked with many eyes, and a cluster of feelers and finely-furred tubes protruding from their jaws. This one had a body of armour-like segments, its many skins drooling cool pus and trembling filthily as it drew air through its body. Its legs were lank, powerful things, strangely jointed. It sprang at her with all that strength. She sprang back. They collided, struck the floor, and rolled apart.

The black notch in her hand coiled. She looked at it, and found the stub was elongated and spilling away from her like a rat-tail. It was black, a part of her hand yet not part of it, a whip without depth or substance. It was her own thin trailing shadow that she must have caught as she'd fallen. The flea-beast, morbidly silent, sprang at her again. She turned the shadow-whip awkwardly in her hand. It missed the creature's attack and cracked harmlessly against the bed. The flea trampled her chest and knocked the imaginary breath from her. It sprang away, landing on the wall and gluing itself there with the pink gunge dripping from the pores of its legs. Greenaway, when she'd been Mistress Piper, wouldn't have tolerated such *mess* in her home.

She stood warily, but the flea didn't leap. She put all her effort into her hand, to learn the shape of her whip, to make this unexpected weapon an extension of her arm. She didn't flail, she didn't strike in fear or anger. She persuaded it and made it twist a clumsy circle round her feet. Her opponent jumped; she brought up the whip and smashed it down. An accident, it could easily have gone wide, and the flea was now up again and charging. Whirling the whip above her head – letting it score the walls and demolish what furniture it touched – she charged back. They exhausted each other, smashing their way round the ghost of Thomas Piper's room, against the walls and the window, the ceiling and the bed, among the wreckage. Neither found a lasting advantage or a killing blow, not before they were fortunately interrupted.

The window exploded just as Greenaway had a slight edge; they were at close quarters in a corner, pummelling each other against the walls, she desperately trying to pin its oozing limbs to stop them thrashing at her. The pane shattered inwards, setting slow glass shards floating through the room. The noise make her jerk her heard round; she lost her grip on the beast, which shoved her away. A thousand pieces of darkness were swarming through the cavity they'd made, malevolent shapeless imps whose no-fingers snatched and tore at the walls, taking away chunks of brick, wood, and plaster. Their no-bodies were no-coloured and un-heavy with no-scent, like plague. They fell on Greenaway; she snatched at them, but they rolled over her, up her legs and body, pinning her arms. They blattered against her face, exploding, dying in their rush to smother her. She snapped her whip, but they clung to it and made it heavy with thick shadows. She tried to scream, but they filled her mouth. She fell back under their clustered weight, as they clawed at her clothes and her flesh and her soul...

The radiant outline of the enormous flea rose over her. Its flesh was suffused. It glowed deeper then pulsed hard clean light, a shriving burst. The light washed over her and the sticky darkness evaporated. She fell back gasping for air that she knew she didn't need. The swarm was driven back and out of the window. The light dimmed, the insect sagged and slumped back into the corner where she had lately beaten it. Behind her, the curtain twitched uncertainly on a breeze that was not truly there. Tired and knowing herself defeated, she scrabbled back on her haunches, her shadow-whip trailing after her like a spent thing. Opposite from her, the insect's many sacs bulged and wheezed; it looked how she felt.

~ *That will not work again ~ I am exhausted* ~

The voice was supple and worn down by time, like the world around it.

'Then what?' she snarled back at it. Let it not think Little Sister Greenaway was off her guard!

~ *Then they will come again and kill us both* ~

'So, there's no point in us fighting much more? Pax, eh?'

~ *Indeed ~ Pax* ~

'Not that I would give you quarter otherwise. You have killed Nathaniel Silver.'

~ *No, I was against that ~ I argued with the others ~ Their case had some merit, but I wasn't swayed ~ Besides, I have studied him and don't think he can die so easily ~ They will die first* ~

'He wouldn't harm them! He is a good man and deserves his life.'

~ *They will die anyway in the solid world ~ It won't sustain their spirits for long ~ But we were besieged and hopeless* ~

Greenaway felt secure enough now to be distracted, pulling off her mask to wipe the sweat and stray hairs from her blotched red face.

~ *Human* ~ The flea might have laughed; it sounded surprised.

'What sort of thing are you then? You are no angel, whatever Nate might think.'

~ *We are neither angels nor devils* ~ *We are pilots* ~

'That means nothing,' she protested.

~ *We are your children* ~

'I have no children, sirrah,' she told it, but imagining she would get no more sense from it softened her tone and told it: 'I am Faction Paradox.'

The pilot-flea shuddered, laughing, weeping ~ *Then we are discovered* ~ *We strived to keep ourselves concealed from powers like yours* ~ *We have no desire to be dragged into your war, but you have wrought so much damage in our history, and we must correct it where we can* ~

'I've done you no harm,' she protested, 'apart from just now. What's your quarrel with Silver?'

~ *And what is yours?* ~

'I asked first!'

From outside there came again the scratching and skittering of plague-imps.

~ *You shouldn't have come here* ~ *They'll attack again, and then you'll die* ~ *You should leave* ~

'Leave? How?! I hardly know how I came to be here. And they will kill you too!'

~ *They will extinguish this spirit* ~

'And you'll die!'

~ *This part of me will die, but this part is only a projection* ~ *My corpus mundus lies sleeping on Civitas Solis* ~ *It will wake unharmed millions of years hence* ~

She sensed evasion. This creature had tempers like any man, and she found she could read them – and it in turn was reading her, for it continued ~ *though I'll know that some tulpa-part of myself has been lost forever on this mission* ~ *I'll haunt myself by not being there* ~

'Then you should leave too.' That was harsh of her, knowing that if it spoke truly it would wither and die in the solid world.

~ *My mission is failed* ~ *I can only stay and wait for the siege to break itself or break me* ~

Greenaway bunched her fists and felt the shadow-whip tickling the palm where it was crushed. She rose from where she'd crouched, and moving slowly so as not to alarm the pilot, went to the window to gaze out for their attackers. Outside she saw a hazy picture of her lost and tranquil garden.

~ *You won't see them* ~

'What are they?'

~ *I don't know* ~

Was that honest? Was it being honest with her? 'Your mission's failed and you're going to die, so why would you not tell me what your stake is in Silver?'

~ *I could ask you the same question* ~ It was behind her now, and not moving. She had turned her back to it, a sly gesture of trust.

'I don't know much. I'm a novice in my order.'

~ *You must know something* ~

She weighed her response, but she'd already tipped the balance with her own argument. 'I've been told that he's out of place, that he lives when he should not. My superiors tell me he must be sustained by some power, and it would be to the Faction's advantage to claim that power. I imagine your motives are similar.'

For a moment she thought it wouldn't answer. Then, ~ *Silver is an anomaly* ~ *In Civitas Solis we observe the historical probabilities that sustain the hegemony* ~ *Above point six six is tolerable and requires minimal adjustment* ~ *Most war events fluctuate within the upper quartile* ~ *But Silver is a distortion and his impact grows exponentially after his lifetime* ~ *If unchecked, all probabilities will tend to zero and permanent ontological extinction* ~ *Then who knows what your children will be?* ~

Impassively, she said: 'I grasped not one word of that.'

~ *Our mission was arranged* ~ *We descended into a praxis fugue, and concealed in this infinitesimal, sank into prehistory to find Silver*~

'And kill him?'

~ *To contact him* ~ *To deal with him in exchange for biodata that could be returned to Civitas Solis and studied so his power could be contained* ~ *He was reasonable; we gave him what he wanted and then descended to claim what was ours* ~ *It was there that we discovered the most terrible thing* ~

'What thing?'

~ *That is he just a man* ~ *That there is nothing unusual about him whatsoever* ~ *There is evidence of tampering with his biodata, but we were attacked the moment we completed our dissection and could investigate no further* ~

'So his power…?'

~ *Is no part of him* ~ *We have been decoyed, and so have you* ~

Greenaway slumped exasperated back in her corner, staring at the disgusting thing that had somehow become her companion. If this gargoyle was indeed her child, then she dreaded to think what kind of grotesque had fathered it upon her and how it had been nurtured unnoticed in her womb. She studied its fat undulating grub of a body with a mother's concerned eye, and a sly smile on her face as the thought crept over her.

'There is a saint of pilots,' she ventured, 'of navigators. His fire burns round the masts of ships and sailors pray to him. *Erasmus*,' she concluded.

~ *Your point being?* ~

'You are a spirit, are you not? You could leave here, but you would fade and die in the light.'

~ *We are productions of time* ~

'You are *loa*.'

~ *Whatever you wish to call us* ~

'You are *loa* and you could live in the solid if you had a body to ride. We have similar missions…'

~ *They are not quite the same* ~

'But not at odds, and even a brief alliance would be better than waiting to die. I've done enough of that.'

Its response, when it came, was a slow and noncommittal ~ *Maybe* ~

She knew then that she had him; or perhaps not, maybe their negotiations took many hours of this infinite moment and she had only stitched and sutured her memories in the aftermath. Whatever the truth of it, Erasmus was persuaded. She took the pilot's spindly limb in her naked unweaponed hand and shook it, and they had an agreement – not between the pilots and the Faction, but a personal pact between one little sister and one stranded spirit.

Their thoughts turned to escape before the final surge could break and overwhelm them. Erasmus – as it allowed itself to be called – would guide her way back along her original path. She took its *loa*-weight onto her shoulder, where it settled as an abiding presence. She wouldn't make Orpheus's mistake by turning, but would consider the pilot a constant spirit haunting the back of her head, as much a part of her mind as it would surely be in the solid world. Erasmus described in difficult terms how time was compressed within the infinitesimal; only a spit of a second would have passed in her absence from the world, though the Earth would have moved fractionally along its celestial path in that time. With Erasmus's weight on her, they crept slowly from the room, anxious not to alert the besieging army. The front door was a final marker; if they could but make it *outside* the pilot could guarantee their escape.

They were almost there. She had her hand on its knob when the door exploded inwards.

Greenaway staggered back with Erasmus dragging at her. She had false splinters in her eyes and the pain imitated life so closely that she bled. *~ It is not real ~ See with my eyes while yours adjust ~*

She took that advice, blinked away the blood from her face and opened the pilot's half-dozen dozy lids to let in the light and face down the attacker who strolled purposefully into her parlour. The plague-thing had stitched itself into a single being that walked in a man's shape, but was the colour of a starless night; also moonless, unless she counted the craterless globe of its head. It had no face; it smiled.

It lunged. Greenaway brought up her whip, the faded black of her shadow slicking visibly across its fuligin chest. Her hand scorched on contact and she snatched it back. The black dome inspected her quizzically and it killed its advance, a moment's respite. It was sniffing her, teasing out her perfume and her name. Its glossy shoulders shrugged, as if dismissing any threat she might pose. There would be no longer pause than this; it would not toy with her, it would not drag out a fight to standstill, it would not be given to conversation in the lull. When it charged again it would kill her and Erasmus both.

~ Greenaway, we must go now *~*

It was still between her and the door; there was no gap. She made small steps, almost tiptoes. The plague-man stood motionless, its fingers slicked with blood not yet spilled. She wished it would speak. She prayed it would not. It sprang.

Greenaway ducked and threw out her arm in a wide circle with the whip extending to its fullest length. It missed her attacker, but found its targets in the house all round her. Its tip slashed through walls and door, through the staircase, the furniture, and the ornaments in an arc of demolition. The walls crumbled and fell, the ceiling and upper storey came down, the stairs collapsed. A rain of dust and destruction smothered the scene. Gloves fell from their lines to lie in the rubble with their empty fingers scrabbling to escape before more brick and plaster might crush them. Inconvenient tonnes smashed down on the intruder, while Greenaway twirled her whip like a shield, feeling the weight of fallen beams bouncing off it.

The door, that narrow aperture, was split into a wide jaw with tongue and teeth ripped away. She ran for it, toward the light. Erasmus barked a warning and she whirled, seeing the monster's hand diving for her. Still running and with her eyes shut, she brought the whip up and stung it; her shadow went through its head and set it screaming. She broke contact as she stumbled into the light, but not before its agony had filled her palms and sent her reeling with revelation. *I know this thing! I know its provenance!*

She fell into the light, Erasmus soared inside her, and they were spat back into the solid world.

∞

The light expelled her, less than a mile from where it had snatched her, onto a bed of snow that sizzled and evaporated in the heated discharge. Later she learned that only an instant had passed for her, but the fine gradations of that instant had been infinite. She lay gasping on a dried patch of hot grass.

They found her in the field and carried her, still half-stunned and moaning, into the warm safety of the shrine. A week she lay traumatised and shivering on her low bed in an anteroom. All of her cousins had survived the fracas at Salomon's House, though it would take some days before they could describe, before they knew certainly themselves, what had happened in her absence. The last scrap they gathered was the most heartening – Nathaniel Silver had escaped whatever fate had been planned for him, and was now in Paris, spirited there by M. Valentine and the power he served.

Greenaway would also listen tight-lipped as her cousins described their battle with the pilot-spirits, and how Erasmus's allies had died. The pilot was silent, but she sensed an equanimity in him. His comrades were not dead – they were sleeping in a distant city – and their mission would continue in other hands. She resolved she would tell her family about her new *loa* when the right moment presented itself, but as time passed that moment proved ever elusive. He stayed hidden inside her, speaking occasionally, but unrevealed to all but her.

She couldn't talk or move when they had found her. She could only stare up at them and marvel at how badly her imagined death had shaken them. Amphigorey even cried; Suppression sat beside her in the early hours of her paralysis, with his hand resting comfortably on hers; Hateman beamed joyfully; only Mother Sphinx stayed impassive, watching her through the hollows of her unremoved mask. Overhead, her reflection in the shrine's shiny ceiling was skeletal and blanched.

Only Hateman was with her when she first moved her lips again. Her cousin turned and bellowed for the others: 'Hey, you lot! Amphigorey! Get your arse in here! Our cousin's talking!'

Cousin?

Hateman saw the unspoken question. 'You've armed yourself. You've gone into Hell and come out again. Whatever happened to you must have been a tougher ordeal than anything we could've cooked up. Mother Sphinx says *Cousin Greenaway*, so *Cousin Greenaway* it is. You don't argue with that voice.'

She shook off this praise; it didn't matter. All that mattered were the words, the message she was screaming unheard inside herself. Her mouth struggled again to form sounds. Hateman gave her the smile an indulgent adult might give an infant, so Cousin Greenaway snatched her by the lapel and pulled her so close their faces touched. Finally the words came out of her.

'Homeworld!' she gabbled. 'It's from the Homeworld!'

Book Three: The Golden Age

⇒ Chapter 11: *The Juggler* ⇐

A boy fell from the north tower, dropping with a geometric precision that bisected the line of the old building. The effect would have pleased the architect had he seen it, but though he was on site that morning, he was conferring with his surveyor and the foreman on the far side of the abbey precinct. He didn't see it, but he heard it – the impact of body against stone, a fruit exploding under a hammerblow – though he was now over seventy years old and in other respects his hearing was faded. It was almost as though he had been expecting it. He drew a tongue over his lips before the first sounds of commotion could reach them from the west front. He tasted raw meat on an unsmooth pagan altar. It was delicious.

Within moments of the fall, the other labourers had downed tools and clustered round the dead boy; others called for the foreman, who came followed by the surveyor, and hobbling nimbly with one hand on his stick, the architect. It was then that the intruder wandered unchallenged into the grounds. He was almost upon the scene of the tragedy itself before he was found and questioned. He was an unassuming and – in dress – somewhat old-fashioned fellow, of perhaps forty years; he claimed to be an old friend of the architect, and had come to offer his greetings. The architect was close enough to be summoned with a shout. He made a play of his irritation and elaborated his stumbling gait, until he came face to face with the intruder. Then all pretence slipped away; the distraught pantomime he had performed over the fallen boy's body disappeared, replaced with a genuine and sober dread. They stared at each other, across the gap, paralysed and silent. The workers, having better and grimmer things to do, left them alone.

'I thought you were dead,' the architect said, at length. 'I heard it. I didn't know for sure.'

The intruder, the younger man whose hearing was perfect, ignored what he'd said, but looked instead to the bloodied thing the workmen were digging out from its half-grave of dislodged masonry. 'Was that your doing?'

The architect shrugged. 'An accident. They happen on every site. One comes to rely on them.'

'For blood?'

'Yes,' he nodded, 'for blood. Think of it as a sacrament, without which the building is incomplete. It has form and substance, it has geometry, but without blood... without blood, it is no living building. It has no soul. But see that boy, now, who would have cared for him otherwise? He would have been one of history's anonyms, leaving no mark on the world save perhaps the pollution of children born into poverty and misery. Now he will live forever in the fabric of these stones.'

'I'm sure he would have rather lived in the fabric of his body.'

The architect shook his head. 'I didn't kill him. These things happen.'

'You were ever a wicked child. You were lucky I never beat you.'

'Yes, and you were always so fucking holy. You could've taken a slap or two yourself.'

The younger man stepped forward, his hands held straight up. The architect, whose skin was withered tight on his bones, and who had never felt so ancient as he did now alongside this clean-skinned interloper, stiffened for a blow that didn't fall. Instead, his old friend took him by the shoulders and hugged him, and in truth that winded him almost as much as a punch might have done.

'Fuck!' he pronounced, once he was broken free – and once he had scanned the vicinity to make sure that no one had seen this reputation-shattering display of affection. 'You have not aged. A year or two or five, perhaps, but look at me!'

'You've done well for yourself these last forty years.'

'I have not. Look, I'm raddled. I'm become a struldbrugger while you might be my son. My grandson!' His own body smelled of tired old meat, while the Magus's was still sprung and fresh.

'I meant your works – Sir Nicholas Plainsong, the master architect. I would never have dreamed you had such talent. And these towers…'

The architect scoffed. 'Them? Oh, they're but a joke! My real work's elsewhere. New churches mainly. Fat Anne awarded me six commissions, the same number as the Houses of Heaven.'

'So you have left a mark on the world?'

'Just on London. I never wanted the world. That would be greedy. But Nate, what brings you here? After our last meeting…'

Nathaniel Silver didn't answer at once, but let Nick's now tired voice rattle off into ellipsis and silence. He was looking at the dead boy on the ground, at the corpse-lips that still twitched as the life and the air expelled slowly from his body. The workmen tugged down a creamy dustcloth from their scaffold and laid it over the dead face like a makeshift shroud.

He looked back to Nick: 'I'm going to die today,' he said.

The trees along Whitehall were pinking with the blossom of a Hanoverian spring. Their track into London's thoroughfares took them past the spot where Nathaniel Silver had, almost eighty years past, seen a king beheaded and a new future inaugurated. It was not *this* future, he ruminated, this strange *today* that they'd stumbled into blindly and by chance. He had thought his life bound up with the fate of the beheaded king, but it had not been so. Those storms that had battered England for so much of the old century had now passed, and a strange interruption now held, a moment of uncertain peace that might one day be thought an idyll.

Silver remained troubled. He could see the dangers strewn ahead, the unwitting traps set by history throughout the isles, but they would not affect him. He was dying, and if there was some true golden age beyond life, a metropolis not of death but salvation, then he hoped he might be forgiven his transgressions and accepted into it. He could imagine paradise as a city much like London or Paris; how could it not be when it was built by the same hands, all the hands there had ever been? The parks, bridges, and boulevards of all cities would be there, all the buildings of the Earth now belonging to all souls equally. He was certain also that there would be another Nate Silver waiting for him, a much younger and coarser man who had rightly died at Edgehill and was ignorant of what had been done on Earth in his name since.

He said nothing of this to Nick Plainsong. It was hard to believe that this was the same boy – no, it was all too easy. The skin might be leathered by time, but the eyes and the gestures were the same. So was the gait; his stick was wholly for effect, or to beat at insolent passers-by who (it seemed) were given to calling him an old fart to his face. He still slouched slightly at Silver's heels, letting the Magus set the pace. And his lusts were unchanged. They were off to Covent Garden to find a brothel.

Neither of them had been in much of a mood to explore the architecture of London Redux, splendid though it was. Plainsong was in fact gloomy about the prospects of the city, imagining how the capital would one day be consumed by pillars of glass and steel, buildings fit only for men who had debased themselves to the level of ants.

'But still men,' Silver cautioned him. Around them burst the teeming humans of the Hanoverian Age, including the young – running chattering playing children heedless of the world around them, their faces never troubled by the hardships of the last genera-tion, and so seeming, in Silver's eyes, unfinished and terribly vulnerable. Nick had no more work at the abbey today, where in any case the men had been spooked by sudden and careless death. Nick's career was not unknown to Silver: his shadowy apprentice-ship to celebrated names; his tours of Mediterranean and North African architecture; his return to England bearing arcane secrets of antique geometry like a crusader carry-ing back profane knowledge...

'I have a question or two for you,' Silver ventured, once they were out of sight of the abbey, once he judged that Nick would be unwilling to beat a retreat, 'about Salomon's House.'

'God's ballocks! That was nearly fifty years ago. You can't still bear a grudge...'

Sixty. Nearly *sixty* years ago. His memory was going.

'No, no grudges. To tell the truth, I thought you did me a favour that night when you stole the pilot's egg from me. I was ready to be done with it. Nor do I hold any ill will about our subsequent meeting. You opened my eyes to many things I had allowed to be hidden.'

'I was cruel to do so,' Nick replied, and that sounded as close to an apology as he could manage.

'You were, but you're Nick Plainsong. Cruelty's in your nature. No...' He heard his voice trail off, but couldn't feel his own body; he was momentarily dislocated some-where else, into a *corpus* that was dying or already dead. Then he was back, and felt well and undying. The power that raised him had done an uncanny job in tailoring his healed body, which did not age or wound as it would have before Edgehill, but the life-force that sustained it was running out. He would not last long when it was gone.

'Why did you do it, Nick?' he asked. 'That's all I need. A little clarity before I die.'

'For Christ's sake, will you stop saying that?'

'No. No, I won't. Why, Nick? Was it Jeova put you up to it?'

'See, you need not ask, you already guess. Yes, it was Jeova suggested the theft, and in truth I was angry because you'd spoiled my sport.'

'Did he tell you why?'

'He suggested it as a mischief. Oh, he framed it cunningly, like I would be *liberating* you from a curse, though it was ever his own interests that guided him. He wanted your egg for himself, I've no doubt of that.'

'Greed? That's a shame. I expected more from him.'

'Not greed, pride. He was stung that it was your gift and not his, when he could do so much with it. Also, he was lonely, and I don't think he'd ever really loved a man before, or a woman. I was kind to him.'

'Because you wanted another Magus.'

Nick shook his head. He had been hatless earlier, and most of the hair had gone from his scalp. Long strands of it now slipped dislodged down his back to decorate the shoulders of his coat, white on black. 'I'd've died of boredom within months. You made for a more exciting life. I missed it when you were gone.'

'You found other patrons,' Silver said evenly, so slight that he wasn't sure that Nick would see a prompt.

Ah, but he was a bright child – he saw. 'Oh yes, but my patrons were never concerned with you, only the others you attracted. That's why they've had me prime the churches.'

'Which others, Nick?'

'You know –'

'Yes, I know and it still hurts. You needn't mention their name, but I don't see what these churches of yours have to do with them.'

'They're coming back – to London – in force, and soon. Look at these children, it will be in their lifetimes, though not mine. Some future George is going to strike a compact with them, and that'll involve a grant of *time*. Not land, you understand, time. Eleven whole days of our empire, this mangy hound commanded by the Hanoverian flea, will be given to them. Those days will be theirs to do with as they will.'

A girl ran past them in the mud, with her skirt hoisted and flapping, a poor ruddy-faced cheerful thing ignoring the old men on the sidewalk. Her mouth made hard regular puffing noises, imitating a kettle or a Savery fire-engine; she seemed to be turning into a machine. The breeze shook blossom from the overhanging trees, and Silver saw that they weren't pink as he'd thought, but a mixture of oranges and reds, with some petals plain white and shot with bloody veins. They were dying, he thought, killing themselves by trying to spread. The world was accelerating toward a future that Nick thought was certain.

No, Nick had planted a spoke into its wheel. 'London will be theirs, including your churches.'

Even as an old man, Nick Plainsong had a lad's evil smile.

Silver parted his hands wistfully and let the petals that had gathered there drift away, onto the barren walkway, or to the fecund mud where they'd be trampled by children or buried under horse-dung. It was hard for him to imagine a welcome in Heaven. He thought of the wavering line of fresh-trained soldiers on the field at Edgehill; he had been there. He'd fallen there, but rose again, while so many others hadn't. He saw skulls split by musketballs, stomachs rent open, limbs spilling as free as blood; he saw heads lopped off by Prince Rupert's cavalry or the anonymous cannon; he could taste gunpowder and hot metal on the air. How could any of his fallen comrades or fallen enemies have accepted the welcome of Heaven? When the light had descended on them, with their jaws or the eyes gone, their stumps seeping with faint beads of blood that no longer flowed or spurted, how would they have reacted to the beneficence of Christ? He could imagine only a great mutiny and the pillage of Heaven, as the betrayed once-living men tore down the palaces of the God that had birthed them into Hell.

'I can understand,' he said at length, 'why you might side with them, but I will not.'

Nick looked at him curiously, and saw that he was smiling. 'Well even if you are to die today – and I doubt that, Nate, I doubt that – you have stuck to your purpose, I see.'

Silver shook his head, and as he spoke they reached the threshold of his final destination. 'No, Nick. I am a broken and disillusioned man.' But he kept smiling nonetheless.

∞

The brothel was one of Plainsong's favoured retreats. Silver remembered it, though not fondly or in great detail, as Corinthian Tom's House of the Infernal, which had – fittingly – been burned out one night during the years of Silver's exile in Paris. It had been a squalid dive then, but now at least the façade had been prettified. The shell had been rebuilt and painted, even decorated, so it looked as respectable as a town house, even if the curtains were ever drawn. Inside was fine furnishing and genteel decoration, overseen by a silver-haired matron and her elderly retainer; the pimps and procurers were well-hidden, the back-stage squalor smothered by heavy perfume and rare madak tobacco. Outside there was even a prosaic wood plate on the door, with the establishment's latest name chipped awkwardly into it, and engraved with images of rabbits.

'*The Cunicularii*,' Silver read awkwardly, stumbling as ever on the Latin.

'So named at the height of this last year's rabbit fever,' Plainsong explained, then – seeing this was no explanation – added: 'The papers were full of it. No? 'Twas a hoax. The lady in question was exposed as a liar and an hysteric, so I imagine this will be the old Inferno again soon enough.'

They knew Nick Plainsong here. The women of the house greeted him with exaggerated whoops, claps, and smiles, welcoming him back as they would an old friend, or at least a very generous and untroublesome client. For all his age, wealth, and status, he turned again into a child, a youth newly-encumbranced by loins and lusts, and happily willing to try every sweetmeat or confection that was laid before him. He was soon swamped by voluminous prostitutes, while Silver – who had had most of his appetites burned away in long fits of hope and disappointment – sat back and watched them smother him. He only wanted a drink, and they served him gin. That had been new once, when he and Nick had crept round these houses decades ago, a foreign tipple brought back by sailors from Cromwell's Dutch wars. Now it was everywhere, a craze like the rabbits. All the girls had forlorn, floppy rabbit ears sewn onto the tops of their caps, the smooth felt dangling down the backs of heads and across bare shoulders. They tried too hard to make this place elegant and modern. Silver found he missed the rough and honest seediness of these places.

Nick introduced him; he forgot the names and faces instantly. He had no need to remember any longer, and he had no desire to spend time with any of these women. Nick didn't believe he was dying. He thought Nate was being morbid again, and he was right. Silver *was* morbid – like the egg, he had carried that with him out of the grave. The does of the *Cunicularii* stroked his hair, his face, and his chest, and drifted away sadly when they discovered he wasn't paying. Only one caught his attention, but she was sitting in her own corner of the parlour, not looking at him, not looking to anyone, but rifling through a pack of stiff oblong playing cards.

'Who is that?' he asked Nick.

The old architect punched him playfully on the shoulder. 'She doesn't fuck.'

'What does she do?'

'She can sing a bit. Mainly she plays French Tarot. She's from the city of your old exile, you might have met her.'

'I doubt it, she looks barely old enough.'

'So? *You* don't look a hundred. Come on, I'll introduce you.'

And Silver found himself being drawn reluctantly out of his comfortable loll and marched across the room to meet the mysterious whore who wouldn't fuck. Silver plonked himself down in the chair opposite her, and she gave no more reaction than a faint scowl, barely detectable in the intense scrutiny she was giving each card. Silver tried to make himself seem presentable, tried to smile. It wasn't even as if he found her attractive; she was a little too heavy for him, her cheeks and neck no longer puppyish but still hinting at lost rolls of fat. She had a pronounced round chin and a mouth of crooked teeth, which might have explained why she wouldn't smile.

Silver had fornicated with more women than he cared to remember, especially in the bleaker times when *le Pouvoir* were still eager to secure his attention; he had romanced perhaps a dozen; he had loved two, and been befuddled by a third. He knew already that this one wasn't going to be a grand passion, even if by some miracle he lived to the end of the day; but she was interesting.

Plainsong loomed over him, not sitting, but resting with one hand on his stick and the other round the waist of a skinny child about a fifth of his own age. She was powdered and practised at her arts, but somehow contrived to seem much more innocent than this sour creature sat opposite him.

'Nathaniel Silver, may I introduce the famous Mademoiselle Machine? She doesn't speak any English, which isn't usually a drawback in her profession, but since she refuses to do much else this makes her a mystery. Wouldn't you agree, mademoiselle?'

Mademoiselle Machine made daggers of her eyes and glared at him. 'Little English,' she spat. Her voice was guttural, a parodic Parisian growl. Silver realised at once that she wasn't French, but had, like him, spent enough time in their capital to make a crude mimic.

Silver rolled his eyes at her. *I'm sorry about him.* 'Do you play cards, mademoiselle?'

The dagger-glare came round to face him. She cut her cards abruptly and extended the topmost to him. It was *arcane majeure*, a gaudy fellow at his workbench, *le bateleur*.

'She knows you, Nate,' Plainsong announced, bellowing it out to anyone interested and setting his companion giggling, possibly from embarrassment. 'And what of Sir Nicholas Plainsong? What is he? *Le diable*, I hope? Or master of *la maison dieu*? Come mademoiselle, I will accept anything but *le mat*.'

Bored, Mademoiselle Machine cut her deck again and held out another card, this time towards Nick and his catch. '*L'amoureux*,' she pronounced, voice dull as a rusted sword.

Nick clapped his hands delightedly and pulled his catch closer. 'Excellent!' he declaimed – it was always hard to tell whether he was truly drunk, or feigning it to indulge his rowdiest instincts – 'I think that's my cue to take this young lady upstairs and ravish her to within an inch of my life. Inches are thinner nowadays, Nate, and I fear I'm more likely to expire today than you are. If that should happen, you'll be sure to tell my good lady and our children that I died screwing a cheap whore and that I'll see them presently in Hell.'

'I will do, Nick,' Silver promised, but the sound was obscured by the girl complaining about being called *cheap*. Plainsong silenced her with a proffered penny, then seized her by the waist, and with a strength obscured by his age, hoisted her over his shoulder and carried her in the direction of the stairs.

'Goodbye, Nicholas Plainsong,' Silver said softly to his retreating back. And it seemed that as Plainsong left his life for good, the whole chorus of raucous noises and yells that had once filled this whorehouse parlour now seeped away, along with the bodies of the women who – seeing no more party or pickings to be found here – became grim and tired and left to take a moment before the afternoon's next gruelling performance. He was left alone with his thoughts and the sound of Mademoiselle Machine paying out her cards on the tabletop. *Le bateleur* and *l'amoureux* were swallowed up when she shuffled again.

Slap. The cards came down. *Slap. Slap. Slap.*

'Do you have a card of your own, mademoiselle?' he asked leisurely.

Slap. She pinned her latest card with her fingertip, and Silver craned awkwardly to study it from the corner of his eye, afraid that if he looked directly she would take offence and snatch it away. It was her own soul she was displaying naked to him. It wasn't a trump, just one of the suits. It showed a three-pointed crown – meant to be gold, but faded brown as if exposed to a surfeit of sunlight – impaled on a thrusted rapier.

Silver, emboldened and dizzied by gin, thought it looked like a seed, or a moment of conception. His eyes shifted from the card and met those of the mademoiselle, who blushed and looked away, then looked back fiercer. She scattered her cards, took his hands and led him to her room on an upper storey where a quickly sobered and excited Silver discovered that – as in so many other respects – Nick was wrong and Mademoiselle Machine was thoroughly prepared to fuck after all.

Nick had promised to pay all debts, but it didn't matter. Silver had money, and no longer had any need for it. He tried to tell the woman that he was dying as they undressed one another, but she wouldn't hear it, sealing his lips with her fingers, and then, unusually, with her mouth.

She was the sort of girl he would have liked when he was a younger, other man. In the years before the war he would have been impressed by her maturity and found her stubborn façade enticing. Young Nate Silver had ridden wild crushes, that had rapidly tamed and gone timid if the subject succumbed to his advances. He couldn't believe he had ever been that boy. Soldiery – and his interment in the earth – had changed him forever. He had been baptised as surely as one of Nick's Satanic churches, the innocent stone activated by violence and blood so it could serve some great power of the heavens or the depths, but – whatever its provenance – heedless of human hope and suffering.

He was baptised again by Mademoiselle Machine's slippery vagina. This time he felt cleansed.

After they'd coupled, she climbed off him and left him spent but hardly tired on her bed. It was a narrow cot in a narrow room, furnished and decorated in a hasty and perfunctory style unlike so much else in the house. It suggested a temporary engagement. Silver raised his head slightly from her pillow and saw Machine clean off her thighs with a cloth, then put on a gossamer blouse and nothing more. She was humming something to herself, a little tune or poem, and he strained to catch the words.

'No gods and no devils,' she sang, 'no servants and no masters, no riches and no poverty, and no laws in the universe but one command: love.'

He recalled where he had last heard these words, and laughed. 'That's a pretty sentiment, mademoiselle, if a trifle naïve.'

She didn't look at him, but went barefoot across undisguised wood boards to the window. The afternoon light was harder than it should have been, passing through glass, and suffused a blushing red from the blossom in the trees outside.

'Mind if I open this?'

'Be my guest.' She wrenched it open. It allowed in the scent of blossoms and a hard breeze that had been building up since he and Nick had met at the abbey. Motion had been let into the world. The wind tickled but didn't trouble his naked body. The air was scented and precious; he took pleasure from each breath.

'You speak more than a little English,' Silver observed. 'Any fool can tell that.'

'Not Sir Nicholas,' said the woman who called herself Mademoiselle Machine; she was sitting on the windowsill, with her blouse and thighs open to this warm March day.

'Sir Nick is easily distracted, where women are concerned. There again, so am I.'

The wind that shook the petals from the trees wafted them through the window and into the room. Their scent – which had until moments before been faint, like a suggestion, like a memory – now turned immediate and heady. He saw the first orange buds flutter onto his stomach and his thighs like the onset of plague, but this was a sweet sickness. It brought up thoughts of lost summers, sticky days in the heat of July, spilled water slaking the hot stone fronts of houses.

The prostitute was still talking, distantly: 'I wish I'd met you earlier, Nathaniel.'

'No one calls me Nathaniel. Such a mouthful. I prefer Nate.'

Did he say that? He must have, as Machine replied, 'I know exactly how you feel.'

More petals fell, trickling then streaming through the window. They clustered on his chest round the tufts of his nipples, and in his navel, and sticking to the slow-drying juices on his diminished penis. The blossom-scent was overwhelming, as if all the other trivial momentary smells of the solid world had expired and died, revealing the perfume of spring as the true and eternal state of things if not obscured by sin and the works of man. Heaven was waiting for him. Christ's pilots had warned him they would come for him at the end of his life, and his soul was prepared; he hoped they had forgiven him whatever mortal but unwitting transgression he had made against them, and that they meant no longer to punish him as they had at Salomon's House. The stream of flowers was a torrent, flooding the room to drown him. Great drifts fell upon him, caressing him, as Ann had, as Alice had, as Aphra had. Buds and seeds were drawn into his mouth and his nostrils by shallow breaths, there to mate and root. It was his second burial, but this one was blissful.

'I heard what you said to Nick outside, and I envy you, Nate Silver. Everyone would, if they only knew.' But Silver could no longer hear her.

Time unravelled, turned, and fell back into itself. He was sucking his sperm back from Mademoiselle Machine's body through the tip of his penis. They dressed each other playfully and skittered downstairs, to be joined by crowds of whores, then Sir Nick Plainsong. Sat in the corner, Silver looked away from Machine and forgot he had ever seen her. He and Nick left soon afterwards and strolled backwards down towards Westminster. Then they parted, and Silver was immediately wracked by fear and uncertainty of what would happen when they next met, a sentiment that bloomed suddenly but felt as if it had been rooted deep in his heart for many years. A dead boy flung off the stones of a makeshift tomb and leapt many dozens of feet into the air, rapturously restored to life.

Silver accelerated backwards through forty years of wandering, losing short-lived friends as he went, forgetting new facts and undoing quiet achievements. Then he came again to London, and a slow bitterness that had welled in him in recent years was suddenly expelled from his body into blissful ignorance. He was captured and transported back across the channel to France, where he fell into the waiting arms of *le Pouvoir*. They seemed reluctant to take him, greeting him with a surly coolness that was surprising given how many insights and achievements they'd attributed to him in the past four years. It might have been in jealousy then that he undid all of these, even the mirrors he had made for them, which he now smashed and unfurled and rolled back into the shape of an egg. Alice was at his side in Paris. One morning she stole the angel's egg from him, and he found the years of happiness slipping away, but Alice was still there at his side, always a comfort. He grew increasingly fearful, as *le Pouvoir* brought him more stories of how the English Service were hunting him and the tortures they meant to inflict on his body and mind if they caught him. Nevertheless, after a few more short years they delivered him back into England. He charged back across a snow-smothered wasteland, determined to confront the Service in their own house outside Cambridge.

No, once there his energies were spent. The angels appeared, and forgave him, and restored the lost egg to him. The world became a calmer place, and over the next few days he casually dismissed all the people who had come to see him fail, sending them back to their homes and institutes across the country. Eventually he was left only with Alice and Nick, and they returned to London together, where they began to erase all traces of Silver's career as the Magus. The time came when he had to be alone, and he left Alice whoring in a Cheapside tavern, and abandoned Nick in a city beset by plague. He had few friends then, though Donald Taylor reappeared and slowly stripped him of his knowledge. He had forgotten the threats of the Service, and they came when he least expected it, throwing him into gaol and implanting a metal stud into his skull – a pain that endured for the rest of his life. The agonies of imprisonment were undiminished whichever way he faced them, and he was relieved to be let out and put in charge of a small and failing commune in the south. Under his tutelage it thrived. He even found success at restoring the dead to life, and found in one Ann Brownlow his Dorcas, his true risen love. But she quickly forgot him once the commune – nursed back to sturdy health – began to disband.

And then what? Then there were many harvests, on rich brown fields that yielded pieces of flesh and bone that could be sewn back into a joyous crop of living men. These new-born men formed corps that swept across England, leaving it healed and whole in their wake. There was a king again and he brought his nations more battles, more bounty, more injuries undone, and more blessed dead awoken to life. Silver was there for them all, emptying his book as he went. Then he was stumbling backwards across a hoar-coated hill, his retreat undoing the commotion among the hospitallers. He had an egg in his hand; he noticed it, then thought of it no more. He found a crude hole in a patch of fresh-turned earth, a grave filled with bodies wrapped only in cloth because they were so plentiful and wood was so scarce. They would live again soon, so he clambered back down to join them in their rest. There was a shroud waiting for him. He wrapped himself into it, then clawed the cool brittle earth down on him to cover his face and make him warm against the winter frost. He snuggled in his shroud and stitched it back up around him. And then he died.

He had died, he knew that – he had been restored from death – but he was surprised that he couldn't parade any earlier into his life, to undo Edgehill, to march back home with the parliamentary irregulars and present himself for the first time to his mother and his father. That reversal, though he struggled for it, was beyond him. Instead, he saw himself spread out on the lazaret of the pilots, in a room that seemed through the addlement of his senses to be much like Mademoiselle Machine's at the *Cunicularii*. He was naked and whole, until the bright intimidating angels drew tender scalpels. They had remade his body, which had been struck down by the King's bullet, but now – reversed – it felt as though their instruments were undoing him. Here, at the end of his life, they were cutting him open to remove his lights and leave him hollow. Their divine, invisible blades sliced away flesh, then humour, then bone, destroying all the physical parts of him until all that was left of Nathaniel Silver was his soul, the very gifts of his life.

The slow dolorous hoods of the pilots clustered closer to see, and there was consternation in their ranks. The immortal part of him they had teased out now confounded them. He peered closer, looking into himself to see what had disappointed them about his soul. It was profoundly and unmistakably that of an ordinary man; but it had been *stitched*; it had been sewn and remade by another hand, subtler even than that of angels. The soul of Nathaniel Silver ended here – at Edgehill, in the grave – but it had been extended, spliced with another man's life entirely. So he had endured more than four score years when he should by rights be dead.

Silver could see this – how he could he not? It was *himself*, it was *true* – but the pilots were confused. They probed the suture, and it exploded outwards in a jet of evil ink that smothered their light and drove them back. And as he died, Nathaniel Silver found his likeness reflected on the surface of the dark the angels had unleashed, and knew at last and without pleasure that he was in the presence of his creator.

I was made to be an instrument of war. I was beset by falsehoods and illusions to justify that war.

No longer.

═ Chapter 12: *The Public Burning* ═

Gabriel Suarez died on the fourth day of January in the sixteen hundred and forty-third year of Our Lord. The date was said with confidence – whatever else they might be, the Spanish Inquisition were meticulous in their record-keeping.

Suarez, a man as old as the century, was a citizen of Toledo, a tanner by trade. He had been suffering for some weeks. Humid Spanish prayers were made for him by his wife and children, and they had grown accustomed to grief by the time of his passing. They were unprepared when Gabriel, no sooner confirmed as lifeless by reputable doctors, sat up on his deathbed, cured beyond all doubt. They rejoiced anyway, while the chirurgeons opined he had passed through death as a necessary station on the way to recovery. The Inquisition was unconvinced.

Suarez and his wife were brought before the tribunal under suspicion of practising witchcraft. Señora Suarez insisted that the only power she had invoked was prayer, the only intercession sought that of Christ and His saints. Subject to the garrucha, *Suarez confided his suspicion that he had been truly dead and truly restored, but claimed ignorance of how this might have come about, what spirits might have granted him their favour, or what their motives may have been. The inquisitors grew increasingly perplexed, describing their deliberations with terse embarrassment (these being officials of a more worldly and legalistic tribunal than the hotheaded Italians who had imprisoned Galileo and burned Bruno). Eventually, they found Suarez innocent, at least of the intent of witchcraft; his penance therefore was meant not as punishment, but to prevent him from being used, unwittingly, as a further conduit for spirits.*

They cut out his tongue, to keep him silent.

Edward Coleman did not die easily. Nor was his death meant to be easy. It was set down in the judgement; he was required to suffer the full vengeance of the state. He was led to his place of execution, to Calgary-made-London fields, in a state of fear and incomprehension that quite shook the congenial mood of the crowd. They had been expecting a bold traitor's brash performance, but no – he was seen crying as he was led on the hurdle, and his tears infected the throng. How much easier would this be if it were a highwayman, a rogue, a perjurer, or a starter of false fires? *They* could be expected to dance for the hangman. They might crow or even feint, hoping at the last to slip the noose, cheat Jack Ketch, leap into a prepared saddle and make a famous escape for the next day's pamphlets. This was Tyburn, the great stage equal of any of the city's theatres, so why was Coleman refusing its lure? It wasn't as though he was the first innocent to go to the rope and the roller.

Afterwards, some said that it was an act all along, that the traitor's toothsome fear was a cruel parody of the terror he and his black-clad paymasters had visited on England and her Protestant sisterlands. They whispered that beneath the vizard of tears burned the fanatic heart of a martyr, pleased to die and promised sainthood already in the unholy pantheon of Rome. The perfidious Papimane, it was opined, lacking all human sensibility, could only mimic the agonies of his victims. He was a parody of the true Christian, a mummer and a puppet of Satan. Coleman had learned to semble the arts of misery from the death-throes of poor murdered Sir Edmund, whom he himself had cruelly stabbed on Greenberry Hill (*oh come now, even if we grant all the other allegations, no one has ever said that Coleman took a direct part in that business!*) He would have learned it, no doubt, from his superiors in the Society of Jesus. They are all 'in' on it, the whole damn'd lot of them. I myself heard that there are some two hundred and five Catholics in the Royal Household. (*A ridiculous figure, plucked out of nowhere.*) From the lips of Ezreel Tongue himself, a more loyal subject than you will find in all England. And Master Oates, who speaks with authority on the Jesuits, having bravely turned his back on their vile order, says there are some seventy plots to do away with the King or murder England's innocent multitudes. (*Your reason is Popishly affected!*) Indeed? And why would an honest Protestant woman throw in her cause with this wicked religion? Unless she is a far from honest Protestant – does treason beat within that breast, my lady Astraea? (*My loyalties are in no doubt. I am for the King.*) Ah, but then is it not a womanish faith? They may pretend a devotion to our Lord, but the creature they worship is a woman, virgin and whore both, whom they elevate above God – not the Christ but the womb that birthed Him. (*Your sophistry is degenerating into the merely vulgar.*) And this king you are for? Is it not the case you are a truer admirer of his brother, and would happily see him on the throne? (*The Monarchy is a divine office appointed by God, who will put there who He will.*) But it won't be God who puts James on the Throne. One way or another it will be Rome, when his brother grows too weak or the Queen slips poison into his beer. (*Sirrah, you are beneath contempt.*) She's another of your favourites, eh? And she dances to the Pope's tune, same as any other Catholic when they are called to it. (*The Pope couldn't find England on a map and you know it.*) Oh-ho, I wouldn't claim to know what the Pope thinks. (*And Oates is a pig-faced pederast whose lies were exposed by the merest breath of inspection! Sir Edmund likely took his own life; it was said his thoughts were turned inward and morbid. This terror you invoke, this shadowy conspiracy besieging England is a phantom menace that would have seemed crude and childish a hundred years gone! And those who speak of it most – why, they are Whigs who see only an opportunity to exclude the Duke, reject toleration, and shackle us forever to their politics!*

I was there! I saw Edward Coleman die! I saw no conspiracy, no performance, only the fear we had put into him before we tore out everything else. We have damned ourselves. Innocent blood. We are all damned!)

Aphra Behn was at Tyburn that day, and did not enjoy herself. It seemed to her that barely any time had passed since the early years of the Restoration, when she'd heard the first reports of the regicides dragged to the gallows to be throttled, emptied, and destroyed. She had received the news with a fit of joy, and had begged her family to raise funds for a trip to London to enjoy the spectacle. The touring display of the dismembered parts had not excited her; it was nothing more than old meat, that might have come from a horse or a cow or maybe an ape. The money had rolled in too slowly though, and she had been taken with a winter chill, and by the time she'd been fit to travel the new king had called a halt to the executions. She had despised Charles for his weakness and his compassion, and had begun – long before the disaster in Antwerp and her days in prison – to shift her admiration to the sterner, less squeamish Duke of York.

She watched Edward Coleman die, and was suddenly uncertain of herself. It wasn't that she was convinced of his innocence – he was condemned by prattling out foolish fantasies, the unhappy toss of that idiot coin whose converse was the good fortune Titus Oates now enjoyed – but by his demeanour. His agonies were palpable but contained; he was too scared, too paralysed, to let out any protest but a whimper. He transmitted to her a fear that would disturb her for many nights afterwards, turning in her breast from the specific horror of one man's death into a broad sickness of the soul. Some nights she would wake and have to push her fist into her mouth to keep the taste of it contained. She wasn't afraid for herself. She was afraid for England, for what it was becoming.

She sat on her bench at Tyburn chewing on a winter apple – tastelessly sour – that she had bought from a stallsman and held on a spike. She tried to ignore the thrum and mutter of the crowd around her, who though disquieted, seemed thoroughly prepared to watch Coleman – innocent or no – suffer before he died. She wished she could rise above them, as in those waking dreams of Surinam, to oversee the crowd in the body of a bird, a mite, or an angel. So many terrifying faces would be reduced to distant anonymity. So many evil human sentiments would be obliterated by the leap into another species. She could not. She stayed on the ground, in the crowd, as one of them – one of the ugly callous humans. She felt no kinship with them.

Neither did she feel kinship with the wretch they had come to watch die, not immediately. He was hanged, as the first part of his sentence demanded, by the short drop. He thrashed like a landed fish on a line. The noose throttled nine-tenths of the life out of him, so that what they cut down was no longer fully human, but some shit-sodden feral creature. He had enough of his wits left to know that he wouldn't die yet. The vengeance of the state, like any other, was cruel and unseeing.

That was the moment that Aphra Behn began to fear for Edward Coleman. He had condemned himself by incarnating his soft Catholic fancies in the intractable medium of ink. If that was his first step to the gallows, then how much further had she climbed? She'd made no secret of her politics – even her foibles and odd tolerations that would have scandalised her good Tory comrades – and it was no hardship to imagine herself into Coleman's place. What suddenly struck her was the sheer injustice – intolerable even if he were guilty – that a man might die for dreaming and for transmitting those dreams.

Having been hung to within an inch of his life, Edward Coleman was then drawn. He had swooned, his face blanched from the noose, so the executioner sprinkled water on his skin before they dragged him to the table and the brazier. Aphra was far enough from the stage that she couldn't feel the heat or catch any of the blood, though the sizzle was a perceptible buzz under the murmurs of the crowd, and the smell when it came would carry across the field, and for a week afterwards she would barely be able to taste meat without recalling it.

The first on the fire were his privy parts, which were struck off by the executioner almost as soon as he was on the table. His screams, shrill though they were, didn't drown the brazier's whisper. His member and balls were soon followed by his lights and organs. A slit was cut into his stomach and his guts were drawn out; not by hand, as they were too slick to be grasped tidily, but spooled out on a spiked spindle. His head had to be twisted, in its agony, and his lids thumbed open, so that he was forced to inspect each new gory trophy before it was thrown onto the flames. Closest to the brazier were the beggars, London's starvelings, whose stomachs – shrunken but safely intact inside their trunks – were not satiated by the smell but at least pleasantly reminded of their last good meal. There were similar scenes at the city's slaughterhouses each morning; they were inured to Edward's agonies.

She had, by now, started to think of him as Edward.

The trick, in these cases, was to keep the client alive for the entirety of his excruciation. Whether they succeeded or not, Aphra couldn't tell, and made no effort to discover afterwards. It was only made certain when the executioner struck off the traitor's head and displayed it for the crowd. And finally, the sentence was completed as the carcass was quartered; the headless gutted torso that had until moments before been a living man was divided into four pieces, to be displayed around the nation. The head would go to the Tower, to decorate the riverbank. His offal cooked and blackened in the brazier, not meant as tribute to any god, yet still somehow consumed by a spirit that lived in the fire and accepted it as an offering.

Aphra Behn crept away from the field that day, hating herself for her quietness and her complicity. *So you sympathised with the traitor, did you, as he lay dying? That would have been a great comfort to him, had he but known!* She spat appleseed onto the field, which was salted to ward off the snow. They might grow into a tall tree some day in the future, but she doubted it. All she'd left to the world were inkstains, and that sort of business had done Edward Coleman no good.

She quarrelled over politics with her current lover that evening, and withheld her favours. He contrived to take them anyway. For a week after, she hated him, and everyone, most of all Edward Coleman, and confined herself indoors. It was winter again, as the world turned interminably through time, and her anger made her only a little warmer. She didn't write. She was afraid of the theatre, afraid even of private verses that might – in years to come – be seen to endorse the wrong man. It was prudent to stay away from the Duke's anyway – the name alone made it the object of scorn and suspicion, even if acting hadn't been seen as such a Popish profession. One night, agitators had broken in and left a bucketload of fish-heads under the stage, and though it had been hosed and perfumed, the stink remained to drive away even loyal customers and unsettle the current production.

Not *Sir Patient Fancy*, thank Christ, which was over and done with long since. Critics like that could kill a career.

Still, she was in need of funds, and with the stage doors of Tyburn and the Duke's both closed to her, she was left with few options. Which was how, barely a week before Christmas Day, Aphra Behn found herself trudging through Covent Garden in search of a brothel. She was defiantly alone and unarmed, a little protest against those voices who warned that escorts and the bearing of arms were the only surety against the murderous Catholic hordes lurking in every doorway. Such 'precautions' were about as effective as the mail-lined underclothing that had recently become London fashion, and whose manufacturers had at least shown ingenuity and originality when it came to milking the credulous. Aphra was determined that her fear would manifest itself as defiance, even nonchalance. Besides, she knew these streets.

Even so, she couldn't help but glance anxiously at the deeper shadows she passed, a kernel of doubt taunting her, her hobgoblin of introspection. But – no. The idea that all England's Catholics – who had, it seemed to her, lived blameless lives for generations and asked no more than their due as Englishmen – would by some whispered command below Saint Peter's dome transubstantiate into fanatic killers, seemed thoroughly implausible to her. Besides, if she were done to death in a Soho field, she doubted she'd care to ask her killers' faith.

It was another bitter cold December, with rain-dampened snow on the air and low clouds in the noon twilight, which in turn trapped hot coalsmoke in the streets. You might almost swear that London was burning again, and certainly there were many cunning Whigs who would have it that this was just one of the many plots made against the city. But it was second-hand smoke, the spark long gone out of it; it did nothing worse than make her gag, dirty her cloak, and remind her of the smouldering meat-smell of traitors. *As a woman, you would be spared his fate; they would only burn you or crush you.* Anyone who thought that fire purified knew nothing about fire or purity, and certainly nothing about London.

They were already in Covent Garden's prematurely eveninged streets – the traders, hawkers, streetwalkers, swindlers, pickpockets, buggerers, gangsters, jugglers, singers, butchers, and Godbotherers that she expected, none especially perplexed by plots, Popish or otherwise. Even the preachers, already half-mad on hellfire fumes, seemed cheerful in this new atmosphere. For Covent Garden folk and Covent Garden professions, there was nothing like religious mania and impending apocalypse to drum up business. It was difficult – though not impossible – to be a lone woman on this street without picking up company and maybe pennies. Aphra herself was propositioned once or twice, and drove the enquiries away with a withering glance. She took heavy steps, careful not to slip on the sleet or the dung. There were still clean and full-bodied patches of snow on the edges of the street, not yet turned to shit-flecked sludge or broken by footprints. Children in mufflers, masks, and fingerless gloves were picking up clumps with their hand and filling buckets; others were doing the same for manure, making sure to keep both separate. Aphra supposed there was a new alchemical craze for both substances; both were *pure* in their own way, and could no doubt reveal the secrets of the cosmos (for a fee). Clean ice, in particular, was being sought as a substitute for rare crystal churned out of volcanoes on the edge of the arctic fimbulwinter. The crystal itself was worthless, but it was rumoured that if you looked through it – at the right angle, in the right light – it would reveal the shape of the future, and such visions were beyond price. Aphra didn't care to contemplate the future, which span the Earth ever further from the Golden Age, and now seemed on the verge of shutting down for good.

The boys and girls, having filled their buckets, took them into a nearby house that Aphra knew to be a brothel – though not the one she was looking for, not the House of the Infernal. Ah, there was no mystery. The snow was for baths, icy water being the quacks' favourite cure-all for most kinds of privy diseases, or to shrivel and kill semen in its natural home (not a method of contraception she believed to be effective – it would be so much more satisfying to slice off the bastard's prick with a rusty knife then make him eat it and hope he fucking chokes on it); and horseshit had a thousand and one practical applications, all unrelated to *science.*

She was trying not to think about her destination, plastering words around her like a layer of insulation, not against the cold but against her task. The House of the Infernal was half a street's-length away. She trudged through the smoke pall to the door, which was if anything narrower and dingier than she had expected, and rapped on it sharply. She looked at the jamb, finding no lamb's blood drying on the post. The Jews had fled London as quickly as the Catholics, quicker even. They were the children of the passover, who smelled blood on the air and knew from sixteen hundred years' experience that the mob – once roused – was indiscriminate in its mercy.

A metal shutter on the door flapped open. Suspicious eyes flicked back and forth, surveying her. She glowered back. 'Fuck off', the door demanded, and the shutter snapped closed.

Aphra sighed. It was all too easy to see what the doorkeeper's eyes had seen through that tight oblong: a stout sour woman in widow's black – not intentional, just the most anonymous choice of shawl she had in her wardrobe – stood on his threshold in a stolid yeoman's pose and clearly wanting to be somewhere else. She might be a mother come hunting an errant daughter. She might be a churchly shrew come to pray for their souls – there was a lot of it about – and poke a prurient but disapproving nose into the house's succulently sinful business. Aphra knocked again, this time making sure to hold up a coin.

The same eyes reappeared. Aphra wiggled the coin insistently. 'The Jesuitess,' she said. After a moment, the door was opened, and she was let into the Inferno. She went briskly, to give the impression of being in command of this inner world. Like the caffé house she'd once smuggled herself into – in a disguise that had been obvious to all but the blind – it stank of masculinity, though here the overwhelming miasma was the honest perfume of spunk, not the dishonest whiff of newsprint. The bricks around her whispered of poverty and heartless love. It was, she reckoned, a touch cleaner and prettier than might be expected, no doubt a consequence of women living here and working here and giving birth within its walls.

She was pleased to find, when she entered Corinthian Tom's parlour, that she wasn't the only woman gathered for the display. True, most of the crowd were London disreputables of all classes – some of the more finely-dressed visibly the worse for drink or night-long benders on the gaming table, and she had no doubt they were the house's ideal audience, to be seduced and fleeced once the show was done. But there were a couple of towngirls here as halves of a brace, persuaded by their beaus and now clinging to male shoulders out of a twittery fear that they might otherwise be dragged off into darkened parlours and never seen outside again; she envied them their girlish fantasies. One maidenly soul seemed to have come alone, and bravely clung to nothing more reliable than the walls of the house as their host held forth.

The Pimp of Pimps noticed Aphra as she entered, and broke his patter. She didn't let his attention distract her, but took off her cowl and stamped the soil and sleet from her shoes as though she'd just walked into the home of one of her worst critics.

'Any more latecomers?' Tom hollered theatrically. The story was that he'd worked his way up to whoremaster by his own endeavours and good-fortune, but he had the bark of a carnival man or a royal herald or the worst kind of actor, who thought the trade was all about bellowing so loud that the words were rendered meaningless. His parlour was partitioned by a bland yellow cloth, like a theatrical curtain; Aphra smelled cheap stagecraft. She shook her head.

'Then shut the door, before the cold freezes our bollocks off! Be kind and think of my loss of earnings. Pounds, shillings, and pence, madam! Pounds, shillings, and pence!' She slammed the door, grudgingly, but Tom wasn't done with her. 'I've seen you before, I'm sure. Are we graced by a famous face' – she shook her head brusquely – 'or some courtly lady? I've been permitted entry to any number of aristocratic openings in my time.' Laughter broke from the mouths of men; she gave them an enigmatic – if embarrassed – smile.

Corinthian Tom coughed out some phlegm before resuming, and she took advantage of the lull to insinuate herself alongside the other woman, thinking of safety in numbers; also she was quite handsome – chestnut-haired, thin-hipped, and prettily scarred on her face – but Aphra was ignored. Her would-be companion kept her hands and cheek pressed to the wall, one ear listening to the rhythms of the whoremaster's speech, the other to the silent cadences of the building.

'Now,' Tom declaimed, 'where were we?' He was an enormous ham. He was solid meat, feigning delicacy; he was an actor, feigning high-rank; too many clothes and jewels, too many gestures, too many words. 'The Jesuitess!' someone shouted. 'Show her!' came another call, and soon hands were clapping and feet stamping to make a ragged chorus of demand. Compared to Tyburn it was so innocent.

Tom, his scarf flapping, his green coat reflecting candle light, skips into the air to find a perch on a chairseat. Not just to make himself taller, or better command his audience, this is a leap into the heart of his story. Overdone it may be, but he's good at it. He makes it look easy.

'Yes! The Jesuitess!' he barks, resuming his interrupted prologue. 'Now, we have heard this name before. It has been granted, in some sections of Protestant society, to any number of orders of holy women, to Christ's brides, to those who offer their bodies and their maidenhoods up to the most sacred of Catholic devotions. To' – he breaks, gasps, teeters on his chair. 'To nuns, good gents, good ladies. To fucking *nuns*. To *this*.' His arms rise to a peak over his head and become a whimple. He half-parades on the seat of the chair, taking step upon step without ever reaching the edge, his shambling legs pretend-caught on the folds of heavy skirts. 'To gangs of frustrated old biddies and little girls who lie each night below the crucifix but whose hearts would stop if a real man's prick were ever shown naked unto them. These plump-arsed waddling birds, are they the equals of the Jesuits? No, never! The one lies awake of a night plotting the deaths of kings, he can spin from his philosophy perfect lies to justify any Papal atrocity, he dangles the destinies of nations on puppet-strings' (now his arms and legs dance in a marionette parody, before he spits) 'The *Jesuit*, terror of all Godly men! And the other? The nun? The little sister of mercy? *She* lies awake of a night *fucking herself up the arse with a candle!*

'The Jesuitesses? Do me a favour!' (and his voice skips from Cockaigne bawdiness to the gravel mutter of a preacher) 'What we have here, good people, is something altogether more diabolical. A creature with the wits and malignance of the Jesuit, but the body and the guile of a woman.'

Aphra found her legs and spine were contorting from the pressure of standing and listening. She grumbled and shuffled a wider space round herself, enjoying seeing the tide of bodies ripple away from her. Most other eyes stayed focused on the scene, on the performance; if she was running this house she would have planted pickpockets to take advantage of these distracted moments.

Corinthian Tom continues, clambering from the seat to balance tiptoed on the back of the chair: 'I wouldn't care to say that the Jesuitess is a true woman. Chirurgeons from around London, from the Royal court, from one end of this island to the other, have been summoned here to inspect her, learned men from Oxford and Cambridge, the greatest brain-priests and thinkers of our age, and they are – to a man – baffled. I have sworn depositions from the masters of a dozen colleges that her *physiognomy* – for the benefit of our Surreysiders, that means her body, don't get impatient gents, you'll see it soon enough! – her physog is improperly ordered. She has parts and organs where those parts and organs have no right to be, yet she is in no outward way imperfect.' He contorts himself, making an easy deformity in his spine, extending his arms to twice their natural length and plucking at the throats of the closest spectator. Ape-like, he capers, prancing on the wobbling edge of the chair, but he doesn't fall.

'Nor does she speak any language known to our finest scholars. Could it be that the wisest minds in Christendom are as hopeless fools, that all those retorts have shrunk their brains as well as their pricks? It's' – a smile – 'not impossible.' One hand now scratches his scalp, the other his arse, and there's more laughter at the dunce. He throws off the idiot face and makes a devil-mask.

'So where has she come from, if not from nature, if not from God? Could even the Prince of Darkness' – (he makes horns of his thumbs, by his temples) – 'conceive such a beautiful monster? Or perhaps it is sinful men? There is in the world a certain city called Rome, and embedded in this city is a smaller city called the Vatican, and it is said that under the Vatican is a tinier city yet, the flea on the back of a flea. Here the Jesuits perform their science, to remake men in their own image. Ladies, those gents of a more delicate disposition, you should cover your ears, this won't be pretty – oh, come, we're not all fishwives, someone must cover their ears! You, yes sir, you sir! You look like you'd wilt at what I have to say, do it for my sake. Right then, do it and I'll halve the price for you. No? Suit yourself.

'So in the pits of the Vatican, the most vile practices are imposed on willing and unwilling females alike, all to make them gravid with a new and miscegenated human species! Women are said to couple with apes! With snakes! With pigs! I warned you, don't say I didn't! It's too late to go pale now, madam! Women are even said to couple with machines, to give birth to babes that are half-flesh and half-metal. They would raise artificial men, called *homunculi* or – in the language of science, *androids* – as an unnatural army dedicated to the Hierophant of Hell. Could our Jesuitess be such a creature? You'll have to judge for yourselves, if you dare, and if you can pay.'

And he leaps, tumbling through the air, leaving the chair to teeter and finally topple in a corner, while the acrobat twirls at his zenith and descends softly to land on tiptoes and bow, and proffer his hat, the bowl held out, its lips a dry and empty oval –

There were mild grumbles as the assembly reached for the purses. Even Aphra, who was spending someone else's money, made the ritual noises of complaint.

He becomes good-natured, sharp-tongued, prancing Tom again, and makes a flourish of his body, a death-rattle of his tongue. 'Be warned sirs, you may look but you must not touch. One of our more' – he mimes a jug – '*excitable* regulars, a certain Mr Perkin, was lately roused by lust and other more tangible spirits' – jug-jug – 'and thought to introduce her to his particular pleasures. But she would have none of it and did him a grievous injury. We call him *Miss* Perkin now, and we keep his Mr Perkin in a pickle pot – stop wincing, sirs! I say a pot but I mean a thimble – stop grinning, madam!'

Aphra flattened her lips, but Tom ploughs on regardless: 'Are these walls strong enough to hold her? They say she broke skulls and tore off arms when she first introduced herself to London society. Imagine, good sirs, good ladies, that you were parading down that street on that cold morning not many weeks ago, that your head was full of unsleeping thoughts, and – for some reason accounted only by God – you could find inspiration only among the sights and calls and scents of Westminster's most whorish, poorish, and villainous alleys. Why then, you might have seen her appear from the aether in a galvanic *flash*!' – as one, the lights on this side of the parlour are extinguished (impressive for amateurs, but still, Aphra scoffed, a cheap trick) – 'of dark and Popish magic.'

Now the only illumination in the parlour is the blonde light that falls through the partition curtain. Tom himself is cast into darkness, and his voice shrivels into a whisper.

'You would be terrified by this brutal and most unnatural explosion, and more frightened still when you saw the costume of the creature that emerged once the smoke had settled, for she was dressed in Jesuitical black and armed with a knife blessed for the purposes of regicide. The violence she met out to those who would greet her made her intentions transparent. By good fortune and God's will there were strong plain Englishmen on hand to restrain her, so that now she is no longer a danger to anyone outside this room, but you, ladies and gentlemen, are trapped inside with her...'

And as Tom talks, the shadow play unfolds. Through the fuzzy layers of light and fabric, she appears, stumbling into the yellowed oval at the centre of the curtain. The silhouette, indistinctly nude and feminine, pulls up abruptly as if commanded to a halt, then sways gormlessly. At the next inaudible order she shuffles one way, then the other, displaying her diffuse profile. Sweet music flutters up from the edges of the room. The shadow-woman lets her arms dangle and never raises her hands from her sides, so she seems disarmed, helpless below the shoulder. More female figures, somehow firmer and heavier in the same light, flutter in from both sides of the curtain. They trill round the woman at the passive centre, cooing like songbirds. They dress her in clothing plucked from the invisible edges of the parlour. Once the costume is complete, they twitter away to those same edges, leaving her solitary and presentable.

'Ladies and gentlemen,' says Tom, his prologue slipping to its end, where fewer words are needed, 'I give you the scourge of Christendom. The Jesuitess!'

And the curtain falls, and brightness wells again in the parlour, and the woman is revealed.

In the long silence that followed, Aphra found herself staring not at the woman, not at her face or her lips, but at the line of spittle that had drooled up from her throat and threatened to break and drip. Watching the build-up her heart had sunk – she had for a moment resigned herself to the prospect of a children's dumb-show, with the Jesuitess wringing all the familiar shadows of birds, rabbits and steeples out of the movement of her hands – but this had an altogether different quality of disappointment. She recalled her slippery discomfort at Tyburn.

'Is she drugged?' someone piped up from the crowd.

'I fear so,' bellowed Tom. 'It's better, you'd agree, than keeping her in chains.' He had found a staff from somewhere, tipped with a bulbous metal sphere, which he brought down on the knuckles of a hand that reached excitedly across the line of partition.

'Can we hear her speak?' came another voice, as plaintive as the first. 'I want to hear her speak.'

'Well,' Tom responded, turning inquisitively to the woman who shuddered under his gaze but still didn't make to move or protest. The pimp's fingers tickled along the holes of an imaginary flute, and Aphra's lips curled, a childhood memory stained. 'Will you speak for us? No? Will you sing something in your bird voice, my pretty black canary?'

The Jesuitess didn't respond.

She wasn't, in spite of Tom's mendacious prologue, a great beauty. She was in fact rather ugly, albeit of the kind of wide-eyed heavy-jawed ugliness that Aphra found *differently attractive*. She was only a little taller than Aphra herself, though much leaner, and nothing in her appearance would have given the mob pause in more placid times. They had dressed her in black, but the clothes were worn ill-matched and ill-fitting, the closest the House of the Infernal could find to a uniform that had either been stolen or never existed outside the rapidly-grown legend of the Jesuitess. The blackest thing about her was her hair, worn loose and straight down to her shoulders; otherwise she looked pale and harmless. She didn't move when the curtain came down, not at first; her eyes shuffled from left to right, over the latest gang of baffling faces, finding nothing there to intrigue her. She lost interest, and tilted her head down to inspect her fingers. Then she slumped onto the daybed that ran against the back wall and sat there listlessly, with her legs crooked, her arms dangling, her eyes and mouth gaping.

Whatever the House was putting in her food, it had left her with enough wit to lick, after a proper pause, the spittle off her lips. She made a contented, idiot smile. Aphra almost screamed: *Why not put in her shackles and leave us in no doubt?! Was she really so formidable that you had to destroy her before putting her on display? Why not kill her, gut her, and parade her parts around the country?* There were held breaths in the dark, and she hoped that at least some among them shared her offence; no, all she sensed was a slight discontent that Corinthian Tom had exaggerated a wretch into a miracle. What else did they expect? He was a *pimp*.

A body – the taller woman, she guessed – moved between her and the object of her attention. She had the chance to look away, in that moment, but didn't take it. For all their disappointment, they were fascinated, she was fascinated. No, this 'Jesuitess' wasn't a monster or a beauty or remarkable, but her audience made her marvellous with their hungry eyes. Aphra found it unbearable. It was unconscionable that this woman – whoever she might be – should be a slave.

That made her afternoon's business all the harder.

'No,' Corinthian Tom intones sadly, as the display draws to a close, 'she will not sing to-day.'

In ones and twos the audience dispersed, some out into the winter streets, some to spend more of themselves in the warmer crevices of the house. The Jesuitess, having done nothing but occasionally hum or scratch herself or fail to rise off the daybed, was concealed behind the curtain again and then removed – no doubt to some less pleasant cell where she was kept between shows. Corinthian Tom retreated from the parlour, shucked off his coat and his wig, then turned and seemed unsurprised to find Aphra Behn had followed him. She stared at the man, with his props. He said nothing to her, but began to wipe the greasepaint from his cheeks with a cloth.

'Who is she really?' Aphra said leisurely. 'Some poor girl off the boat from Ireland? Didn't like the work you had lined up for her so you've made her into a freakshow instead?'

Tom didn't reply until his face was naked. He was older than he contrived to appear. 'No,' he replied. When he wasn't performing, his tone was clipped, as was any man's whose business offended against the public good. 'She's what I said. Be mad to claim I'd got the Jesuitess if she wasn't the genuine article. They could tear the place down. Lose my livelihood. I'd be mad.'

'They?'

'Anyone who wants a crack at the Papists. Sir Edmund Berry Godfrey, thou art avenged.'

Aphra was open to the possibility that her intelligence was wrong, that Tom was only a bluff for the real pimps who ran this house, who were altogether more anonymous and perhaps more respectable; his colour and vitality distracted the eye from their indistinct grey. It was said there had been more than one Corinthian running this house over the years, and he might just be the latest user of the name, but she couldn't imagine him settling here long without some stake of his own. Like all bad actors, he was looking for the day's take.

She forced a flirty little smile and asked, 'She speaks no English, you say?'

'Not a word. Not any tongue we know. Nothing moves her. Not even insults.'

'If she speaks no English, then am I right to assume that your stories aren't wholly true? That she wasn't heard to shout *Die heretics, in the name of Holy Mother Rome* or *Out of my way you dogs, I am here to kill your king and put a tyrant on the throne* or even *I will do for you as we did for that meddling magistrate*? That these might, in fact, be inventions?'

'*Embroidery* is the word I'd use. We didn't start the stories. You must know what playhouse gossip is like.' He grinned at her, and – while he grinned – he took out some of his teeth. So, she was recognised. 'Thought I knew you. You're Aphra Behn, the famous wit. Go on, say something funny.'

'That will take time, sir, and money. I'll be as witty as you like if you care to pay for it.'

'Yeah? I should be coining off the likes of you. *Actresses* already have one foot in the whorehouse. Look to your Nell Gwyns and Elizabeth Barrys, they're kept women both. You're not even that, you just put the pretty words in their mouths. Is that your business here, Mistress Behn?'

Aphra shook her head, she hoped coquettishly. Corinthian Tom deflated into the nearest chair. His skin had the swell and the odour of long-extinct arousal, as if the business of the house had been slowly poisoning him over the years until he could no longer take pleasure from his surroundings. That made things easier. When she produced and dropped the purse, she made sure it landed on his lap. The coins jangled.

'I want to buy her,' she said.

⇒ Chapter 13: *Voodoo Honey* ⇐

The child was nameless, or rather no two accounts could agree about it; the same was true of her age, and even her sex was in doubt, as one described her as a boy. Most thought of her as Polish. The most detailed reports said she came from Kraków. Dating the precise year was difficult, but it was winter, definitely winter, because she had been walking on the river, on delicate ice. Some said it broke, some said she slipped, one suggested that she had been intentionally drowned. Only once she was dead did the accounts converge.

Her body, blue with cold and bloated with water, was dragged and taken home, so she could be buried. She woke on the way back, before her parents had even heard the dreadful reports; she spent the next week coughing out water, trembling, unable to speak. She sat dazed, staring into nowhere as if contemplating the void of death she had escaped. When she found her voice again, it was clear that she had lost her wits. She no longer recognised her home, her family, or her friends, and her mother and father became convinced that whatever spirit now animated the child it was no longer their daughter. She was lost to them. They sold her possessed corpse to a carnival.

With a new name and spurious title, she became famous. She toured Europe with the show, attending on nobility and even royalty as her reputation grew. She spoke in a child's voice and a dozen languages, spelling out visions of the times yet to come. In her madness she had become an oracle. No one understood the nature of her pronouncements, but wasn't that expected of any prophet? What to her family had seemed hysteria became wisdom in the public gaze. Fakes and imitators cropped up in her wake, until it was no longer possible to tell which of the many performers was the original little girl. One day she fell silent, uttering no more prophecies and no more pentecosts, and the stories began to dry up. It was said she starved herself, but her painfully thin body still refused to expire, as if death itself had rejected her. Three decades had passed since the river gave her up, but she was still insane, and still – despite the gap of years – unaged, a child indeterminately young.

Cousin Greenaway couldn't help but imagine the timeships of the Great Houses as being like ships of the sea; and as she grew acclimatised to her routine journeys back and forth across the channel, she found the vessels of her enemies turning comfortable in her imagination. They might be friendly old hulks, like this one now carrying her back to London docks, the *Lady Newcastle*. True, there were warships whose dismal profiles she'd spotted on the horizon on occasion, and which – even when only distant grey dots – seemed to bristle with invisible cannon and the prospect of violence. She had never, thank the Grandfather, seen one of those up close. But there must be timeships like the *Lady*, whose only threat was in their uncertain seaworthiness and ominously creaking timbers, which were pregnant with mundane cargoes and sickly passengers, whose berths were haunted by the presences of a hundred wambled journeys. Nothing that people called a home, nowhere *lived in*, could be entirely awesome.

The others dreaded the timeships, but could barely describe them. Hateman had tried to explain, first by getting her to imagine ships that sailed through the air, and beyond that, between the bodies in the heavens. They were simple enough to conceive, but then it became complicated, and the pictures Hateman tried to paint were vague. She described machines that could travel *under* the solid world, not merely burrowing through the Earth but through the fundamental terrain on which the world rested; vessels that didn't simply put in to port but were themselves the entirety of the port, all its peoples and all its stories; so that the whole of life itself might only be the shadows cast by the ships as they passed before the sun.

Erasmus had also tried to explain ~ *The timeships of the Great Houses are like your own memories come to life* ~ but how could she explain Erasmus? His presence became harder to reveal to her cousins with each passing day, with every moment she had failed to declare him looking increasingly like a deliberate concealment. Eight years had gone by since she'd taken her *loa*, for her if not for Mother Sphinx and the others, who still spent much of their lives sleeping outside of time. He hadn't been much of a presence at first, but gradually he had rediscovered a voice inside her. He was a part of her now, not merely a rider or a temporary possession by a friendly spirit, but a living knot under her skin. She found herself dreaming of wondrous and impossible lands that seemed – on first sight – totally natural to her, and unsurprising. *Part of me now is an invisible insect, tied into my flesh and bone more tightly than any church wedding.* It didn't feel remotely ridiculous. In fact, it made her feel safe.

She was still young, even now, and looked younger. Possibly this was a side effect of her possession, but she doubted it. She knew unnatural youth when she saw it, whether it was in the faces of her cousins met again after a year for her, a moment for them, or in that of Nathaniel Silver, whose retarded ageing was becoming noticeable even to him. Not that he had expressed such thoughts to his confidants, not even to Alice Lynch who had followed him to Paris, but like so many of his resentments it was ever more apparent. He had become sullen since Salomon's House and his forced employment by *le Pouvoir*. Once Greenaway had recovered from the infinitesimal, she found she was still tasked with observing him, more closely than ever now that they'd learned of his connection to the Homeworld. He was no longer the opportunity they had hoped, though Greenaway found it hard to conceive of him as the danger they imagined. If he was somehow in the thrall of the Great Houses, then he betrayed no sign of it. Alice, who knew him better than anyone, believed he was his own man, and Greenaway carried that intelligence to the Faction. The family had agreed that he must be watched and studied, at least until his loyalties became plain. Life as a cousin turned out to be little different from life as a little sister, and she had still found no cause to use her whip in anger or self-defence.

No, it was Erasmus who kept her safe as she travelled back and forth between England and France. So many of her fellow passengers saw a timid young woman travelling alone and marvelled. *Do you think it's safe and proper to be abroad without a companion?* they asked in astonished, querulous voices. 'I have to,' she replied sincerely. 'My husband is dead. I have no one else.'

But the risks are incredible, a young and – if I may say so – attractive woman such as yourself, unguarded and unchaperoned. Anything could happen!

'I have prayed. I'm sure one of Christ's saints walks beside me and will protect me.' She would give a twinkling smile then, and add, 'And my virtue keeps me safe also.' That usually put them off, that small hint of pious mania. The last case had been her trip out to France, when a respectable and elderly couple had tried to persuade her that she would be safer sleeping in their bed on the crossing. She didn't mind, these types never became aggressive; at worst their disappointment turned to wheedle, and they distracted her from a journey that was becoming familiar and wearisome.

She had requested that the shrine be moved permanently to Paris, but Mother Sphinx herself had refused. Since Salomon's House, Faction Paradox had grown much more cautious, afraid of attracting the eyes of its enemies. Cousin Hateman tried to explain to her why such a *complex space-time dislocation* would create trouble, and she had been sceptical until Erasmus had concurred in the recesses of her mind; the pilots, the children of men, feared the Houses as much as the Faction. Besides, there were practical considerations: Silver might become suspicious if she were constantly at his side, and it would make monitoring his communications a lot harder. Despite – or perhaps because of – the Cambridge fiasco, there were still many scholars in England who wanted to keep in touch with the Magus. That the Service were seeking him made their interest more furtive, but in no way discredited him. He still wrote letters daily. *Le Pouvoir*'s agents carried all but the most secret and the most sensitive. These he entrusted to Alice Lynch, and it was simplicity itself for Greenaway to intercept them. She had become a courier on their behalf, Silver's personal *Thurn und Taxis*, ferrying messages across the sea and returning with replies.

He had written at least twice to Nicholas Plainsong, but had received no reply. The Faction had no idea where the boy had disappeared to, and Greenaway entrusted the letters to other hands who might be better placed to find him, but she had heard nothing. She had a bundle with her now, in a pouch that she kept taped to her stomach using a sticky band that left irritable red marks on the skin. She came up impatiently onto the deck that morning, standing at the prow as the London docks drifted leisurely towards the still body of the *Lady Newcastle*, to embrace her.

The docks stank, as always, and were uncommonly sullen. She still saw signs of the old devastation on the waterfront, the burned-out or crumbled sites seeming curiously dignified among new or tattily-repaired warehouses. The silence was, she expected, a condition of the Popish paranoia that was gripping the nation. It was the talk of Paris already: *the fuckoffs have gone mad (again)!* There were the usual shrieks and catcalls as she disembarked, yells of *cunt!* and *Catholic slut!* and – if anyone presumed she was English – *traitor!* She'd brought a parasol in case anyone fancied chucking vegetables or rotten fruit or dead fish, but these didn't come. Europe was presumed thoroughly Catholicised, and anyone returning from the continent was believed contaminated; but the docksiders seemed oddly cowed this time, as if afraid that any newly-landed ship would open its belly to disgorge file upon file of the French troops that (it was widely believed) would be required for the Duke, the Queen, or even the King to maintain public order after the change of regime.

Unrained on by excrement or offal, Cousin Greenaway strolled along the waterfront until she spotted Cousin Suppression, waiting for her with a horse and trap. He was reading another one of his *Homeworld Chronicles*, oblivious to his surroundings. She was almost upon him before he looked up. She took his hand; it clenched. She felt the elation of being back in the bosom of the family.

'How are things?' she asked.

He stowed the thick pamphlet in his pocket. 'Bad,' he told her. He hadn't changed. Suppression was still older than her, though only by a few years. She had already overtaken Amphigorey and Hateman while they slept. Soon only Mother Sphinx would be older than her, but Mother Sphinx was older than everyone.

Suppression lifted her onto her seat on the trap, and then took his place to drive them the short way to the ruin where the shrine was concealed. He didn't elaborate on the situation; in fact, he didn't talk at all. Greenaway knew better than to try to engage him in conversation, even if she wanted to. One of the few things she liked about her constant travels was the solitude and the silence, where she had no voice to listen to other than her own and that of Erasmus. She was growing accustomed to that lack of companionship.

She turned to her uncompanion now. Erasmus stirred in her head and her heart; he didn't command her, but when he woke out of their shared wholeness he made her acutely aware of the extent and potential of her body; he would never be completely familiar and settled in her physical shape – so unlike his natural one. Every inch of her skin, inside and out, bristled as if rediscovering that it could feel.

~ *Will you declare yourself this time, Cousin Greenaway?* ~

No, we're too far gone for that. They might think me a traitor to the Grandfather.

~ *Does it occur to you that by taking me as your* loa, *you might have genuinely betrayed him?* ~

They'd had this argument before; she'd resolved it in her own mind. Nothing you've done has compromised my loyalty to the order. We all have secrets. Suppression has secrets, but I don't ask them of him. Hateman has secrets. Amphigorey would have secrets if he didn't talk in sleep. Christ, where did we leave things with them last time? *They* remember. I never do.

~ *You parted on good terms with them all* ~

That's probably the easiest way, is it not? I'm getting used to this.

~ *Remember, you're their equal now* ~

In the ranks of the family perhaps, but they all know things that I don't. I only ever stumbled into becoming a cousin. I'll never be a mother. Hateman knows that. She looks at me like she knows one day she'll be a mother but I won't because I'm not good enough. It's sympathy. I don't need her sympathy.

~ *Do you want to be a mother?* ~

I don't know. What are the other options? She pulled a face, and Suppression – his back to her – didn't notice. Let's talk about Silver. Have you reached any more conclusions?

~ *No* ~ *I see him through your eyes and can only make surmises as you do* ~ *If he had the egg it would be different* ~ *I could monitor him* ~

And influence him still?

~ *Perhaps, but you would know* ~

We don't know where the egg is. Plainsong has it, that's all we know.

~ *It's programmed to find his way back to him* ~

It's been lost for eight years.

~ *It's patient* ~

But are we any closer to knowing what the Great Houses want with him? They must have some purpose, but I can't see it. He's working on whatever projects *le Pouvoir* order. I can't see how that would affect the cosmic order, one way or another.

~ *But have you noticed how he resents* le Pouvoir*'s instructions, and tries to moderate them if he imagines they might be put to selfish or violent ends?* ~ *Even without the egg, he has a reserve of knowledge and a formidable grasp on application, but he withholds this where he can* ~ *What does this tell you?* ~

That he resists. That he thinks more of his work than to let it serve the profit and power of Earthly estates. That he's a good man, but I believe we knew that already.

~ *It says to me that he will not allow himself to be used* ~ *He is innocent in many ways, but he is no one's fool* ~ *He understands that his work has its implications, and his sponsors don't always have the best of intentions* ~

So?

~ *So I wonder if his impact on the world is less to do with his methods and philosophies than...* ~

Than what?

~ *Than the fact that he lives at all* ~

You mean, it might simply be that he exists. That he changes everything by breathing?

~ *One human being, a point so small that he might as well not exist* ~ *He may be their secret doorway into our history* ~ *And once he is opened, who knows what he'll let in?* ~

But the trap was slowing as they approached the hollow shell of the building where the shrine had, these last eight years, concealed itself. Greenaway bade Erasmus to recede back into her mind; their conversation could wait until later, maybe when she slept and was free of her waking anxieties. Once stopped, Suppression lifted her down from her seat, but put a restraining hand on her shoulder while he glanced up and down the length of the row.

'Be careful when you go in,' he warned her gruffly. 'Make sure no one sees you.'

This was a new precaution. 'Why?' she asked.

He shrugged, not ignorance but a general incomprehension of the ways of humanity. 'Strange days,' was all he'd say, but when she pressed, he added: 'Half the country's afraid of terror cults that don't exist. It makes life harder for the ones that do.'

'I'll be careful,' she promised. While he tended to the horse, she slipped down the side of the ruin, running her fingers along the wall and seeking its impression. It was secure, comfortable with its old wounds, the blackened wood now healed, the stone now cool. There was a coy tremor, as if it had once been the object of more than idle curiosity, but those prying eyes had moved on. She glanced up and down the alley, and seeing and sensing no one, ducked under the beams that blocked the entrance and slipped inside.

The interior was little changed in the last three months. The roof was in good repair and hadn't let in much of the autumn or winter, though browned and flattened leaves still carpeted the stone floor. A place like this was designed to trap heat, and light – especially light – so it was brighter and warmer than a casual observer might have imagined. Rats and mice still made their homes here at their own peril, as this was Faction Cat's territory, though the spiders at least were left alone to weave their webs. There was some unspoken truce between the cat and the arachnids, something like respect, or paralysing animosity. The shrine door still sat incongruously at the blunt end of the main chamber. Greenaway's family was sitting at the entrance, on brightly-coloured canvas chairs, waiting for her. They looked up half-heartedly as she approached. They were maskless, and their unhidden faces were disquieted.

One thing had changed, or grown, in her absence. They had begun, after Salomon's House, to set up wood totems around the door to the shrine. At first she'd assumed they were designed purely to ward off the curious, while she was in Paris and the others were in their timeless sleep. They were like witches' hexes, or miniature scarecrows, tiny wood figures with damp strings threaded between their hands. Then others had sprouted, hanging from the more secure beams of the ceiling, dangling lines of leather or weed, knitted with tiny bells. Then came more items, never more than the size of a man's head, but in increasingly strange shapes and material: twisted devices made of meat that never stank or rotted; symbols burned into metal or unmelting ice; relics that might have been dug out of the earth, old coins and teeth and Roman combs spread out in patterns of diabolical significance. The old furniture had been broken up and pushed away to make room for them all on the floor. Eventually she had asked and learned what they were: *loa*-casts. Not *loa* themselves, but totems that symbolised the *loa*, little material bodies in the solid world where they could make their presence felt.

In the past eight years, Faction Paradox had been raising and binding more and more *loa*, in readiness for the coming of the Great Houses. Come the day, these uncanny, un-likely, ugly objects would speak as one, calling out a warning of impending doom. And here they all were, shivering, humming, wailing, bells tinkling and strings thrumming. Cousin Greenaway halted and looked to Amphigorey – fists balled, mouth pursed and frightened, to Hateman – rising from her chair, brisk, concealing her anxieties behind smooth movement, to Mother Sphinx – slow-blinking, brooding, smiling like a subtle thing.

'They're here,' said Cousin Hateman.

Faction Paradox had taken a house-proud young widow from Hornsey St Mary and somehow transformed her into an expert burglar. In Paris, it had been a vital skill to negotiate the complex rookeries where *le Pouvoir* had hidden Nathaniel Silver. Most buildings resented their occupants, the human parasites whom they saw as an essen-tial but intrusive part of their reproductive cycle, and could be persuaded into petty conspiracies against them. It was this skill they needed now, along with Greenaway's natural acquaintance with the customs of England.

So far, the incursion had been causally insignificant, but that could change. Immedi-ately on her return to London, Cousin Greenaway had been put on surveillance, spend-ing three days learning the building that was now the epicentre of the incursion. The next stage was contact. That would give them a better idea of the scale of the threat, though they would have to reveal themselves to the Houses' scout in the process. They didn't put it to the vote until Greenaway was certain of the territory, but they all con-curred. Hateman had spent the meeting scribbling frantic figures and mathematickal formulae on paper scraps – Greenaway was minded of the letters she'd brought to de-liver for Silver, now abandoned and forgotten in her quarters in the shrine – before breaking into a broad, relieved grin.

'Good news,' she had announced. 'It's still statistically very unlikely that they're going to blow up the entire planet. Unless we provoke them,' she'd added as an afterthought.

That evening, three of them gathered shivering below the eaves of the solved house, out of the slow-drifting descent of the snow, but still close enough to feel its tickling cold. Hateman and Amphigorey wore their appalling Faction armour under their clothes, but there had never been an opportunity to find something suitable for Greenaway. She was glad of that; she had no desire to wear that writhing cartilaginous fabric against her skin, nor did she suspect it would provide her with much warmth. They dared not risk moving the shrine at all, not with the possibility of timeships lurking close by in the submundane, so Suppression had stayed with it, and Mother Sphinx – who was more frail in the aftermath of Salomon's House, and was hardly fit for combat – Mother Sphinx had…

Mother Sphinx had wished them all well, given each of them a tiny red stone that turned out to be edible and fruity, and disappeared, her huge silhouette dwindling into the London snow and London fog.

'She doesn't think we have a chance,' Amphigorey opined. The Mother had appeared the least convinced by the plan they'd conceived, and seemed almost on the verge of vetoing it before throwing in her approval.

Hateman had an inkling of what she was up to: 'Maybe she's got something more important to settle.'

'She goes where the *loa* tell her,' Greenaway whispered, but no one was listening to her, and her voice was obscured by an outburst from Amphigorey.

'More important? With the whole of the Second Wave getting medieval on our arses?'

'Yes! We deal with the action, she handles the reaction. Besides, we don't know it's the Second Wave. We don't know anything.'

That was the sentiment they carried as they went into battle. It was midwinter, and night had come early to unsleeping London, but the city kept itself warm, and lit itself with flames in braziers, candles in windows, and the strained reflected half-light from the settled snow. The skins of the whores and costermongers were cast in grey – a bland uniform shade – as were the hides of the passing horses. Greenaway could easily believe that they had stepped onto a spectral battlefield half outside the real. A shrill went up, battle clarion, and Greenaway's heart thumped, but no attack came and the harsh whistling faded into London's raucous symphony.

Erasmus was sleeping inside her. She'd woken him before leaving. He accepted the possibility of her death – and his – stoically. He agreed to come to her aid, if she needed it, though what he could offer was uncertain. He could do nothing that she couldn't.

She touched the front door, prayed to it, solved it. The locks and bolts, flattered by her courtship, politely unfastened themselves while the hinges swung themselves open. The doorkeeper looked up, startled. Hateman was prepared for him. She put a finger to her lips and hushed. He decided that the time was right to curl his body into a tight warm ball and rest on the floor. Faction Paradox closed the door after them, so there would be no draught, no drifting snow to freeze him. They stepped carefully over his murmuring body, mumbling old rhymes he'd last heard at his mother's breast, and slipped into the house.

Once inside and out of public sight, Hateman opened her bag. 'Masks,' she insisted, lifting out the first skull and passing it to Greenaway. The bone-faces were more than a disguise. Greenaway understood something about their shapes disturbed the Home-worlders, and that might give the Faction a little leverage and provide some protection from Homeworlder magic – the capacity to see into the mind and the soul. More than that, they were a diplomatic nicety. They might be at war, but there were still protocols to be observed. She lowered the clean white bone over her head, rediscovering the smell of it, the ancient weight of it, the soft whispers from outside the world that echoed in its cavities.

Greenaway pressed herself to the nearest wall, mouthed questions, learned answers: 'The attic,' she told Hateman. 'She's alone. No one likes to spend time with her.' On her tongue the words sounded lonely.

'Ship activity?'

Greenaway shook her head. 'There's nothing. Just people, coming and going, nothing unusual at all.'

Hateman nodded. 'Can the house make us unnoticed?'

Greenaway asked and was answered. They went through the parlour as a ghost parade, moving like warm drifts of snow through the smoke-filled theatre, home this evening to a live shadow-coupling behind the yellow curtain. Crowds of whooping onlookers parted for the skull-faced marchers, without even seeing them or hearing their tread. The curtain seemed to twitch on an unfelt breeze; the bodies rutting artfully behind it weren't distracted from their routine, and Greenaway imagined that if she tried to touch them her fingers would break like beads of steam against their flesh. She wasn't foolish enough to try.

They found the back stairs, and climbed to the topmost storey and the cramped attic studios where, off-duty, prostitutes of all ages, sexes, and colours chatted, smoked, danced, drank, gambled, and dressed wounds by candlelight. The day of the dead walked unnoticed through their most ordinary intimate scenes. Greenaway, leading her cousins into battle, saw all the small furtive gestures around her, the hidden scowls on sun-starved faces, the lips kissing bluntly to pass apple-slices from mouth-to-mouth, the stray hairs scratched from otherwise smooth legs by rusty blades; she had never felt so separated from the solid world as now.

They arrived at the final door. Greenaway placed gloved palms flat on its surface and heard the tingle of the lock springing open in the back of her head. *Thank you.* The interior was harder to judge; the Homeworlder herself was a blind spot and distorted her impressions, but there was enough of the familiar around her to make out the shape of the hole in the real.

'She's drugged,' Greenaway had reported the previous night, as they finalised their plans for confronting the Homeworlder.

Hateman had shaken her head, her loose hair fluttering from out of the folds of her skull. 'Her biology ought to be able to metabolise natural toxins and narcotics, even in this world. On its own the worst it could do is make her that tiny bit slower. No, she's disorientated by the *loa*. Break their hold over her and she'll recover quickly enough. We have to be ready for that.'

'Why break the *loa* at all? They're our best defence.'

Hateman ran a motherly finger down the ridge of her bone-cheek. 'The *loa* are no defence against the Houses. A timeship would punch a hole through them, though at least we'd be forewarned. But she didn't come in a ship. It's just luck that the *loa* snared her at all.'

There had been no timeship. The Homeworlder had impaled herself into the solid world by other means, cruder in some ways that Greenaway didn't quite understand, subtler in others. She had fallen to Earth where the *loa* caught her in their many webs. The twitching of the strings and the jangling of the bells outside the shrine were the sound of her caught on their lines, tugging helplessly to free herself. Most of their arguments that evening had been concerned with the ship that wasn't there.

'The simplest explanation,' Hateman had volunteered, 'is that they know we're waiting for them and are trying to sneak past the *loa*.'

'Simplest?' Suppression had rumbled – he had the most direct experience of the Homeworld, he knew the most about their minds, or was the least ignorant. 'If there's a spider in *your* way do you try to sneak past it?'

'Sometimes, yeah.'

'Maybe, and this is just a thought, boobs, don't put it down before you've heard it – maybe they've stopped using ships. Maybe the ships have declared independence at last.'

'Big presumption. Possible, but we can't afford to rely on it.'

'It'd make life a lot easier for us.'

'Easier? Are you out of your fucking mind, Amphigorey?! Rogue ships?! Everyone's fucked!'

Mother Sphinx had made the growl at the back of her throat that meant she was about to speak: 'Perhaps' – her mouth was full of tombstones – 'we ought to ask her.'

The Jesuitess was waiting for them on her narrow cot in her narrow room. She didn't move as they glided inside, didn't raise her head or make the faintest sound. Hateman, as the senior member of the party, the armed member, had gone first, and raised her hand to her mask to cover the smell. 'Bloody hell,' she ordered, 'get the window open.' Greenaway went wordlessly to obey.

The quality of the stink was unusual; it wasn't rank or wet or bemerded, as might be expected of a cell or a neglected room. It wasn't from the Jesuitess, who was quite clean, her skin bland and odourless. It must, Greenaway decided after some reflection, be the smell of Tom's poisons seeping out of the Homeworlder's body; one of the Faction's tenets of faiths was that breathing expelled spoiled air from the lungs. Whatever its source, the miasma was dispelled once she'd pulled open the shutters, to let in the clammy London air, the low-hanging soot-clouds, and the babble of the street.

The Jesuitess had been left scraps and stew, which had turned cold and wasted in the bowl. Under the bed, a chamberpot was dry and unused. The bedsheet, though ruffled under the weight of the woman's body, wasn't as crumpled as it might be. The cell's occupant was no longer in the borrowed black costume of her displays, but a gauze-thin cotton nightgown, though she gave no sign of feeling the cold. The body tangible beneath was so unremarkably human that Greenaway dared hope they'd made a mistake, and it was just some harmless innocent who'd blundered into the *loa*'s snares. There was drool on the Jesuitess's lips, glistening under the inspection of candlelight. Greenaway reached instinctively to wipe it away, as she would for a child, but Hateman blocked her and shoved her back towards the door.

'Don't touch her; don't talk to her; stay at the door,' the once-older woman commanded, fear in her voice, fear in the strength of her push. 'Don't look at her if you can help it.' Greenaway couldn't help it, her eyes staring through ivory tunnels to the creature on the bed. *They look so much like us. How can we tell?*

'They're nothing like us,' Suppression had told her. 'They're beyond love and death. They're not born, they're grown on machines, and they don't die, not properly. They just rise again, like... like the Phoenix, but changed.'

'They sound miraculous.'

'*Monstrous*,' Suppression had insisted. 'You should see some of the things they've become. Once they would have grown back looking like ordinary men or women, but since the War started... ' Then he had stopped and refused to say more.

Still, the Jesuitess hardly seemed a monster. Nor was she much of a miracle.

Amphigorey dragged a stool to the middle of the room and sat, facing their prisoner. He was the family's diplomatic specialist; he'd studied in the Empire under Father Raban, which made him the closest they had to an expert Inquisitor. Hateman passed him her bag, then stood aside with her sword hand open and swaying, the blade sheathed in the deep shadow round the edge of the room. Amphigorey kept the bag on his lap as he rifled through it; he didn't want either cousin to notice his erection, though Greenaway knew immediately it was there, she would have known even without Faction training. The Homeworlders were sexless – Greenaway could just about imagine that – but that frigid blankness was said to be powerfully erotic in itself. 'Grandfather help us all,' Amphigorey had told her, 'if they ever work out it could be a weapon.'

Suppression had been more reassuring: 'They won't. It'd never occur to them. Not ever.'

Amphigorey found the token and held it out in front of him, in his delicate fist, carefully not crushing it. It was a wood-cancer, so they'd told Greenaway, cut from the roots of a dead tree, from the soil of another, older world. Its browned, withered tendrils had knitted together in a fugue of tortured growth, sucking the life from its host vegetable. It was irreplaceable now, priceless. 'Look at this,' he instructed.

The Homeworlder blinked, sullen eyes under a sullen brow, under a long fringe of black hair.

Amphigorey would have been smiling, beneath the bone. 'This is called *syrinx*. This is the totem of the *loa* that binds you into the trap of mundane biology and disrupts the language centres of your brain. This is the *loa* of your confusion.' He tightened his fist and the *syrinx* imploded into a fine powder that guttered between his fingers and carpeted the brothel with alien dust.

The Homeworlder's hard jaw twitched, not opening but shuffling side to side.

'You can talk now,' Amphigorey told her, 'but remember, you are bound by other *loa*.'

She breathed hard; it was the first time Greenaway had noticed her breathe, even at the displays under Corinthian Tom's guidance. Without shifting out of her posture, the black-haired woman suddenly looked stronger, more confident, more powerful. Her pupils shifted carefully, assessing her three captors and the shape of the room around them. Hateman raised her sword-arm slightly, a mild warning.

'Do you know who we are?' Amphigorey continued, his voice the same formal tone as before. This was still diplomatic. If she requested a formal introduction, all sorts of odd rules were enforced, *supposedly*. From the way the others talked, the Great Houses had abandoned all their most revered principles and laws the instant they'd felt threatened.

The Homeworlder created a smile. It made her uglier.

'House Paradox,' their prisoner said, at length. Hateman and Amphigorey's unreadable masks exchanged glances, an unexpected frisson Greenaway couldn't understand. The Homeworlder didn't seem to register anything, only smiling deeper and stretching on her cot, rediscovering control of her body after the days under the *syrinx*'s *loa*-bind.

The next question came smoothly: 'Have you had formal dealings with our... House?' It was Hateman who spoke, which wasn't supposed to happen. Greenaway kept herself still, but she had the impression that they'd lost control of the situation already.

'Not really.' The eyes moved again. Something like disappointment on her mouth. 'You're all human, aren't you? Interesting.'

At a gesture from Hateman, Amphigorey continued the planned line of questioning: 'Do you have a name?' She shook her head. 'A title?' Another shake. 'Then we'll call you Homeworlder.'

'No.'

'Then we'll call you nothing.'

'Good,' said *nothing*. Before the next question she chimed in: 'I was caught in temporal deflection trying to materialise. Your *loa*?'

'Yes. They do what we ask of them.'

'Quaint.' Her head went down in monkish devotion, then up again: 'This is what you'll do.'

'You're in no position to –'

'Be *quiet*! This is what you'll do. You'll remove all the restraints and paradoxes around this space-time period. You'll do it immediately. You'll get out of my way. If you don't, I'll destroy you.' She was still smiling. 'Don't trust that I can't. I can.'

There would have been a long silence then, if it hadn't been for the rowdy yells and breakages drifting up from the floors below. Then Hateman chipped in again: 'You're not House Military, are you? You're something else. You're something new.'

~ She's something old *~ But your Cousin Hateman knows that already ~*

'I've said all I need to.'

Another gesture from Hateman sent Amphigorey reeling off a list of their demands. 'This is what you're going to tell us. Where is your ship? Why were you not travelling by ship? What are your strategic and specific purposes on this world, in this century? Do you represent the whole Homeworld, the House Military, or an individual House? Who else is with you and what are your numbers? What are your numbers of ships? Do you have auxiliary support? Some of this we know already, but –'

The Homeworlder cut across him, laughing. 'No, you don't. You know nothing.'

Contempt. That's what the Homeworlders were, she saw, pure contempt.

'Don't laugh at us.' Amphigorey was angry, but containing it well. 'Not when you've burned so many worlds. Not when you're at *our* mercy for once.'

Then suddenly there was no contempt. 'Worlds?' she said, curiously. She looked away. 'Is there a War King at last? Who is he? *What* is he? Dvora?'

Another masked glance between Greenaway's two senior cousins, real confusion in their careless movement. This was going very wrong, but the Homeworlder looked back to them with something like sympathy. 'I don't withdraw my threat. But I'll tell you this. You know nothing about my numbers, my ship, or my superiors, because there aren't any. It's me and me alone, House Nothing. Now get out of my way or I'll destroy you.'

'We can't do that –' Amphigorey's blunt insistence was undercut by another crash and round of yelling from below. Hateman's mask turned, its ragged snout bristling at Greenaway.

'Check that.'

Greenaway bobbed a mild curtsey and withdrew, grateful to leave the tension of the cell, grateful to have a free moment to consult her *loa*. She caught one last glimpse of the tableau of interrogation through the jamb – her cousins poised in unconfessed confusion, the arrogance of their prisoner now sprawling on her prison cot – before the door clicked gently closed. She was afraid it might explode from the pressures building inside.

It was noisier out here, the sounds carrying clearer up the storeys. The air was pocked with unboisterous sounds and joyless shrieks. It might be the casual vandalism of London rowdies out on a spree. It might not be. Her whip uncoiled from the shadow of an empty hand and she made for the stairs.

Erasmus.

~ *Yes* ~

You know something. About the Jesuitess.

~ *Nothing you don't know yourself* ~

There is something. They saw it. I didn't. What's House Paradox?

~ *An old name* ~

How old?

~ *It hasn't been used for hundreds of years* ~ *Since before the Faction left the Homeworld* ~

We started on the Homeworld? I suppose I knew that. What am I missing *now*?

~ *There was a time when the Great Houses didn't bother the rest of the Spiral Politic, except to observe it* ~ *There was a time when the War would have been anathema to them* ~ *And Homeworlders are practically immortal, barring accidents* ~

More retorts and screams rose from below, and from the windows. Chants and crashes were leaking in from the outside, from the front of the house. Greenaway turned away from the stairs, pulled her head off cautiously, and went to the nearest window, leaning out through the gap to look down on the street. A small mob was picketing the façade, directly below her, at the door. A dozen or more men stood in a crescent blocking the entrance and chanting. Behind them others buzzed like flies, dropping out of hiding long enough to hurl stones, bottles, and other objects thrown too quickly through too little light to be described. Spotted, Greenaway reeled back as a brick splintered on the sill by her head.

She looked again, more cautiously. The crescent-men were chanting and stamping. 'Out!' They called. 'Out! Out! Out!'

She risked craning out further and saw the protesting bodies being repelled from the main doors, prodded or shoved back with staffs and makeshift spears. Another figure, faintly flamboyant even in the flattening lantern light and still recognisable as Corinthian Tom, was railing against the mob; he hopped about like a gadfly, ducking punches and kicks with some success, though his imprecations clearly weren't placating them. Perhaps he'd given up and was sarcastically egging them on.

'Out! Out! Out!'

One of the mob grew bold enough to grab at a jabbing spear, which snatched away too slow, was seized and twisted, dragging the pikeman with it. She thought she recognised the doorkeeper, before he was pulled into the crowd and buried under a flurry of fists and footprints. Small pieces of stone clattered around her – they'd seen her again, marking her as a target. A hard-pitched bottle span towards her, still half-full, spilling its content out into the thirsty air; she demolished it with the point of her whip.

Below her the crowd surged, and Tom, his skill with an audience expiring, vanished into a swirl of violence. There were further impacts, crackles of flame and lightning. They were throwing brands now. One went through another window, which began to vent fire. Below her, the clamour of angry voices and destruction gave way to sharper, fiercer sounds – panic – flight – and at the door, a dozen men were piling their way into a building they'd already begun to burn.

'Bring her out! Bring her out! Bring her out!'

~ *Greenaway* ~

Her hand was on the cold wall. Even through fabric, she could taste the house's distress. It didn't fear death; it wasn't alive. Ugliness. That's what it feared, that's what was being visited upon it, the scars cut and burned into its skin, inside and out. The mob, in a way, knew its terrors and were going for the heart of them. I'm sorry. I'm so sorry. A half-dressed man jumped, fell, was thrown from a first storey window – a gaping wound on the house's made-up face – his naked legs flailing even once he'd thumped into the snow.

She turned to run back to her cousins.

~ *Greenaway* ~

We have to get out of here.

~ *Greenaway* ~ *I've calculated a new probability* ~

Later!

~ *We won't have the opportunity later* ~ *It's closer than it's ever been* ~ *Not physically, but this is the optimum moment to recover it* ~

She became irrationally afraid someone might hear Erasmus echo in her head, and restored her mask to muffle him. 'What?' she demanded.

~ *The egg* ~

A moment later, she pushed back through the door of the cell, to find the Jesuitess on her feet, Hateman standing a careful, respectful distance away with her shadow poised ready to strike, while Amphigorey bound their prisoner's hands behind her back. Greenaway could see at once this wasn't going to be adequate, the Homeworlder's insouciant smile told her that, the whole heavy mask of her face gave it away.

'We worked out what's going on,' Amphigorey said, not looking up from his work.

'They want the Jesuitess brought out,' Greenaway confirmed. 'They'll kill you,' she told their smirking prisoner.

'They won't.'

'No, they won't,' Hateman told her. 'We'll make sure of that. Cousin,' she added, voice cooing as she turned to Greenaway, 'we'll fight our way out. You've avoided this up to now, but we're going to have to hurt these people, and maybe even kill some. I'm sorry. For the Grandfather, you understand.'

That hardened her heart. *Don't you know how much I've killed already, for the Grandfather?* 'No,' Greenaway said solemnly. She took off her mask and threw it onto the Homeworlder's bed. The Jesuitess pursed her lips, staring at the exposed human face as though Greenaway were naked, as though she were food.

In the passage beyond the door, the window burst inwards, showering wood and brick pieces and clumps of flaming pitch into the wooden attic-space, which was rapidly eaten by fire.

≡ Chapter 14: *Doctor Bendo – Cures All* ≡

Proctor Harrow was not the first man to be hanged in the town of New Beulah, but he was certainly the first to be hanged more than once, more than twice, more than a dozen times. The settlement had been founded a little over fifteen months earlier, by a sect who had – in raising Harrow, an orphan – nurtured a sinner in their bosom, and transported a serpent across the ocean into their fresh paradise. He and another youth were accused of persistent sodomy; both were strung up by their necks, but only Harrow was still alive when they were cut down. The citizens of New Beulah took this as a sign that God wanted Harrow to suffer more than one death, so they tried again, and again, and again.

They were gallows-mad in New Beulah, according to Dufresne's account. The old French trapper was the only reliable eye-witness to the many killings of Proctor Harrow, and sold his account to le Pouvoir *before he died. He fancied that the settlement had been driven crazy by the quality of the light, the season, and the strange, unsettling continent. Being the sternest of Puritans, they had done away with the celebration of Mass Days, and their relentless, frustrated attempts to do away with Harrow now became – in the Frenchman's eyes – a new and insane midwinter ritual. His refusal to die grew more offensive with each fresh survival.*

Eventually, Proctor Harrow had escaped and fled into the warped and mapless interior of America. He may have died; he may have found a life among the Indians or as a hermit; he certainly became a story, the white man with the scarred throat who could lead strangers on the safe paths through the wild land. Those stories were still in circulation almost two-score years later, while New Beulah was withered and gone, its people extinct, its houses overgrown by wilderness, its spent gallows wreathed in green.

Stars had fallen from Heaven to decorate the Earth. Glistening, they caught her eye. *Broken glass*, she realised, and trampled over them. Doctor Bendo's purse, concealed in her skirts, bashed carelessly against her hips. This must be what a scrotum feels like, swollen and ungainly on the thigh – the wrong side admittedly, but such deformities were not unknown. Among the skills attributed to the good doctor was an ability to reshape the human form at will beneath his magic blades, turning men into women, women into men, and both into beasts. *Horseshit*, he wasn't even a real doctor! Not that you could tell that to his army of supplicants; women queued for his ministrations, to be cured of the diseases or infertilities that were in the main – Aphra suspected – their husbands' fault.

That was the public face of Alexander Bendo, the *soi-disant* Doctor. He'd been sent down from Trinity in disgrace, despite his brilliance. No wonder he preferred the company of low-born riff-raff and levellers; the poltroons of Cambridge had denied him his proper station in life. He had been recruited to the Service anyway – *they* at least were prepared to concede the superiority of his intellect and his hands. He had taken Astraea under his wing after Salomon's House. He mocked her airs and tradecraft at every turn, yet also seemed to admire them. It was hard not to feel belittled by his praise nor find crumbs of comfort in his scorn.

After eight years' acquaintance, Aphra Behn was still unsure what to make of her Master in the Service. She approached his wagon with a sense of ambivalence, with his moneybag scraping against the curve of her thigh. It hung heavier than the package that she carried from the House of the Infernal, the large but cloud-light bundle swinging loose at her side. She hadn't quite succeeded in her mission, but at least she could bring Bendo a prize of sorts in consolation.

The sun was long sunk – it was midwinter, so who could say for certain that it would rise again in the morning? – and Bendo was no longer performing miracles for the crowds. His wagon was parked in a crevice between warehouses, either one of which might conceal his true headquarters. His assistant, Serviceman or stooge, shone the light for her up the steps to the door. This was the entry she'd turned to – and found open – in her despond after Tyburn. It was decorated with crude stick pictures of swell-bellied women, crudely painted in pink lines so their breasts looked like sleep-shadowed eyes with drug-pricked irises, drooping over the promise of distended stomachs. The wagon itself was a wooden womb, vaster inside than the narrow exterior suggested, where Doctor Bendo's works gestated. To step inside was to return to Salomon's House, lifted whole from the Cambridgeshire hills, squeezed into a tiny box, and set on wheels. It was a trick, of course.

Mirrors, Aphra guessed. The tight and musty interior of the wagon – the birth-channel – was wreathed in gloom and an air of stale sweetness that distracted the senses. Disorientating mirrors fooled the unwary into slipping through a secret door into one of the adjacent buildings, decorated in the style of Salomon's House. The furniture may well have come from Cambridge, and the windows revealed pictures that – from a distance – seemed authentic views across the Gogs. She did not care to inspect them closely. She made her way to Bendo's *laboratorium*.

No one challenged her. Indeed, she saw no one. She was expected.

The workroom of the alchemist was exactly as she imagined it. She suspected that it was contrived to appear so – a stone-walled dungeon (this was deception, there were wood beams beneath grey paint), lined with workbenches on which a dozen and one experiments all seemed to be taking place at once, all involving bubbling fluids and pots of frothing green scum. The distorted ephemera of nature were gathered in bottles, from ill-nourished flowers to deformed and pickled babies, while some pots contained clockwork automata in the form of tiny humans, who danced and cavorted and bared their arses at curious eyes. Bendo claimed he was trying to breed them. Aphra had seen this all many times before, and grew less impressed with each new visit. She slung her package onto the nearest free surface, mindful that it would be impolitic to disrupt his *experiments* and risk his temper. His latest arcane decoration was the rug, placed at the centre of the room and squeezing the rest of the contents into the margins. It was black, and chalked with astrological symbols and intersecting geometries. Bendo had pinned it down with pots that she'd almost dislodged. The largest, in the middle of what she felt idly must be a chart, was a Russian *samovar*.

The jars would contain *fruits* of some description, albeit not the kind that hung from branches. Not all of Bendo's boyish paraphernalia was meant to trick the unwary; he genuinely believed a lot of his own twaddle. These pregnant pots would hold blackened fingerbones, mystic substances, and shrivelled horrors – not the sort of child that any woman would want to heave and squeeze into the world.

Bendo had asked Astraea, once and once only, if she cared to avail herself of his skill at treating the barren. She had fixed him with her sternest glare: 'Sir,' she told him, 'my country way should be a one-way path. I would rather it were used for deliveries only, and would not care to make it an exit.' She had thought it tremendously witty at the time.

Curious, she lifted the lid of the teapot, peered inside, and was met with an unexpected glare that set her blinking and put a short-lived green haze over her eyes. She looked again, cautious this time, but the steady light was still settled in the guts of the pot. It was a tiny sun, though not hard enough to blind her. It was elongated, not quite a sphere, and it was solid. She dipped her hand in to touch it. It was an egg.

~ *Aphra Johnson?* ~

She snatched her hand back and slammed the lid. For a moment she crouched on the rug in confusion. Her fingers, where she'd made contact, were unmarked, untingling, unwarm. She licked them cautiously with the tip of her tongue. Her skin was unscented, finely-ridged, mildly salty from the effort of walking to-and-fro about London. *God's ballocks!* This is some trick of Alex's. He's watching me through a spyhole and projecting his voice like a mountebank with a puppet.

She pulled open the lid again. This time she didn't even have to touch.

~ *Aphra Johnson?* ~

'Don't fuck me around Alex, you know I'm not in the mood.'

~ *We are not Alexander Bendo* ~

'This whole thing's just a way of getting me on my knees, you dirty sod.'

~ *Take this with you* ~ *The egg does not belong to him* ~ *It must be restored to the one for whom it was made* ~

'If you want to talk, come out and show yourself.'

~ *He would be grateful to you* ~ *If you refuse to help we can show you terrible things* ~

That got to her, somehow. 'Terrible things? I've already seen enough of them! This isn't funny Alex, I thought you had more sense than this.'

~ *We are* not *Alex Bendo* ~

She plonked the lid back on the *samovar*, killing the light. Still, its voice seemed to permeate out of the jar, and she began to scramble on her haunches back towards the edge of the chamber, where she hoped it might be quietened. She reversed into something solid and unexpected. She turned and found herself looking up a line of skirt.

'I wouldn't look in there, dearie,' crooned a shrewish voice. 'It's got a funny light to it. Nothing good's got a funny light to it.'

Stingingly embarrassed at being caught on her hands and knees, Aphra stood and found herself eye-level with Mistress Bendo's exaggerated bosom. She was rouged, her fat lips full of skinny teeth; they welcomed Alex's guest lustfully. Mistress Bendo flounced into the middle of the room, her considerable weight wobbling like molten butter, her bland summery dress and matronly cap looking utterly incongruous in this subterranean folly. She was a superbly ugly woman. There were times when the good doctor's clients had wary husbands, who – wisely – wanted to keep another man's fingers well away from their most prized possessions. In those cases, Mistress Bendo was on call to offer the same cures as her husband, but with a reassuringly womanly touch.

'You must be the Lady Ass,' Mistress Bendo shrilled.

'And you look ridiculous,' Aphra shot back, witheringly. Her hostess capered.

'He calls you worse than that behind your back. He calls you the Lady Buffoon. He calls you Kit Plumparse, Ben Noballs, and Mrs William Pricktease.'

'So? Half of London calls me a trollop for daring to pick up a pen. Your husband at least has the good manners, reading, and wit to associate me with playwrights I admire, even if they long ago passed out of fashion. Get him, I need to talk Service business.'

'Ooh, hark at her,' said Mistress Bendo, but nonetheless she began to strip out of her clothes, starting by shedding the voluminous tent-dress, that had pins concealed up and down the seam for easy access. Christ, Aphra thought as she watched the ritual undressing, is this what he thinks all women are like?

Mistress Bendo looked up from shedding bags of padding around her stomach. 'How did it go?' she asked in a duller voice, closer to the natural tone. 'Deal?'

Aphra fished the purse out of her skirts and tossed it across to a bench where it landed with a crunch. 'No deal,' she said. 'He guessed I was on crown business and can stand more cash. Also, he has other offers. Haggling, probably, but I thought better of it.'

The woman shrugged; she had lost weight and hair, the lurid blonde wig she habitually wore now decorating the astrological rug, revealing underneath a tight black buzz around the scalp. Her moustache came away too; even that wasn't natural. 'We made the offer in good faith. Now we can resort to other means.'

'You mean kidnap her? I'm not sure I'd agree to that.'

'You don't have to. You've done your bit. Besides, it's not as though Tom *owns* her. It would offend Aphra Behn if he did.' The rapidly-slimming woman purred and her voice sank further. 'And yet the girls who're forced to sell their sex for Corinthian Tom's betterment are in no wise better off than slaves – but that offends you not a jot, does it?'

'You're mistaken, sir. It upsets me a great deal.'

'*Upsets* maybe, but not *offends*.'

'Fuck you Alex, I'm not here for a lecture.'

All that remained of Mistress Bendo was scattered on the floor around her husband's naked feet. He was already dismantling the scaffold of branches and wires that had helped foster the illusion of her corpulence, not dropping the delicate components but placing them neatly on a felt surface on the nearest table. Beneath that, he was skinny and naked. Mistress Bendo was as overblown a grotesque as Salomon had been. The real Doctor Bendo was quite a different creature. Once free of his imprisonment within his own imaginary wife, he took Aphra's hands and put a mollifying kiss on her forehead. 'Aphra, I'm sorry.'

He smelled like a barber's shop, like her father's old workshop in Kent. He swept past her to the corner of the room where he kept water jugs and soaps to wipe away his disguises' stinks, and she, still frothing with a little anger like one of his own fabulous fake experiments, kept her peace as he washed. Her carnal interest in men had been grievously wounded of late, but still she wondered why so many women were happy to march into Bendo's embrace, if that was entirely down to the success of his fecund cures. There must be something more to it than that. She wondered if he might, as a lover, be that most elusive of creatures – a gentle-man?

'He's right, though.'

'What?'

'Corinthian Tom. He does have other offers for the Jesuitess. Reports of her physiognomy have travelled. They've probably reached Germany by now. That sort of thing always attracts dilettantes.'

'They could be lies.' Aphra shrugged. Tom was concentrating his efforts on his groin and upper thighs, which were vanishing into a grey foam of suds. At that moment, it looked like the most disgusting thing she had ever seen.

'They might be, but we have reliable reports. We won't know until we actually see her with our own eyes. And it's not just quacks who're after her. Guess who's resurfaced this last week. No? Guess.'

She shrugged again. 'The French?'

She couldn't see his face, but she could imagine it contorting into the shape of his laughter. 'Has France been hiding for eight years? Last I checked it was just off Dover. Head south-east, you can't miss it. No, not the French! Faction Paradox.'

A third shrug. *Faction Paradox* meant little to her, just another party to the chaos at Salomon's House, but it was an obsession of Bendo's, and it seemed hard for him to grasp that others didn't share his interest. Nonetheless, she suddenly realised that she must owe her position on this particular assignment to having been woven up, in Bendo's eyes, with the events of eight winters gone. He might have marked her out in the Service files as a likely agent for any *situation* arising from that old disaster.

Her hips complained again; she looked round for a chair, but found none she was willing to trust, and sat instead on the rug, watching young Doctor Bendo sluice his face, then his genitals, with cold water. He was seven years her junior. What must he have looked like under the decrepit guise of Salomon when he was so much younger?

'Faction Paradox,' she said. 'So what are they up to?'

'We have a man watching them, a good man. He thinks they're going to try to kidnap her. We'll have to get her out first.'

'How? You can hardly raid the House of the Infernal. It would be over-conspicuous.'

'We can stir up feeling in the mob. We'll snatch her while they're busy trashing the place.'

He spoke so blithely about the prisoner, as if she were nothing. Aphra suddenly saw that Bendo didn't see her as an object of interest in her own right – there were so many curiosities brought to his attention, ninety-nine out of every hundred just as interesting as the case of the mysteriously-appearing Jesuitess. No, this was a trap for his enemies, who were no doubt as substantial a threat to him as the vast Catholic conspiracy was to Protestant England, ready to storm the citadels inside his head while leaving those of the solid world untrembled. No, more than that – he was only interested in the Jesuitess because the Faction had showed its hand first. Tom's instinct – not to sell – had been right, though he would probably lose his business in consequence.

'People might get hurt,' Aphra said, waving a gesture that Bendo wouldn't see. He was dressing, at last, hiding his untempting firm young body beneath a robe.

'Only uninvolved bystanders,' he quipped.

'Of course,' she said wearily. 'Have you thought any more about what I asked?'

He had, until this moment, been jolly. Now he blinked and turned into a solemn statue. 'The law must take its own course, I told you that.'

He had rehearsed all his reasons with her, and she knew immediately that arguing further would avail her nothing, but she owed it to too many friends not to try, and saw from his demeanour that he would at least listen patiently before refusing her.

'I have acquaintances – actors for Christ's sake! Only players! – who are gaoled now because they wore their faith on their sleeves and so made themselves intolerable to the mob. Is that the law? They're held on no charges that I can discern, while their accusers may never face the uncomfortable prospect of having their weasel words tested before a court. You talk of law? I would remind the law that it is required to act in their defence! My voice may not be heard, but yours is loud enough to break down doors.'

Bendo sat cross-legged on the floor opposite her, and took her hands. This is it, then, the brush-off. 'How do you think the mob would react if they saw agents of the crown acting for your friends? They'd see a weak king sucking up to Catholics. Who'll taste the brunt of that? More Catholics. Mistress Behn,' he said, and his tone – meant to calm – only cut her further, 'this madness will be done in a year or so, and when it collapses it will destroy the reputations of all those who pitched in behind Oates. The exclusionists will be exposed as fools and the wind will be against them, at least until James finally becomes king and fucks it up royally –'

She snapped. 'Do they despise weak kingship? Well let them have a strong king! The Duke will give them bloody assizes.'

Bendo rolled his eyes. 'You think that the way to deal with people driven by fear of monstrous Catholicism is to subject them to a Catholic monster? James won't be the tyrant they fear or the paragon you hope. I know James. He's a fool, nothing more than that. I can't do anything for your friends.'

She put her hands over her face. 'So they must rot in gaol? For the rest of their lives?'

'They might be safer there.'

'Safer? Jesus! You know nothing of prison! Why not lock up all the innocents and have done with it, because they'll be *safer.*'

'Don't think it hasn't been discussed. Your friends might find solace in the pen. Many a literary career has begun behind bars. It's the fashion of the times.'

'Hah.'

Bendo stretched and stood, the hem of his robe flapping so she could see the coarse black hairs tangling up and down his pasty legs. 'I'm gladdened to see you've found your sense of humour. Mistress Behn, this age will pass. Take comfort in that.'

Aphra wiped a surprising slick of dampness and snot across her sleeve – no blood though, she expected blood. 'Will the Queen be safe?'

'She's tougher than you'd think. And Rowley won't let her go, not ever. When it comes to her well-being, he's unusually afflicted by loyalty and affection. Guilt, I reckon.'

He had turned to display his back to her. She stared insolently at its impenetrable dullness, at the shabby robe over the skinny body that was all the magician truly was, under his tricks and retorts and false cures. *At least he doesn't deceive you*, she heard a part of her say – the part of her whose voice was the most reasonable and Puritan and shrill – *nor hold out any false hopes.* She bared her teeth at him, though he wouldn't see, and snatched back her package from the bench. Bendo didn't notice, he was busy with his coin.

'This is lighter than I remember,' he said, patting the moneybag on his palm.

Aphra shrugged, invisible to him. 'The Corinthian isn't displaying her for free, you know? For Christ's sake! Whatever else I may have been, I was never a thief.'

He looked round to show her his smile. It was easier to hate him when she could only see his back. She held her parcel tighter, unwilling to let it go. She put her free hand to her face, and made a play of wiping out stray tears with the fleshy mound at the base of her thumb.

He had one more question for her before he sent her on her way.

'The Jesuitess?' he asked. 'What did you actually make of her? What is she?'

She remembered an emptied mouth and emptied eyes. She couldn't decide for a moment, then it came: 'I think she's a lost soul.'

It was snowing again when she left Bendo's wagon, and she set off home under a strange starless, moonless sky that was black from horizon to horizon. This is what she found, when she looked inside herself: the fear was gone, but it had left nothing in its place. Her meeting with Doctor Bendo hadn't relieved her, it had merely left her drained, like a bottle, like a fen, like a cup of cooling tea.

She took the package into her bedroom as soon as she got home. She had spent as little time as possible in here in recent days, even preferring to sleep on a mat before the

fire in the parlour rather than suffer draughts and bad memories. The parcel emboldened her slightly; rational though she was, there was clearly some mystery and some
strength at work. It would certainly prove earthly – it had already proved fallible – but
it was *there*.

Her fumbling attempts to haggle with Corinthian Tom hadn't lasted. He was a shrewd
man, a businessman as flinthearted as anyone in the world of theatre; he could see from
the first that she wasn't his equal. He hadn't even made a game of his refusal – the
Jesuitess was simply not for sale on any terms she could muster – but still, she had
money and he was happy to help her part with it. He had produced the bundle as a
tease, swaddled carefully in the same grey, gently-greased wrapping. Perhaps he hadn't
expected her to take it seriously, but she had, and handed over a few coins. She thought
Bendo would think it *interesting*.

Bugger Bendo. Aphra Behn found it interesting. She'd already had half a mind to
keep it for herself even before leaving the house.

She unwrapped her prize under the gaze of a single candle, and the fabric within
stirred in response to the light, the reflection slicking down the length of the material
as if it were a liquid bead of fire. It was familiar already, the texture of it as her fingers
brushed it, the smell of it, the way the fabric stretched easily where she prodded it as
though it were made of slow and supple water. *I've seen this before, in antic Jerusalem* –
Lifting it from its wrapping felt like peeling a newborn creature mewling from its caul.
It seemed to warm and brighten under her touch, and when a rogue gust rattled her
window frame and put out the candlespark, she found she could see perfectly well by
the costume's inner light.

'So much for the legend of the Jesuitess! I thought she wore a black uniform,' she'd
snorted. Tom had shrugged.

'She did. That's long gone, before we ever got her. A half-dozen different bodies claim
they've got it for sale, but chances are none of them are right. Whoever's got it will want
to hold onto it.'

'But you don't want to hold on to this?'

'It's worth nothing to me,' Tom had said, but he was lying. He wanted rid of it. It
wasn't that he was *scared* of this odd, neatly-folded garment he'd unveiled for her, he
was too solid a man to entertain that sort of superstition. It simply wasn't part of his
world, where all costume was calculated to conceal, to flatter, and to deceive.

'She was wearing this under her uniform?' Aphra suggested.

Tom shrugged again. 'Way things are at the moment, people will wear just about
anything if they think it makes them safer. Never does though, does it?'

Aphra had cast her eyes up at the ceiling. 'No,' she agreed. She'd bought it anyway.

It was a translucent skin to cover trunks, arms and legs, perhaps tight, perhaps –
given how readily it stretched – not so tight. It was light as air, though it was pricked
and riddled with strings, bones and metal tokens – like a magician's cloak sewn with
heavy talismans. But no, they added no weight to it, and looking closer it seemed all
these pieces of obscure and occult machinery were *inside* the thin lining of the magical
translucent cloth. A few solid items were slung round a belt at the waist, but the rest
looked more like subtle tattoos written onto the garment's skin, tattoos that swirled
when she moved them. She put it down on her unslept-in bed. The wrapping drifted
down the side and onto the floor, forgotten.

Impulsively, Aphra Behn removed all her clothes, throwing them into a heap in the corner, to reveal her heavy body. Around her the bedroom was unthreateningly blank; its memories couldn't touch her. Her unhappy fingers inspected the roll of flab above her throat, the second chin that made her feel portlier than she was. Her bedroom trapped cold air, and she felt it acutely on her skin which turned to gooseflesh. Her legs were still sore, stitches tugging particularly hard up the length of her right thigh. She ran her hand down it, finding no bruise, finding nothing more than cool pimpled skin. She moved her hand to the windowsill and found dust had gathered. She retrieved the Jesuitess's strange shift from the bed. It felt luxuriant. It was warm, the heat welling from the same uncanny source as the light. She held it to her stomach. It burned, wonderfully.

The skin unseamed itself to admit her body; it slid on smoothly. She could feel the fabric tightening and sucking round her legs and waist, moulding itself comfortably against her flesh. Where it touched, she felt not just warm, but less weary, more healthy, more *alive*. The new seams knitted themselves together once they were no longer needed, as if there had never been a join. She was covered from her throat to her ankles, but she still felt naked. She moved freely. The cloth clung to her almost unfelt. It seemed to whisper as she moved, reassuring her. She liked this kind of magic.

A sharp pain – a sting – bit halfway up her right arm. She looked and found a notch had been cut into her skin and was seeping blood. It rippled, trapped between her body and the bland surface of her new costume. Swearing, she tugged her arm free, and the cut tore as she pulled it from the sleeve, loosening more blood to sluice into the lining of the fabric. Was there a barb she hadn't seen? She looked – nothing. Phantom prickles worried at her from the inside of the skin, and she tore it off hastily, the costume unwrapping itself as freely as it had come on. Her forearm hissed with pins & needles, so she pressed her left hand over the cut and let the sticky flow of blood congeal under the heat of her palm. Aphra left the Jesuitess-skin in a shabby heap on the floor, and redressed in her own unspiked clothing.

As she finished, a polite knocking carried in from her parlour door. She went to it, cursing her luck that the caller had chosen this moment, when she was so shabbily, thoughtlessly dressed.

Here was a most unlikely visitor – an African woman, with scorched-blue exotic skin. Her face, ancient, was an outcrop on solid grey whimple; her habit was topped-off with a winged but fragile paper hat.

Aphra Behn opened her mouth, but could think of nothing to say.

'I hear,' said the nun, in an accent like fermenting fruit, 'someone's raisin' a daughter here.'

'No. No, children here. This is only a small house,' she found herself saying. 'Are you collecting for an order, sister?'

'Mother,' said the Negress. 'And yes, I'm collecting. And no, I can see into your head and you're wrong. Mother Sphinx ain't from Africa, except by three thousand miles and three hundred years. She's taking the long way round. You going to let her in or what?'

'What?' Aphra shook her head, but realised she was being asked something entirely reasonable. 'Do you want to come in?'

The old nun had perfect teeth. 'Cup of tea?' she asked. 'That's the first thing I'm collecting.'

Aphra went to make a cup of tea, just the one, not for herself. She brought it for Mother Sphinx, who had seated herself at the parlour table as if taking up an old pew worn down to fit the shape of her posterior. So perfectly did she fit into the room that Aphra found it hard to shake the impression that she was a constant and familiar visitor. Aphra watched, fussily anxious about her skills as a teamaker, as the mother drained her cup.

'That's a good cup of tea,' she said agreeably, and houseproud Aphra found herself beaming. 'I oughtta apologise for what I'm doing to you, but it saves messy explanation. Someone's gonna raise a daughter here tonight and I want to see it. Make sure it don't get out of hand. That's rare and dangerous shit. You gotta name?'

Aphra told her. The old black woman whistled. 'You gotta *interesting* name there. When the daughter rises, you go and hide. Save yourself.' She shrugged into a new and comfortable shape on the chair, a little saggier and closer to the ground. She wasn't African, but she couldn't be from London, Aphra reasoned; the city took heavy folk from poor orders and made them lean.

'Second thing I'm collecting,' said the Mother Superior, 'is in that room over there. It ain't the daughter, but it's bringing the daughter down on us.'

Aphra squinted, tried to concentrate, and realised this made no sense. 'I don't –' Mother Sphinx seized her arm and pulled down the sleeve.

'Thing that did this to you,' she said, heavy fingers stroking the tender line of the cut without enflaming it. 'Nasty bite you got there, not a tasting I reckon, a *reading*. Go fetch it. I ain't gonna steal it. Mother Sphinx, she's an honest thief.'

So Aphra fetched the Jesuitess's slick undergarment, bearing it back carefully on her fingertips. She laid it out on the table, and saw that her smear of blood was still percolating through the veins inside the fabric. She shuddered until Mother Sphinx took her hand and pressed reassurance into it. The nun had donned eyeglasses to inspect her prize. 'Now this is interesting. This weren't what I was expecting at all. Some kind of technohoozit, I thought. The *loa* play with this sort of shit, *play* like a cat. You like cats?'

'Who doesn't?'

'You just made a prayer to Bast. Only god Mother Sphinx got time for. No, this ain't the kind of thing you'd find the Great Houses using. Look at it, it's worn 'gainst the skin. They're not big on *bodies* on the Homeworld. Know they're there, put up with 'em, but secretly wish all that biology would go away and let them play in their dream gardens, is what they call a *necessary evil*. No way a Homeworlder'd wear this unless they were sick or needy. Or both. You got more tea?'

She got more tea, reusing the same cup as before, rinsing it out carefully until the browned rim looked clean and (almost) new again. Rebecca, her latest maid, was away visiting a sick sister or similar, and though Aphra had grumbled about this she was now glad of the girl's absence, because it would be very hard to explain Mother Sphinx otherwise. When she bore the fresh tea back into the parlour, she found the Negress unfastening a thin metal wand from the Jesuitess's belt. Not a wand, more of a needle –

Larissa, she thought, but then it was gone.

Behind the pale moons of her spectacles, the nun's eyes narrowed, but the moment passed. Icelandic-white teeth beamed again. 'Now this is a different order of thing. This here is *clean* technoshit. This is the sort of thing the Grandfather would have seen, when he was a young fella and still existed.' She took the wand by its end and weighed it, before moving it through elegant practised moves, stubby sword-strokes. Then she shoved it into Aphra's hands, her nose wrinkling in disgust. 'Don't care for it. No respect for the *loa*. Takes the fun out of the funeral.'

'What does it do?'

If Mother Sphinx was offended by this impertinent outburst, she didn't show it; her face inflated with good – if solemn – humour. 'I reckon,' she said, 'it raises daughters.'

Aphra put the needle aside on her table, and then returned the suit to her bedroom, leaving it on the floor in the same place she had found it. When she returned to her parlour, she found the mother kneeling by the fire, lighting it. As it caught, the storm blasted down the chimney and the heatless flames danced.

Mother Sphinx didn't look up, but threw her voice over her shoulder. 'Don't worry about me no more. I'm just gonna sit here and wait and watch for the daughter when she comes. I'll do no harm and you'll be okay with that. You might want to make some more tea now and then. That ain't a political thing. Mother Sphinx just likes the taste. Right?'

Why not? Aphra smiled. 'Right,' she agreed. She looked round her empty parlour, wondering who on Earth she had been talking to. It had been a strange day.

She sat, not on her favourite chair – which she felt was somehow out of bounds to her this evening – but on the harder seat. She wanted to write, but wanted also to stay out of the bedroom, which was where most inspiration struck. She couldn't face returning there while the Jesuitess's suit lay crumpled on the floor. Its shape was ominous, un-folded and ungainly, with stabbing-victims arms and legs protruding from the heap, as if she had the very carcass of Sir Edmund Berry Godfrey stashed away in there. She dreamed of Oates and his bodyguard breaking down the door of the chief conspira-tor's home. So she had never been a mere 'concerned subject', but the true Jesuitess all along! – the Popess of Rome, God having granted her the short-lived gift of testicles to pass the fondling test of Saint Peter's Chair – the truth of it known not even to her waking self.

She found herself staring at a blank sheet with nothing to say, with ink drying unspent on her nib. She broke off occasionally to make cups of tea, always in the same bowl. She didn't drink them, she wasn't in the mood. The act of making the tea itself became a comforting ritual, distracting her from work and the itch round the scab on her forearm. She brought the tea out and placed it on the table. As the evening drew in, she would check and find the tea had drained itself out of the bowl, at which point she would return to the kitchen to wash it out and pour a fresh brew from the pot. Her best chair creaked contentedly. She didn't write. She was blocked.

She was brought up short from her doodling by another disturbance – a terrific crash from her bedroom. Her first thought was that the snow had grown heavy and blown the window in; her second revived her fears of the mob, now turning on those who spoke out for the Papists. A night ago it might have cowed her, but now she felt irritated – as if she had been put-upon all day by enemy forces and this was a final indignity that served to goad her rather than crush her spirit. She snatched up the poker from the fireplace in one hand – warm metal snug in her fist – and grabbed a candle with the other, and charged howling and unthinking from the parlour into the bedroom.

The window was indeed smashed open to let in the snow, its pieces spread like heaven on the floor. The brown candlelight fell upon the intruder who hunched over the gar-ment Corinthian Tom had sold her. Aphra recognised the apeish face at once.

The Jesuitess had come to reclaim her property.

⇒ Chapter 15: *Raising a Daughter* ⇐

And there were other, less reliable stories, from less reliable parts of the world. Suarez and Harrow and the mad Polish girl were documented by credible witnesses, whose accounts could be checked, but it was all but impossible to confirm the truth of the folk stories, even those from close quarters like Denmark and North Africa. And what of the world beyond easy reach? The dead might rise from their graves in Persia or Cathay, but wasn't that sort of tale expected from those parts of the world and never quite believed? If the dead rose among the unlettered tribes of Africa or America, then who in Europe – even if they heard the stories – would not dismiss this as savage superstition? And beyond the fringes of the known world, were there other lands as yet only dreamed of – Australis, Greater Ireland, El Dorado, Utopia, and Atlantis – from which no reports had yet proceeded?

His rooms now overflowed with documents of the phenomena. One winter, thirty-six years gone, the world had been visited by a plague of resurrections. An Angel of Life had passed over the Earth and raised the dead. Not all, just the fresh, just those with wounds that could heal or fevers that could be conquered. They were too few to cause general distress, so perhaps the animating power chose only as many as it needed to carry out its task, maybe anticipating that many pairs of hands were needed because one could so easily fail. After all, isn't that what happened to Suarez and Harrow and the oracle of Kraków? They never claimed to have seen Christ's angels. They had found no divine duty. They had been driven mad or into exile, or were purposefully silenced. Salomon's House had given him doubts about the angels, and now he found he was no longer unique. Nathaniel Silver knew only one thing –

Among the papers, bought from him by le Pouvoir, *was a jar containing a relic of his doubts. Pickled, preserved, kept locked away in a Toledo warehouse for thirty-six years, was the severed tongue of Gabriel Suarez.*

– there but for the Grace of God go I.

By the end of the night, the House of the Infernal was standing but gutted. Fire had eaten through walls and floorboards, while its anonymous façade was left streaked with black-smoke makeup. Small flames still flared, but were doused naturally by the weather. One floor had collapsed, showering flaming chunks onto anyone who had yet to make their escape from the storey below. The mob itself had scattered once the alarums had been raised, leaving Tom and their other thrashed victims to salve their wounds with clumps of snow and frozen soil. Most of the fire-fighting was done by Servicemen who had arrived in the guise of concerned citizens, carrying convenient long ladders to reach the upper storeys. They came wearing skins and hoods coated in oils blessed by Service rituals to protect them from the elements of fire and water.

Faction Paradox had escaped by climbing through the attic window, onto the roof, and away between the chimneys of adjacent buildings. Reports passed rapidly from hand to hand before arriving with Doctor Bendo – the three cultists, distinct in their skull masks, were pursued; Ratcatchers had their scent. He sent orders back that they should be kept under close observation until he could join the hunt.

The Jesuitess was rescued, along with various other souls who found themselves trapped on the upper floors. Three Servicemen had smashed through the window to the Jesuitess's cell, already half-broken by the Faction's escape. They'd found the woman seated calmly on the edge of her bed in her black costume, unexcited by the flames that crackled round her. The largest of the men had slung her over his shoulder and carried her, without a struggle, back down the ladder to the ground. He'd set her on her feet, and for a moment she stood forlorn and helpless in the street, quivering on the winds that squeezed hard through the canyons between buildings. Around her more survivors were clambering and dropping from windows, while those already rescued were wailing as their homes and possessions and livelihoods were swallowed up before their eyes. It was the Great Fire again, flickering up from the hell where it had these last twelve years been frozen. The locals looked to the blank-eyed woman in the middle of the chaos and shivered, absorbing all the cold that she didn't feel.

The Servicemen bound her, and half-led, half-dragged her before Doctor Bendo. The alchemist, cackling behind his robes and his staff and his birdnest beard, inspected her with a squint, with a leer. He ran his fingers over her face, leaving a grease smear behind. 'Put her in my *laboratorium*,' he commanded, between barked and spittle-dripping Enochian syllables. 'Keep her chained. Keep two pairs of eyes on her at all times.' Doctor Bendo looked away from her. He had other, more pressing priorities for the moment. He made a prayer to his God, then set off in pursuit of Faction Paradox. He galloped, surprising men who thought he could only hobble on *those* legs, with *that* stick. His prisoner was taken through the streets to Bendo's wagon, and from there to the old madman's workroom.

The arcane quality of the wagon's entrance didn't confuse or disorientate her, as it was meant to. The springs that deadened the sensation of movement but inflamed the perception of size, the rotating floors and secret doorways designed to couple seamlessly with the *laboratorium*, the false perspectives in the surrounding passages – all failed to move her. Such things reflected dull and commonplace on her sullen eyes, which slid round her surroundings, patiently searching for an invisible prize. She said nothing in all this time, which one of her guards found unnerving and the other convenient.

The Jesuitess had a vivid smile, a crooked red line full of angular teeth and arrogance. It was her most distinct feature. Cousin Greenaway's impersonation wasn't perfect, but it was fair, and her guards couldn't look at it.

The first thing Aphra thought to say was both ludicrous and untrue: 'Put that down. It isn't yours.'

The Jesuitess ignored her. She had changed since the afternoon's performance at Corinthian Tom's. Aphra hesitated for a moment, wondering if it was the same woman. Her eyes, her empty eyes, were filled with devilish life. They had flickered momentarily to Aphra when she burst into the bedroom, but didn't look to her.

'This is my home!' Aphra protested. The woman shrugged so insolently it was impossible to tell if she'd understood the words. She wrapped her skinsuit over the crook of her arm to carry away. Finally she turned, finding Aphra, inspecting her as though through a microscope.

She didn't drool, not any more. 'I saw you today,' she said.

'Yes,' Aphra responded sullenly, then – realising she was losing the initiative – jabbed the poker at her threateningly. The Jesuitess blinked, reached out for it and tugged it free. Aphra felt something twist in her forearm that wasn't meant to be twisted. The healed cut broke open again and began to weep. She stumbled back, clutching her double-wound and protesting: 'This is my bloody livelihood, you bitch!'

The Jesuitess's head twitched in a series of gentle nods. She seemed to be listening, learning new words. She smiled, and that at least was a pretty decoration on a plain face. She inspected the tip of the poker curiously, then set it down on the floor. She'd come dressed in a chillingly-thin white gown. It had been shredded in places, as had the skin of her legs below the hem. The flesh was lacerated, and blue with cold. Her toes were almost black. She took a step, and Aphra saw the glint of glass pieces grinding themselves into open wounds in street-soiled soles.

'You're hurt,' she said, hoping she sounded sympathetic despite her anger.

The intruder shook her head. 'I need to go.'

'At least come out of the cold. At least let me look at you,' Aphra said, though she wasn't sure why. A cunning part of her thought she could lull this woman – slip *something* into a drink, then raise the alarm – but she knew even as she contemplated it that she wouldn't. Her concern was simple fascination. Even at the House of the Infernal she hadn't wanted to look away. She wanted this creature, this marvellous monster, in her gaze forever.

The unlikely burglar stood stockily for a moment, then made a curt nod. Aphra took her hands and led her out into the warm parlour. The woman paused on the threshold, casting her eyes about the room suspiciously before allowing herself to be tugged – however gently – further in. Wordlessly, Aphra persuaded her to sit by the fire, though she was less successful at prising away the skinsuit that the woman held jealously and tightly in her arms. She knelt, like a servant, to inspect the tiny, frostburned, shredded feet and undo the damage as best she could. Her hands came away from the first attempt bloodied and glassed.

There was cunning and there was fascination. There was also guilt, she realised. She was picking out fragments of her window from the woman's feet in penance for Edward Coleman, who – in her cowardice – she hadn't saved. As she worked, the intruder's hands came down to stroke at her hair.

'Do you have a name?' Aphra asked, without looking up. 'I can't call you the Jesuitess. That's not true, is it?'

'I don't think so.'

'Have you forgotten?' Aphra asked curiously, not looking; hearing the voice was enough. 'Do you remember anything?'

The reply was one hollow word. 'Yes.'

Aphra couldn't think of anything to say after that, so she kept digging out glass. The woman's body, where it wasn't sliced or frozen, was smooth and hairless. Aphra put her face close and found no smell to it. She tore a long strip from the hem of the white gown, to make bandages, to bind her feet. It had been a mistake to bring her too close to the fire, she realised suddenly, though her dainties were suffering from more than just chilblains. Parts of her feet were charcoal-black and hideous and far from dainty.

'Who tried to wear this?'

The question caught Aphra by surprise, as she was straightening up. The Jesuitess held up her suit, with the patches of Aphra's blood still visible through the naked skin. Another bland question came from her lips. 'Was it you?'

Aphra nodded. The eyes below the overhung brow shuffled from side to side, considering. 'Good,' she pronounced. 'The blood will help it. It's learning who you are.'

This new decisive note frightened Aphra. She backed away to fetch water and a cloth, still wanting to look, but grateful nonetheless to get away from the parlour, if only for a minute.

When she returned, she found her guest had discarded what remained of the gown and was pulling herself into the suit, one leg at a time. She had a smooth back and plump buttocks and a curve of breast visible in the gap between her flank and her armpit, all pleasing to Aphra's eye until they disappeared into the tattooed fabric of her suit.

'How did you know it was here?' Aphra asked, only mildly curious.

The sharp blades of her naked shoulders shrugged. They were not so smooth after all – they were marked with white shadows where the skin might once have been broken. 'It's unique, in this time. It wasn't hard.'

'That's all I have of yours. The mob took everything else.'

'This is all I need,' the Jesuitess told her, sliding her arms into the gently-yielding sleeves. Her hands went down to the belt, fingers ticking each decoration hanging there. They found an absence, an empty notch. With her hands, not her eyes, she panicked. Her head angled downwards to look closer.

'Is something missing?' Aphra asked, but she knew already. She found her treacherous eyes giving her away, turning casually to the wand she had left resting on the parlour table. The Jesuitess looked up and noticed. The wand sat in plain sight before them both. Simultaneously, they leapt for it.

Aphra got there first. She grabbed it and backed towards the door. She held the wand low and close to her stomach, so the Jesuitess would find it less easy to snatch it back. The ugly woman prowled. Her face was inscrutable, but her hands begged.

'Give that back to me,' she ordered, asked, pleaded.

'And then?'

'Then I'll go.' She moved between Aphra and the fire, making of herself a shadow with a shivering orange nimbus. 'Give it to me. It's dangerous.'

'It's not dangerous.' Aphra prodded her palm with the wand's blunt point. 'It doesn't even scratch.'

The silhouette of the woman said nothing and didn't move, and Aphra readied herself for the pounce. A thought popped into her mind and blurted out of her mouth before she could stop it: 'Come to bed!'

The lump of the Jesuitess's head cocked, almost overbalanced. 'What?'

Emboldened, Aphra kept blurting. 'Come to bed and then you can have it. Don't go yet. I don't want you to go!' And the woman wavered, delaying her leap for just a sliver of a second too long, as if she were seriously considering it, as if the wand meant that much to her... But then suddenly she was no longer looking to Aphra or her stolen needle. She was retreating, the spring in her body uncoiling, her palms displayed limp in the common gesture of surrender.

Aphra looked around, and found the tip of a pistol pointing just past her face. She skidded backwards until her backside collided with the edge of the table. Her plates and bowls rattled out of their places, and one almost threw itself off onto the floor but checked and righted itself, trembling precariously on the edge.

'Doctor Bendo!' she exclaimed. She was shot a contemptuous look from below the cowl, above the beard. Alex Bendo had come in his public disguise, the face and robes and sickness of Salomon. He hadn't brought his stick or his infirmity – he moved fluidly, with temperamental guns in both hands.

He spoke in Salomon's mutter: 'Which do you think is more persuasive to our guest, Lady Ass? You or these?' he asked, shaking the pistols.

'Alex,' she seethed, but there was no hint of the real Bendo here. This was Salomon, his were the goatskin whiskers and the oil-slicked skin, his was the leather strap covering a diseased pit of a nose that was in fact whole, his was the tortured curvature of the spine – all unreal. 'Show me your proper face, Alex, I can't deal with you like this.'

He ignored her, instead shuffling a little further into the room with his weapons trained unwavering at the Jesuitess's chest. 'This one I followed across London. Faction Paradox abducted her. They substituted another, but I knew her face and wasn't fooled. The others tried to take her to the river, but she fought them and fled. There's no love between you and this Faction?'

Their prisoner blinked and said nothing. 'He means you,' Aphra mouthed.

'And you come here,' Bendo said, 'which is half a surprise to me, and find the Lady Ass is about to kiss you goodbye and wave you happily on your way, because she has a soft heart and soft brains. Not the first one you've let slip, is it girl?' Aphra groaned inwardly.

The Jesuitess, who had stood unmoved – even listless – as Bendo spoke, took a surreptitious step forward. She froze as he jiggled his guns.

The woman's head turned one way and the other, casting freakish shadows across the floor in front of her. Aphra realised she was still focused on the wand, more so than Bendo's pistols. She made her fingers tighten, in case the woman leapt to snatch it. It would do her no good, anyway – Bendo would shoot before she could reach Aphra.

Her guest spoke at last. 'You won't stop me,' she said. Not defiance, just a practical statement.

Bendo's lips inflated into a smile. 'I will. We know how your kind can be bound, with cold iron.' Carefully he put aside one of his pistols and raised his free hand, a nail held up between his forefinger and thumb. 'Driven through your skull into the front quarters of the brain, it will make you quite docile.'

'Jesus!' Aphra exclaimed, but Bendo rattled on:

'Then the studies can begin. Vivisection. Perhaps insemination. You aren't the first mermaid or undine to beach herself on our shores, but you are the best preserved. I want to see what kind of monster we can grow in your womb. Half-man, half-well... whatever hellish thing you are.'

The object of Bendo's vicious intentions didn't even shrug. 'No. That would be impossible.'

'That remains to be proven. If you try to flee I *will* shoot, and I can learn almost as much from cutting up your carcass as I would from your living body.'

Aphra suddenly realised that the spymaster had her wrong. She wouldn't run. She wanted the wand, she *needed* the wand; to be deprived of it was a worse prospect than any fate Bendo's lurid imagination could dredge up. She would have come to bed to get it. She would, she would, she would, and it would have been wonderful! *Too late now*, she thought. *Shame*, she thought.

She'd risk a bullet for it. Aphra saw that. She saw that the Jesuitess would leap, a second before it happened.

The Jesuitess pounced; Aphra raised her arm, offering the wand; the first of Bendo's pistols barked.

The woman's stomach split open. Aphra saw what she first took to be light – red and liquid – guttering from the hole, and dropped to her knees with her hands covering her mouth, a scream whistling between her fingers. *The war! The war! The fucking war's starting up again in my house!*

The wand was gone. The Jesuitess had snatched it back and clutched it in a white-knuckled fist. Her free hand went to the hole below her ribs and sank inside, the fingers disappearing up to her knuckles. Her face fell, forlorn. Doctor Bendo had swung his second pistol up, adjusting for her sudden proximity, brushing the snout against her flank as it rose. The wand pulsed with a clean light – white like the sun creeping into a December sky – and she brought it curving up in a hard, violent arc. The pistol levelled below her jaw. Aphra, crouched by her table-leg, breathed spent black powder and coughed it back out again.

The second and final pistol fired. The woman's throat exploded, killing her scream as quickly as it was born. The blast didn't slow her or deflect her. Her fist, still clutching the wand, slammed into Bendo's chest. The tip – which only minutes before hadn't made the smallest impression on Aphra's skin – rammed through Bendo's breastbone into his heart.

The two combatants fell away from each other. The Jesuitess went the most theatrically, toppling back onto the floor to drown in her own blood. Her head lolled on the rug and settled so that the face turned bitterly to stare at Aphra across the room, a whitish froth drooling from her lips along with the blood. She might have been mad as she lay dying but Aphra could only see terrible sanity in her expression.

Aphra wrenched her head away and found Bendo dying quietly and at length. He remained on his feet, staggering about with his hands clasped at the wand, and at a wound that seeped light. His pistols were discarded on the floor. He refused to join them, though his false beard was dislodged, revealing the lips of a better Doctor Bendo than the wretch she had just seen killed. He lingered on in the room for what seemed like an age, while his killer lay thrashing on the floor at his feet. He released his hands at last – and the wound was dry and blazing – so he could claw at the air, at nothing. The light that shone along the spine of the wand now flickered up and down his body and pulsed – and pulsed again –

No longer screaming, Aphra reached for him –

She was still reaching when Doctor Alexander Bendo exploded. He vanished into tiny gunpowder pieces, dwarfed by dust, leaving no other trace but the flare of his silhouette on Aphra Behn's eyeballs. The needle dropped out of the blast and rolled close to the Jesuitess's twitching body. The mortally wounded woman lurched painfully closer to grasp it, and press it to her body. Aphra barely noticed.

There was nowhere else to go. Aphra buried her head on the floor and passed out.

Her skin was not African black, nor even brown, but it was far richer than her mother's sunless pink. The colour of her hair fluctuated with the seasons, darkening in winter and lightening when the sun was out. In the cold months, it was sometimes burnt umber, sometimes mute burgundy. In summer, more startlingly, it turned blonde, and that brightness made her delicate skin all the darker. She strolled sometimes on the beach, with her chaperone, bare-headed and unafraid of sunbeams. All the eyes of this sight-obsessed world turned to her, all but those of the fussy, cowled men who clambered over the slime-coated rocks of the headland, measuring and collecting. Sometimes they found eggs, which were so old that their yoke had ossified and become stone. These were more fascinating to them than the unsweating, beautiful girl.

The older woman and the younger left ponderous footsteps in the white sand behind them. The sun was out and fiercely hot, but only the elder was afraid of burning, and carried a parasol whose shade trekked obediently up the beach in front of them. The younger collected brittle shells when she could, and talked guilelessly to men who were all guile, and who yearned to collect her as though she were herself a fruit of the sea. Her chaperone let the girl off the leash to play, while she rested wearily on the beach, reading from sweating books. She wore a broad straw hat that cast an obscuring shadow over her pages, making them unreadable. When she raised her hand she found the words imprinted on her palm in sticky ink.

Sometimes her charge came back and blocked her view of the sea, an accusation. Her dress didn't tremble on the breathless air. It was a white sheen of sunlight round a body of smoke. This child had been blown, not born. She had questions.

Tell me about America. Was it as hot as this?

Hotter but wetter. They had slaves there, building a new world for us. But I prefer it here.

Why didn't you bring him back from Surinam? Were you afraid?

He didn't belong in England. It was too small for him, like it's too small for you.

Am I like him?

No, nothing like him. You bring me delight.

He didn't?

He did, but yours lasted.

Later, the older woman watched as the younger waded out to sea, holding the hem of her skirt above the surface, her body dissolving into a slick of gold on the water. Soon there was nothing left of her. Aphra Behn cried tears of hot butter and hot milk.

She was my beautiful, beautiful daughter.

Aphra was woken by the chanting and the lack of pain in the arm she'd trapped under her stomach. Every other part of her hurt, but her arm was so numb she was afraid it had been shot off. She rolled onto her back and tried not to open her eyes to let in the stinging light. They flickered anyway, and the parlour was gloomily red. Her eyes were damp; she blinked that away and lay still, breathing.

The chant – the song, almost – trailed off once she moved, dwindling down into a fruity funereal chuckle. Aphra hadn't caught or understood most of the meaning, but it sounded to be a lament about a woman called Ursula or Essaly, shrilled out in a degraded provincial version of French that slurred or corrupted half the words. The singer stepped over Aphra's prone body and into another room. Aphra was still in her own house; she recognised the atmosphere.

She turned her head towards the nearest source of warmth. The fire, she noticed, was burning down. She didn't try to move. She wanted sleep, dreamless sleep.

After a few minutes the footsteps returned. A hand reached down and tickled her face until she opened her eyes.

'I made you some tea.'

Mother Sphinx helped her sit up, then held the cup for her, with the lip pressed to her mouth so she could drink without any further effort. She swallowed thirstily, missing the milk, missing any hint of sweetness. She didn't try to take the cup, afraid her hands would shake out all the fluid.

The old woman, ebony skin turned scarlet in the dying firelight, sat beside her patiently as she recovered her strength and her wits. Aphra smelled blood, a lot of blood, decorating her parlour thick as an abattoir. Once her cup was emptied, the nun left her to light the lamps, and she looked round for the Jesuitess's corpse – but she must have crawled away or been taken.

She shook her head to clear it, but that just spread the smell of blood deeper into her skull. 'What happened here?'

Mother Sphinx pottered over to the wall to inspect a stain, squinting then grimacing at it. 'You got a burglar,' she surmised. 'Broke in your bedroom. You must've caught them and put up a fight. Looks like they came off worse.'

'She got away, though?' Aphra said, focusing on her recent memories and finding nothing.

'Ain't no body here but us,' the old woman said solemnly, though she was smiling like a mad thing.

'She got away.' Aphra felt almost pleased to realise that, then she had a bleaker realisation. 'All that blood. She won't last long.'

'I heard shouts and smashes and seven kinds of hullabaloo,' she explained. 'Got here just too late, I guess.'

'You might have helped scare her off,' Aphra said graciously, though there was nothing scary about the squat presence in black, save the possibility that she might overbalance and crush passers-by under the immensity of her body. 'You know, I must have taken a blow to the head. Everything's hazy. I don't remember if I ever asked you your business?'

'I'm looking for a fella name of Bendo. Doctor Alex Bendo. Name mean anything?'

Aphra wracked her brains, and found it. She laughed helplessly. The nun seemed unoffended.

'You don't know him?'

'Oh, I know him, but he's not what you think. There is no Doctor Bendo. He's a guise. He's Johnny Wilmot... Rochester, that is. Whenever he gets into trouble – which is often, Johnny being Johnny – he pops on the beard and the robes and goes touring and whoring and having fun until he's forgiven. Which he usually is...'

'I seen him once. He looked solid.'

'Smoke and mirrors,' Aphra said happily. The chance to flaunt local knowledge was invigorating, she felt good health flooding back over her. 'Rochester's a natural actor and wit. If it weren't for the accident of his birth, he'd be a darling of the stage.'

Mother Sphinx nodded sagely and backed away, a mountain in motion. 'Guess he ain't solid any more. You be okay now?'

Aphra nodded. 'Bendo's skill was foisting children on the childless, so he claimed. Surely you're not interested in that?'

'Mother Sphinx got children of her own. They're trouble enough.' Then she was gone.

Once she was alone, Aphra got to her feet, threw out her arms wide, and breathed. She'd come through a close brush with violence and (who knows?) maybe even death, and emerged bruised but triumphantly alive. The world beyond her walls was galloping rapidly into madness and imminent apocalypse, so she would savour her every sane and waking moment as if it were the last. She would laugh in the face of republicans, Whigs, and holy fools alike, let them make a bonfire of her vanities, let them do their sacred worst! Her home had been broken into and torn apart, but she would find time to resent that later when the euphoria was past. Aphra Behn knew – for one glorious magical moment – that she was immortal.

Once she'd had a daughter, but she'd already forgotten.

∞

Cousin Greenaway was unwrapping the shadow of the whip from her guard's neck when the paradox rippled across her. It was good timing; a moment before, and it might have thrown her off her stride. She might have killed him in her confusion, and she wouldn't kill.

Erasmus wouldn't kill, and Erasmus was part of her. He didn't forbid it, he simply made it impossible for her by restraining her anger. She settled for hurting them instead. Hateman's insinuation still cloyed in her ears. She was neither too frail nor too innocent to use her whip in the Grandfather's service. She'd proved it.

~ *Faction Paradox rarely murders its enemies* ~ *Your Mothers and Fathers consider it an inelegant way of doing business* ~

And you, Erasmus? Do you think it's inelegant? Or does it turn the stomach of insects to see men killed?

~ *I have ontological objections* ~

In any case, these two men had done her no more wrong than getting in her way. She didn't treat them any the gentler for it when she finally persuaded her chains to unlock and fall away. Her guards didn't react with the surprise she'd hoped for, but drew nonchalant clubs and stepped wearily to subdue her, maybe punish her too if she read their flat, pinched smiles right. She unfurled her whip and took away first their weapons, then their wits.

Then the paradox washed through the *laboratorium*, changing the world completely but leaving it unaltered. The guards, if they'd been awake, would have felt nothing. Cousin Greenaway noticed it lightly, as if it were a fine spray of rain that didn't settle on the skin but evaporated immediately under a renewed sun.

'What was that?' she asked Erasmus, aloud – that was how much it had rattled her. She felt the quease in her stomach, she felt Erasmus itching inside her. What had only brushed her had scarred him.

~ *A probability realignment* ~ *Something has been physically inserted into or excised from the continuity of the Spiral Politic* ~ *Local conditions are rewriting themselves to compensate* ~ *Think of it as patching a hole in a bucket to stop it leaking* ~

Is that bad?

~ *Define bad* ~

Is it harmful to us? To anyone?

~ *Not to us; this was small scale, almost zero, so it's self-healing* ~ *We call them daughter events* ~

Why?

~ *The compensation generates short-lived spontaneous timelines as part of the process, like children* ~ *They don't last long* ~ *Too much heat, too little space, they burn up quickly* ~ *The holes in the solid world are plugged with the skins of dead universes* ~

You didn't answer my other question. Is it harmful to anyone?

~ *If the thing that's been excised was a living being then yes and no* ~

If I didn't know you inside out I'd swear you were just doing this to confuse me.

~ *Flatterer* ~ *Yes, it's harmful because they've been destroyed* ~ *No, it's not harmful because they never existed in the first place, and the world heals over everything they ever were and ever did, leaving a scab* ~ *Greenaway?* ~

Yes?

~ *This is important* ~ *Your people are at war* ~ *What you've just felt is a report from the front* ~

'I know,' she said. She meant it. 'I know.'

She was eager to finish their business and get out of the Service's prison before... someone? She couldn't recall his name or picture his face... came back for her. Erasmus, who had sensed this opportunity from as far away as the House of the Infernal, guided her to the egg. It was concealed in a fat pot being used to hold down a rug in the middle of the workroom. She lifted the lid and recognised the light within.

It recognised her. It recognised Erasmus.

They must have captured Plainsong and got it from him. It's not damaged?

~ *It can't be damaged* ~ *Not by the science of this period* ~

She shoved the egg deep into the folds of her dress. We need to get this back to Paris.

She praised the building all the way to the exits, ensuring they made a rapid escape. From there it was a long and cold but not particularly eventful trudge through the glow of night-time London to the river, and her cabal's hiding place. Mother Sphinx and her cousins were all waiting for her, along with her mask that she'd had to surrender so that they could smuggle the Jesuitess from the House of the Infernal. Judging by Amphigorey and Hateman's bruises, that hadn't ended successfully.

The *loa* totems were all silent and still. The Homeworlder had got away from them, or died in the attempt.

'So where does that leave us?' Greenaway asked. 'Are we still in danger?'

'We're always in danger,' Hateman said. 'They'll come again. They *will* come.'

'Not today,' Mother Sphinx chimed in. No one else shared her air of satisfied confidence. Eventually, they drifted back to the shrine, one by one, to find their beds. In her cot, Greenaway heard the others move around, first shifting as insomniacs on mattresses that became too saturated with effort to be slept on, then gradually migrating into each other's rooms, partly to make love but mainly to avoid being alone. She imagined she heard Amphigorey with Hateman, Hateman with Suppression, and then all three together. She was almost – *almost* – tempted to join them.

No. Not with her *loa* there watching her, afraid that – unguarded – she might reveal him.

She left the shrine and went to sit on one of the hard wood benches in the ruin outside. There was no light, except that radiating from the egg now pressed cold against her stomach. A little warmth would have been welcome tonight, when small flakes of snow were falling through the gaps in the ceiling.

She sat gazing into darkness. Then she spoke. 'So?' she asked.

'So,' said Mother Sphinx, 'has he gotta name?'

She nodded, not doubting for a moment that the mother could see that little movement in the dark. 'He's called Erasmus,' she said.

Give us the future.

Le Pouvoir were losing patience with Nathaniel Silver. He had expected this from the moment he'd arrived in Paris, eight years earlier. He was no longer the Magus they expected. He had lost his lustre when the egg had been taken from him. Not that he needed the egg to make himself useful – and he did, within the limits of his abilities and his conscience – but he was no longer brilliant, and he no longer trusted the power in his hands or his heart. *Le Pouvoir* protected him, and he was grateful; they had reunited him with Alice, and he worked hard to repay them; they indulged his investigations into affairs that seemed impractical, even trivial, and he knew he was accruing a debt. On the first day of the New Year, M. Ladre and his *danse macabre* came to him and presented him with a full bill for services rendered.

Le Pouvoir wanted the future. They wanted to conquer tomorrow, and they believed Silver was the man who could do it.

He didn't enquire as to the penalties that would befall him if he didn't comply, but they used elegant loaded words to insist that they would not hurt him. 'How could we? You are a man who cannot feel pain.'

'I can feel pain,' he told them, sitting solidly at his desk. 'I'm sure you're aware of that.'

They stood around him, the five kings in red, in their scarlet hats and tunics and paint-masks. Silver hadn't risen from behind the desk, which was covered in documents pertaining to the case of Señor Suarez, one corner pinned down by the pickle pot that contained the Spaniard's tongue. He'd been studying them innocently in the early hours, but now they seemed ominous.

'You refuse to die, then,' said M. Ladre. 'You are unlike so many others in that respect.' And Silver nodded, absorbing the implications and thinking he would have to send Alice away if he failed, somewhere far beyond the clutches of *le Pouvoir*, if there was such a place on Earth. Then he thought of Suarez and Harrow and the girl, who had been turned back by death, unwanted.

'I'll do my best,' he told them, smiling blandly, as the *macabre* filed out of his room to evaporate in the dawn light. In truth, he didn't have the first idea of how to begin. *Le Pouvoir*'s ambition was driving it to the edges of a finite, shrinking world. There was still so much undiscovered, but the cartographers were confident it was only a matter of time now before the Earth's four quarters were thoroughly mapped. Then eyes would have to turn inwards or outwards for new discoveries, into the microscope pointed down or the telescope aimed at the heavens; and once the worlds above and below were uncovered, what frontiers remained, except those of time?

They didn't mean it that way, of course. They just wanted to secure their legacy, for as long as possible, maybe until judgement (when, it was tacitly agreed, the wealthy sinners who could outrank Heaven's opulence would have somehow *won* the human race). Nevertheless, Silver's thoughts turned to the more abstract notion, that the future was real and could be assaulted.

Any man who makes war on the future would be destroying his own children, he thought idly, *but isn't that what we do anyway?*

He went out for his regular morning walk in Paris, stopping for a drink and the latest gossip in an inauthentically Ottoman caffé house, then to Rue Slaughter for a quiet meeting with Reinette – who was certainly handling him for *le Pouvoir*, but agreeable company none the less – followed by a stroll through the less salubrious back streets and quarters of the city in search of inspiration. Today he went looking for fortune tellers with shrew-stones and beryl mirrors, but found mainly charlatans. He was shown a specula, liberated from the palace of Montezuma II, supposedly cursed; more likely from some provincial glassworks in Normandy. The mirror reflected his own face back on him, unremarkably. He had stayed clean-shaven since Salomon's House. He had lost a lot of weight. He had lost none of his youth. He put it down, declined to pay for it, and walked home with his head still in a miasma of thought.

As he climbed his stairs, he spotted that his door had been opened and left ajar. He continued climbing casually. He felt certain this must be a simple burglar – *le Pouvoir* were watching this place, and the agents of another crown wouldn't be so careless as to advertise their presence. He reached the half-landing slowly, then threw himself into his rooms, his cane raised to fight off the intruder.

Back on the battlefield, Nate Silver, as if you never left. Was it le Pouvoir *who made you a soldier again? Or is it part of you? Do you carry the black earth of Edgehill in your soul?*

He tumbled through the door, landing gracelessly, sending a twinge through his ankle and knocking all the air and the fight out of him. The woman at his desk shrieked and half-ducked as he fell into the room. Silver stared at her for a moment, bewildered, then threw his stick away, mortified by her tears.

'Alice!' he exclaimed, half-apology, half-delight. 'I didn't realise you were back.'

He ran to her to comfort her, but she fought him off. He gave her his handkerchief and backed into the corner to wait while she dried her eyes. She was getting older now; there was no trace of the girl she'd once been, except maybe in those eyes that were presently obscured by her red blotched skin. If they walked out together, he'd still be thought the elder, but in another few years she might overtake him. He would start to grow young in her eyes. That was a day he wanted to put off for as long as possible.

She staunched her tears and threw the grubby cloth he'd given her down on a pile of Inquisitorial paperwork.

'What's the matter?' he asked.

'They know where you are. They knew the name of the street and the number. They knew *everything*,' she snarled. 'I was so scared for you, Nate. I was scared for me. She stopped me in the street. I thought she'd kill me.'

'Who?' *Le Pouvoir.* No, that didn't make sense. The Service, then?

'Faction Paradox!' she spat the name. He almost didn't recognise it. 'From Salomon's House? The skulls? Remember?!' He recalled them at last and nodded. 'They sent a woman after me. She was wearing that mask. I could smell it like it still had meat on it.'

'Did they hurt you?' She shook her head. 'Did they threaten you?' She shook her head. 'What did they want?'

'They wanted me to give you something. She said it was a *gesture of goodwill*. She said she wanted you to think of them as friends.' And the strength in her voice broke at last and she descended into burble – 'Nate, I'm sorry. I only brought it here because I was scared they'd kill me' – into panic that didn't subside even when Silver held her and kissed her; and she would still be trembling and frightened later when they made love. She had always preferred the dark. Tonight she would insist on light.

She gestured to a small wood box that she'd put on a table on the opposite side of the room, as far from the desk as she could manage. Gesturing her to kneel behind the desk, Silver went to it, touched it gingerly, found it cold, flipped open the lid.

Alice thought it might explode. When he saw the light he imagined she was right.

Then he recognised it, and the shape at the heart of it. He thought he was rid of this. He didn't want it, or the debt he had incurred to Faction Paradox by taking it back. Still, he found himself smiling and mouthing to it. All the questions he had longed to ask rose to the forefront of his mind.

And the egg whispered his name back to him, and forgave him.

'It's safe,' he said. 'You can come out.'

'What is it?' Alice asked.

He didn't turn to answer her, but remained fixed, staring into the depths of the light. It was the future.

⇒ Chapter 16: *Astraea, at the Dawn of Time* ⇐

There was a road that ran past her home. It had grown from the path trod by a penitent king as he'd shambled barefoot to the tomb of a friend he'd had killed; over a half-thousand years, it had been smoothed from a track into a proper road by the soles and cartwheels of the pilgrims who followed and then returned, all the while telling themselves lewd stories of a sort that Eff's mother refused to let her hear because they were *swinish and filthy, full of effing and blinding and the Devil knows what else.* Master Rooke had a book of such tales, and read to Eff from it, behind her mother's back.

Lately the road had carried armies, strutting out in pomp and slinking back in shame. It had carried heroes and traitors. It had carried the dead and the dying, and sometimes those wagons stopped at the hospital to unload their cargoes of corpses-to-be. These convoys grew rarer as the country settled. Much of what replaced it was, in Eff's estimation, boring. She would sit by the road in her idle moments, watching the wheels spin past but caring nothing for the dull commerce they carried back-and-forth between Dover and London. The road was a boundary her parents forbade her to cross, but she wouldn't be told. She went straight across it now, making for the boundaries of Blean.

Eff was alone. She was a popular-enough girl, and had already turned the heads of boys and – to her surprise and crafty delight – even some girls, but the forest was her special retreat and she wouldn't take anyone with her to taint it. She wouldn't even admit Tom Culpepper, whom she called brother, though he had in any case been forced to flee, like Master Rooke, like so many others. Crossing the road was like flight, she imagined, and Blean was a singular exile. Her schoolmaster had explained its significance to her. The forest was a fragment of an older world, when wildwoods had covered the whole of the British Island, before the New Trojans had arrived to make farms and cities and gardens, putting to the axe trees numbering more than the quantity of all the men who had ever lived.

'The spirit of old Britain lives on under these trees,' Master Rooke had told her. 'Walk there a time and you will notice the light does not fall as the wan light of our current age. These are beams that drop from an older sun, whose glory has long since been extinguished.'

'Before I was born.'

'*Long* before you and I were born, Miss Johnson. Before Christ was born. Before God made Adam, some say. Before God Himself was made.' And he'd put his finger to his lips, as he did when sharing a secret, and she'd sealed their compact by giving him a fat, rounded smile.

'A very long time ago,' she'd opined. She could hear her voice sometimes, and regretted how shrill she could sound, how self-possessed.

'It's said,' Rooke had continued, now certain of her complicity in his teachings, 'that if you wander too far into the wood, you will be lost forever. There are some tracks that lead you into the deep past, as if that island-forest was still standing. If you get lost, you'll never find your way back. You will live out your life never seeing another man or woman, because those were the days of the age before humans set foot in Britain.'

'I'd be alone.'

'You would not be alone,' Rooke had taught her.

'What lived in the woods,' she'd asked him, 'in the olden days?'

He'd told her. She'd been much younger, and had taken him at his word. She no longer quite believed that she would find giants, nymphs, and satyrs on her forays into the woods; she had more grown-up priorities now. But he was right all the same, the light *was* different. It fell through the branches of the trees in warm pellets, like unwet rain; it was golden. Eff went as deep as she could, trying to lose herself. She ran until there was pain below her new-budded breasts, until the autumn air turned chilly and iron in her lungs, and though she wanted to whoop and holler she didn't make a sound. Twigs cracked and leaves rustled beneath her feet, but there was nothing more. She was afraid she might be followed; she never was.

She walked for an immeasurable period of time, until the green light grew so thick it seemed like evening, though it was the middle of the day. She had explored much of the woods, but there was always more. Sometimes she would spin round and round until she fell, then stagger off in whatever direction she was pointing when her head stopped spinning. She was not in that sort of mood today; besides, she had a bundle with her, and was afraid of spilling its bounty. She didn't quite know where she was going, only that she'd recognise the spot when she saw it.

Her resting place proved to be a dry slope overlooking a pool where two streams met and mated and became one. Their currents fought and whirled around one another before draining downhill towards a fiercer river. This was perfect. Eff removed her shoes so she could stand barefoot on the ancient soil. She could imagine Christ's naked soles walking on the same land, and took a little pleasure from the thought that He would have been humbled by His surroundings, just another a shiny deity trespassing in an older world.

She had food with her, wrapped up in a blanket for sitting on – aweful nature was one thing, but she would get a beating if the seat of her dress came back muddied. She'd brought bread, hard cheese, and a bottle of wine, lifted from the tables when the kitchen-maid wasn't looking. More importantly, she'd brought her flute. She sat herself cross-legged on the blanket – which she imagined to be an appropriate posture for the worship of small, old gods – and began to play.

In the open air it sounded strange and halting at first, but she soon lost herself in the music.

She didn't believe that she could charm the birds from the trees or coax the creatures of the woods out of their setts and burrows, but a girl could hope. They would all come to her, creeping or slithering, fluttering on wings or strolling on four legs, to make her audience. While she played, she would restore harmony to the world and tame the savagery of nature. The owl would not snatch the mice. The wolf would not prey on the rabbits. The badgers would generally refrain from being vicious little buggers. They would do nothing but sit and listen, until, as she reached a crescendo, the deer would come to applaud her from the ridge, the bucks parading around her with heads lowered, offering their antlers to her in supplication. She would sing the lost ages of the world back into being, if only for a moment. The animals would eat the music from her hands.

She had never seen anything larger than a fox in these woods, and they had been mangy things with sad, terrified eyes.

Sometimes she imagined that Cromwell would come this way, riding on the back of an enormous black hound. She would see him as he truly was, not as his deluded followers saw him – bewarted, stunted, and ugly, driven to his fits of treachery by his repulsive aspect and pious mania. His faults – that a better man would have striven to overcome, so they were no excuse – had turned him into the worst of all men, the worst of all criminals, and the worst of all tyrants. She imagined herself leaping from her pose to throttle him with her bare hands, at the cost of her own life if needs be. She breathed such daydreams into her pipe.

A raucous crowing from the high branches distracted her. She put down her flute and scanned the woods for some disturbance. Probably not Cromwell, she guessed. More crowing. The birds were going bloody mad in their nests. The green canopy of leaves shook as a flock took flight, so Eff was looking up when the explosion came.

Her head came down in time to see the wet aftershock of the blast as a plume of water was hurled up from the pool, splashing over her. *Cannon*, she thought instantly, but then dismissed it. There would be other signs of battle, and only a madman would be firing at random into the forest. No, this was more like something had fallen from the trees, or the sky – a bird perhaps? No, no, it was too big.

She ran to the water's edge.

It was a body. Shocked, Eff leaned forward and saw that it was still alive, thrashing violently. She couldn't tell it were a man or a woman, an adult or a child; the murk and the light made it impossible to see. Its face seemed to blaze like an earthbound sun, a glare without features, though that was surely the reflection of the afternoon light on the water – ah, yes it must be! As the clouds moved to obscure the sun, so the light grew dimmer and cooler. Eff thought of her dress, already coated with mud to the knees, sure to get filthier. She plunged into the water and *grabbed*.

The hand she found was slippery, but she squeezed hard. The pool sucked the body down and almost dragged Eff with it. She fought back, the muscles and bones in her shoulders screaming, an unbecoming grunt on her lips. The pool surrendered, and the body surged upwards toward the air. Eff grunted again, elation this time, and hauled and hauled until she'd raised the drowning head and shoulders above the line of the water. A further tug drew her prize to the shore. Eff fell back into the clammy mud, ruining her dress for good. She wailed. She feared she'd done nothing more than fish out a bloated corpse.

It was a woman. It was the most striking woman Eff had ever seen, though bedraggled, with her pretty face smeared with long dirty streaks of red hair. Her skin was white and cold. She opened her mouth and coughed up water, which came out pink. Her eyes came open and they were glazed as if she were blind. One hand rose shaking to her throat, clutching it desperately as if trying to expel more bloodied pondwater, but nothing further came; her other hand was a fist clasping some object tight against her body.

'Are you alright?' Eff asked. How polite and how odd to ask such a foolish question!

The woman pulled herself up out of the mud and scrambled away from the bank. She managed about half-a-dozen graceless steps before her strength deserted her and she came crashing down onto the grass. Eff went patiently to kneel beside her.

'I have some food,' she said, 'and a blanket. I'll fetch them.' The woman sat up while she was gone and folded her arms round herself – not from cold, Eff thought, but something else, some inexpressible fear about her body. Was she wounded? Eff saw there was a rip in the fabric of her clothes above her stomach, though the skin beneath seemed whole and unbroken. Her costume itself was unusual and deeply immodest; from some angles, she appeared naked, but she was in fact wearing decorated red armour tight against her skin. Eff wanted to see more, but kept her eyes low and incurious, afraid she'd scare this woman off.

If this *was* a woman.

'What's your name?' she asked. 'I'm Eff.'

There was no answer. She tried again: 'I didn't see you till you were in the water,' she explained. 'Did you slip?'

Her catch was silent. She stretched out under a patch of sun, her lank limbs extending and giving Eff a clear impression of how tall she must be. The hair that matted like weed on her face would be a lighter red when it dried. Her eyes had sharpened and were prowling, suspicious of her surroundings. There were men who came back from the battlefields like this, with life still in their bodies but their spirits burned out or fled. Cannon-fire was said to bring its own madness – or maybe she'd struck her head in the pool and dashed out her wits. Eff smoothed back the woman's hair and surreptitiously felt for a wound, but the scalp was unbroken. The woman's body was warm, below the layers of damp.

There was another explanation for her demeanour, but Eff didn't care to contemplate it. When the thought rose, she pushed it back down. She busied herself with practical matters. She handed over her food and watched fascinated as the woman sniffed it and tasted it cautiously (like a mouse) then gobbled it in wide mouthfuls (like a wolf). Eff gave her wine to wash it down.

'Do you have a name?' she asked again, but the woman paid her no attention. 'I'll have to call you something!' But she couldn't think of anything. Perhaps she should take her back to the village, maybe to the hospital? No. The longer Eff spent sitting here, the less certain was she that her catch had suffered any physical injury besides shock and cold; and there was something in the woman's furtive manner that wanted to stay hidden. Maybe she was on the run, like the prince. Maybe she needed to be kept secret.

'I'll have to go home soon,' Eff said, at last. 'Will you come back with me?'

The woman stopped chewing but said nothing. *No*, then.

'Where will you go?' Eff asked, and received the same blank response. 'I can come back later. I can bring more food. Would you like that?' More dead-eyed silence; this time Eff chose to interpret it as a *yes*.

Her companion was staring over her shoulder. Eff turned slowly, and found herself gazing back down at the pool, which babbled and churned as it had always done, as if it had never been disturbed. The suspicion came back to her, and she still couldn't voice it, not directly.

'Did you come from there?' she asked, carefully. 'From the water?'

She didn't expect an answer. When she looked back, she received a jolt. The woman's gaze had not moved. She hadn't been looking past Eff at all but directly at her, into her face, as if trying to wring out its secrets. Eff, shuddering in the warm sun, should have been afraid but wasn't. This was *exciting*.

The time came when Eff had to leave, as the sun began to climb down the horizon into evening. In all that time, the woman didn't speak or move from her spot, and Eff simply sat with her basking in the silence. She understood that some parts of the world had laws that made a rescuer responsible for the life of anyone they saved, and though England would not compel her to this, still she felt she had acquired a duty. She waited until the woman's hair had begun to dry, then she made her apologies. She promised she would return. Afraid the woman would leave without her, she went back to her resting place on the slope and fetched her flute. She held it out on both palms, open, a gift.

'This is the most precious thing in the world to me,' she explained. The creature took it from her and held it against herself, wrapping her arms tight round it. Eff felt she had been understood.

She collected her shoes and folded her cloak to disguise the dried sludge on her skirts. The mild afternoon was becoming a warm, insect-thick evening. She hurried back, taking the shortest route through the woods, then cutting across the common back to the village. She was already late, and lost her breath on the way. Some of the boys whistled her as she ran past them, but she ignored them. They were Rud Sturrock's mob in any case, and their interest in her was not wholly flattering.

She stopped just out of sight of her house, brushed away more dirt from her dress, then turned her trot into a saunter for the final few steps. Her mother grabbed her arm as she came through the door, and dealt her a hard blow on her backside with a flat hand.

'Effy!' she screeched. 'Where in God's name have you been? You won't be found when there's work to be done! Such a lazy girl.' Such was her anger that she didn't even mention the poor state of Eff's clothes, or – there was a glass on the wall for Eff to see herself – the dirt on her face and hands. Her mother dragged her to the kitchen and scrubbed the worst of it away with a cloth. Eff was used to this rough kindness, and made the least protest. She had a secret that might slip in anger.

Once she'd got her daughter as clean as she could manage, Eff's mother thrust a laden tray into the girl's arms, and directed her through to the parlour. 'Your father's entertaining. Take these through to the gentlemen. Be polite, and don't make me ashamed.'

Eff was an ungainly maid. The tray shuddered with each slow step. She kept her eyes intently on the jugs and plates, willing them to stay still and unbroken, and so didn't see her father's latest guests until she was almost at the table. Unannounced visits to the House of Johnson were no longer rare events, and she had grown used to strangers, whose names were never mentioned and who seldom appeared more than once. There were two this time, both still dressed for the road and both weary. One fellow was as old as her father but heavier, a sour Falstaff she thought. She knew the name from Rooke's volumes of the obscure old bard, never having seen a stage. The other – younger, leaner, sharper – must be the Hal; he would have been more handsome if he'd taken time to attend the state of his beard. In spite of their obvious exertion, both men were in good humour, and she – the plump shape wobbling dangerously towards them – was their butt.

'By God,' cried Falstaff. 'Here's one who's been in the wars!'

Self-consciously, she set down the tray and poured wine for them. Her cheeks were reddening prettily. Blond Hal reached out to brush a hair from her dirtied forehead. She fussed on her feet. 'How old are you, girl?'

By their accents they were not local. Nor Londoners. They must have come far. This would be their final stop before Dover. Then where? Antwerp? Dijon?

'Twelve,' she said. She breathed in hard to let him appreciate her chest, but a voice cut in from behind her and spoiled the effect.

'She'll be eleven years come winter, and she's my daughter.'

Blond Hal nodded and withdrew his hand. Eff cringed, her crimson cheeks now prickling uncomfortably. Her father strode commandingly across the room to join his guests at the table – and perhaps that's what these weary men saw, a confident and prosperous patriarch, where Eff could only notice how old he seemed, how timid and how weighted with burdens.

'She'll make a good wife some day,' Hal said primly. 'I meant no harm, sir.'

'No harm was done, and you're right, she'll have good prospects if the world rebalances itself. If it stays topsy-turvy, then who knows? I worry for her.' Both Bart Johnson's guests were nodding at his wisdom and his proper concern. Eff, standing to one side, found herself discussed as if she weren't there.

A smile formed on her father's face, between the greying beard and moustache. 'You'll play for us later, won't you?' But he was looking to his guests, explaining: 'She's a fair flautist.'

Eff agitated. This needed a convincing lie, but she was good at that sort of thing. 'I've had bloody teeth all week and can't get a note from it. I could dance,' she suggested brightly. And sure enough, as the evening wore on she was called out to gallivant before the fire, but slipped and fell on her arse, to the amusement of all. She didn't feel stung. It wasn't cruelty. These men, her father included, had seen much they couldn't bear. Laughter was the sound of their forgetting.

She spent most of her evening in the kitchen, as her father and his nameless guests conversed in low tones. She tried hard not to listen to them as she came out, though one snippet caught her ear. They were discussing the colonies. Her father had spoken sometimes about investing in a prospectus of land in the Americas, but she'd known immediately that it was an empty aspiration. Her father wouldn't abandon England, no matter how much he yearned to leave. She would have to go one day, but on her own.

'...can only hope the colonies will stay loyal,' her father was saying as she shuffled in with another tray. 'So there'll still be some bolthole for free Englishmen, and maybe leverage across the ocean.'

'That's what Willoughby's doing in Barbados,' Falstaff rumbled, through a mouth full of food.

'Won't last,' Hal shook his head. 'The fleet's gone to the Indies to force him to terms.'

At that, her father let out such a groan as she had never heard. All the air went out of him. The party stopped talking entirely as Eff reached the table, and she served them in silence. There was nothing remarkable about this gathering of old men, though she might once have thought there was. She had a better secret waiting for her in the forest.

She made preparations for her return. She was left alone in the kitchen for a time, and used that to squirrel away some more wine, cheese, and a cold portion of lamb. She doubted she could find clothes to fit such a long woman, and in any case, that might be a theft too far, but she found another blanket and a coat to add to her hoard. When she was sent to bed, she collected it on the way, carrying it in a basket with a busy look on her face as if this were just another ordinary household task before she could retire. She retrieved one final practical item from under her bed: a comb.

She made her escape through a window, with a lantern and with her hoard wrapped up in a bundle. She hit the earth below the sill with a dry soft thump; more grime on her dress. The windows on the ground floor illuminated her escape; she stayed low, hugging the shadows until she was clear of the edge of the village and near the road. As she lit up her lamp, Eff considered how changed the familiar landscape was by night, and feared she would lose her way in the wood. If the light in the Blean fell from the sky of another age, then the same must be true of the dark. In the gloom it was much easier to believe her deepest suspicions about the woman she'd rescued from the waters.

She was still there by the pool, but sleeping. She had Eff's blanket not just pulled over her, but coiled round and round as if she'd woven herself into it, like a cocoon. Eff held the lantern carelessly over her face, and the woman muttered and wrinkled her sharp nose but didn't wake.

Something flapped like a flag overhead. Eff lifted her light and saw the woman's armour slung over the branch of a tree, barely catching the breeze. It hung like a cobweb-wisp, Eff's beam glistening off its surface and off the beads of blood and water that slicked it still. It no longer looked big enough to contain a whole body, and in the strange light, the tattoos and designs written on its surface seemed to dance. Eff lowered her hand, placed the lantern on the ground close to the woman's sleeping body, and extinguished it.

Eff spread the fresh blanket on the comfortable grass, lay down, and wrapped its folds around herself. The body beside her was close and sweltering, throwing out heat like a freshly-spent gun. Their faces were close, their foreheads butted and their wilder hairs tangled together, but otherwise they did not touch. Eff had not planned on sleeping out here under the protection of the trees, and even now thought she would stay awake all night, but soon she was insensible in the throes of odd dreams until morning.

She woke with a thickness in her spine and cramps in her arms, but otherwise refreshed. This was the first time she'd woken in a truly strange place, and the most surprising part of it was how natural it felt. She rolled onto her side and gazed at the empty blanket beside her. The chrysalis was broken, the butterfly fled –

– but not far. The woman was crouched at the edge of the pool gazing into the waters from whence she'd risen. Her shed skin was still dangling limp – its drooping sleeves tickled the top of Eff's head as she rose – but she had wrapped herself in Eff's father's coat. It was a little too short and a little too broad for her, but it served its purpose. Her hair, now dried, was a frizz of stray and tangled strands. But she was more concerned with her face, which she touched and prodded with uncertain fingers. Her reflection, visible on the surface of this still backwater, seemed compelling to her. *Narcissus*, Eff thought. She brought food to the water's edge and offered it. Her charge took it, still not speaking but nodding gratefully.

Why wouldn't she speak? Was she mute or mad? Was there some quality of her voice that would betray her? She used her mouth only for eating, less ferociously today than before. In fact she was rather demur, and looked embarrassed when she couldn't finish a huge lump of cheese. Eff took it from her, inspecting the marks left in its soft body by the woman's teeth, before finishing it off herself. She was dreadfully hungry now, having had little to eat the previous day.

She didn't try to talk, but instead gestured to the woman's head, holding up the comb to show her intention. This seemed understood, and the woman sat patiently while Eff began to smooth her wild hair into something presentable to polite society; she made no complaints as Eff ripped through hard tangles. As the child worked, she talked, turning out whatever subject came to mind, from village gossip to affairs of state.

She didn't reveal her political sentiments. Such words might be dangerous in foreign ears.

'I had a pleasant night,' she said, starting a new paragraph of chatter, 'but it was disturbed by odd dreams. I get these a lot. My dad blames it on the turmoil of the age. I've never known a quiet year, you see, not since I was in the cradle. Master Rooke – he was my teacher, he thought different. He said I'm *blessed with a life of the inner mind*. Not that he'd say that to my father. Dad wouldn't have liked a lot of what I learned, if he only knew. Pagan things, he'd call them. Heathen things. But I must be an educated lady if I'm to get anywhere in this world.'

Did that get a reaction? No.

'Last night,' she wittered on, 'I'd a dream I think was about England, though at the time I didn't feel it was so. I was dreaming of a great building, vaster than any I've ever seen before. How I imagine Rome must look – or Jerusalem. I think it *was* Jerusalem. The old Jerusalem from antiquity, when it was a Jewish city and they still had their Great Temple. That's what it was, that building. I knew they must be Jews because of the hats they were wearing. You know, the type of skullcap that Jews are said to wear, though I'd be lying if I said I'd ever seen a real one...

'Where was I? Oh, yes. There was a great procession of the Jews into the Temple. It must have been some feast or ritual. The council of the rabbis filed in to fill every seat and bench in the inner temple, which is circular, like a great eye peering out from the centre of the world watching everything. They had all come to praise a man – a great man, in the most magnificent robes and with such a proud face. I think I would have fallen at his feet and worshipped if I'd been there. Did I say I wasn't actually there? It was like I knew I was watching something ancient, hundreds of years past. I was seeing how it happened, in antique Jerusalem –

'So, this man... He was their leader and they were hailing him, because he had been such a great leader, and because they wanted him to be king. They were making a crown for him. He only had to speak and it would be his... and that's when I thought *this is a dream about England*. It was Cromwell. Parliament will want him crowned, sooner or later. King Oliver the First. Can you imagine that?

'But before he could accept, all the doors swung open to admit soldiers in bright red uniforms. They burst in and declared that the whole thing was illegal and that everyone was under arrest. You see, that was Pride's Purge. The soldiers wanted to arrest the leader before he could name himself king. He opened his mouth to speak, but one of the guards pulled out an odd gun and shot him – just in the mouth so he couldn't speak. And the weird of it was the soldier. Because she was a woman, you see.

'Isn't that odd? Do you think it's prophecy? It's my fate to shoot Cromwell and restore the kingdom? Do I have to? Master Rooke taught me that the old Greek gods were always giving men and women dreams like that, and woe betide them if they fought against their destiny!' She laughed, and slipped in the question she wanted answering. 'Do you know anything about that?'

No answer. She'd finished with the woman's head and turned away, to brush out hairs caught in the comb's teeth. She knelt to wash it in the waters. 'And what about you,' she asked idly, 'did you dream?'

'Yes.'

Eff turned as she heard the word, and studied the woman's face, which was immobile as if no sound had ever preceded from it. She risked another question: 'What did you dream of?'

This time she saw the lips move: 'Peace.'

Such a simple word, but she made it sound so complicated and so lonely.

Eff wiped the comb dry on her hem, thinking hard about what to say next. She might as well come out with it. 'You're a nymph aren't you? You rose from the waters. You don't belong here. You're from an older world.'

The nymph nodded. There was force in her face, as there had been in the face of the

Cromwell of her dreams, but this just made her more beautiful. There was no softness there, that was all in her voice, which came again. 'I'm from an older world,' she agreed.

Eff was startled to find herself crying. 'You poor thing,' she blurted, between sobs.

The nymph was still anonymous, and though happy to respond to Eff's questioning in her new-found voice, she was less than precise in her answers. By the time noon passed, Eff was none the wiser, but had made herself hoarse describing the stories of the Greek gods and demi-gods that Master Rooke had taught her in the gaps between the more conventional and ladylike aspects of her education. The nameless nymph sat there and smiled and occasionally nodded, which Eff took as acknowledgement rather than agreement. She gave nothing of herself away.

There remained on the demi-goddess's face a terrible hunger that Eff felt was directed entirely at her. Some of the local boys stared at her like that, the older ones usually. In their eyes it was desire and it was crude. Here, in the eyes of this woman-shaped miracle, it was more of a yearning appetite. It didn't want to possess Eff. It *needed* her. She was an immortal, transfixed by brief human life like a moth flattened onto the glass of a lit window. Without this urge, she would be merely pretty. With it, she was beautiful.

Sometimes it became hard for Eff to stop herself leaning across the often-narrow gap between their faces and kissing her.

'How did you come to be here?' Eff asked, after wetting her dry mouth with a little stolen wine.

'I followed you,' the nymph explained.

'I would have heard you or seen you.'

'Not physically. I followed your blood. I followed your life.'

'I don't understand.'

'You don't need to.' The nymph sighed and sprawled back on the grass. She still wore the coat, but when she fell back the fold came immodestly open and Eff made a show of shading her eyes. 'Have you ever gone on a journey and found that a tree has fallen across the road? How would you get to where you need to go?'

Eff shrugged. 'Take another road.'

'What if that's blocked by another tree? What if they're all blocked?'

'That's not likely.'

'Say you have an enemy who doesn't want you to get where you need to be and has deliberately closed off all the roads. You can't turn back, so what do you do?'

'I'd try to work out where I need to be and beat another path to it.'

'That's what you are to me. You're my path. I came here because this is your quiet time, when I knew I could recover. Also, it's very close to the original entry-point, though not close enough that I can find my way to it. I'm sorry, Eff, this must be confusing for you.'

Eff. She had always been called Eff. It was a cheerful name, but it was woefully inadequate on the lips of this wonderful ancient monster. 'Aphra,' she said. 'Call me Aphra.'

'Aphra,' the nymph agreed.

'Where is it you need to go?'

The demi-goddess shook her head. 'I don't know yet. I'm hunting.'

'What are you hunting?'

'A man,' she replied leisurely, 'or a woman. Maybe something else, but those are the most likely. I don't know who it is.'

'Could it be me?' Eff asked, suddenly afraid of being pursued by this mistress of the hunt, pinned and skewered by her barbs and her fury. Artemis was a goddess of the hunt, also Diana. Was she a *Diana*? She didn't look like one. Whatever her name, she was shaking her head slowly.

'I would have known when I first saw you – it's not you. But I know your life. My suit read it in your blood. Twice in your lifetime, you will come close to the creature I'm hunting.' She paused then, and her tongue poked out to lick her lips. '*Possibly* a third time as well, but the reading was confused.'

'What is it?' Eff asked.

The hollow need in the nymph's eyes wasn't brutal or dark, but it had those things in it, and they were revealed now. Eff looked away, unable to bear the sight.

The woman's voice remained pleasant. 'The worst thing that has ever lived,' she said.

Eff nodded, and believed her. 'What will you do when you've found it? Kill it?'

'If I can.'

Eff lay down on the grass like a faithful pet beside her mistress. The nymph kept her eyes fixed on the overhanging trees, as if trying to stare through to the sky beyond. It was not, Eff thought, that she didn't look like a killer, because she had seen so many boys come back from war trying to feign innocence and disguise their deeds. Her innocence was uncertainty, as of an apprentice on the edge of making the leap to journeyman and afraid he'd slip on the way. She took the limp hand that lay beside her, but the nymph didn't react. 'How long have you been hunting?' she asked.

'Longer than you could know. There are so many worlds he could have chosen, and it took me so long to catch his scent.'

'How long?' Eff asked again, not forcefully.

The nymph's eyes closed. 'Nearly four hundred years,' came the reply. Then she rolled onto her side to address Eff directly. 'Will you help me? I need your life to be my path. Will you let me use it?'

Eff considered. 'And if I said *yes*, what would you do?'

'I'd get up. Put on my suit. Follow you until you led me back to the hunt.'

'And you'd do that when? This very minute?'

'This minute, if you said yes.'

She didn't beg, but the need was there and it pleaded. Eff hardened her face and turned away, unable for the moment to look at her nymph. She got to her feet and walked away from the pool, back to the slope where she'd sat the day before, before this eruption from the older world had overwhelmed her. The nymph didn't follow. When Eff turned to survey the scene, she had shed the coat and sat naked by the banks of the pool. She looked less supernatural from this distance, so pale and freckled, so skinny – starved almost into a skeleton, still beautiful but altogether more ordinary. The fabulous armour that hung from the tree was remarkable, but not beyond mundane explanation. It might be that this was just some poor mad woman or a malicious prankstress. Eff came here to fantasise. How easy it would be to mistake the solid world for the whispering lies inside her head!

No. She wanted to believe. She looked around the woods, which seemed as ancient as Master Rooke promised, and – even now – were undisturbed by human presence. They were spirits, the both of them, on the borderland of a heavier world. Beyond the edge of the trees there was endlessly-grinding traffic, there was starvation and war, there was tyranny and an anointed king fleeing for his life. There was the death-rattle in the throat of her own father as all he lived for was squeezed out of him by each new appalling piece of news. Thus was all the magic and wonder throttled out of the slow-dying world.

Eff made up her mind, walked back to the nymph, and dropped to her knees.

'I will do anything for you,' she pledged. 'My life is yours to do with as you will. I'll serve you as best I can, above and beyond any other cause. I'll be the best path and the best weapon and the best servant you ever had, I promise.' And this time she leaned in close and kissed the woman, who seemed entirely unsurprised by this revelation of her servant's true colours.

'Is that a yes?' came the reply, said so solemnly it couldn't be a joke.

'Yes, but on one condition. Just the one,' Eff gabbled, before the woman could react. 'It'll be no hardship. You've already waited four hundred years.'

Impatience ticked in that beautiful face, as invisible as her hunger but just as palpable. When she took Eff's hands she was gentle, she didn't squeeze too tight. One day soon these would be killing hands. 'You want me to stay?' she asked.

Eff couldn't help herself. Her face creased and the tears squeezed out of her eyes and the snivel from her nose. 'Just another night. That's all. You can be here today and gone tomorrow. Just stay another night, please!'

The nymph pulled her closer, agreeing wordlessly. It was such a small thing, the least of all possible boons, to hold off her hunt for another day just to keep Eff happy. It didn't staunch Eff's tears, but it changed them utterly.

Even so, when their embrace broke it hurt like a parting, and when the nymph released her grip Eff felt as though all the glory of the world had slipped away.

She had to go back to the house for the afternoon. She had work to do, more than two days' worth stored up for her now, though at least some of that would be given to the servants, while she would face a stern lecture and an equally stern beating. She left the forest with regret, but not uncertainty: the nymph would be there for her. She was a fey thing, and constant in a way that the solid world was not.

On her way back, Eff also realised that she would have to account for her absence to her parents, and also – vaguely – that they might be distressed; but the house seemed deserted when she arrived. Her father would be in Canterbury today, of course, and her mother might have business in the village, and they would take the servants with them leaving the house hollow and unwelcoming. Eff felt aggrieved as she prowled the empty rooms. She had been abandoned!

Not quite! A hand snatched out behind her, caught her ear and twisted it. She catyowled and corkscrewed her body to escape, but the grip held fast. 'And where are you going in such a hurry, girl?' came her captor's voice. Its owner manhandled her through passageways to one of the bedrooms before releasing her. She fell back against a wall, breathing hard and spitting. Her captor clomped to the guest-bed, which remained unmade – *one of your duties today, wasn't it?* – and perched on the edge. Falstaff.

He pointed to a jug by the bed. 'Pour us some wine, will you?'

She did as she was told, then slammed the jug down hard so that splashes leapt from the rim. 'Where's your friend?' she asked, not politely.

Falstaff downed the meagre volume she'd served him in one gulp, as Shakespeare's man would have done, though with less warmth and wit. 'With your father. Just me and you here now. Most of the day it's just been me. You know this morning I saw your mother thrash a maid to the blood for stealing food. Not that she stole nothing, y'understand? You're a fat little thing. You want to know where the food goes in this house, look who's got the tummy on her.'

Eff stood and bristled – she was rather pleased with her firm and swollen belly – but he ploughed on. He wasn't drunk. She wished he was drunk, it might drain the sour out of him. 'And you weren't in your bed this morning, either. Your mum and dad were goin' mad, so I piped up for you. I says you were up bright and early and I sent you on an errand. That's two beatings I spared you. I don't care what you were up to, but you owe me now.' And he leered at her.

Fuck, she thought, not this. She recoiled, folding her arms protectively over her body and trembling. The door was slammed, and any screams would not be heard. If only it were Hal, who was at least young and handsome, and not a blotched old broken-nosed sot. She turned away from Falstaff so he couldn't see her cry and began to pull her dress over her shoulders.

Fury bellowed at her back: 'God's hooks, girl! What are you doing?' He rose from his perch, span her round and wrenched cloth back down to cover her. 'You think this is a game?! I'm trusted by the best man in England, do you think he'd do that if I fucked children? Oh stop it, stop crying you silly bitch. Here,' he thrust a smeared cloth into her hand, not even a handkerchief. Eff held it unused and didn't dry her eyes.

Falstaff rummaged through his bags, then sat waiting until Eff had stopped blubbing. He used the cloth to wipe her face, then pressed a sealed note into her hand. There was no name on it, no writing whatsoever. 'You'll have more guests these next few months. Ask every man who comes if his name is *Maynarde*. One will say no, it is in fact *Tyrell*. When you hear that, you'll curtsy and blush and make all the apologies you can. Later, you'll find that man again and give him this. Make sure no one sees you.'

Eff stared at the clean folded sheet – 'Will I get into trouble if I give this to the wrong man?' – and something like realisation dawned. There was blood inside her mouth from where she'd bitten it, still a better taste than salt tears and snot. 'Will my father get into trouble?'

Falstaff sank back on the bed, which sagged. 'No. This is a trifle. If you're caught it won't matter, but you'll never be asked again. If you're successful, then, well, you may be asked more favours.'

'I only owe two,' she reminded him, but her heart was pounding already.

Falstaff grinned at her. 'You have a pretty mouth, but it prattles. Looking at you I'd say there's never a thought comes into your head that doesn't immediately vacate itself by way of your tongue. No one would see your fat foolish face and think you had the wit for plot or subterfuge. Your father's loyalties are well-known, and if he does anything unusual it'd be noticed – but you? How could *you* have any secrets?'

She bridled, but kept herself unmoved, because she knew she had secrets, and Falstaff knew it too. Had he seen her sneak away on the edge of the light? Had he noticed her thieving or just guessed? 'These favours,' she said, at length, 'they're not really for you, are they?'

'I ask them on behalf of the best man in England.'

'And how is that man?' Her tears were almost forgotten. She even managed a cunning smile.

'I believe he'll shortly be taking a pleasant sea voyage, and in good time will be accounted safe and well. Does that reassure you, Miss Johnson?'

She nodded, holding the letter to her breast. 'And if Mister Tyrell asks from whence this letter came, what name should I give him?' She almost asked to say *Falstaff*, but she doubted it would be appreciated.

Falstaff thought slowly, his head nodding to the rhythm of his brain. 'Mister Knot,' he said.

Knot-Falstaff provided her with an alibi for her absence, and one that could usefully be employed again. She skimped over her chores as quickly as she could, and left the house before her mother returned. She took some more wine with her, not for the nymph but for herself, to keep her warm by night. The woman no longer seemed to have an appetite for food, eating only sparingly on her second day. Eff recalled Rooke's rhymes about unwise children who accepted fairy-food or goblin-fruit. These songs rarely had a happy ending. Men must look like goblins to divinities and deities. Human food must leave a bitter taste in her mouth.

The stars were coming out as she crossed the road back to the forest. She hurt her neck staring up at them. Each tiny light was the prick of a pin, trapping the gods on the dome of the sky. For the first time, Eff – who was not quite convinced by her teacher's insistence that they were distant crystal spheres – could almost believe that they were literally gods, their bright eyes distantly appalled to look on the works of men. This Earth had been their playground once. Now they only came down from the sky to hunt, and she regretted that – but oh, how dull miracles would be if they took place every day, and how much more precious was her Earthbound nymph for being unique.

Lamplight bobbed ahead of her through the forest. It shone on the water when she arrived to join the nymph, who still sat there as if she hadn't moved in Eff's absence. She leaned over the edge of the pool, no longer inspecting the reflection, but running her fingers through it as though it were clean and fresh, not soiled and murky. Her hair fell in neatly-combed strands so long that their ends trailed on the surface of the water. She stood as she saw Eff's light. She was naked and nameless. Eff ran to her.

As the evening became night, Eff drank herself silly.

They strung Eff's clothes on the low branches, one piece per tree. Eff invited the nymph to kiss her on the mouth, and the nymph accepted, though gracelessly. How could a half-goddess be so clumsy in love? Perhaps she didn't fancy goblin-maids? It couldn't be Eff's youth – the gods were typically above human laws and customs. 'You need a name,' Eff told her.

'I don't.'

'You do,' Eff insisted. 'Gods have names, though we can't speak them. The Jews say that, about their God. His name will destroy the world if it's ever spoken.'

'That must make praying difficult.' It was hard to tell in the meagre light, but Eff wasn't sure this was meant as a joke.

'They use another name,' she explained.

'I see.'

They were lying on dry soil together with the blankets covering them, though the night was still warm enough to do without it. Eff hadn't realised how much colour there could be in blackness, or how clean the earth could feel against skin. She was absorbing the greater life of the woman beside her, whose body felt unnaturally smooth where it brushed hers. She was glad not to have tried to lure her away from the woods. The nymph wouldn't survive away from here. She would diminish in the human world.

Later they slept, and Eff dreamed again.

She dreamed she was a little Jewish girl. She saw her reflection on a sheet of gleaming, dented metal. It was dark-haired and short and plain, adult in its ugliness. She was young. She wasn't sure of her age. She was far from home.

They had separated her from her playmates and marched her over the mountains. This was punishment, but not for her. There was madness in the family, a taint in the blood, so the children were scattered to the nine corners of the world for their own protection. She was still too young to understand the reasons, the scandal and disgrace her elders had left behind. She had been carried everywhere all her life, and hated walking. Her new and temporary home was a small house in the mountains, so tiny it was forgotten and flew no sovereign banner.

Days fluttered by, each one disappearing with the flick of an eyelid, faster than a slow, nocturnal breath. The house smelled odd. The odd thing was that it smelled at all. She took lessons here. She played with new friends. She was inducted into the mysteries. Sometimes she ran riot and brought the wrath of the caretaker down on her head; the old woman was wizened and hunched, scary because she was so old and deformed when it was so unnecessary. The girl had come to dread the shambling sound of her approach, the padding footsteps, the many keys clanging on the metal ring at her belt.

This was a strange old house, with strange stories. She discussed them with her truest friend, her favourite cousin who had been her companion on the long march. They had been brought into the world at the same hour; they shared the same dorm; they were closer than close. But her cousin had a tongue on him, and told untrustworthy stories. Most nights he didn't sleep and went out to explore the house. He told of secret ceremonies in the lower depths; great caverns filled with machines and ships; the nocturnal delegations of the wild things, whose sharp bright teeth and claws gleamed in the dark of their robes. Sometimes she believed, sometimes not.

He told her a voice was calling his name from the deepest, innermost sanctum. She hadn't believed. He insisted. Over days and weeks, he had insisted, he grew agitated. But – she protested – this is a spooky old building full of emptiness and silence that our minds try to fill. We're still undeveloped. We're still, what's the word? (What word?) The old word for what we are.

Oh yes – children.

But it knows my name, he protested. So? We all know your name!

It knows the name I'll have in the dead lands. It knows the name I'll have when I won't exist. Lord Yellow Dog of the Thirty-One Cuts, they'll call me. It's been itching inside my head. Don't laugh.

Ha ha ha ha ha hah! Lord Yellow Dog of the Thirty-One Cuts? You idiot!

You'll see, said her cousin, I'll prove it to you.

Then it was months later and she lay on her cot, reflecting on that old boast and what came of it. Her cousin had gone the next night into the depths of the house to find the thing that called his name. He had come back ashen-faced and silent. He never revealed what he'd seen in the warrens, and he never spoke of the voice again. They had grown apart after this time, and she was left alone.

Except –

Except now she could hear the draught blowing through the narrow corridors and it seemed to be calling a name. It wasn't her name, not yet, but one day it would be. It would fit her like a glove, or a suit of supple armour worn tight against the skin.

Larissa, it called. Larissa, Larissa, Larissa, endlessly, but she wasn't tempted to go.

There was more to the dream, but Eff forgot when she woke. She would try later to coax it out in writing, but her pen would always stall after the first three words, setting the scene of how it was 'In antic Jerusalem –'

Eff woke with wet eyes. Green sunlight greeted her. Her face twisted as she realised that all her time was gone.

But the nymph was there. She hadn't melted with the dawn, like dew or memory. In fact she was all too physical. Their cheeks were pushed together and spit mixed from both their lips, which were close, if not touching. Their bare limbs were tangled, and the nymph had half-rolled in the night so the weight of her body pinned Eff to the ground. The pressure was unmistakably real, as were the fingertips pressed to Eff's stomach, the smallest nail buried in her navel as though it were a fascinating blemish.

The nymph was still asleep. Eff hadn't expected that. 'I love you,' she whispered. It didn't wake her.

Then she had to go. Eff cried and begged, but knew it was hopeless. She sat despondent on the slope, watching as the nymph dressed herself in the armour. It took only a minute. Once she was fully dressed, she looked as naked as she'd ever been. Against her skin, the costume came to life. The patterns that riddled its surface began to move, frothing red, animated by the touch of a higher power. They were little engines, Eff realised, little machines.

The nymph turned to Eff sadly, before she went a-hunting.

'I know your name,' Eff told her. 'I dreamed it.'

'Tell me when you see me next,' she instructed. Eff nodded.

Before she went, the nymph returned Eff's flute, held out on both palms. 'Have you done anything to it?' Eff asked. 'Is it special?'

'No.'

No, it wasn't. Eff took it back and held it to her chest as she watched the nymph go. She retreated backwards to the pool, all her attention still directed on the girl whose life she had chosen to guide her in pursuit of the worst thing that ever lived.

Eff thought the demi-goddess would sink back into the pool, but she didn't. She didn't make it to the water's edge, but faded from view with each backwards step, as if lost to darkness. The last Eff saw of her, at least on that evening, was as faint as a glass-echo, with the dense cluster of trees in the distance visible through her clothes, her skin, her whole body. Then she was gone.

Eff gathered herself together and left the forest, one step at a time.

She changed as she walked home. The wrench of parting grew less painful as she moved out of the ancient world and back into the modern. She had found a purpose in the cruel world of men – even if that was nothing more than delivering letters– but she also had a role in the cosmic order, serving a greater purpose even than the King's. All other eyes were blind to the better world, but hers were not. Who else looked to the constellations to find gods? Who else had seen a nymph rise from the waters as though they were giving her birth? The Earth, as Eff had always suspected, was a shadow. She had seen the substance. By the time she reached the road, she was happy, she was laughing, she was running.

Eff Johnson knew the truth of it. The age of miracles was gone, but not completely lost. All gold was not yet transmuted into lead. There was still wonder in the world. Glory, glory, glory!

Book Four: As Above, So Below

⇒ Chapter 17: *In Antic Jerusalem...* ⇐

Eff dreamt she was a child of another time and world, tangling up her memories with those of this warm leaking mind beside her. She dreamt she was asleep on a grassy bank below alien boughs and a colourless fresh-sunned sky. She had left her home only once, and had never looked back. In this she was unusual – most never left at all. She was no longer a girl. She'd grown older and taller, though no prettier. She closed her memories and opened her eyes –

The sun is precariously low and swift across a horizon of undulating dunes, a sullen beach without a tide. It's a swollen thing, barely brighter than the archipelago stars. She doesn't know these constellations, the distant suns that so disturbed her mother, but she can tell that she's far from home. Still, the light is a bland and reassuring red. Is it? That might just be the blood on her eyes. She wipes it down her face with the flat of her palm. It's still wet as water, so she hasn't been out long. The sunlight remains an unwavering crimson. Her once proud and bony nose crunches queasily below her hand's soft pressure. She rolls the corpses off her legs and finds the strength to stand. She isn't dead. She isn't dead. She isn't dead. Everyone else is dead.

Eff dreams. Eff dreams of all the battles fought and lost. Eff dreams of a foreign country.

Infantrymen sprawl across the sands, nursing wounds they could barely have believed, dead as much from the shock of their own mortality as the blows or the slices that felled them, blows too harsh even for her people to survive. Her uniform feels inadequate and flimsy on a suddenly vulnerable body. The boy at her feet looks so young, though appearances can be deceptive. He no longer has hands. She unbuckles her helmet and flings it away. Her hair falls loose in thick black sheaves.

From the distance – and the air is rare, so it's hard to judge how far – comes the death-howl of some vast unliving thing. This is not a pleasant thing to hear, and she hears it in the blood, in the marrow, in her very gifts. She knows, in her clotted memory, that the soul of a great ship is dying; the ship itself feels no pain, and its screams are only the sizzle and flash of lost futures burning. She can do no good; she turns away. She contemplates the bodies of men and women who were never born and never expected to die. A patch of her skin below her right shoulder burns in the shape of a hand, fingers-splayed. There's nothing and no one behind her. She clambers over the fallen towards a clean patch of green sand.

There are a dozen bodies around her, and more scattered in smaller heaps further across the landscape. What a pattern they must be from above, from the vantage of the crucified man! This is less than half the company; the others must be sprawled and dead out of her sight. Some will have attempted to flee, and that won't have done them any good. She wonders how she came to be spared, with nothing worse than a broken nose. It wouldn't have overlooked her. It is, after all, meticulous. Best to assume this is no accident, and it will be back for her once it's done, once the ship's soul bursts and dies.

Her gloves come up heavily, weighted down by blood-slicked sand. Here's one of her mother's mordant epigrams: *There's blood in all our bodies, and shit, and all kinds of filth. There's no clean biology.* (So unlike her true mother, in the waking world.) *Remember that, little book.*

How could I forget?

Where is the mother of the order? Somewhere on the sands, perhaps; still alive, perhaps? It might not have killed her. It shouldn't be able to kill her, not without damaging itself, not while the ship still kept them bound together. No, no, it would have tried in spite of that, maybe even because of that. After half a thousand years, it would want to feel something again, even pain. Still, if she is still alive, she needs to be found and destroyed before she can die. You'll need to do that, Eff. You were trained for it. It must be you.

Do what's practical.

Last she saw, a trooper had held the needle. Like her, he would have been at the centre of the violence when it had exploded, and he would have been among the earliest victims. Playful though it was, the crucified man would have recognised the threat as its priority. That should have been anticipated. Then again, any wonder that it wasn't? The crucified man had been planning this escape for five hundred years, before Eff was born. *In her dream, five hundred years was hardly a heartbeat, hardly a breath. Nothing changed. The old Anarchy came again.*

She haunts the battlefield like a scavenger or a bereft lover, turning over corpses and body-parts in search of booty or tokens. There'll be others after her, probably lurking already on the dim edge of the field for the danger to pass and the feast to unfold; raven-kind with a taste for the trinkets of time. If she lives, she'll stay and fight them away. This is a tombworld. For the first time ever, she learns a frantic disgust at the prospect of disturbed graves. There are more to these bodies than mush and residue. They're so heavy! It's hard to turn them! How is it that the dead can have such weight?!

The fallen myrmidons broadcast their final secret to her, from the screens of their eyes, from the blank ovals of their flesh: nothing secure is real. We all knew that. Didn't our mother try to teach us that? We knew, but we didn't believe. Listen, she can hear a ship dying. She believes. She believes.

She finds the needle in a soldier's glove, in a severed hand tossed casually onto the beach. The sun whirls in the sky as she prises it free, one finger at a time. Reports of battle will have reached home by now. Even outside the order, the loss of a ship will be noticed. She places the empty hand reverently down where it had fallen, fits the needle in her grip, and recalls the code that will wake it to life. The light flares along its spine. It doesn't feel changed.

She staggers, one heavy footstep after another, up an incline to survey the sands, to find the body she's searching for. It's close. She clambers down the sandslide, finding the descent as hard and stodgy as the climb. She leaves long uneven prints in the soft ground behind her. No need to cover her tracks. If it wants to find her, it will find her.

The mother of the order – who'd raised her, who'd named her, who'd led her unwittingly here – is spreadeagled and bloodied on a slope. Eff thuds down the slide towards her, finding urgency and fear again. There are wounds visible and seeping on her mother's neck and wrists, made by her own hand, but perhaps not of her own will. She's prone – ah! her head turns and her lips move, and it's no trick of the heavy light – she isn't dead. So there is still a chance. Eff drops to her knees beside her mother. She puts a blood-coated hand out and finds warm feverish skin. The older woman's unwide eyes open. They find her executioner. Her eyes smile; there's something in them that isn't quite pain, but can't be pleasant. The lips twitch. Last orders.

'Kill it,' she says. 'Kill me.'

Eff puts the annihilating point of the needle over her mother's lightly-rising lightly-falling chest, ready to strike. The physical point of impact isn't relevant, so long as it penetrates deep into her life-gifts, but this feels right. With her other hand, she clasps her mother's fingers.

When she strikes, her mother will be gone. She won't simply be dead, she will never have lived, not even in memory.

Eff's crying. She doesn't want to be crying. She frees her hand to clean away the tears, and leaves long streaks of sand-flavoured blood over her face. When she finds her mother's hand again, it's lifeless, and her breast no longer breathes, and the flickering needle is suddenly useless.

A shadow stands suddenly in front of her. She has no idea how long it's been there, watching her try and fail to kill their mother.

Her signature was one of the seven on my life-warrant. We're both orphans.

Eff raises her head to look at him, the worst thing that has ever lived, the crucified man. Her eyes are too wet and slippery for anger, so she shows it with her bared teeth, with the curl of her mouth.

She rolls in her sleep, and her dreams change their shape as readily as clouds or tortured flesh.

'Give me a child of eight years, and I will show you the man, or the woman.'

It was the first thing that the housekeeper had said to her – to *her* personally – since she had joined the order. The housekeeper had grown younger, taller, and healthier – *in her dreams this didn't seem at all surprising* – but she still managed to inspire the same sense of fear in the young and unease in the older. When had that happened? Eff guessed it must have been recently, during the worldquake or even the goblin infestation. When she was recruited, she hadn't expected to be recognised, but the housekeeper's words told her she was wrong. She made an appropriate ritual response. The doyenne of the order rolled her eyes.

It was rare to see her eyes so wide.

'I remember your cousin, too. The interventionists appealed to him too much. Pity.'

It was strange that her life should lead her back here, to this place that she'd come to loathe so much when she had been growing. It was one of the lesser Houses; she and her cousin had named it the Least House, as a joke. To her embarrassment, it turned out that this was the order's nickname, too. They spurned any claim to greatness.

They? *She*, the housekeeper. She dictated policy and philosophy. She'd made the order in her own image. Eff was flattered and flustered in equal measure to have caught her attention. She'd been at her desk analysing field reports when the summons had come. She had descended hurriedly into the chthonic storeys where the architecture of the Least House was mirrored and reversed. The housekeeper lived underground most of the time; she was a pale thing.

Eff was still getting used to her uniform, which was much looser, particularly round the legs, than the formal collegiate gowns, or even the casual skirts she'd worn when her old House had finally readmitted its prodigal cousins. It was black, without even the gold lining of myrmidon armour, so in the subdued light of the lower floors she felt herself invisible.

The housekeeper was a confident woman, sat poised behind her desk in a cone of light. Some called her smug. She had a habit of looking through half-closed eyes, so that she seemed distracted or lazy. Her lips were fat, and she liked to purse them until they were thin, making a line of her mouth. She kept her arms folded whenever she spoke. She was formidably insolent. Eff was flattered by this levelling effect, which she knew would be shown to lords and chancellors as easily as underlings and servants. To talk to the doyenne of the order was to be admitted into her conspiracy of the moment.

She had brought down a Presidency. There was nothing she couldn't do.

She put aside her paperwork and indulged Eff in a little small trade-talk, nothing remarkable, nothing testing. What were her assignments? How was she settling in? Was she comfortable with combat training? Did she have any interest in fieldwork? All the time, those eyes were remembering the little girl who used to flee before the measured tread of the old woman, with her stick and her jangling key-belt. She still wore the keys, and they still rattled. There were countless locks in the Least House.

'You have mnemonic training,' the housekeeper said, introducing the topic abruptly. Not a question. Eff made an affirmative gesture. 'That's a neglected skill these days. None of the colleges teach it. Where did you learn?'

'Here.' As she spoke, she realised her answer was already known.

'Not at Dvora?' She was making a common cause. They shared a bloodline. Both women had once been devouring hounds.

'No, here,' Eff insisted. The older woman inspected her face, as if looking for a trace of a lie, or the trace of a truth not understood. She closed her narrow eyes and didn't smile. With hindsight, her subject realised this was a good sign. This woman never bared her teeth except in anger.

'I need a mnemonic,' she said, at length. 'Would you like to move from your current post? I warn you, I'm demanding and unpleasant.'

Eff stumbled on her words, because the first thing she wanted to say was that she couldn't imagine the mother of the order being *unpleasant* in even the most testing conditions. Still, something was being demanded of her now, something more than a simple *yes* or *no*, so she tried a question: 'Why do you need a mnemonic? Wouldn't it be more effective to use private registry?'

Still no smile came. 'The Imperator relied on private registry. At his trial, he was condemned by his own words. I don't want recordings. I want someone who can talk with my voice.'

Eff rolled in her sleep, and abruptly she found she had been part of this world for years, for decades, a trusted member of the housekeeper's permanent staff. The past stretched behind her as a series of perfect and indelible memories. The housekeeper had filled her up with words, not just briefings and memos but all her confidential thoughts, not just secrets and cyphers, but aphorisms and anecdotes. She had become a living diary, to the extent that all she had once been – the girl who had been marched to the House in the dwindling past – was squeezed out by this new creation, the living thesis her mistress was shaping out of words.

'You're my little book,' the housekeeper had told her, in one of her jollier moods. The name had stuck.

She walked with the housekeeper through the levels of the Least House. The structure had become her theatre of memory. She made it the mental structure in which she could hang all her observations, fleshing out each room and passage and annexe with more and more detail as the years passed. She had exhausted the storeys above ground, and extended her skills to exploring the lower depths. They had become symmetrical and inseparable in her mind. It was a dangerous strategy. She risked turning an everyday walk between different offices into a turmoil, each glance or step raising myriad images and impressions. Eff looked at little book in the mirrors of the Least House and no longer saw herself, or a girl, or a woman, or a mortal. She no longer thought this Jerusalem. This was the hive of Heaven.

They descended to the lowest level, to the silo at the very base of the Least House. This was one of the few secrets that had not been trusted to her. It was a great black cylinder with a permanent guard and a dozen invisible locks. It was the housekeeper's retreat. She went in alone and pensive, and came out alone and surly.

'What's in there?' little book found the courage to ask.

Her superior smiled, with her teeth. 'Mistakes of an earlier administration.'

Eff breathes in the damp scents of grass and soil; in her dream, she's seeing the face of the woman she imagines to be her mother. It's a lean face, still young, but formed by experience. She's lived through interesting times, she's shaped them.

'Is this really our problem?'

It was late. The sense of night weighed heavily, even in the permanently-dark deep of the Least House. Little book was reclining in her chair, and wouldn't have let the question slip if she'd been fresher and alert. The housekeeper paced. She stopped at the desk occasionally, not to sit, but to pour herself another black-skinned drink from her flask. She looked up quizzically over a rim of glass. They were talking about the War.

The mother of the order had moods and secrets. Little book had heard, from others who knew the housekeeper better, that her mnemonic's presence mollified her. There were stories of her temper and her impatience, which seemed exaggerated, though could easily have been a side effect of the physiological changes in her lives. As far as little book could make out, the time of the Imperator's fall had been a period of personal turmoil for her, beyond the merely political. They had cast him out of the Homeworld. She imagined him – though she knew this image was nonsense – falling like a coruscating star through the void. The order never admitted any role in his exposure and expulsion, but during the trial and its bloody aftermath, the housekeeper had gone into seclusion.

Some who knew her from that time had said that she'd put a gun in her mouth. It was a drastic course of self-improvement.

No one in the order carried guns now. Even the myrmidons only had knives, pocked with tiny airholes so that the metal breathed and sang as they were drawn. The housekeeper herself had a ceremonial sword in her office, but it was never taken down from the wall as far as little book knew. The memories of these objects were denied to her.

The Imperator had been troublesome even in exile. He'd been executed eventually, his body burned cleanly and scattered, but she imagined sometimes that his head had been struck off first by a falling blade, the warm and bloody-wet dreams of the human child intermingling with her own.

The Imperator was often in the housekeeper's thoughts. Little book knew, because her mistress talked about him incessantly, just as she talked about the War that was to come. The War was her obsession, so it became the order's obsession. Those departments not directly involved in counter-intelligence were increasingly turned over to planning combat scenarios. Little book watched and remembered, as a permanent roster was drawn up of thirteen potential external aggressors – other names were added and removed almost on a whim – and five internal organisations liable to encourage an aggressive foreign policy for their own profit. The housekeeper pored over the endless reports, looking with an open but feverish eye for the enemy that would bring the walls of the Homeworld crashing down. It remained elusive.

And now they were talking about it directly, and she had asked the impertinent question, and her mother's face went blank and stared at her, ready to leap one way or another into furious rage or mocking humour.

Little book shifted and straightened up. 'A war would be an external affair. Outside our remit.'

'You think so? Anything that affects the common weal is our problem. The War will *deform* our society. We'll destroy ourselves in our eagerness to fight.'

At that moment, little book understood the ferocity of the doyenne's obsession. She wasn't seeking the best or swiftest method of fighting the War to win it for the Homeworld. She wanted to anticipate it. The weight of history – an imperceptible quality that most Houses thought had been banished since the anchoring of the thread at the dawn of time – was driving them, but she believed it could still be deflected. Little book wasn't sure. She wasn't convinced that the War was as profound a threat as the housekeeper believed. The last person to feel this weight so compulsively had been the Imperator – and it had destroyed him.

Little book left her doubts unspoken.

Pollen fills her mouth like sickness, reviving that memory – her mother on her bed at home, *sweating and shining with illness. For a moment it is* her *mother, in that familiar old house in the village, and she almost panics herself awake, but no...* no, it was the Least House and little book was diligent at her bedside, sometimes with flannels and water and potions, other times with strange alchemical apparatus that even she didn't truly understand. Translucent lines and strings drooped into the invalid's body, connecting her with the healing womb of the Homeworld.

The housekeeper had begun to spend more time away from the Least House, and little book was invariably left behind, often with effective charge of the order in its mother's absence. She had kept up a pretence that the doyenne was inspecting fieldwork at first hand, spying personally on the rashes of invisible cults like the Seedless Stars, the Dronidites, House Paradox, so many harmless little blisters. In fact, she had requisitioned ships and left the Homeworld altogether. She was out among the suns and histories of the Spiral Politic, hunting the enemy. As these trips grew more frequent, little book would draw her aside to remind her about the self-fulfilling character of prophecy, but the housekeeper wasn't a stupid woman, and most of the time she was careful, she was meticulous.

And now it seemed she hadn't been careful, she hadn't been meticulous. Little book hadn't learned the circumstances of that mission, but she had come back feverish and babbling, strapped down and guarded by shaken myrmidons. Little book watched over her for interminable days until she recovered, sitting vigil alone in the gloom, waiting for words to memorise, words that never came. They were unpleasant days and unpleasant dreams. The housekeeper had lost control of her biology, of her stomach and her bowels. Little book tended to her, uncomplaining, hating every moment.

Then suddenly it must have been days later, and the housekeeper – now recovered – was leading little book through darkness, down through the layers of the House to the silo. She had decided this unprompted, but had insisted on precautions. First, little book had been bound with oaths of secrecy. Second, her eyes had been covered to prevent her seeing which of the keys were real and which of the locks truly turned. Third, a gentle warning: 'Don't let it distract you. As far as it's concerned, you're a novelty. It's seen no faces but mine in nearly five hundred years.'

Deep in the silo, suspended from the ceiling in an ühle-prism as though nailed into the empty air, was the order's oldest and only prisoner. Little book stared. It was perverse and fascinating that such a creature should exist. Its body was colourless, the blackness of light invisible, harder than shadow. She thought of it as a man, though its body was smooth, ideal, and perfectly sexless. It had a globe for a face, without eyes or markings or features, that nonetheless turned as if to look at her.

You came at last. You heard me calling.

The housekeeper gestured for her to stay silent and still on the edge of the silo.

And you brought me a new thing, mother? These must be interesting times.

'This is my secretary. She's going to be observing all of our conversations from now on. You won't address her or acknowledge her in any way.'

No? But I've been so good and so accurate. Have I not told you truth? Have I not been valuable?

The housekeeper ignored the complaint, which issued pleasantly from a sleek mouthless mask. She began to pace in circles round its prism, and its head swivelled and swivelled to keep up with her. The housekeeper rarely kept still in any case, but little book felt that to be stationary now was to become a vulnerable target, under the merciless head-sized gaze of the crucified man.

The housekeeper cleared her throat; maybe not for effect, maybe she was still ill. 'I want to recap the discussion we had yesterday. Not the technical specs, just the outline. You understand?'

I understand

'Tell me how we can win without fighting.'

If it could have moved, it would have preened. As it was, it could only talk. Little book strained to catch and remember the nuance of every word.

We adopt the guerrilla tactics of the secondary war-powers as broad strategy, and recruit another species to fight on our behalf. Rather than use localised remote conditioning, we rewrite the entire species-continuity. I propose we turn entire biohistories into a weapon for use against the enemy.

'How? I need specifics.'

Use me. My biotelegenetic cycle was designed as a defence for the Homeworld's noosphere, but can also be employed in a mirror capacity as an offensive weapon. Release me into the noosphere of the specified world. Within F-generations I can prime the dominant species to accept the military protocols of the Great Houses. They will fight for us as though the interests of the Houses are their own.

'Noosphere infiltration can be detected.'

Remember the timescale. An exponential change in biocontinuity over F-generations would be near imperceptible.

'Not good enough. *We* would notice the change. We must assume the enemy would as well.'

Then we make the point of entry one when the noosphere is beginning to coalesce out of rudimentary physical communications. There will be no detectable infiltration of the noosphere, because I will be its organising principle from the start.

'Do you have any suitable world in mind?'

There are a number of possibilities.

'How effective will this be against our enemies?'

At worst it will swell your ranks and demonstrate the extent of your powers. I see you're not impressed. At best – well, an attack of this kind in the right place could destabilise them completely, or at least put them on the defence. It depends on the nature of the enemy.

'Yesterday you suggested you could predict something of their nature.'

That was yesterday. I can only see probabilities, and they change from moment to moment.

And she was no longer nodding: 'In our last session you intimated it was more than a probability. You *know.*'

You misunderstood. Besides, if I had some presentiment about the enemy, do you think I'd blurt it out in front of a mnemonic? This lacks your usual finesse; is something getting to you?

Vexed, the housekeeper parted her lips. 'This session is over. Oh, and your plan – it's utterly unacceptable. I would never permit it.'

There'll come a time when the presidency and the military will disagree with you. They will find I am more useful to them than the Imperator's other enduring mistake. And what will you do then?

'I won't let it happen.'

I know you. You'll do what's practical.

Silently, the housekeeper led little book out of the silo. The walls of the cell radiated behind them, saturated with the crucified man's droll mockery and malevolence, and neither woman spoke again until they were safely above-ground, in airy rooms with vast windows that filtered the sunlight so it seemed yellow. Only now she was well away did little book realise how oppressed she had felt in the cell, as if it were herself – and the housekeeper, the whole order – who were the prisoners, and the crucified man their gaoler.

How long has this thing been influencing policy?!

'It knows,' the housekeeper muttered. 'It knows who the enemy will be. It's always known, but it won't say. It wants them for itself.'

'I don't understand.'

'It has an inbuilt imperative: *Destroy the enemy.* That's all it wants to do. That's all it is.'

She still didn't understand. 'Then maybe we should let it. It would solve our problem.'

Then the housekeeper smiled. 'You need to see the private registry of what happened when it reached maturity. You need to see what it did when it escaped.'

Little book watched the record. Later, she tried to forget, but of course she couldn't.

The housekeeper held her and comforted her, reversing the roles they'd played during the older woman's sickness. '*Destroy the enemy.* It's not an order. It's a justification. And *enemy* is such a flexible word.'

Eff's eyes flicker in her sleep, while little book filed in and out of the silo, the great blank spot of her memory where she kept details of these meetings contained. The voice of the crucified man remained unwavering over the years, barbed and sickly and patient, while the housekeeper's withered. She was using it as an oracle, to see out into the malleable probabilities of future time, searching for the right choices and numbers that might reshape the Spiral Politic. She *believed*. She might feign scepticism or boredom in its presence, but she was haunted by whatever honeyed words it dripped into her ears. Little book watched and listened and remembered, and kept her thoughts unspoken.

There were more and longer periods when the mother of the order commandeered ships to explore the Spiral Politic. In those stretches, little book felt no desire to descend to the silo or speak to the crucified man, and ignored the whispering voice that seemed to come to her in the night, from the lowest level and from her dreams.

Reports came to the House on beams of light and time, carrying instructions from the housekeeper. She requested little book's presence, among other things. This would be the first time little book had left the Homeworld, and she attributed the shudder of apprehension to novelty. Ships weren't that different to Houses, except that they moved and lived and thought. She joined the housekeeper aboard a ship stationed on a dead world at the edge of time. A detail came with her, guarding a sealed cargo whose identity she would have guessed if only she'd realised how obsessed her mother had become or how far she was prepared to go.

Her mother took her into the stateroom in the humming abdomen of the ship and told her the truth, and then little book howled in protest.

'It's a calculated risk. We have to know what it knows.'

'You can't cut it loose. You saw what it did when it escaped. You were *there*!'

'It won't happen again. There are safeguards, and we're not letting it out on a populated world. We're going to a barren rock on the edge of time. Even if it broke free, it would have to destroy the ship in the process. It can't escape without a ship.'

Little book stared at her, over the narrow distance of her desk. She searched the housekeeper's face for signs of illness, but there were none. 'Why now? What's happened?'

And then she seemed ill after all. 'I saw the future,' she said; it came out as a wheeze. 'I saw the future, and it was exactly the way our prisoner said it would be.'

'We need another guarantee before we try this,' little book blurted. 'We have to be able to kill it if something goes wrong.'

The housekeeper nodded; she had already thought of this. 'There is a way. It's designed to bond with a host. If something goes wrong, we destroy the host.'

'Kill the host and you'd only accelerate its lifecycle. It would just find another host.'

'I didn't say *kill*. I said *destroy*. Look at this.'

The housekeeper took a case from behind her desk, unfolded it, and revealed the needle. Later, little book would have trouble conceiving of a time when it was new and unfamiliar, when she wasn't used to the shape and the weight of it in her hand, when she didn't know what it could do.

'Another of the Imperator's mistakes,' the housekeeper explained. 'He was good at mistakes. This is a continuity weapon. It doesn't just kill. It purges an individual's biodata from the Spiral Politic. Kill the host with this, and it will be as if she never existed. And it will take our prisoner with it.'

Little book replaced it in the case, determined never to touch it again.

Still she had doubts. 'You're asking the host to take an enormous risk.'

'No. No, I'm not.'

The housekeeper filled a glass with lightless fluid from her flask, took a sip, then held it out to little book as an offering. Her mnemonic, always slow on the uptake, had reached halfway across the gap before realising. She recoiled, back to the wall, and watched helplessly as her mother finished her fill.

Eff shifts again into a new sleeping poise and shakes all these strange thoughts loose, forgetting them in the way that little book can't. The dream lurches, back into the bleakest memories.

The death of the ship swallows the sky; the flares are its mortal wounds, the colours are fluids seeping and unseeping through time. There is a puncture in the horizon where the sun had been, matter and energy flaring and mutating in black patterns round its ragged edge, time winds howling. The Spiral Politic itself is breached and wounded. It hurts to watch, but she can't look away.

The crucified man stands between her and the broken sun. It is its own shadow. It's wounded, its perfect skin cracking and peeling, its flesh oozing from between ever-widening gaps, but it's still formidable. It offends her to see it there, standing over the housekeeper's body.

'Did you do this to her?' little book asks.

I made her do a lot of things.

'Are you going to kill me?'

I killed everyone else.

The needle waits in her hand. She can still attack, but it will kill her before she can get near it.

It'll kill her anyway.

Can't do any more harm. She moves her hand. The crucified man lashes out, and sends the needle arcing into the sand, far from her reach. Her fingers burn; she brings them back and finds them twisted and bleeding. She remembers she should feel pain. She clasps her smashed fingers.

If it's any consolation, our mother loved you. She had such a kindness in her hearts for strays and freaks and mediocrities and nothing else.

'You don't have a ship. You're trapped here,' she snarls between bursts of pain. 'There's nowhere you can go.'

Its curved head seems to turn gently from side to side. It's laughing at her. The aweful hole in the sky churns behind its crown. *I don't need a ship.*

She throws herself up the slope towards it. It descends. They fight.

She loses.

She loses badly. It breaks her. It breaks her skin in two dozen places. It breaks more bones than it leaves whole. It breaks her tolerance of pain, and she screams. It breaks her nerve. It breaks her spirit. She realises, as it crushes her throat and lacerates her thighs, twists muscles and shreds tendons, that it isn't trying to kill her or leave permanent damage. It doesn't want to push her to a point where her body will have to blaze and consume and reform itself. It just wants her to feel pain. It wants her humiliated and ruined. It wants her submission. It wants to destroy her and leave her alive to know it.

This realisation makes the beating far worse.

With its fists, with its nails, with its burning jaws, it describes to her what it's like to be its enemy. Once she knows this thoroughly, it drops her bleeding and gasping onto the sand. She can no longer speak with the blood bubbling in her mouth, and can hardly see through the swollen bruises round her eyes. Still, she makes out the shape of the crucified man looking pitifully down on her.

Go back to the Homeworld – it tells her – *Go back to the Least House. Tell them I'm going to destroy the enemy. Then they'll forgive me anything – and so will you.*

And having said that, it throws itself into the sky, into the shipwound, and is gone.

Once alone, she claws her way into the sand to bury herself, and lets the grain suck into her wounds. She plants herself deep in the darkness, away from the renewed turning of the sun in the sky, away from any hint of time, and any clue that will fix the memory and make it inescapable. In the sweltering dark, she heals slowly. She has no life-threatening wound, only pain and defeat.

In her hot shallow womb, she decides that she can't return to the Homeworld and its thought-clotted houses, not while the crucified man is loose, maybe not ever. She leaves her hole and cleans herself as best she can. Around her, the desert is undisturbed. She tidies the bodies of the company but digs no graves. The clean mouths of the timeships will tend to them when they arrive. She closes the eyes of her mother and kisses her on the forehead and forgives her. She finds the needle and tucks it into her belt.

She sheds the name *little book*.

While she was buried, the scavengers descended from the chronosphere in their pseudoships and timesuits. Slim pickings here, the ship having died and collapsed on itself leaving nothing worth looting. They won't disturb the bodies, these ravens of time, they're not interested in Homeworld flesh, not if it's cold. They look like us, like Homeworlders. They're so corpulent and so clumsy and so ripe.

Limping, she goes to them.

⟹ Chapter 18: *The Uses of Pleasure* ⟸

For a second morning, the sails hung limp on the sullen breezeless air. The crew made the usual propitiatory sacrifices to un-Christian elementals, though without the jolly solemnity they had displayed on the first becalmed day. Odd boots, coins, and bottles were cast into the mild German Sea again, this time nervously. Sailors were rarely as superstitious as the comedies painted them, and it was impossible to become stranded so close to land for too long, but balanced against these simple truths was the occult fact of their prisoner. He was a man of unholy ken, a black-hearted sorcerer, and who knew what powers he could call down to confound their passage?

There were the usual mutterings about having women aboard. Give it another few days, Astraea worried, and they'll have me over the side. She doubted the Ratcatchers would be in much of a hurry to fish her out afterwards. The *Queen Christina* didn't usually take on passengers; it flew under Swedish colours as a flag of convenience, but the Service owned every plank and nail in its hull. Most of the crew knew nothing of this, so Astraea's presence – and the prisoner's – was a baffling irritation to them. She did nothing to make life easier. She had her own worries. The ship was becalmed. Her latest dreams were coming true.

Bloody typical. It's not the *good* dreams that pay off! Never the glad omen, ever the doom...

She put a hand on the small of her back, which was aching, which had ached since she'd left Paris. All this travelling, all these strange new beds in motion, it wasn't good for her.

She wasn't superstitious. They were becalmed because the serjeant had insisted they sail for London, rather than the quick and sensible option of Dover. The sailors weren't so afraid of a feminine presence when they spied on her through knotholes, and took her coin readily enough when she needed meals or clean clothes or the other niceties of civilisation. The Magus was a reedy, helpless fellow, who was defeated by a few ropes and a gag, and certainly wouldn't have the magics to stall a ship. Besides, this didn't have the flash and thunder of a magician's bag of shallow tricks; his kind would create great winds and thunders that would swell the *Christina*'s sails and drive the ship to Arctic straits, not suck the air from them and strand them in naked sight of England's coast.

She prowled the decks impatiently, until the captain ordered her back to her cabin. She stood her ground and complained about the delays.

'Tell you what,' he suggested. 'Why don't you go aloft and fart the life back into the sails? I don't doubt you have enough wind in you, and that it proceeds as readily from your arse as your mouth.'

Five minutes later, she'd come up with an ideal witty riposte that would have put the grotty little man in his place, but he was gone, she was back in the sweat-stinking bowels of the *Christina* and the moment was lost. She took heavy steps, thumping angrily among the berths. She needed a distraction. She didn't even have a book, except for the Bible, which bored her despite the occasional pleasing turn of phrase.

That God! she thought to herself. What a shit that God was!

And Man, created in His cumbersome image, was just as bad. She complained to the Ratcatcher-Serjeant about the captain's insolence, and watched the furrows of impatience and ill-temper form on his brow. She pushed her case harder, venting her full righteous force, but this left him unswayed. She was not a part of his world, she was an interloper. Her contribution to this mission had been nothing more taxing than the delivery of a letter to a certain address, as vital as the sheep driven onto a field to draw enemy fire.

The weary air that slipped the serjeant's lips was just about the only breeze the *Christina* had felt in a day. 'Here's your problem,' he said, 'you've got too much freedom and too little to do with it. You need to busy yourself.' He made some suggestions that – because he was a couth fellow – were practical and not at all bawdy, though still objectionable. The least evil of them was that she might skivvy for the prisoner, which was how she came to be carrying food to his cabin that becalmed morning, as if this were Kent, he a furtive guest of her father's, and she had never left home.

The Magus's cell aboard ship was a private cabin, albeit one locked and guarded by alert Servicemen, who peered at her as if she were a specimen of a wholly new and exotic creature. Still, she was known to them, and they waved her through and locked the door after her. She would have to knock to leave, or yell if the prisoner caused a scene or took advantage of her intrusion, but since his capture in Paris he had been no trouble at all. She had forgotten his name. *The Magus* would do.

He was asleep as she came in. She was dismayed to find that he had been afforded a larger cabin than hers, and a brighter one, with a porthole placed just above the sloshing line of the sea to admit more sun than Astraea had grown used to. She banged the tray down by his bedside, sending stew tipping out of its bowl and cracking the brittle old ship's biscuit. It failed to wake the man, who must have been lulled to sleep by the regular undulation of the floor beneath his bed. The last she had seen of him, he had looked desperate and feral. Now he slept like a babe, though a truculent one whose parents had shackled one wrist to his bedpost.

Sleep brought out the severity of his features, and Astraea found him quite the handsome monster. She was sure he'd had whiskers when they'd met at Salomon's House, and though he'd lately shorn them, a whisp of blond stubble was reasserting itself on his chin and jowls and the ridge of his lip. He'd been stripped of coat, hat, and boots, and was reclining on the bed in his shirt and breeches, both now grimed and exhausted. His bare feet were smooth and clasped together. Astraea found her mood altering; she'd taken every step from the galley in a foul temper, resenting the prisoner, but it was no longer possible to hate him so. She rattled his spoon around the rim of the bowl until the noise caught his attention and woke him.

The woken Magus was softer in the face; Astraea struggled to dredge up what she'd learned of him in the aftermath of the débâcle at Salomon's House, and recalled that he'd been a soldier in Parliament's army. The sleeping man still wore a warrior's numb vizard, but in his stirring, this fell away to reveal a naked and alert face. Most of the male sex were contrarily arranged, displaying their true natures only when insensible, but to watch him wake was like seeing a healthy chick hatch from a petrified egg. If he had seen war as a Roundhead, he must be considerably older than he looked. She remembered his name at last: *Silver.*

'We've been here before.'

She hadn't realised he was properly awake, and his voice was weak, but his eyes were open and watching her as she poured water for him. 'Beg pardon?' she brusqued.

'Water,' came the mild reply. 'Fuck that shit.'

She hid her confusion and proffered the cup to him; he took it with his unchained hand, his fingers knocking clumsily on the soft underside of her palm. He emptied the mug, then explained: 'At Salomon's House. You were my prisoner then, and I brought you water. And you said *fuck that shit.*'

The memory came to her and she laughed, no more than a single breath but still good humour. She was under instruction not to engage the prisoner in gossip or chit-chat, but those orders pressed less forcefully away from the serjeant's presence.

'This time,' she told him, 'you're my prisoner, and water's all you're getting.'

'You're less suggestible than I was. Sensible. I've become a sterner man since then.'

'You have a good memory,' she observed. 'Those days are a fog.'

'Not to me. You gave me some good advice, but as you can see' – and his attempt to throw his arms out expansively was thwarted by the short chain at his wrist – 'I didn't run far enough.'

This time she caught herself, and didn't laugh. 'I brought some food. It's not much, but you won't get any more till London, so you'd better eat up.'

She pushed the tray as close to the bed as was sensible, then cast around for somewhere to sit. The cabin was not merely larger than hers, but less cluttered. Doubtless the Ratcatchers had removed anything that Silver might be able to make use of as a weapon or a tool, but it left her with no perch except the precarious bedside cabinet, the bed itself, or the floor. She elected to stand, though it was unpleasant, the bone in her right flank still grinding from the effort of walking the ship's length.

He lay still, his loose hand unstretched towards the spoon and the bowl. Astraea rolled her eyes up in the direction of Heaven, took a spoonful herself, and shovelled it into her mouth. She ground down the horrid stew of stale bread, thin vegetables, and day-old meat, then swallowed visibly. She made a play of licking the spoonface clean before dumping it down in the brown morass.

'We're not going to poison you,' she told him.

'Was it good?' Silver asked.

'No. It's horrid. It's fit only for dogs and it will grumble in your guts, but it won't kill you.' There was a splodge of stew on her lips; she wiped it away on her knuckles.

Silver's gaze went from the spoon to her mouth and back again. She couldn't read his expression. 'Do you know,' he asked, 'that the human body contains many hundreds – maybe thousands – of creatures so minuscule they would make fleas appear giants? Don't mock, their existence is well-known to the community of science. I think of them as *trivialities*. They carry disease, and they can spread from body to body in the merest droplet of fluids. I wonder how many trivialities you've just licked onto my spoon? You're laughing. You don't believe me.'

She *was* laughing. 'I don't disbelieve you. I'm laughing because you call yourself part of a *community*. Science-men! What pompous loons you all are!'

'We're all of us trivialities,' he replied, took the spoon, and began to eat. He grimaced – 'You're right. This is vile' – but he didn't stop eating.

Presently he looked up from the bowl. 'I have questions.'

'Ask all you like,' she retorted, 'you won't necessarily get an answer.' But he'd judged her well, she realised. He had already tested the limits of what she could and couldn't say; besides which, she doubted the Service would much care. The serjeant had seemed frustrated by this mission, which was rated so highly by his superiors, yet seemed to involve nothing more than nursemaiding this unwilling traveller on his voyage back to England.

'I've one important question. I was captured in Paris. Was I alone, or were others taken with me?'

'I can't tell you.'

'Please.'

'Literally, I can't tell you. I don't know. I didn't know *you* were involved till I found you trussed up on my bed. I'm one of your trivialities in all this. Those men out there are the giants.'

'They're the fleas. The giants are in London.'

'All I know,' she finished, 'is that you're the only prisoner on this ship. If I guessed, I'd say *no* – no one else was arrested with you.'

He rolled his head on the pillow to look away from her, towards his bound wrist, which was chafed red under the metal band. 'I ought to be happy she's not suffering this.'

'You had a lover in Paris?'

He nodded. 'More than that, a friend.'

Having nothing to say, Astraea flapped her arms. Her prisoner returned to his water and stew, and ate with less enthusiasm than before. Watching him eat was like watching a man digging a pit; he chewed each gristly piece into slow fine pieces before swallowing. He didn't try to talk with her while he ate, and she stayed upright, suffering on her feet, watching him fidget unhappily on the bed.

He finished the bowl and the biscuits, and washed it all down gratefully with bland gulps of water. She refilled his cup. Her hand was shaking – not from fear, from the stress of standing – and soaked his cuff. The accident broke the grim seal on his mouth.

'Mistress Behn,' he addressed her.

'Astraea,' she corrected.

'Aphra Behn – I learned about you after I got to Paris. *Le Pouvoir* told me everything.'

'Not quite everything, I imagine.'

'Enough to impress me. You're a poet, you've left your mark on the world. Why do you do this? Work for the Service, I mean, when you've got so much else in your life?'

She shrugged. 'I'm a patriot,' she said, but it was an inadequate reply, and his smile revealed he knew it. So, maybe *le Pouvoir* did know everything, after all? She felt with some certainty that she had more pride in her pen than she had in a nation that behaved so shabbily, and repaid its debts niggardly if at all.

Was he trying to persuade her to help him escape? She hardened her heart to the possibility, but no – he was only curious, already turning over new earth in the conversation. 'I've never been one for the theatre, but I know it's my loss. What did Mister Behn make of your calling?'

'He died before I started writing. The plague,' she explained.

'Ah, I'm sorry.'

'Don't be. He was a drunk and a lout and a lech, and he barely spoke English.' She conjured an image of the man in her mind and smiled bitterly. Then an afterthought: 'And it was a long time ago.'

He tugged again on the short metal leash holding him to the bed. 'Can you do something about this? I'd like to stretch my legs.'

This was permitted, and she showed him the key. 'But I have to stay with you. I remind you there are two sentries on the other side of the door, and they'll be more than happy to shackle you hand and foot if you try anything.'

'I won't try anything.'

'And if I let you loose, you'll be sure you won't overpower me and ravish me or anything like that?'

'I won't. Promise.'

She pursed her lips. 'Shame,' she said, and sprang his lock. Silver rose from the bed on quivering feet, rubbing his red wrist. Aphra – she was Aphra again, there was no point in being Astraea with this man who knew all but one thing about her and yet seemed so far removed from the secrecy demanded by the Service – lowered her backside onto the warm rut left by his body and relaxed. She showed nothing of this to her prisoner, who stood with his back to her and stretched his arms and spine in a posture of ecstatic prayer.

'If you need to piss or shit then I must stay, but you'll spare me the sight, I hope?'

'I don't,' he said, sounding curiously embarrassed by this admission. 'I may puke if the sea gets rough.'

'Don't say that. I had some of that stew as well.'

She stretched back on his stiff mattress, indulging herself while Silver paced back and forth around the limits of the room. The walls that had seemed spacious only a moment before now became tight and unyielding as a cell. Sweat and bad air was the lingering scent of all such prisons, but this one was briny with it. She felt saturated with salt, and it made her body heavy and treacherous. The mattress was not comfortable, but it yielded to her buttocks and the small of her back readily. She propped herself up on one elbow. Her other hand went to the back of her head, to massage the lump of her skull through a thicket of dry and tangled hair. The muscles below that lump were taut and hard under her thumb, weary from holding up the weight of her brain. She felt very lazy.

Silver stopped pacing, and stood staring at the door, as if he had forgotten her. She thought for a moment about a story in which a woman happened upon some enchanted item that concealed her whole presence from society, some belt or jewel that would render her invisible. Such thoughts led inexorably to an obscure and lonely death. She wouldn't have that. She tried to sit up and failed.

Silver removed his three-day-old shirt – by fuck, he *has* forgotten I'm here – and put it over the doorknob where it hung roguishly. His fingers paused to inspect the thinning patches of the cloth, before rising to make a more ponderous and painful examination of his torso. He didn't turn to look at his gaoler, who craned forward, mildly interested. She couldn't see what fresh bruises he might be tending, though she had no doubt they were there. As far as she could gather, the Ratcatchers had instructions to be gentle with him, but this went against their nature, and he might have taken a few extra blows and shoves for it. Yet it was the old wounds that absorbed her, making his back a bleached map of all his ancient wars. A laceration here, a lump there, an eye-catching yellow blotch where a bruise hadn't recovered. There must be bones beneath that skin that had broken and never properly healed. She looked for them, but – she being untrained in anatomy, despite her father's calling – they escaped her.

For the first time, she believed he was truly as old as was said, that the years and experiences that went unwritten on Nathaniel Silver's face were nonetheless recorded on his body. These wounds were gained in the battle for England's soul, given him by men dying to preserve her world when she was still a child. He was no mere blight or nuisance. He was a true enemy.

She blew air out of her mouth. The war was over. The war was over.

'So,' she tagged the word on the tail of her breath, 'what is it you believe in?'

He shrugged. How complex that plain gesture seemed, the ripple forming out of a dozen twitches among the muscles of back and shoulders and neck. *Turn round*, she did not say, *turn round and look at me*, but he only inclined his head to the wall. 'Not sure. Everything changes. I suppose liberty, levelling, love. These are constants.'

Aphra felt herself slide a little further down on her back; she was in a proper slouch now, and didn't care if he saw it. Her fingertips found crude lumps everywhere on the mattress. 'Liberty and love, eh? It's not strange to me that men are the most vocal advocates of free love. While your sex spends freely, mine picks up the many costs.'

This made him turn, to correct her: 'Not free love. Just love.' He kept his arms folded high, as if ashamed of his flat breasts and listless nipples. Yes, there was a fresh patterning of browns and purples below his ribs, and cuts both red-new and white-old, but she found she could not look at them. He had torn a rag from his shirt tail, and went to the water jug to soak it.

'Just love then? Nothing more?'

'Love is the first step from which the rest of the journey proceeds.' He brought the wet cloth over his chest, not concentrating on the wounds as she expected, but sloshing generally to wipe away all the grime and sweat and sloth he'd acquired since Paris. The unwrung rag dribbled long trails down his stomach and flanks to wet the tops of his breeches. She looked there. She found it easy. All this talk of love. Is he more than a republican eunuch, more than a castrato in reason's choir? Does he have a cock under there?

Is that a lump? He does have a cock!

Fuck, am I doing that to him?

'You ought to be careful saying that,' she warned. 'You'll end up nailed to something.'

'Too late for that,' he remarked. Then he tipped the dregs of the jug over his head. There was barely enough left to wet his long lank hair. His skin was left pocked with tiny beads, the tops of his breaches soaked and darkened, but most of the water lay dribbled on the floor in miniature puddles that diminished slowly through the cracks. There was no cloth or towel, so he dried himself on the discarded sheet from the bed, in the process making himself no cleaner. There was something of the Christ behind him, Aphra thought. She had never before thought of that man as an imposing figure in any way, but here He was – or a decent-enough effigy of Him – dabbing himself dry meticulously and almost prudishly in front of her.

Her knees ground together beneath her petticoats. 'And what has science –' she began, while he at that moment also began to speak, 'Would you do me a great –' Their questions battered against each other, and there was an awkward stumbling moment as each gestured the other to speak. Silver shuffled and pinked, as if noticing her interest for the first time; he took the shirt guardedly from its hanging place, but didn't dress in it, instead holding it between his forepaws like a housecat presenting a dead rodent to his mistress.

She cleared her throat. 'What does natural philosophy say about love? It doesn't command the sun and the stars. What use is it if it's not visible under glass?'

The question rankled with him, though not greatly. Still damp, still clutching his soiled and ragged shirt, he perched himself on the bed beside her. 'You know I first embraced science because it promised to liberate mankind from all these mystic forces that have for so long oppressed us –'

'Womankind has been so disposed, but her oppressor is all too tangible.'

'If you want to keep interrupting –'

'No, sorry.' She waved, regally. 'Go on.'

' – but all I found is that the invisible forces are real, and their rules are iron hard. At least kings and tyrants are prey to whims and fancies on their better days. Science doesn't command the universe, it reveals only the precise dimensions of our servitude.'

There'd been no anger; his words came from a cool dark place inside himself. Aphra fluttered numb eyelids during his lecture, but couldn't help feel the heat of his too-close skin, the nimbus of damp that still clung to his body. His mood was the kind that stimulated the ardour of youths, but distracted from the same in men of mature years. Was he young? Was he old? Her palm rested on the bed a spider's-step away from his crotch.

'There's still love?' But she was wondering aloud, and he had not heard her. He bowed his head, and seemed to be inspecting the hand that lay beside him, insolently close.

'I wish I could name the forces that have driven me,' he murmured. Then he unfolded the remains of his shirt, but Aphra stopped him with a gentle hand, took it, made a ball of it, and tossed it away.

'No,' she instructed.

His body, his slow flesh, gave away no hint of surprise, not then and not the moment when she kissed him. She pretended later, when she rewrote the scene in her mind, that he had moved first to kiss her, but in the true moment it was all her. It was her tongue in his mouth. He tasted of wound, of raw meat and rust-coated teeth. His eyes were still open, so were hers, boggling at each other across the narrow gap. She lifted her hand to his groin. Fuck it! She slid her hand down his front, hungry skin against hungry skin, to find his stiff and inquisitive prick. It wriggled like a salmon and wetted her palm.

He broke away, as if she had punched him or shot him. She saw shock – good, that could be overcome, and a little disgust – not with her, but with what he thought her motives might be, but he was wrong. She wanted nothing for the Service – if the Five Masters wanted his lust, then let them come here and beg for it in person! – nor any toll that a gaoler could demand of a prisoner in exchange for an easier life. Everything she wanted was in the flesh, his and hers alike.

'This isn't love,' he protested.

'So?' she retorted. She pulled her hand free, and pressed it against his mouth to silence him. His eyes bulged. She gestured frantically towards the door and raised a shushing finger. He nodded, understanding. When she took her hand away, he stayed silent, and they moved mutely on the bed, so as not to distract the Ratcatchers without.

She couldn't bear to let him see her naked, not so early when it would spoil the mood, but she was lustful for his body and tugged his breeches down. He blushed and again tried to cover himself, coiling one hand and forearm over his member to hide it. He had a long, narrow cock that was neither the greatest nor the least that Aphra had ever found pointing her out. She made hooks of her fingers, to weigh his balls on her fingertips. She tickled. He winced. Sensitive fellow. She kissed furiously around the groin, letting his rough thigh-hair prickle her lips. How many cunts had wetted him before hers? She didn't care, but she was curious.

She looked up at Nathaniel Silver, and he was as startled as a maid on her wedding night. She almost despised him for his innocence. Had he thought she was planning some ruse to sneak him out of this cabin to freedom? Not a chance of that, Magus, not even if I willed it, not even with all the science and magics and forces at your disposal! The only escape she could offer him was into her body, to separate him from this world, if only for a few seconds. She no longer despised. She had gone beyond that, into mercy.

She marvelled for a moment at the sight of his body. He had a fascination of wounds. She wanted to kiss each one and learn its provenance. Each was the death of a good royalist on the fields of long ago. He wasn't beautiful; men weren't beautiful as women were beautiful, or as princes like Oroonoko were beautiful. The male form was so ugly and impractical, proof – if any more were needed to be heaped up on His list of failures – that God was an artless imbecile. But Nate had a spring and a leanness in his flesh.

She laid him unprotesting down on the bed and straddled him, her arms a V at the joining of their bodies, her hands guiding his cock through all the demanding layers of her clothes. She was always gentle, not touching too crudely, nor stimulating him. He left her to this, and devoted his hands instead to unpeeling her upper body as though she were a ripe exotic fruit under skins of cloth. A bit over-ripe, she thought, but – too late! – she was breached. He brought her shoulders and her breasts out into the open and looked undisappointed, though you could never trust men's eyes. Her tits had felt like lead bullets these last few years, complaining as bitterly as her spine about the weight they had to bear. He touched them with his young man's hands, his thumbtips massaging the teats until they were so sore she was afraid they would, for the first time ever, yield milk.

She cried. He released one heavy breast to thumb away her tears. These last years, she had taken as many youthful lovers as would have her, and she wondered – now the ancient but unaged Nathaniel Silver treasured her body – how much she had needed them for a pretence that she was still young and supple, not the fat old cripple that fashionable London mocked. *Tell me again about women 'playwrights', they jeered. I would laugh. I have seen Mistress Behn's work, and find in it nothing but a fishwife's prattle, that convinces me more than ever that women are oafs uncomprehending of human nature, while all men who pretend to find worth in her plays are eunuchs and cuckolds too. Do I hear you rush to her defence? I hear a choir with many horns but not one true testicle!*

She didn't need to be defended against London farts any more than she needed to leech youth from virgin boys. She was herself. That should be enough. She took Silver's penis into her cunt, into her beautiful cunt, and he gasped, and it was very far from being a complaint or an apology or a sigh of disappointment. Fuck, let him not make so much noise when I start pounding him! She gagged him, first with her tongue, then with the flat of her hand. They sweated and copulated, and she grimaced, his cock kneading her sometimes clumsily and sometimes too hard, but always pleasantly tickling. It was hard not to cry out, alternately from pain and from excitement. She would not climax, she would not climax, she rarely climaxed when a man was involved, they squirted their seed willy-nilly then had it out and into running water before she was even hopeful of satisfaction, so quick to wash away the smell of her, the bastards! She would not climax. She would not climax.

She would not –

His hands fought to keep her mouth shut when it came. He had to sit up violently and that brought him off, and she hardly felt his flow spitting out in the midst of her orgasm, any more than a few spots of rain are felt amidst a hurricane. He was so red, his body bright with their shared effort. There was no mirror here; she dreaded to think how she must look. Half a dozen pieces of hair obscured her eyes. She thought he would brush them away for her, but he didn't.

Why did we work so hard to keep those rat-men outside from hearing? Doubtless, they were expecting this. Doubtless there is a spyhole in some wall. So let them stare. That was a good fuck!

Silver sagged back on the bed. She fell with him and pinned him there.

'That was good,' she said. She grinned at him. She wanted fruit now. She wanted a big juicy orange. She wanted its pip and pith and juice on her lips, there to drip on his face. She jiggled her thighs to convince herself that his cock was expelled, and to shrug off the skirts still flapping round her legs. She felt superbly soiled.

He seemed less happy, but then he had a girl in Paris, and had been forced to give her up. She rolled off him, falling fat into the thin gap between his body and the wall. They lay together for a while, contemplating the steady rock of the ceiling. A melancholy humour crept over her.

'I lied,' she said suddenly.

'About what?' He was dozy, but not unalert. Should she risk telling him? Yes, yes, she would.

'My husband,' she told him. 'He didn't die in the plague. He never lived. There never was a Mister Behn. I never married.'

That caught his attention, and he sat up – though not too quickly – to look down on her. She was almost wholly naked now, and all her poundage was visible to him, and all forty-three of her years, too. Her stomach was still adorably plump, and she was pleased when he planted a hand there, then a kiss. 'I don't understand.'

'I made him up. It wasn't too difficult. I met him in the colonies and married him aboard ship. He died in the days when corpses were so plentiful they'd stopped counting. That took care of the records. The rest was easy. I'm a writer. It's easy to conjure up a whole man out of words and stories. A few carefully rehearsed anecdotes made him real. By the time I was done, there were a dozen men who'd swear honestly before God that they'd known a Johann or Joachim Behn all their lives. You men, you're so easily led.' She jiggled his diminished, saggy bollocks. He liked that.

'But why?' Silver probed. 'What possible good could a nonexistent husband do for you?' He wasn't protesting. There was an unfaked curiosity in him that pleased her. She had shown him too much scepticism. Whatever else he might be, his sense of inquiry was quite genuine.

'His *death*. He gave me his death, and it made me a different person. A spinster couldn't drink and fuck and swear and exhibit herself like I do. Aphra Johnson couldn't have been a writer, that would be scandalous, but they can tolerate Aphra Behn because of her circumstances. I have a widow's freedom.'

She expected him to laugh, but he didn't. He said nothing for a while, then began to trace whorls on the inside of her thigh, his nail sharp as a quill. 'Does it bother you that it's his name that will be remembered?' he asked, but he was making small talk, not expecting a proper reply. His fingers continued their exploration of her lower body. So they passed the hours. They wouldn't couple again. They wouldn't couple. They wouldn't.

Maybe they would.

She wasn't bothered by his question. *Johnson* was her timid father's name. *Behn* was hers alone.

Eventually she had to put things back the way they were. They dressed in moody silence, and he let her chain him back to the bed. They would dock almost as soon as there was wind, so she doubted she would see him again. To her relief, her indiscretion seemed to have gone unnoticed by the Swedes and the sentries. These last were playing cards on the floor when she emerged. She stepped over them, dislodging their formations with the trailing hem of her skirt.

In the years to come, she would wonder how genuine had been her passion for Silver. It certainly wasn't love, but nor was it just the latest encounter with a joyless prick. She felt unsatisfied, but only in the way that the effects of a full meal must give way to hunger. She dumped her baggage in the galley, avoided the stares and the crude hooting of the men who bumped into her, and went up on deck. A sullen grey sky awaited her. Rain, she thought. Rain and wind. They were to be carried to London after all.

Had her magnificent fuck done this? Had her primal rutting worked magic to summon the elements? Had she created this weather as easily as she had created her phantom husband?

Her clothes were unsettled, and the first blast of cold air went through them. No lonely prowling on the deck for her, she decided; she would go back into the belly of the beast and find somewhere warm to lie. She turned away. She almost turned. She didn't move. She saw the woman-shape poised on the prow, as if the figurehead – brought to life – had climbed up onto the deck to confront the crew with the needs and lusts of its wooden soul. It was wrapped in thin, tight armour that rippled on its body. Its hair whipped round its head; the colour was impossible to tell in the grey light but

Aphra knew it to be the richest of reds. Wetness shivered in the cold air between them, obscuring the unwoman's face, but Aphra remembered every detail.

She had lain with Nate Silver so passionately that gods and goddesses had fallen from the sky to attend them and adore them.

'Larissa,' she said. The apparition – who could barely have heard over the churn of the sea – nodded, and stepped down from the prow. She was six feet away, no more, and solid. Aphra took a shaky first step towards her.

═ Chapter 19: *The Terror in Paris* ═

There is a land on the far side of the world, as yet unknown to Europe. In the dry scrubs under the baking sun lives Aki, alone now except for Lizard and the faces of the sky. She had a people once; they were nomads, but they no longer welcome her to walk with them. Aki tries, though not hard, to remember why they parted. It was a dispute over a child, and a piece of meat, and the markings made in white urine trails on a flat black rock. No, forget, forget, that was another time. She walks the lines away from them, into another world, surviving on the berries and the bark of trees, on water from the moonpools, and sometimes the meat of wild dogs and lizards. Not from Lizard himself, who walks with her, and changes shape with every new sun.

Aki has dreams. She dreams that if she sits at the foot of a certain tree by a certain pool, then the bone people will come for her. They have made peace with the spirits and live in the earth. They have watched her and want her for their tribe, which has no such rules about children and meat and marked stones. Come and join us in the sunless lands, they beg her – you will be loved. She wants to know if she can bring Lizard, and the bone people smile, yes, you can bring Lizard, so she is happy to go with them. And it will be good that she goes with them. Soon their world in the earth will be threatened by the witch-woman, whose stomach breeds grubs bigger than men. She will come to devour the sunless lands, and when she comes it will be Aki who stands against her to save the bone people. Aki will be the Grandfather's hand.

She walks to the end of the world searching for that certain tree by that certain pool. She finds it, just as it is in her dreams. She sits above its roots and waits, and the face of the sun comes and goes and comes and goes, and Lizard capers for her until he grows too hungry and too slow, and she waits and waits and the bone people do not come.

'She would have been a Mother,' Hateman had said. 'She could have been a God-mother.'

Instead, Mother Sphinx's cell had turned their attentions to Nathaniel Silver. When they'd recruited their fifth member, they had to choose from someone in England, someone from the here and now, who could spy on Silver without drawing attention, without difficulty. Cousin Greenaway had taken Aki's place in the cabal, and it would be another cell who recruited the strange foreign child for the Faction, if she were recruited at all, if the Faction could survive their setbacks in the War.

Their occasional meetings in London had grown ever more strained. The escape of the Homeworlder four years earlier had had no repercussions, which on the one hand was good for them, as it became clear the Houses would be sending no ships and no more agents, and London wasn't about to become a battleground. On the other, it had left them with no greater advantage than before, and no better grasp on Silver's mystery. They'd resumed their endless vigil over him, waiting for the moment that he might reveal himself. Cousin Hateman was now convinced that this moment would never come. Suppression and Amphigorey agreed, though quietly.

Only Mother Sphinx was urging patience, which Hateman – bristling with frustration – took for exhaustion. It was always difficult to tell with the Mother, who rarely showed her naked face these days, even informally. She might be a wolf waiting for the unwary prey to walk into her jaws, or she might be a fox on the run, cunning but panicked. One thing was clear, she was the only member of Faction Paradox who still had any faith in their mission. Greenaway certainly didn't, but she sided with Mother Sphinx anyway. She *liked* her tasks. She enjoyed spending time in Paris, watching Silver and reporting back on his activities to London. There had never again been anything so arduous or dangerous as their night at the House of the Infernal. These last years had been pleasantly tedious for her, even as Silver immersed himself deeper into *le Pouvoir*'s latest project, and even as the channel crossing grew ever more familiar.

At the last meeting, Hateman had stood up angrily and denounced her complacency, then stormed out of their hiding place then, clomping down the nave in her armour and mask and out into broad daylight. Suppression had flustered; Amphigorey had said something droll and uneasy about someone called Anastasia; while Mother Sphinx had sucked sweet wine impassively through a straw, and her mask pulled a sour face on her behalf. Greenaway had simmered furiously under her mask, first angry with Hateman for singling her out when she was only following the Mother's lead, then with Sphinx for putting her in this place, then only with herself, because it was true – she had become complacent in Silver's company – and because she couldn't change. Faction Cat, always happiest when there was harmony among the humans, had yowled grumpily and spat at them.

Amphigorey had taken off his mask and gone to fetch Hateman back in. No damage had been done; no one had seen her but some impressionable children, and a few stories about skull-headed bogeymen would do the Faction's reputation no harm. There were still plots abroad in England – some more real than others – but the imagined Popish conspiracy had been forgotten, and those who roused against it had since been suitably humiliated or punished. Later, when heels had been kicked and tempers cooled, Hateman had taken Greenaway aside to make apologies. She had told her about Aki. Greenaway had seen at once that her younger cousin was hoping for an equal in the cabal, someone as sharp as her and as bright as her, but had ended up with a dull, ordinary woman who'd been snared out of chance and necessity.

'But I wouldn't've loved Aki,' she'd confessed. 'I would have been too much in awe of her.'

~ She loves you ~ Didn't you see that? ~

As far as she knew, Mother Sphinx had told none of her cousins about Erasmus. More complacency? Possibly, but the fox knew better than the wolf how to cope with the unexpected.

And now she was back in Paris, ascending the latest flight of stairs to Nathaniel Silver's newest quarters. *Le Pouvoir* liked to move him around, though it was hard to judge whether that was for his own protection as they claimed, or just to foster in him the impression that there were English spies forever on his tail. That was true, but not quite in the way that he – or *le Pouvoir* – imagined. Still, she liked these changes of scene.

Disorientating though they were, they gave her an opportunity to explore new parts of Paris, and prevent the old from becoming over-familiar. It wouldn't do for her to start imagining the city to be a mere island off the coast of London, or vice versa. There was always power to be drawn from the distinctions between places.

She just wished they would stop putting him on the top floor, and giving her so many damn'd stairs to climb. Had they no respect for her advancing years?

~ *High ground ~ It makes his defence easier ~*

It also makes it harder for him to get away, should it come to that. She groaned heavily as she reached the attic. The building around her whispered subtly, trying to convey a message it didn't want overheard. It might be a sign that Silver was being entertained and gently interrogated by another prostitute paid from *le Pouvoir*'s pocket. He no longer bothered to conceal that from Alice Lynch, still his lover after all these years, who had realised that to raise a complaint would have put her in *le Pouvoir*'s black books, and from there very rapidly into the Seine with bricks tied round her ankles.

Alice was devoted to Silver, though it was a strained sort of devotion. Greenaway liked Alice, though she no longer felt that they had much in common.

Ah! No, there was more to the walls' warnings than the sizzle of distant sex, and when she came to knock meekly on Silver's door, it gave way – unlocked – below her knuckles. She pushed inside, into a space that felt gloomed even though glorious ochre sunshine was falling through the windows. Much dust had been thrown up, casting a thousand tiny shadows, and the furniture had been overturned. Silver never kept himself too neatly and was prone to the occasional dark mood, but that rarely amounted to more than scattered papers or a dent in the wall where he had kicked out his anger. Now everything had been smashed, except for a small civilised island round the desk where Nate's papers had been stacked in neat but tottering piles for the inspection of subtler vandals. The men were poring over them, taking notes or copying, sorting some into boxes and others into the fire.

They were three. None of them was Silver. Of him there was no sign, and the door at her back whispered of his absence.

Greenaway recognised them, and acted the scared girl she'd once been, stepping back in fright. They wore the blue coats of *le Pouvoir*'s *bêtes humaines*. They were not masked. They were all ugly, even the handsome ones. They were all much bigger than her. They stared at her, seeing prey, no – not even that – just a detail, an outstanding but minor problem to be accounted for with the minimum of effort.

'Where's Nate Silver?' Her voice came out reedily, a helpless thing.

Their chief didn't even smile, didn't even look at her. He gave a plain, clipped order. 'Find out what she knows, then take her away. Do anything you have to, short of killing her.'

The nearest of the men nodded wordlessly. He reached for her. She threw him out of the window.

The second man she blinded. She brought the third to his knees with her whip coiled round his throat. His fingers clawed at the impossible throttle, scrabbling on hollow air, while his face reddened and whitened and blued as though his neck were in the grip of an expert strangler.

Eventually, because she needed answers, and because Erasmus began to fret in her head about the damage she could do, she slackened her grip, a little, only a little.

'Now,' she said, pushing her face against his – she found she didn't need a bone mask to be a holy terror – 'where's Nate Silver?'

'In England,' he gasped. 'The Service took him days ago.'

That was volunteered a little too easily, so she choked him for a little longer. 'Took him?'

'He was handed over... The mirrors're finished... So's he...'

On the wall, her shadow made to tighten its whip once more.

~ *That will kill him* ~

Maybe I want to kill him?

~ *You don't* ~

She didn't. She slackened her whip, and the man fell gasping at her feet.

'Run,' she said. 'Run as far and as fast as you can. It's not me you'll be running from, it's *le Pouvoir*. Run to a place where they can't find you. Run to the unknown countries on the edge of the world, and there's a chance *le Pouvoir* might not follow.'

I'm good at this, she thought.

~ *Good is the wrong word* ~

She left before either man could get back to his feet, well aware that they would still be dangerous. She wouldn't be able to return here – no great loss. Silver travelled light, ever surrounding himself with new things but ever prepared to abandon them. Only Erasmus's egg was important to him, and that was in *le Pouvoir*'s possession already. No, the priority had to be to get back to England, alert the Faction, and locate Silver before the Service could do away with him.

She skidded down each flight of steps, tearing her spattered skirts behind her.

A pall of debris filled the air on the street outside, all the pieces of the house displaced when she'd hurled her attacker out. Glass and plaster and wood fragments decorated the ground round his fallen body. She didn't get close enough to see if he had survived, though it was possible, always possible. She saw the white of his shirt; boys had already snatched his prized blue coat, and were careering down the street with it trailing like a banner behind them, their legs skipping, their mouths whooping like Indians. There was a cluster of people on the street, consternation, passers-by helping a fainted woman into a cool doorway, fish-eyed spectators gathered at their open windows along all the walls, but no one took the petite woman in the tattered dress to be its centre. She reacted like an innocent.

'Quelle horreur!' she bellowed, as she burst into the street, and no one paid her attention. She was not yet pursued, but she ran anyway, and by the time she was three avenues gone she was laughing with the exhilaration of the chase.

There was a brick archway below a riverside wall, where prostitutes gathered of an evening. Greenaway took a risk hiding herself there, and it would grow riskier once the sun was fully down and the lamps came up, but it was open and public and escapable. She'd abandoned her bloodied and torn overskirt in an alley, hanging on a nail at the back of a respectable garden like a flag or an accusation. She hoped that it might be found, become a celebrated local mystery, growing into a story and perhaps even a *loa* one day. She could pose as a harlot in her underskirts until the opportunity came to find (~ *steal* ~) more suitable clothing.

She sat on her haunches under the arch, listening to the nearby murmur of the Seine, and the efficient chatter of the working girls as they prepared themselves for the night. She had a good grasp of French, but like English, it merged into a seamless babble when heard from a crowd and at a distance. They could be talking about her. They could be prepared to hand her over, if they recognised her. She trusted to their ignorance or their better natures, and ate some bread and a pie she had found (~ *stolen* ~) while making her escape.

Must you keep mentioning that I'm a thief? It's necessity.

~ *Stolen or not, one pie fewer is one pie fewer* ~ *All actions you take will affect the statistics, though admittedly the effect is negligible on this scale* ~

I thought I was the one with a mouthful of dead meat.

~ *I mean you should have died twenty years ago* ~ *You're potentially as big an anomaly as Silver* ~

Then maybe I'm your problem. You should compel me to kill myself. It would make everyone's life a lot simpler, my own in particular.

~ *I doubt that* ~

She wolfed down the pie. She refused to make her thoughts plain to Erasmus as she ate, out of politeness more than anything. She'd had good manners beaten into her by her father. The pastry was days old and stale, the meat unpleasant on her tongue. She hated the thought it might be her last. She had stolen nothing to drink, so each half-chewed piece went raw and hard down her throat. Erasmus waited patiently as his precious numbers resolved themselves into nothing in their shared stomach.

Greenaway's back was pressed against a wall so hard that the brick patterns were impressing through her clothes into her skin; but she read nothing from it. Its voice was a muttered catalogue of all the bodies that had passed by, from one part of a transaction to another, all the betrayals and heartbreaks and crimes played out below the arch. The streetwalkers went about their business around her, like tradesmen in a market place, like the wares displayed on hooks and poles. A few curious faces and masks looked to her, a few prospective customers too – the dusk making them all indistinguishable, sidling and pale predators – but no one approached. She was dirtied and ragged. She was not an attractive catch.

~ *So, what now?* ~

We have to assume we've already lost the initiative, and Silver's back in England. So we need to follow and report to Mother Sphinx. Which will take time, even if I can book passage and get out of France without being challenged.

~ *There is another matter* ~ Erasmus said, and the voice that lived in her was cautious. What?

~ *Silver's egg* ~ *It would be useful* ~

Le Pouvoir has it.

~ *True, but we may never have another chance to retrieve it* ~ *Also, I think there is some conspiracy to keep him apart from it* ~ *This is the third time he's been forcibly separated from the egg; the first instance might be put down to circumstances, but the second...?* ~ *And now this...?* ~

There's the question of finding it first. Nate told me it was meant to be moved to Versailles.

~ *It's still in Paris* ~ *I can sense it and lead you to it* ~ *Once it's moved to the palace, our chances of getting it back will be immeasurably slim* ~

They're slim to the point of starvation already. We can hardly just walk into a *Pouvoir* vault to burgle it.

~ *We can walk in* ~ *We would not necessarily walk out again* ~

It sounded like a grim joke. It took her a moment to hear the serious intent in the chimes of the *loa*'s voice. She couldn't imagine what Erasmus meant, so he told her.

Cousin Greenaway carried her face in a bag that swung pendulous at her hip. It was the bag itself that weighed her down; the mask – when she wasn't touching it – was light as a trifle. She concealed herself in the dark edges of the street and under the eaves of houses, not so much to stay invisible, but to keep her shadow hidden. If they were efficient as was claimed – and they were – *le Pouvoir* would have caught up with their failed agents by now. Stories about the woman who struck them down with a whip-shaped shadow would not be trusted, but neither would they be discounted.

Erasmus was leading her, through slummish boulevards, down brick crevices that were too narrow to be called alleys, under bridges and over low rooftops, through the hollows of derelict houses and the unlocked doors of occupied ones, to the vault of *le Pouvoir*. The *loa* still had his secrets – or at least a greater part of him was deep and incomprehensible – but they had been familiar with each other for so long it was impossible to believe that he might be deceiving her, or leading her unwary into a trap. She recalled the last time she'd broken into a house, but this time she was alone, with no cousins to back her up, or even aware of her predicament. She had nothing but her whip, her face, and her *loa*, the sacraments of the order. She wouldn't go invisible this time. She would put on her mask and becoming a living terror.

Le Pouvoir's treasure house was a growth of buildings close to the Seine. What might have been built as prosperous warehouses had declined over time, and became jostled, squeezed, and finally impacted by new outcrops of wood and brick around them, until they resembled no construction planned by man but a strange natural petrifaction. The night hid its outline, but she could read it, even from a distance. This building was tortured by the infestation of man, and yearned for the entropy that would collapse it back into its component parts. Her whip unfurled in the oily air. The darkness didn't mute it here, it gave the whip weight, as if the whole of the night sky were a weapon extruded from her wrist.

Will they be afraid of me?

~ *Put your mask on* ~

Yes, they'll be afraid of me. She took her skull-face from the bag and held it up close to her eyes, to catch the reflections of the night-lamps on ivory. It was meant to intimidate the Great Houses, not mortal men, but she would still look a monster. I'll teach them to love their lives.

We'll both look like monsters; it's Erasmus's face as much as mine.

She breathed through the holes of her war-face, and the bone scoured and purified the air. She went under skull, with whip, in petticoats to knock politely on the door, and – when her enquiry went unanswered – to split it in half with the force of her shadow. The warehouse hummed with pleasure, welcoming demolition.

Cousin Greenaway ploughed into the anteroom, where tables and chairs were up-turning as their occupants – unprepared watchmen in shirtsleeves – abandoned their positions and went for their pistols. It was a tiny, sweaty, brown-tinted room. A pair of streetgirls huddled like tame young cats by the nearest doorway, and she could safely ignore them. She swung her whip round the room, slicing gun-barrels and castrating candles. One pistol exploded as she cut through it, singeing her fingers and turning its holder's hand into a stump of blood and bone-splinters. The flash lingered on her eyeballs, lighting the room after all went dark. The wounded man screeched, a second vanished into silence; the third had the nerve to swing at the intruder, but Greenaway commanded the night and twisted his body round into the wall.

These sentries were only in her way. Someone was crying, a man or a woman, she couldn't tell.

'Run,' she told them. What did her mask-voice sound like? She could hear only how frightened she sounded, how tiny, while to them she must be a fiend with an ivory growl. She left them and pushed further into the building, whose occupants would now be warned against her, and whose resistance would become more formidable and more pronounced.

Her big surprise that evening in Paris was discovering how much more sensible women were in combat than men, who more often than not stood their ground and tried to fight when she'd already shown that she could divert bullets from their arcs and move much more steadily and stealthily in the dark than they. Erasmus guided her, seeing with those parts of her eyes that were normally dormant, but now revealed patterns of heat and motion in the black. The tortured house whispered its encouragement, applauding as she hammered heads and ribcages against walls and furniture to remind *le Pouvoir* of the limitations of mens' power.

She felt no particular desire to hurt anyone, and that made it easier.

Still, the armed whores of *le Pouvoir* showed either a better grasp of tactics or a better sense of self-preservation, removing themselves rapidly once they'd realised they were lost. Most likely they were regrouping, banking on the prospect that the intruder could only get so far into the house, and once there she had little chance of escape. She had the face of a monster and could deflect bullets? Those magics could easily be brought down with a sustained volley. Three times she was stopped and forced to fight in the passages, and with each delay she felt certain that *le Pouvoir* were concentrating on slowing her and tiring her in readiness for caging and slaughter.

The final door in her way wouldn't give. She put her shadow-hand to the lock and felt the metal and wood dissolve into its elemental parts. After that there was no more resistance; she slammed the door after her and dragged shapeless furnishings out of the dark to barricade it. She would need an undisturbed moment; after that, *le Pouvoir* could do what they would.

The three monoliths had been erected in the centre of the room, like some abandoned pagan stoneworks, their outlines visible as different shades of darkness. This was her first glimpse of them; Silver had not been permitted to reveal his work to anyone. They were presently lifeless and unreflective below wraps. She wrenched away the coverings, and the glass surfaces flickered with enough light for her to see them properly.

~ *Not glass* ~

They were responding to Erasmus. He was calling up the light and the vision.

These were Silver's last four years' work, the oracles he had promised *le Pouvoir*. The images welled up now on the flat silver eyes of the mirrors, glazed pictures of other worlds that seemed to address Greenaway directly: a triumphal military march bearing trophies back through the gates of its home city; flawlessly-twinned sisters naked and fondling as their husband leered; two distant figures skipping into the air above a twilit valley, to exchange perfectly-matched blows; a furtive red-headed boy in pursuit of a cocksure fellow through the choked alleys of a city more dismal yet and sprawling than Paris; two shapes in chess-coloured robes, their feet planted and smouldering on a *mappamundi.* Through the hollows of her mask, Greenaway was transfixed, and would have stayed longer if the first hammering hadn't come from the door to distract her.

~ *They're testing our boundaries* ~ *We still have a few moments* ~

The reflection of a woman appeared on the glass, but leaner and taller than Greenaway, maskless and clean-cheeked. She was slow-burning from the inside. Her skin blistered under invisible heat, ripening until it was the same scorched-black as her eyes. Where she burned, her body turned glossy and unmarked. Her already-brazen hair fell out in clumps, making her bald and smooth. The burning consumed her face, leaving it a featureless curve, no longer capable of displaying pain. The fire consumed her until there was nothing left but an ashen parody. It was hard not to go untricked by this illusion; she felt her skin prickling from an unfelt fire. It was harder to turn away. In her ears, Erasmus's voice shivered with effort, and the glass dimmed and the prediction faded.

~ *He grasped more uses for the egg that we ever intended* ~ *It was never meant to be a weapon* ~

Greenaway heard herself give little gasps of relieved laughter below her stoic face. The hammering renewed itself, then just as quickly stopped.

~ *Break them* ~

They tested it, Silver told me. *Le Pouvoir* brought in strong men with metal hammers. They were invited to smash the mirrors. They wore themselves down with the effort and they didn't make a scratch.

She weighed her whip, then brought it down on the central of the three windows. The impact was the most satisfying part of it, more than the sound, more than the shower of glass-like pieces across her body; but it was the noise that caused the most alarm. The attackers resumed their pounding on the door, no longer making soft impacts with fists and shoulders, but the more precise blows of axe-heads, hammers, and picks. They couldn't wait for her to come out. They could hear her destroying their futures.

The remaining mirrors fell with two more cracks of her whip, and as the last pieces shed from their frame the lights dimmed, leaving only a haze glowing behind the lines of the door and the shimmer of a dozen dozen egg fragments carpeting the floor. Greenaway put a bare palm down to touch them.

I hope this will work.

~ *It will work* ~

More light erupted into the room as an axe gouged a ragged hole in the nearest door and a searching lantern was raised to it. They had a clear shot at her, if they just wanted her dead. She prayed to the Grandfather that they would want to take her alive, to question her, to break her, or to revenge themselves on her. She prayed to the *loa*, and no shot came. They thought they had her trapped.

The unglass pieces on the floor shimmered and flowed.

~ *Good* ~

Will this work without Silver?

~ *It will work with me* ~

How many fragments were there? It didn't matter. They were seething towards her, droplets of eggstuff merging into pools, then puddles, no longer trickling like a stream, but rolling with the weight of tiny stones dislodged on a hillside. They rumbled silently under her hand, their numbers diminishing as they grew larger, as they grew whole, a shapeless mass bulging below her palm.

The upper frame of the nearest door splintered again and again until there was nothing of it left but a gap, filled by a creature with eyes of light and many squabbling arms. Some of its hands held hammers and axes, others pointed pistols and cautious lamps. It babbled to her in French; they were calling out to her to surrender and offering her mercy. ~ *You may have impressed them* ~ *They might be offering you a job* ~ *On their terms, of course* ~

Concentrate.

She held the egg up to her bone face, trying hard to listen to the soundless words her *loa* was intoning, the sacred Enochian commands that would unlock its secrets for her. At the door, her makeshift barricade fell away after a few concerted shoves from the many-armed men.

The egg broke into streams of light that flooded the gaps in her mask. It filled the cavity between her face and the bone, and for an instant she was drowning in breathless light, the egg-substance coating her mouth and her nostrils. It slid over her eyes, insinuating under the lids and into the soft bloody corners; it dribbled through her lips and her teeth, up her nose, and down her gullet into her lungs and her stomach. It went smoothly down her throat, barely swallowed. It clung to her cheeks and her forehead, sinking into the layers of her flesh and then into bone. It crawled inside her. She was impregnated. She was eaten by the egg.

It was her *loa*. It had been part of her *loa* all along. The part of her that had been Erasmus sang throatily as he was reunited with himself.

There were more French shrills and barks around her. She had forgotten the language, the meaning of the words, of all the words in any human tongue. The egg was made of words, words of power and violence. She pitied *le Pouvoir*, who – being only men and tied to the solid world– could only mimic real power. They were like Barbary Apes swaggering mannishly in imitation of uncouth sailors. They were like – and Erasmus made her smile – insects.

She had sunk into an unthreatening crouch on the floor as the egg devoured her. She had her legs crossed beneath her now, and her arms folded across her chest – in part to show meekness, so they would not shoot her immediately out of fear, but also to clutch onto her clothes, which she wouldn't care to lose, especially if Amphigorey was on the prowl.

She realised she was laughing like a mad thing, and her captors could hear it plainly through her mask. At least a dozen pistols pointed warily at her head, and no brittle bone – no matter how uncanny – could survive that many shots.

She looked up at the closest, bravest man, and the halo of his lantern was white and dazzling. 'Au revoir,' she said, and the world lurched, and when the flickering glare patterns faded from her eyes, the lamp and all the agents of *le Pouvoir* were gone, and the mundane remains of the mirrors and the walls of the house were gone, and the warehouse itself was gone, and Paris was gone, and she had exchanged them all for a friendlier darkness.

She experienced a moment's unthinking bliss. Then she had to wrench off her mask before it filled with vomit, and the remains of a half-digested meat pie.

So that's instantaneous travel? I'm not doing that again!

~ *You won't have to* ~ *And it was not instantaneous* ~ *We moved insubstantially at the rate of just under one thousand million feet per second* ~

She smeared the remains of her last meal on the back of her sleeve. Erasmus had assured her there would be no serious side effects, and she and he both had no option but to trust one another. She could feel the egg inside her, suffusing her with its warmth and its strange nourishing hunger. She thought of the burning reflection, but Erasmus's mood was heady and it no longer disturbed her.

~ *There is some risk* ~ *You will have to expel the egg shortly* ~ *We warned Silver not to eat it, when we first gave it to him, for these reasons* ~ *It hasn't the mass to induce full-scale mutation, but the probability of side effects increases exponentially with prolonged exposure* ~

It's all numbers with you, isn't it?

~ *They're all we have* ~

She restored her mask – which was clean, though her breath still tasted a little of bad meat – and got to her feet, which protested. Erasmus had relocated her precisely into one of the annexes of the ruin housing the Faction's shrine. She walked out into the long narrow lung of the building, and the light of the moon fell on her through the jagged-edged cavity that had once been magnificent many-coloured windows. None of her cousins were here, but she expected that. They didn't know she was coming. They would be away, or sleeping in the shrine.

~ *You don't sound convinced* ~

She wasn't.

There was an atmosphere. No, there *wasn't* an atmosphere. The Faction's presence had made this a vivid house, and that spirit was gone. She went quickly to the door of the shrine. It was cold and grey and unyielding, the portal a sullen face with tired eyes that could barely look at her. She took a step back.

A *loa*-totem crunched under her clumsy heel, and didn't squeal or burst or protest. She picked it off the ground and it was inert, as if it had never been alive. She swung round, casting her gaze across the floor and finding that the besieging hordes of symbols, casts, hexes, and dollies had been lain waste. They had been smashed, or overturned, or twisted into lifelessness; they had been rearranged into evil patterns; vandals might have trampled one or all, but this was ritualism.

This was an attack.

Where was Mother Sphinx? Where were her cousins?

Instinct warned her not to draw her whip. She was in no immediate danger. The hall echoed emptily, and so it must be empty. These places were built to harvest *souls*; loneliness was a rare and tangible quality within these walls. She scrabbled in the hole at the base of the shrine for Cousin Suppression's lightning-powered lamp, found it, and slid the clammy peg on its side. Its galvanic magic was unaffected by the desecration of the shrine. The beam fell on the far wall and revealed her family.

They were there, all four of them, or at least their shadows. She recognised her Mother from her bulk, her obesity transformed into flat comic rotundity; the others were less distinguishable, but she recognised the shapes of their masks and their half-drawn weapons, blades pinning through crooked arms and into their insubstantial torsos. No bodies stood between the light and the wall, but it was them, all that was left of them.

Greenaway ran to them. The light shook as she ran and the shapes on the wall trembled, as if trying to break free. She hoped that was true. She hoped they might be still alive, only pinned and not entombed. She flattened her hand on the closest – probably Hateman, though it was hard to tell for sure – but her fingers found nothing but naked stone.

'What happened to you?' she yelled, but the shadows had no mouths, and couldn't reply.

~ They must have been trapped when they drew their weapons ~ Your technology has been turned against you ~

'Can we do anything?' She spoke aloud, and Erasmus didn't answer. 'Who could have done this? We're Faction Paradox! No one has this power!' But she knew almost before she'd said it that there were greater powers and Great Houses, and they had come at last.

'What can we do?' she blurted.

~ I don't know! ~ Don't use your whip! ~ You'll be vulnerable to attack ~

It was good advice, and her hand bristled, empty and impotent. 'Silver. We have to go after Silver.'

~ You think he did this? ~

'I think he might be the only one who can *undo* it.'

She snatched up her underskirts and ran for the doors. She was halfway there when the voice came, whistling out of the darkness around her.

'Cousinnnnnnnnnn Greeeeeeenaway!'

So she wasn't alone. She whirled, looking for the source, but he was well hidden, whoever he was.

No. She knew that voice. She knew exactly who he was.

'Coussssssssssssssssssssssssin Greeeeeeeeeeeeeeeeeeeenaway!' And he giggled, that evil laugh, old beyond his years, that she hadn't heard in such a long time. 'I *know* you, Cousin Greenaway. I've known since I set eyes on you!'

She turned and turned, and girded herself ready for an attack on her mind and her spirit, an attack of magic and power. So it came as something of a surprise when her assailant stepped from the shadows and rapped her across the skull with a length of pipe. Her mask absorbed the worst of the blow, but the crown still came down hard on her temple and sent her reeling. She slipped onto the patterned floor, the weight of bone taking her down into darkness.

⇒ Chapter 20: *Outside the Cathedral* ⇐

In her haste to cover their tracks, Mistress Behn had shackled his wrist much tighter than before. The metal band cut into the soft flesh below his palm, so what had been a delicate rash was now a livid red weal. He couldn't move his arm without incurring a deeper gash; if he left it, then the blood and the feeling went out of him below the shoulder. He had to shake it painfully back to life. Around him, his waterborne cell was humid and musty; the close air smelled, of his sweat and hers. The light of the outside world faded, and the ship lurched and butted round grey headlands and into England's delta, and Nathaniel Silver could do nothing but lie brooding on the bed in the evening gloom.

He turned his pinned arm in a gentle repetitive motion, that kept it alive while testing the cuff least.

Aphra Behn had been pleasant company, both in and out of bed, and he tried in spite of his mood to think good things of her. It had not been a mistake. She had endeared herself to him, he lying satiated beside her as she bumbled and tossed on the bed, fussing restlessly about whatever thoughts came into her head, and complaining bitterly about her barely visible shortcomings. He liked her, but he had let Alice down by fornicating with her.

I don't blame you, Alice said. *You might be dead by dawn.*

He put his free hand over his face so he couldn't see her, so he couldn't see that she wasn't there.

The mattress sagged slightly as Alice sat beside him; he imagined her as she had been when they last met, circumstances so unexceptional that he had never guessed it might be their final meeting. He had offered to marry her, but that was almost routine now. As always, she'd declined.

'Hah, I'm not exactly a catch,' she had explained. 'You still look young, you don't need to indulge an old spinster.'

'You're hardly that, Alice. It would make an honest man of me.'

'I would only make you dishonest. Besides, you're free now to indulge yourself with other women, and if you couldn't do that, *le Pouvoir* would see me as an impediment. And in any case, there's only one man on Earth fit to preside over our nuptials –'

'So, ask him, if it will please you.'

'– but you can't be the minister and the groom both, Nate. Sorry, but it's still *no.*'

He had tried hard to show that he was unhurt by the rejection. 'Years ago,' he'd said at length, 'you told me all your hopes for the future. They were so humble and so plain, yet full of good heart. *Le Pouvoir* won't own me forever, and once they're done we could make those dreams come true.'

This had darkened her. 'Those dreams were so full of good heart,' she'd replied, 'because they can never be. They've escaped us, Nate. They've escaped me.' And then he'd had to spend much of the rest of the day comforting her in silence, resenting it because there was so much he wanted to say before they parted, and which might now remain forever unspoken.

Soon after nightfall, his prison gave a final lurch before settling into a more playful rhythm on the water. Nothing was visible through the low window, but he assumed they had put in at port. Aphra, who had been incontinent with every secret confided in her, had told him they were heading for London. How far could they be from the place of the King's execution, or his digs after he'd been freed from gaol, the house where he'd first met Nick, or the tavern where he and Alice had been reunited? The ship would be tethered to land by thick ropes, as tight and biting as the chain on his wrist. He longed to be free, if only for a few hours, so he could climb down into this great city again to discover what had changed in his absence. Last time he'd been here, there'd been little to see for miles but scorched timbers and blackened stone shells.

Would they kill him? A key turned in the distant lock, but it was only the sentries. Without their hoods, they seemed less terrifying than before, but also less human. Their neutral eyes and faces refused to recognise him, seeing only an object on the bed, not a man, not something like themselves. The nearest released him from his chain, and despite Silver's best efforts, his arm flopped limp to his side and began to sizzle with pins and with needles.

The men made him stand, with gestures and with orders that were more grunts than words. Tenderly, they let him stagger about to regain his footing before marching him away. The boards were spongy beneath his feet. He went sullenly.

They took him into the open, where the shock of wet mist and chill air did nothing to refresh him. He saw Aphra Behn, though she didn't see him; she was distant and receding, carrying herself alone down the gangway to the shore. Not realising she was watched, she did nothing to hide her limp or the unsensual wriggle of her thigh. She had no stick, and was steadying herself on the railing, pausing every half-dozen steps to muster the strength to go on. He would have called to her, if his guards hadn't warned him away. They were callous men in the Service, not even allowing her a crutch.

Silver was taken down into another part of the hold, into a narrow room where water and a clean costume had been set aside for him. His guards told him to wash and change, and they waited patiently and unembarrassed as he removed his old clothes, bathed, and shaved. The suit was in the latest Dutch fashion and of fine quality, of the type that *le Pouvoir* would offer him when they needed him to present his ideas to dignitaries, or when they were trying to wheedle or bribe a little more activity from him. The new fabrics prickled his skin, but he was comfortable in black. He was given a wig, which he declined, and the guards shrugged. His old clothes they put in a sack, to be tossed in the river or burned. They shackled him again, pinning his wrists together this time, though more carefully than Mistress Behn had done; they had more practice with chains.

Eventually, once the dockmasters had been bribed to look away, Silver was led down the gangway to the shore where a carriage was waiting for them. Its driver and guard were hooded Servicemen; Silver looked idly to the horses to see if they had been similarly disguised, but they were barefaced and cheerful, though they champed and whinnied with impatience and from the cold.

'Where are you taking me?' he asked the driver, as he stepped from shore to land.

He hadn't expected an answer. 'The Cathedral. Saint Paul's.'

'Saint Paul's burned.'

'It rises again.'

He was lifted into the carriage, which was more of a cage than a gentleman's seat. Once inside, the door was slammed, locked, and bolted. He sat on the narrow bench before the wheels could lurch and knock his legs out from under him. Dry land felt no more secure than had the ship's swelling floor. The window was a barred hole by his head, a hollow sucking in cold air and the odour of horses; he looked out hoping they might overtake Aphra Behn so he could call to her, but she was long gone. He didn't settle, but continued to gaze sourly out of the window.

London was a malleable creature. He saw as much as he was driven through its streets. In part, it was because the night hid its outlines, the shapes of buildings and people reduced to twilight fuzz – but more than that, it was a reborn city, moulded out of the chaos left by the fire. Silver could imagine himself at the centre of it, in different circumstances, a shaping presence drawing avenues and boulevards over the desolation, not forcing them, but raising them out of the natural shape of the landscape. He had seen the Palace of Versailles too often to plan great designs; the wilful Sun King might impose splendour on the Earth, but wherever he touched, he left the world burned and barren.

Ah, his guards had not lied to him. They were drawing up to an uncluttered structure north of the river. He turned his head awkwardly to see the new shape of the Cathedral, but it would not come. He saw only blank walls, with mere hints of scaffold behind it. Then his carriage came to a halt, his door was opened, and hands reached out to draw him down.

The new Saint Paul's was not finished; it was barely begun and invisible. The plain walls he had fought to see were nothing but screens – the works concealed behind them, as if the artisans were modest or ashamed. Silver would have been glad to slip behind the blinds to see what progress had been made, how complete the skeleton might be and whether flesh had yet been put to its bones, but the Servicemen had other plans. They led him along the perimeter, and refused to acknowledge his mild questions.

They took him to the door of a wood structure adjoining the building site. Light glimmered behind the window, so it was occupied. It was raised on a step, and seemed weathered and unremarkable, as if it were more than a temporary placing. A surveyor's hut, he guessed, or the architect's. It reminded him of nothing more than the plain house of prayer he had conceived for the Church of Christ Sublime, so many years ago. His guards removed his cuffs and ordered him inside.

'Who's in there?' he asked.

'The Master of Service,' they told him. 'Your benefactor.'

Puzzled, Nathaniel Silver did as he was told.

It was, as he had suspected, more than a workman's shed. Its interior, already tight, was squeezed by the presence of desks and worktables, all submerged by a tide of papers and designs, and models created from stiff card and thin wood. It smelled like a hive in here, the few candles spreading their beeswax-scented smoke further than their light. One day the builders would return here to find that their tiny models had become yellow and supple from the slow accumulation of candlefat, or worse – a candle might upend and send a miniature conflagration through this miniature city. All the plans and shrunken architecture were given to describing the new cathedral, which looked unexceptional to Silver's eyes, and was topped with a tiny dome that might have better suited a pot of beer than a palace of Christ. He would have picked through them in greater detail if he had been alone, but he was not.

The Master of Service sat in the far corner on a humble stool, a confident or engrossed man with his back turned to the door. He was reading in the pale light, holding his pages perilously close to the nearest flame. Silver saw a black expanse of coat, its tails flapping over the edge of the stool into the dust, while a long trail of brown curls – none his own – hung down the fellow's back. The Master was not masked, but gave nothing away.

'Sir,' Silver said, wishing he had a hat so that he might remove it and be fashionably polite. Let him find insolence in that if he could! No answer came, so Silver continued. 'I would introduce myself. I am Nathaniel Silver. I have heard you might be the Earl of Sunderland, though I may be mistaken.'

The wig twitched, a shake of the head. 'You are mistaken. Sunderland is a useful man, but he has no interest in the esoteric business of the Service.'

Silver cocked his head to catch the sound better. The Master's voice was not unknown to him, though he couldn't yet place it. 'Architecture is too esoteric for me, though I would like to see the cathedral once it's done.'

'Done? It won't be done for many years. Another one at least before the lead goes on the roof, more than a decade before it can be devoted to worship again, and even then the supplicants will have to find places to pray well away from the scaffold and the construction. This is a slow building to rise, but such is the price of magnificence.'

Silver sensed the Puritan disdain in him. 'You're not then the architect?'

'No. It is not my art. The architect himself is a bright enough lad, and well known to me. He designed a modest home for our library at the college. That took long enough, but a heartbeat compared to this. Still, God demands patience and perfection. Sir, do you not remember me?'

'Turn into the light and we'll see,' Silver suggested. It came from his mouth like an order, and he was surprised when the fellow, without rising, shifted his arse on the stool. His face became plain, though it was not entirely revealed as the shadow of his beak still obscured one half of it. It was enough. Silver put a hand to his mouth to still his tongue. He had readied himself for any revelation except this.

The Master of Service held up the bundle that he'd been reading. The book was in no better condition than it had been twelve years earlier; no amount of care had saved the lining from fraying, the paper from crumbling, the pages from tearing. Silver had not shed ink in any cause other than *le Pouvoir*'s for so long he had almost forgotten it.

'Yes, it is Jeova Unus Sanctus, come down from Cambridge to greet you. And see,' said his old confidant, 'I still have your book. Now sir, put your tongue away, close your mouth, and sit yourself down. You look a starving student, but we will feed you at length.'

His age, still not far advanced, had given him a gaunt and cruel gravitas. When his lips made to smile they seemed unkind, though Silver knew this was the shape of his face and not his temper. The wig perhaps made him younger than he would have appeared, but it was Jeova more than his prisoner who was marvelling at the other's appearance. 'By the Lord,' he declared, 'you must have some secret elixir, and I will have that formula.'

Silver cleared some loose leaves from the nearest bench so that he could sit. Jeova chuckled, enjoying his fluster. Silver could see that he would be a good Master in the Service, enjoying the little power and mystery he wielded, though not wantonly.

'I wrote to you,' Silver began, 'many times after Salomon's House. I longed for a reply from you above any other, but none came. I assumed I had disgraced myself.'

Jeova shook his head, and wisps of wig fluttered over the candle flames but didn't catch. 'Some letters I received, but it would not always have been politic to reply. I've not always had this influence in the Service. Also, the clerk here tells me you trusted the letters to some damn'd fool of a girl, so other communications may have gone astray.'

'The clerk?'

'He'll be with us soon enough. He has other business, which I take to mean whoring and the pursuit of excess. Still, he stands with the righteous, as do we both.' Jeova shed his wig at last, revealing an ashy-white scalp. He smiled, not coldly, on seeing his guest's discomfort.

'I admit,' he continued, 'there was another reason I made no reply. I was disappointed with your – what shall we call it – *abortive* lecture at Salomon's House. To tell the truth, I was offended. You had promised so much and delivered little. Please! Please, let me finish! It was only later I realised how Salomon had set his traps around you. I was not party to that deception. I would apologise for that.'

Silver shook his head and even that was an effort. 'It was not your doing. You said yourself.'

'Then I apologise on behalf of the Service. Things have changed since then. The incident at Salomon's House is a blot on our organisation's pages. I made enquiries when I became Master, and found a strange cloud of embarrassment obscures all. None of the other Masters is prepared to admit that he was Salomon, or sanctioned his interest in you. His influence has waned. You are among allies, Nathaniel Silver. We snatched you back from *le Pouvoir* for your benefit as much as ours.'

Silver was no longer listening. He had no kerchief, so he used his hands to conceal his eyes. Jeova's patient sigh was audible over the slender gap between them. He rose from his stool, though whether he meant to comfort Silver or just to look away was unclear. Silver rose with him and pulled the man into an embrace.

'Sir!' Jeova protested, and his voice was comical, and his faint struggles dramatic. 'These tears are not seemly, though I forgive them.' Silver broke away before the scholar's feeble shoving could have an effect. The tears were drying on his eyes, and his confusion distilled into a potent mixture of humours, anger and relief and something more, something inchoate rising in his gullet. It was a kind of recognition and a kind of reunion, a homecoming.

'Do you mean that I have been in no danger? Am I safe to return to England, then? I am glad to see you,' he said, 'though everything you say baffles me, but I am so glad to have you welcome me. We are one.'

Jeova waved flat fingers in front of him, to calm him, to encourage him back into his seat, to keep him at a distance. 'Sir, you babble. Sit and breathe and compose yourself. We are kindred spirits, yes, but spirit is best contemplated in simplicity and silence.'

Silver sat, then rose again, then sat just as rapidly, and fidgeted for a time under Jeova's benevolent glare. 'The Service,' he begged. 'Were you in the Service when we met? I thought you only a man of learning.'

Jeova gave a sober smile. 'I was in the Royal Society then as now, and in some ways that body is truer to the Service than the Service itself. They overlap invisibly. To serve God, to serve science, to serve one's nation, to serve one's self – these are the same prospect. They are indivisible, as God is indivisible. You'll learn this for yourself.'

Silver boggled. 'You're inviting me to join?'

'More. The Service is only a part of what we must do. You're right that we are kin. There is a voice that speaks inside you, and it speaks also in me. It is the voice of Heaven.'

Silver unwrapped a sly sad grin, which he sheathed again when he saw how sincere was the expression on the younger man's face. 'Are you sure,' Silver asked kindly, 'that it is Heaven's voice that speaks?'

'God's voice cannot be mimicked.'

'But men's ears can be fooled,' Silver responded, still gently. How could this man be a Master of espionage? He was delicate. He was a soap bubble. Jeova turned his head away, so that it blocked Silver's view of the light. His head jiggled again, as if Silver's soft prompts had brought out the tiny madnesses that compelled it, and once started it could not stop.

'I have faith,' Jeova began his confession, halted, then resumed – more measured, 'and more than faith. I was a witness. I was a boy once, an indolent boy. It was faith that later gave me my will and my sense of purpose, though the voice denies it when I lie half-woken and it is apparent to me. I was a soft boy in need of beating. I lay beneath a tree and –'

Then he stopped again and moved his head back, so that the candle-flame came out of its eclipse. He snorted, his nostrils flaring. 'Sir, you would mock me.'

Silver, who had leaned into a seated stoop and hadn't made even the smallest sound, flattened his lips and shook his head, but his benefactor flustered. Jeova fiddled to re-place his wig, its spaniel-ear coils falling over his face and giving him respite from Silver's gentle questioning gaze.

He stammered: 'You – you – you would think me addled. Better men have been cast into purgatory for telling less fanciful tales. I have faith, I am of the righteous, surely that is all the proof you need? But soft, here is a footstep known to us both.'

Silver, who had heard nothing and took this as a feint to be humoured, looked to the door and found that he was wrong and it was indeed opening to admit another body. 'This is the clerk?' he asked.

'Here is the man who has done more than any other to secure your freedom.' Silver stood stiffly to greet the newcomer, then dropped back into his seat winded by an intangible blow to the stomach.

'This is a night of surprises,' he observed meekly.

The clerk didn't acknowledge him to begin with, but made a play of clearing some space on a seat opposite. He lowered himself down with a satisfied sigh, then spread his legs out into the centre of the room, a man comfortable in his space. Silver couldn't help but notice how Jeova kept his feet folded neat and crossed at his stool, but then Nicholas Plainsong had always been a boy to sprawl, and he had not lost the habit in adulthood.

'You'll remember,' Plainsong said, 'the last thing I said to you before your lecture.'

Silver didn't, but nodded anyway. This seemed to satisfy the youth – the man – and the malicious glint came back to his eye. Before he had looked tired, drained and wrung dry – Jeova had intimated that he'd been out at leisure, but he had dragged himself in with the weariness of a man struggling under a great burden. Like Jeova, he had changed little in the past decade. His wig should have given the man an authority that the boy had lacked, but instead it made him all the more childish, a kitten or a puppy staring plaintively out from a heavy mound of stolen hair.

Oh, he was still sharp-faced and smilingly evil. That much would never change.

He held a silver coil in his hand, wrapped between his fingers. Each end was tied to a tiny metal sphere that, by his flexing, rolled over his knuckles to bash against the other, and away, and back again, infinitely until he lost concentration or grew tired. He did neither.

'So,' he said, staring up and down the length of Silver's body but having the good grace not to comment on how little he had aged in twelve years, 'I bet you almost went off when you first saw *him*' – his unencumbered hand pointed at Jeova – 'I bet that was all kisses and backslapping, but you only knew him a couple of days. Now me, I was your best mate for five years, and you look at me like you found me at the bottom of a chamberpot.'

Was he genuinely aggrieved? Hard to tell. Still, his words gave Silver a small smile. 'I'm tired, I've been dragged unwilling across a sea and not treated softly on the way, and there's only so much surprise I can take.'

Nick's serpent tongue wetted his lips. 'That's a shame. There's more to come.'

'Also, the last time I saw Nick Plainsong, he had just stolen from me and was running. Into the arms of the Service, it seems.'

'Into the guns of the Service, but they all missed. They're rotten shots. When the smoke cleared, they looked at themselves and thought *this lad, he's alright, let's set him up in a trade and put him in our debt.* So here I am, fighting the good fight by night, making sure cathedrals don't bloody fall down by day.' As he spoke, all his impious energy came back to him, animating his face and his hands, while discomfiting Jeova. Silver gazed at him, saying nothing, because Nick knew it already – *you've not changed, Nicholas Plainsong, you've changed not a jot.* He rose to embrace the fellow.

As they hugged, Silver felt Jeova's eyes sweep over them, but the scholar made no move.

When they sat back down, the mood shifted and became more serious. Perhaps it was because he had finally found his land legs, and put the long ordeal at sea behind him; but perhaps it was what he saw in both of his hosts' faces, their uncertain eagerness to please him, their desire to make him feel accepted. He had power over them, though of what sort he couldn't fathom. They needed him. They were all three of them dressed in black, like priests, different cuts of the same uniform. They were recruiting him.

It was Nick who spoke first. He nodded, indicating Jeova. 'How much has he told you?'

Jeova responded: 'Nothing. He arrived very shortly before you did.'

'Typical, isn't it? Takes us nearly five years to get him back from *le Pouvoir* and he turns up here before I do. Bloody typical. You'd better tell him, then.'

Jeova bristled, smoothing down his sleeves before answering. His hands were thinned and jaundiced by candlelight. 'There is war in Heaven,' he said simply, and his voice resonanted with the simplicity of true faith. 'This is no metaphor. There is a real war, it is fought both above our heads and beyond our understanding, but nonetheless we have been called on to fight it on the side of Heaven.'

Silver nodded. 'Against Satan?'

'Against Heaven's adversary. Sometimes he is called Satan, though he has many names, and that is neither the oldest nor the truest. The war against him is eternal. It cannot end by any human reckoning, and for that reason we are content to live our lives as if neither he, nor Heaven, nor their conflict make any true difference in this mundane sphere.'

'That will change,' he pronounced. 'Man must choose his side and take up arms on Heaven's behalf. We are God's finest creation, and so it falls to us to defend Him.'

This was familiar – how could it not be? – but there was a certainty in Jeova's voice that extended beyond the usual hellfire mania of preachers and hotheaded boy-warriors. He spoke as one who had seen the battlefields of Heaven and carried his tales back as reportage. Silver picked his words carefully. 'You'll have a fine time convincing Man in his entirety to take up arms.' *And* – he thought of Aphra Behn – *I doubt Woman would be too happy about it either.*

'It will take time,' Nick interjected. His voice was quiet, and his fervour was Jeova's reflected, as though on water. 'It won't happen in our lifetimes, but if a great general raises the standard now, then our grandchildren's children will be flocking to the cause.'

And in a flash of divine inspiration, Nathaniel Silver realised where this was going. 'You need a great general to prepare us for war, eh?'

'Not just any man,' Jeova enthused, 'but a man made for divine purpose. Nick's told me your stories. God brought you back, Nate. God raised you from the grave so you could be His instrument.'

Silver, who had once believed that to be true, almost snorted.

'Don't mock, Nate. You told me yourself of how you came back changed from the grave – you became a wiser man, a better man.'

'I was a youth of seventeen years at Edgehill. Many men grow to be wiser and better in their later years, and that's no mystery. I saw more of the world and learned more of it, that's all. Besides,' – and he didn't want to dash the expectation in their faces, but he had to, for the sake of his own sanity if not theirs – 'I've discovered something since we last met. I was not alone. God, if it was Him, saved more than just one man from the point of death that winter. I am one of many, and they can't all be the great general of God's army.'

But Jeova was quick to answer: 'Precisely. The divine voice raised many, looking for the one that would endure. Oh, perhaps it hoped that there would be more than one, that they would work to form alliances between nations in the march to war, but they were weak, or they failed, or there was some impediment they couldn't overcome. God cut them loose, Nathaniel Silver, and now there is just you. You have *proved* yourself. You have had temptation put in your way, and sometimes it has led you astray, but you haven't succumbed. You are a truly remarkable man.'

Still, he wasn't convinced. 'What temptations? *Le Pouvoir*? Earthly powers? Women?'

Jeova shook his head sadly. He reached for the book and held it out. 'This should have been your manual for war. The divine voice can guide you, but it does not command you, so you were compelled to find your own path for how we might best serve Heaven. Now, as I may have remarked when we last met, there is much good in it, but it is garbled, it is confused, and worst of all it is skewed, as you fell under the influence of two pernicious philosophies.'

Silver raised an intrigued eyebrow. 'Really? What were they?'

'First, there were the beings you called Christ's pilots. They brought you an egg, but they had an agenda of their own that warped you. They were not divine as you imagined, and no, nor are they beings of the adversary, except by omission. They are insects, timid craven creatures who fear the coming of the great crusade. You would have done best to ignore them, and hurl their egg away. It was a deceitful thing.'

Silver assimilated this, and asked: 'What was the second false philosophy?'

'Your own,' Jeova said simply, and he held the corners of *The Cycle of Sun and Seed* close over the candleflames until the paper's edge caught. Fire curled rapidly up the side, flickering not just the expected yellow or the intensities of blue and red, but discharging as many colours as a rainbow, as if the book had been bound on alchemical pages that, when set alight, revealed all the wonders and enchantments that the words could only describe.

The tongues licked at Jeova's fingers, and he slung the exterminated book into a metal bowl on the table, where it continued to blaze merrily. Silver stared into the obliterating light and could feel nothing stirring, no thought, no humour, nothing. They were making a hollow vessel of him, these two, by their magics.

Nick patted him comfortingly on the shoulder. 'What our friend means is that you had already been a soldier. You wrote your book to put war behind you. You wrote in expectation of peace.'

'And there will be peace,' Jeova insisted, clenching at the empty air with his knuckles as if throttling the life from invisible devils. 'Once we have won our victory and the adversary's hordes have been annihilated, your commonwealth can be made real, but what use is it to a nation of soldiers? Liberty, levelling, love – fine things, no doubt very fine things, but how quickly they would wilt from the heat of our war's forges. Put them aside, they are not needed.'

Silver contemplated his burning book for a few moments more.

'What do you want me to do?' he asked.

'Take command of the Service,' Nick said. Silver stared at him.

'You heard him right,' Jeova confirmed. 'You would have no official position, but unofficially you would be Master of Masters. You would run the affairs of the esoterica, which will be distinct from the mundane divisions, at least at first. Do you understand the power this would give you? You are an instrument, and so is the organisation. Through her you will turn England and Scotland and the Americas. *Le Pouvoir* will race to become like us, and through them we shall have France. So the Holy Roman Empire and Muscovy and the Turk; so the Inquisition and the Church of Rome; through the Service it can be done. Before you die, you could be, quietly and unnoticed, emperor and general both.'

'The Empire of Heaven,' Silver pondered softly.

'The Republic of Heaven, if you will. The title isn't important.'

How long did they sit in silence waiting on his reply? There was no clock to measure them by, and Silver judged time by the ticking of their faces and the slow fading of their composure. Jeova feigned stoicism, but his body couldn't maintain it, not with all the Godly fervour leaking out of him. As for Plainsong, he was the very statue that Jeova could never be, except for his lips, which threw any number of shapes, none of them pleasant or inviting. Nick was a mouth; he was a hunger; he was tearing teeth. Nick and Jeova, what an odd brace they were. *Click*, went Nick's charm, *click, click, click.*

Silver saw that he had raised a hand before his face and was ready to answer. He could speak the request that he couldn't make to Aphra Behn. 'This is what you'll do,' he instructed, 'as Master of Service. You're going to send men to Paris to fetch back Alice Lynch. I want her in England, with me and unharmed.'

Jeova looked cautiously to Nick, who nodded, curt. 'That's already in hand.' Silver looked in the boy's face and saw fluid sincerity.

'Is that all?' Jeova asked, and Nick was grinning behind his hand. 'If we do this for you then you'll accept your role in the war?'

Silver shook his head slowly. He looked at his hands again, which seemed to have taken on a life of their own in the presence of these two tempters, and they were clasped together in prayer. Maybe he was meant to be a holy warrior after all – put away his weariness and take up the sword again. 'If you do this for me, then I will consider your offer.'

He was being too harsh; he waved the sleep away from his face. 'I need time and space. I need more detail. I need to rest.'

'Can the hand of God rest? Can He sleep?' Jeova accused, but Nick cut across him.

'But He wants us to be patient as well. You can have Alice. You can have all the time in the world, after tonight. We're in this for the long haul, aren't we? These aren't the last days, they're the first. Three hundred years this could take, a few more days won't hurt.' He fixed Silver in his gaze, and as always it was impossible to tell what was going inside his skull. 'But one more stop tonight, eh Nate? You've been worked over by higher powers all your life. Give us a chance to prove it to you.'

Too tired to argue, Silver nodded.

Jeova rose. 'I'll speak to the serjeant. We'll leave directly.'

When he left, he neglected to fasten the door properly, and it banged on the breeze and fanned the subdued flames from *Sun & Seed* back to life. There was nothing left of the book but curled black paper and ash, the remains of his warped and misunderstood bible. He wanted to put his writing hand into that flame and never pull it out. Give it back to God, if God would have it.

Plainsong broke the silence with his clicking device, the silver balls now quite rhythmic and irregular. He had sat in his deceptive lull opposite Silver since Jeova left, occasionally turning aside to register irritation at the flapping door, or perhaps to check on his Master's progress.

'You don't believe,' said Silver. 'I can see it.'

Plainsong's smile was unsettled. 'I believe,' he said. 'I have proofs. Not just what *he* says. I have other sources.'

'You believe it is the case. The War in Heaven might be real to you, but Nick Plainsong wouldn't play favourites or put his faith in one side or the other, not for very long. You're no Jeova. You're no more righteous than I am.'

Nick squinted sourly, but he nodded all the same. 'Look at these designs, look at them all. This is what Saint Paul's is going to be, a great building. Oh, forget that pot on the roof! That's just for public consumption – Chris has a far more impressive dome in mind, but even that's just a shadow of what it should've been.'

Then came a bitter laugh. 'It's a great building, but it's deformed. It should have been greater still. Righteous men did that, striking down the early models for their own piddling reasons. Too Catholic, too Greek, too Jewish, doesn't matter to me! Now since I wandered into this job, I've seen drawings of Saint Peter's in Rome, and descriptions from Moorish Spain and from Jerusalem and from Persia and further east till you reach the edge of the world. And I think to myself, why can't we have something like that? Why not something as great as the standing stones and mounds that the heathens made before we civilised Christians fell on them and ate them? And maybe Saint Paul's redux will be that great, but only because we cheated and lied and deceived the righteous men. We snatched the greatness from between their teeth, where they were chewing it like toothless old dogs.

'Their God is petty, Nate. Their God is so, so small.'

Through the door, they could see the shapes of Servicemen detaching from the night to fetch them. They had only a few moments. Silver rose and held out his hand to Nick, who considered it cautiously.

Silver said, 'I never imagined Nicholas Plainsong cared about anything.'

Nick allowed himself to be lifted to his feet. He had been a slight boy, and now he was a slight man, though no less heavy for it. 'You're going to hate me before this night is done, Nate,' he promised.

Silver said nothing to this, but looked instead to the smouldering ash that had once been his life's work. The guards knocked politely on the loose door and waited for their masters to come out.

⇒ Chapter 21: *A Wedding* ⇐

Aphra Behn had hoped to be completely alone, but that proved impossible. She had forgotten how busy London could be this close to the river and the docks, where lights in every door and window turned the night sky into a thin gravy-coloured day. They didn't sleep, the river-dwellers, or not at such an early hour when there was still work to be done or drink to be drained. On the waterfront, there were clusters of gaunt raggedy girls, like petals that disappeared one by one as sailors, shipworkers, and miscellaneous haunters of the docks drifted by to pluck them. Things had got worse, she thought, since she was last here. Many of the old buildings were gone, and in their places were newer structures, either grey and grandiose with window-pocked façades that looked benevolently down on the tribute carried into port; or half-built shanties, the rat-runs of the dockworkers and their families, infesting the walls of this burgeoning empire. It was these latter buildings that swelled with signs of life: with lights, music, the babble of far-off crimes and fights and sullen arguments.

Aphra huddled under her shawl. The serjeant had offered her an escort and a ride straight to her door. She had refused, claiming she would prefer to walk, and he had seemed genuinely concerned for her, though not enough to insist. It would be a long trek from the *Queen*'s berth to her home on the other side of Westminster, but he'd had no reason to know that. She had managed to stagger just out of sight of the gangway, found a cold step to numb her backside and her fingers, and sat upon it. She could see her breath on the air, like it was midwinter. Though she loved it more, London was so much bleaker than Paris.

Larissa would come. She had promised Aphra, in those brief moments when she was visible on the prow, that she would appear again once she was back in London. She had taken Aphra's small and heavy hands into her own, and she had been warm and fleshy and real. She wouldn't break her promise.

'Are you here for me?' Aphra had asked. 'What do I have to do?'

Larissa shook her head. 'Not yet,' she'd said. 'I'll see you again later, when you're alone.'

And Aphra had found that flesh which moments before had been joyously real was now turning into colourless smoke in her hands, and her fingers had suddenly tightened round nothing but damp air. Larissa had slid away from her like a shadow receding into a greater darkness.

The ghost's mouth had moved, and Aphra had strained to hear words. 'Stay close to Silver. Watch him.' Then she'd been gone, into the haze and the spit and the storm, and the wind had carried *Queen Christina* home.

Aphra had dwelled on Larissa's last words in the dark behind her eyes. *Watch Silver.* It wasn't that different to her instructions from the Service. It was common to find men ascribing their own motives to the heavens, quite another to have goddesses descending from their constellations to mimic the designs of men. She was real after all, Aphra thought bitterly, as real as any part of this grubby world, and so tainted by it.

Even so, she'd tried to keep close to Silver, but the Ratcatchers had kept her well away. He'd been bundled away in a carriage, and she couldn't follow. Now she waited by the riverside, lonely but not alone, haunted by distant voices more than present bodies. The streetwalkers were a constant; if she felt for anyone she saw as she waited for Larissa, it was them, because they were so like her, so needy and so frightened. How many would escape their traps, she wondered? Each time she saw one drawn away by a client, she revised her estimate downwards. The numbers – the numbers were against them. She herself was not approached. She had lost her looks and her figure long ago. She was very hungry. She had eaten heavily on the boat, but wambled most of it over the side during the storm, and besides, her stomach grew ever quicker to wheedle. Over an hour she waited, until she almost cried with the fear that she would have to risk the walk back to Soho after all. Once home she would go to bed and not come out again for a week, a month, ever…

Then Larissa came out of the gloom, glistening red like a newborn in the dark. Aphra shook off her tiredness, levered up on her elbows, and went to meet her nymph, shucking off her shawl as she walked.

'For Christ's sake,' she insisted, 'put this over you, or everyone'll stare.'

It was true, Larissa was an imposing sight, especially in the real and sordid streets of London Now rather than the gold-bathed glow of Aphra's memories. The skin that covered her was seamless, but revealed every curve and crease in her body; not just immodest, it was indecent – the twitching of the tattoos drew the eye as if her naked skin were covered in a riot of weevils or lice. Fluid guttered and flowed within the fabric of the suit itself; it looked heavy and rank and sticky, in a way that hadn't been apparent before. It was blood; the nymph wore a suit of living blood. How could that fail to attract attention?

Aphra's anxieties were unfounded. She glanced up and down the alley, but the human huddles were briefly thinner – no doubt why Larissa had chosen this moment to manifest – and no one was paying much attention to this imposing red unnaked madwoman. Perhaps they were used to such sights? Perhaps the foul Thames gave off fumes that inspired brain-fever and visions? Still, Aphra handed over her shawl, and the nymph covered her shoulders and a tiny portion of her upper body, uncomplaining.

'They've taken Silver,' Aphra blurted. 'I'm sorry. What is he?! Is he one of your lot? A beastly god or a brute from the pit?' She found herself crossing herself automatically, a Papist response she must have picked up unknowing while in Paris. Her head was full of stories of gods descending as bulls or swans to sample humanity. She had pinned Silver to the bed less than a day before, and wondered now if she hadn't inadvertently made herself a new Leda or a Semele.

'Silver is as human as you are,' Larissa reassured her. 'He's not my quarry. He's a proxy and a decoy. The thing I'm hunting can do that; it can make its own creatures and disguise them with its scent. But I can use that. He can guide me to the beast, and I no longer need your help to find him. The path has become clear.'

'What?'

Larissa showed her a subtle smile. 'Remember I told you about the falling trees? Well, here it's as though all the trees have not just stopped falling, but have been raised and rooted back into the ground. A path has been cleared that's safe for me to walk, and that path is right now, just after your second meeting with Silver, when you mate with him.'

Aphra pulled away from her, embarrassed. 'You saw that...?'

Was that a shrug? 'No, but it happens, and you seemed to enjoy it. Have I said something wrong?'

She shook her head. Larissa seemed to accept this as genuine. 'Let's say that I'm going to use the clean path to find the people who have been chopping down the trees, and stop them doing it again.'

'You're going to steal their axes?'

I'm joking, I'm joking. Please see that I'm joking.

Larissa was smiling. Good. 'And yes, they are somewhere in the world and by this river. You could walk there easily enough.'

'You might. I have short legs,' Aphra complained.

Larissa looked at her curiously. 'They used to be shorter,' she remarked. 'But I no longer need your help.'

'I *should* come with you. This is my world and my city. I know them both better than you.'

'It's a distraction. It's nothing.'

Aphra pressed her point. She felt emboldened, out-arguing a deity! 'Have you considered that it might be dangerous? You know, trees don't root themselves back into the ground of their own accord. Well, maybe they do where you come from, but on Earth, nothing moves unless it's made to. Men do that, for their own purposes.'

'What are you saying?'

'That it could be a trap. You're hunting something, yes? Not all such pursuits end with the hunter triumphant and the beast in his belly – sometimes the prey turns and fights. If someone has cleared a path for you, then if you follow it you'll end up where they want you to go. Have you considered that?'

And from her face, Aphra could tell that she hadn't. Larissa had her hunt, and she had abided no distractions from it.

'It can't hurt if I'm with you. Besides, I have a duty.'

Aphra didn't breathe again until Larissa spoke. 'You have a point,' she said. 'If there's any danger...'

I won't leave you, she thought, but she said: 'If there's any danger, you won't see me for dust.'

She found Larissa was nodding at her, warily, but not unhappily. 'You can walk with me at least.'

'Good. Good,' Aphra said firmly, and then: 'Is it far?'

'Five minutes' walk if we go briskly.'

They didn't go briskly. Larissa let Aphra set the pace, and indeed, even seemed at times to be mimicking her painstaking steps as she struggled to overcome the clicking of her hips. They did, as Aphra feared, draw the occasional gape or raucous yelp from passers-by, but mainly they walked invisibly. She had to stop and rest sometimes, to sit or prop herself on a wall. She grew so weary she almost fell, but Larissa caught her by the hand, and the nymph's strength leapt between their knotted palms and fingers.

Aphra huffed out a huge long cough. 'The last time we met was at Salomon's House, you remember?'

'Clearer than you.' Her voice was serene.

'Then you'll remember how you moved us by magic, from the house to the snow.'

'Not magic – but yes, I remember.'

'Couldn't you do that now and save my feet?'

Larissa's expression was odd. She looked embarrassed – worse than embarrassed, humiliated. Aphra had expected anger or condescension, but Larissa was *ashamed*. 'It's not a good way to travel. I wear the suit because I have to, and I use it only when necessary.'

Aphra nodded, understanding. 'The power is not yours, but your costume's?'

'If the suit were destroyed, I'd be trapped in this world.'

Aphra felt an instantly-shameful longing to attack the woman's skinsuit, tear it to shreds and strand the goddess here. It responded to her interest, the slippery blood within its folds pulsing hungrily, as a seeping wound might if it were trapped under glass. There was a gap in it, she saw, a tiny hole above the stomach. All she would have to do is reach down and *tear*...

She looked into Larissa's eyes, and found only horror at the prospect at being stuck forever in the world of mortals. The demi-goddess blinked, looked away, and said: 'Once the hunt is done, I don't know what I'll do.'

They resumed their slow walk. Aphra, afraid her thoughts might leak again, tried to strike up a new note. 'You know, that isn't the only such suit I've seen. Since I last met you there was –'

Larissa cut across her. 'We're here,' she said.

Here was a narrow street, among new and unfussy buildings that had been rapidly constructed to replace those destroyed in the fire. The flames would have gone through them quickly, as they would again if the naked timbers and pitched roofs of these replacements caught light. They would hold tobacco, maybe, or oil; one after the other they would explode, shattering ears and layering the body of the inferno with thick smoke. The nearby Thames itself was not in sight, but the lap of it was audible, mixed with the shrilling birds of the river and the horns and bells of slow-moving boats. The freshly-laid architecture had crusted around surviving bricks of old buildings, most of which had since crumbled through neglect or had been purposefully levelled. The stones that remained, sunk unshiftably into the earth, stood like accusing markers. The church was the most intact survivor of its parish, but even it looked like a toothless pauper, a broken-jawed, muddied old skull, worn down by rain. Larissa pressed herself to its walls, which might have trembled below her touch. She looked infinitely stronger, a sharp red stain on grey.

Slowly, she began to clamber up the wall, finding invisible footholds on smooth stone. She scampered, making it look blasphemously easy, like a gargoyle coming to life and searching for a place to shit. Then again, she was the prettiest gargoyle Aphra had ever seen; from her vantage point on the ground, she could appreciate that elegant body all the more. Larissa's splendid thighs and limbs and buttocks and back; they crawled remarkably up the wall to peer through a chasm where the window had once been. Then she flipped backwards, ten, twelve, twenty feet through the air, and landed painlessly on her feet.

Aphra had hung back. Through the cavities that had once been windows, she saw lamplights flickering, and she regained her nerve and went to join her mistress. 'There are people inside. Is it your prey?'

Larissa hummed. 'I don't know. *They're* here, the ones who tried to block my path.'

'Who are they?'

'They call themselves something new – Faction Paradox. Does that mean anything to you?'

'I've heard the name, in the Service. Someone I once knew was obsessed by them. Who was that...?' And she slapped her temple, but it didn't cure her forgetfulness. 'Are they hunting the same prey?'

'I imagine that's what they think, but it will have been hunting them. It'll have run them to ground. They're the *enemy*, you see.'

'Whose enemy? Yours?'

'*Its* enemy. As far as it's concerned, everything's the enemy.' Larissa stepped away from the wall, removed the shawl, and slung it back over Aphra's shoulders. 'Will you do something for me?'

She's playing you, Aphra. You'll do anything she asks. She's using you.

Yes. That's what I want. I want to be used.

Aphra nodded. 'Anything.'

'The last time we met, you stopped me using the needle on Silver. My... my *mother* once told me that those people who boast loudest about killing are the least able, when the moment comes, to deal a death-blow. I've never boasted. I never wanted to kill anyone. Aphra?'

'Yes?'

'Will you promise me that you won't try to stop me this time?'

'Stop you killing a man?'

'Destroying a monster – but *yes*, I would also be killing a man – or a woman.'

'Can you be certain it's the right man?'

'If I have his scent, and if I'm close enough to see him, then yes, this time.'

Aphra's eyes opened wider, fixing on a slink from the shadows. She mouthed: we're being watched.

Instantly Larissa swung round and dropped, a narrow light flickering in her hand, a glowing wand. The shadow prowled forward hungrily to sniff at the outstretched hand, then wrinkled its nose in disdain. It was a patchwork cat, with a long springy white stomach. Once it realised it was not being offered food, it sat up and pulled hungry faces at these strange, over-alert humans. Aphra giggled, as much delight as relief. 'Oh, precious!' She reached to stroke it, and it turned and ran, sliding into a gap between the stones of the church.

Larissa stayed in her hunch for a moment longer, and this was a side to her Aphra hadn't seen. She was a hunter right enough, and a poised and alert one with it, but it seemed to Aphra's eyes too much. She had moved so rapidly, as if she had too little faith in herself, or an overabundance of fear.

'It was only a cat,' Aphra said.

'I know what cats are,' Larissa replied, and she slung her now darkened wand back into its place on her belt. 'We have them in my world.'

As she straightened up, Aphra felt confident enough to place a hand on her back. 'I promise,' she said solemnly. 'I won't try to stop you.'

Voices rose from inside the body of the church, then footsteps. Larissa pressed Aphra back against the wall, and held her there in the darkness.

The journey from Saint Paul's to their next, unspecified destination took less than ten minutes, including the time it took for them to walk through the whitened London mist to their ride. The wheeled cage that had conveyed Silver from the river was gone, replaced by a far more comfortable carriage that still managed to feel like a prison once he was through the door. Silver sank into the upholstered seat opposite Nick Plainsong and Jeova. The first had sauntered relaxed from the clerk's hut, with his fists as ever bunched in his pockets and his wig flapping jauntily with every confident step. Jeova moved stiffly by contrast, as if he were a wood marionette whose every action had to be painstakingly moulded by a greater hand.

'Where are we going?' Silver had asked.

'To disappoint you,' Nick had replied, heavily. 'After that, you'll be put up in luxury for the night, though you won't sleep.'

He'd imagined they might discuss their plans on the journey, but instead they sat in near-silence, broken only by the rumble of the wheels below them, and the clatter of Nick's device as the metal balls ticked up and down his knuckles. Nick himself looked out the window as they rode, while Jeova stared stiffly into the middle distance, not quite settled with Silver's gaze and yet not willing to turn and in turning acknowledge his discomfort. Silver felt inadequate in the company of these very different men. He lacked Nick's self-assurance and sprawl; he lacked Jeova's devotion and intelligence. What quality they saw in him, beyond his few dubious and unplanned miracles, he couldn't guess.

For all that he recoiled from the immediate implications, there was a part of their offer that appealed to him greatly. Had he not devoted himself to the service of Christ? Had he not clung to that devotion as an article of faith, even when *le Pouvoir* made their more practical demands of him, even when Nick dressed him up as a famous monster, even when Ann died and his commune failed? He had strived to serve God all his long life – surely his wariness of the divine plan was no more than an instinctive fear of making that commitment solid? Even if Jeova's faith – and Plainsong's grudging acceptance – of the fact of the heavenly war was misplaced, there was still much good that could be done through the Service and the Royal Society. He had once dreamed of a great dialogue among the natural philosophers, conducted in English, not Latin, and open to all. He had no desire to be the presiding voice, let alone a commanding one, but his could be the founding word.

No. No. Not tonight. He couldn't think of it tonight. He was too tired. Why did Nick have to drag him out here? If he was truly a guest, couldn't this be put off until the morning?

Jeova leaned forward, and said in a conspiratorial voice audible to all, 'You realise, of course, that I have no idea what surprise our young fellow has planned for us.'

Nick didn't turn from the window; he had always, in spite of his earthiness, been a dreamer. His voice was bland and flat. 'I don't want to lie to you, Nate. You look at us both like we're puppeteers looking to string you up, but we're not. Our plans for you contain no secrets and no traps. We have no hidden masters and we wear no masks. *I* wear no mask. I never did.'

'I've never doubted your honesty, Nick.'

The clerk nodded, satisfied, but still did not look away. 'We're here.'

Here was a run of riverside warehouses and storerooms, whose utilitarian lines were flat and modern. As he stepped down from the carriage, Silver realised he was in a row of temporary buildings that had somehow rooted and become permanent, but had yet to acquire character. By contrast, there was a humble stone church, whose scorched and tattered stones whispered of antiquity, and choirs that had sung in the common tongue before English. He was truly back in London when he saw it. Paris's splendid Catholic churches were too proud to let this state of decrepitude creep over them.

'It was desanctified after the fire. Unsafe, you see. Can't have the faithful worshipping in unsafe buildings. Imagine a beam coming down during prayer and smacking them over the heads. It'd be like a rebuke from God,' Nick observed. He had been constrained in the carriage, and was taking the opportunity to pace back and forth, stretching his short legs. 'Most people round here have forgotten it's a church. Faction Paradox did that, with their rituals.'

'Faction Paradox?' Silver was surprised to hear that name, for the first time since they had returned his egg to him, and put him in their debt.

Plainsong nodded and hummed tunelessly. 'They've been using this place as their headquarters for the past dozen years. God might have survived the fire, but *they* drove Him out for good.'

Jeova pulled his coat tight round him, as much against Nick's words as the cold. 'What a hellish place,' he declared. 'This Faction, they're witches? They worship devils here? Most horrible.'

'Yeah, horrible,' Plainsong said, his tongue tasting and mocking the word. 'They're heathens. They worship spirits, not devils, not that you'd see much of a distinction.'

'Indeed I do not. Must we expose ourselves to their wickedness?'

'Yes. Yes, we must. Especially you, Nate. Come in. I'm going to introduce you to someone who'd spit in God's eye.' He laughed raucously, and Jeova shivered again and pulled a face – but it was numb, he must be used to Plainsong's needling humour.

With Nick leading the way, they processed through the yawning doorless mouth into the body of the church. Silver came after him, treading slowly not out of fear, but because the floor was strewn with broken pieces of masonry and stained-glass that Faction Paradox had not, in its twelve-year residency, seen fit to clean away. Jeova came close behind at his shoulder. Behind him, two Service bodyguards followed, lighting hissing oil lamps that cast long primitive shadows of their three charges across the nave ahead of them.

The pews and the eagle and the stations of the church had been destroyed – though that could have been from the processes of fire and time rather than vandalism on the Faction's part – or moved aside to make a great space where an aisle should be. Silver wondered if this was perhaps how a church should be – not a line directed towards a solitary speaker at the head of the hall, channelling the voice of the Holy Spirit through his mouth as instructions or damnations, but a communal space for a congregation of equals, whose joint voice would be a choir or a Pentecost. By turning the church's pews to the side to face one another, the Faction had unwittingly made it perfect.

Why, Nate Silver! How Protestant of you.

In place of a pulpit, there was a cold stone door that was so ancient it must have been erected with the church, but seemed out of fit with the architecture, a curious upright tombstone. No solution to this mystery was apparent, nor to the swell of beached objects scattered across the open floor. Jeova shivered when he saw them, seeing Satanic properties, but Silver wasn't so sure. There was some pattern here, something mechanical and purposeful about these devices. They might be a thousand fresh attempts to create a mousetrap as far as he knew, but they suggested a method to the Faction's rituals.

The skull-headed folk from Salomon's House were not in evidence. Instead, the floor was held by a squad of hooded Ratcatchers, armed with pistols and more lamps. Nick crossed the floor to join them, to address Silver and Jeova. 'As you see, we drove out Faction Paradox some days ago. I won't describe the methods, save to say that the divine voice that speaks in you both provided the basis, and I developed it further with suggestions from other intelligences. They were caught unawares, the Faction. I've been watching them for almost as long as they've been watching you, Nate.

'They're desirous of your power, Nathaniel Silver. Not for its own sake, admittedly, but they would have harnessed you as their swordhand against Heaven if they'd known but how. That's pretty much the only thing they don't know about you. Show him,' he ordered.

His Ratcatchers parted. In their midst, pinned by four men with heavy grips around her arms and feet, was a woman with a Biblical skull for a face. At Silver's side, Jeova gagged and raised a cloth to his nose; he would have seen the Faction before, but in the comparatively sedate confines of Salomon's House. In this unholy ruin, the sight was simply ghastly. The skull topped off an otherwise unremarkably slender body, dressed in torn and shabby clothes that were only just on the good side of rags. The skull face turned one way then the other, surveying the scene with hidden eyes. She fought with her gaolers, but they held her fast.

'She's quite harmless,' Nick quipped, strolling close to her, touching her exposed bone with tickling fingers. 'She has a weapon, but I've made it useless, and without it she's what? Nothing. The Faction likes its waifs and strays. This one calls herself Cousin Greenaway. She's your spy, Nate. She's your watcher and your shadow. What are we going to do with her?'

With both hands, he wrenched the mask from her head, held it aloft for a triumphant moment, then dashed it down on the cold floor, where the bone shattered into a dozen pieces. He strolled away from his prisoner, taking off his wig and throwing it as he went.

When he reached Silver, he laid a comforting hand on the old Magus's shoulder. 'Nate,' he said, 'Nate, I'm so sorry,' but Silver didn't hear him. All his attention was on the woman knelt helpless and unpraying on the church floor – on the woman flinching in his gaze – on the naked unmasked face of Alice Lynch.

Nicholas Plainsong was an unpleasant lad, and Little Sister Greenaway had hated him from the moment she first saw him, his dirty mouth drooling over the sight of her half-dressed and posing as a prostitute. That loathing had grown with every moment she'd spent in his company. She'd hated his ways, his filthy manners, his leering suggestions, and worst of all, the ease with which Nathaniel Silver had taken him on as a companion and apprentice. This was to Nate's credit, of course, but she hadn't had his saintly tolerance. Besides, she doubted Nate had ever caught Plainsong trying to stick a hand up his skirts or mock-masturbating while crooning his name.

There had been another reason to dislike him – Nate might've been blind to all deception, but Nick had been sharp enough to see through her. So she'd gone cold when, one day – about a month after she'd become Alice again to ambush Nate at Cheapside – he'd said, 'You were never a whore, were you?'

'Just because I won't fuck you doesn't mean I wasn't a whore,' she'd replied smoothly, but he'd opened his mouth to show unsmiling teeth and persisted. She'd been washing her hands when he'd come in, and she hadn't been prepared when he'd snatched both her wrists and plucked them out of the water.

'You've been married, too,' he'd observed. 'You never told Nate that. Why is that?'

'Does he need to know? My husband's dead. If Nate asks, I'll tell him.'

'Maybe I'll tell him for you,' Plainsong had said then, but a strange silence had fallen over him, and the expected offer of complicity in exchange for her favours had gone unsaid. He'd grinned and left; if he'd told Nate anything, then she never heard of it. She'd made sure she was careful about her business after that, but she'd been careful before. Plainsong hadn't smoked her out by reason or observation, but pure instinct. He'd been a devious boy, and he'd recognised the same quality, better hidden, in her.

She'd submerged the Little Sister in Alice most of the time, and the memory of that confrontation had faded. She recalled it again only years later, when she woke on the bleak floor of the shrine's hiding place, with light peeking in through a painful crack in her skull.

The light was sitting on the palm of Nick Plainsong's scrawny hand. His other hand was tinkling with the sound of a metal chime, that because of the awkward angle of her mask, she couldn't see.

'Cousin Greenaway,' he said, kneeling over her. 'Two bits of good news. First, I hear a delivery's arrived from Paris this very evening, which is good timing. Second, when I saw you lying there so helpless in your pretty mask, I decided I didn't want to fuck you that badly after all. Times change. I grew up and you grew old.'

Grandfather, he knows, he knows.

Plainsong's expression splintered; he looked on the verge of tears. 'How could you do that to him, Alice? He loved you.'

All she could think to say was, 'I love him too.'

His face went flat and smooth after that, and he straightened up and looked away.

Then he turned back and began to kick at her viciously, his face bedevilled by rage and hate, his feet planting themselves excruciatingly on her ribcage and her stomach and her thighs, until larger men reached out and held him back. They backed out of her line of sight, and she was too pained to move, barely even to breathe. Her whip hand shuddered uselessly at her side.

~ It's not so easy when we don't have a weapon, is it? ~ We grow dependent on them ~
I deserve it. I deserve it.

'You deserved that,' Plainsong said, hoving back into view from another angle so that he seemed to be peering upside-down from the church rafters. 'I won't do it again, but you deserved that.' And he was gone.

His men made her sit up, checked her wounds, and dressed them without making any comment. Once it was clear that the fight had gone out of her, and that any resistance she put up would be no stronger than a few feeble shoves and punches, they treated her almost tenderly. They didn't even chain her.

~ Good of them ~
~ Good of them, Greenaway ~
~ Greenaway ~
~ Greenaway? ~
She didn't answer him.
~ Alice? ~
'Yes?'

She'd said that aloud, and her guards almost looked at her, almost curious, but the moment passed.

~ Did you see the device he had in his hand? ~
No. It was too dark.

~ That's his loa-cast ~ That's what he used to trap your family ~ Destroy that, and you're halfway to getting them back ~

Destroy it? With what exactly? I can't use my whip, and this lot won't let me near him.

She felt the egg-stuff bulge in her throat. *~ You don't need a whip ~ You have me ~*

No, she thought. No. I know what's coming. I know exactly what's coming.

Later, when she saw that Nick had returned and brought Nate with him, she took no pleasure at all in being proved right; and when Nate destroyed her skull-mask, the only part of her that was still Faction Paradox, she howled silently. She was exposed. Nathaniel Silver was here, and could see her naked face and her naked treachery.

'Alice?' he said after long silence, and still she couldn't bring herself to look at him, but shuffled her eyes from side to side in an effort to keep away the tears.

'Alice.' He stepped forward. He was white. Christ, he was white as death. He clearly couldn't bear this any longer, and span to confront Nick Plainsong, to tear his eyes away from her. 'This is some trick!' he spat. 'This is some warped lie of yours, Plainsong. Please tell me that.'

'No,' she said, a dry word from a dry tongue. 'No,' she said again, and Silver turned back to her. He believed this time. He saw her and recognised her for what she was.

Please ask me why. Please, Nate. I could tell you I would have died otherwise, or that I did you more good than harm, and that's true, but they're pleading words and I won't speak them. Besides, look at you! All the things I've done for you are undone now, toppled by this crushing moment. Even the sweetest, most spontaneous kiss now becomes suspect and degraded. But please ask me why. Please, Nate!

~ That's the last thing he wants to know ~

The colour returned to Silver's skin. If there had been any hate or even anger on his face, it slipped her notice. There wasn't a trace of malice to it. He spoke, but not to her. He spoke to her guards, and to Nick Plainsong, and to the trembling streak of meat who stood beside him; he spoke to everyone.

'Don't hurt her,' he commanded, plainly and clearly. 'Don't punish her. Let her go free. Let her do whatever she wants, but don't let her near me.'

He turned, and though he went slowly and at a stately pace, he gave every impression of running from the church.

Once Silver was gone, Nick ambled back to stand before her. She hated him more than ever, and now Nate would hate him too; there probably wasn't a more hated and humbled man in London this night. She couldn't tell whether the slowness in his face was genuine or only another mask, like bone, clean ivory concealing his celebration and victory.

'You can do anything you want to me,' she told him. 'I don't care.'

Click, went the anti-*loa* on his wrist. Click. Erasmus stirred in her heart and her head, urging her to take notice of it, but she wouldn't heed him. Click. Click. Click.

There was a blur of motion on the far side of the church and her guards swung to find it, their pistol-hands slowing when they saw their target was only a cat, pawing forlorn at a shadow on the wall. It was Faction Cat, no hope for her there. Her head bobbed down to inspect the grime on the floor, tracked and trod in by her family over days and weeks and years. Fragments of bone glistened white among the dirt. Nothing was left of Faction Paradox but a helpless woman on her knees, the *loa* stranded in her soul, and a cat scratching puzzled at a shadow that had once been its Mother.

~ Greenaway ~

~ Greenaway, it's now or never ~

Not Greenaway, she thought. Not Alice Lynch. Not even Mrs Thomas Piper. I am Faction Paradox.

'Good cat,' she said. Then she spat as hard as she could into Nick Plainsong's face.

The spittle was a few drops of fluid from a dry and hungry throat, but it was followed by a fountain of gleaming translucent grey eggstuff. It blasted out of her mouth and her eyes, out of all the pores on her face. It had waited coiled round the strands of her, all the things that had been part of her life; it had drawn power from tightening in her soul, and all that sprung energy was now loosed.

It wrenched out her insides; the current ripped Erasmus out of her soul; she screamed.

Plainsong yelled and stumbled back with his hands thrown up wildly to protect his face, but that wasn't the true target. The stream of light swirled round him, then dropped onto his hand. It resolved once again into the shape of an egg, an egg larger than his fist. The light that flared from it washed the sound and the colour out of the room and blasted back the weightless body of the woman who had been Cousin Greenaway, and the heavy limbs and trunks of the men who had been her guards. They tumbled. The egg rearranged the world around them.

~ *It changes the world ~ Maybe it is a weapon after all ~*

Erasmus had told her that, years before as she'd carried the egg up the hill to Silver's latest residence in Paris, so she could present it to him. He had never imagined Alice capable of deception, even when she'd been sure she had given herself away; yet why should he have suspected her? Most of the time there was no pretence. She *was* Alice. She'd followed him and obeyed him and adored him as readily as if there had never been a Faction Paradox, as if she had just found him by chance in the years after the commune failed. She would have loved him even if there hadn't been the splinter of unreal bone on her head and in her heart. She would have loved him even though she would have been dead.

She could no longer hear Erasmus. He was gone. He was blazing now on Plainsong's hand. The boy scrabbled at it, but the egg wouldn't come free. She rolled again and couldn't see him. She slammed into a wall, and felt the impact go through all her good bones and all her bruised ones.

No, not a wall. It shuddered and hummed as she collided with it; the shrine door. She looked up and saw its lights rising as it returned to life.

She pulled herself onto her side in time to see the egg drop from Nick's fingers and settle on the floor. He held up his hand, his glazed face betraying surprise to find his fingers whole and undamaged, and his device reduced to a blackened drooping thread. He looked to her wildly, and she felt the shadow-whip pricking in her hand. She was Cousin Greenaway again.

At the far end of the church, the skinny man who had arrived with Nate and the servants who flanked him had been stilled but not knocked down back by the blast. The heavy-handsome face peered out from under its wig, perhaps a little afraid, but commanded – Greenaway saw – by curiosity and enquiry, a hunger for explanations, no not even that, a hunger for *phenomena*. He took a step forward. Plainsong shrieked.

'Get him out! Get him out of here!'

The bodyguards seized the fellow and manhandled him, protesting – though limply – through the arch and out into the world.

Greenaway was on her feet at last, the whip swirling weakly in her hand. Could he see that? Could he see how weak she was? Yes, yes he could. Around her Nick Plainsong's army were rising or scrabbling for their guns. One was already up and barrelling towards her. She had only a moment, so she flung out her arm and let the whip fly.

It lashed past Plainsong's head, a flea's-breadth. Wisps of shorn hair from his scalp drifted to the floor.

The soldier slammed her. She went back into the wall – the proper wall this time – and her collection of bruises renewed their complaint. The worst of the pain was in her arm, which she still held out taut past the bulk of the man who pinned her. The line of her whip dragged her; the pull of it was agony, muscle-wrenching, bone-snapping pain. She couldn't speak, not even as noise dribbled back into the hall after the blast, but she mouthed anyway.

I didn't miss, she told Nick. I didn't miss, she told the egg at his feet. I didn't miss.

Plainsong turned to follow the line of her shadow, which bisected the air through the body of the church and into the far wall where Greenaway's cousins and Mother were trapped. He would have seen what Greenaway saw and heard what she heard. The calico-patched cat meowed contentedly and no longer stretched out its forelegs into the empty air; now its claws found substance. The line of the whip twanged and frayed, as one great meaty hand then another pulled itself from the shadows along its length, followed by the bleached skull and immense whale-bulk of Mother Sphinx, dragging her way back into the deep.

As Nathaniel Silver left the church, he reflected on his feelings, which he could not face directly for fear they would burn. The world inside him was God's territory, mapped by His angels and named only by His holy terrible voice. It was not a world to be tamed by compasses or the finely-notched rule. He had been hollow; he was filled now with aweful humours.

Hate was the easiest of all tempers to imagine and describe, and he worked hard to dismiss it. He didn't hate Alice Lynch; he didn't hate Nick, if he was honest – the boy was wrong about that – oh, but he loathed the clerk's cruelty and his confidence and his melodrama; he didn't hate himself, not even for being a blind fool. Perhaps, just perhaps, he hated Christ's pilots for backing him into this corner, for taking Ann Brownlow from him and all his dreams with her. Nick and Jeova had offered him God's sword, and showed him Alice so he might wield it wrathfully.

Nick had been right about the other thing. He was honest, he was open; Silver despised his honesty and openness.

Out of the body of the church and the sight of the congregation, he no longer had any need to appear proud, and he felt his legs crook beneath him and his back bend under an invisible burden. He half-stumbled to a wall opposite and plunged his hands into the brick, which held fast. He wanted tears that wouldn't come; instead he wept grit and tiny flakes of dead skin.

He thought he heard his name hissed urgently at his back, and then a whispered spat between two hushed voices, but he didn't turn. Then he heard muddy footsteps, coming closer in short strides, and he ignored them. A small hand stroked his back, between his clenched shoulders. He started and the fingers recoiled.

'Silver?' came an unexpected voice.

He looked round.

It was Aphra Behn who'd approached him and touched him, and she held her hand out as if shocked by it, by the tension and the angry energy it had let loose. She'd lost all her elegance in the few hours since he'd last seen her, her clothes soaked wet first with rain then with mist; her plump shoulders, chest and neck blue with chilly bites. Her eyes were as surprised as his, but cow-soft though they were, they were sharp enough to prick the shell of his moods, and all his anger dribbled away.

'Did you follow me?' he asked. Her head shook from side to side.

She hadn't been alone, and he looked past her to the rust-coloured silhouette below the church's slumbering walls. He recognised it. He recalled being pressed against a tree, with a needle over his heart. 'She's not here for you,' Aphra babbled. 'When she attacked you before it was a mistake. Bloody hell, that was so long ago, I'd almost forgotten.'

Now Silver found his old assailant wasn't even looking to him, so intently was she watching the door. Radiant light flared from the holes in the church wall; his eyes sizzled and he flinched. Aphra turned too – he saw the shape of her head burned white in the black behind his eyes. In that moment of darkness visible, she took his hand hard and squeezed.

When he looked again, the windows were dark, and the red woman-shape hadn't flinched at all.

Moments later, two hooded Ratcatchers appeared at the arch, bustling Jeova ahead of them, out into the yard. Silver saw the woman tense, ready to leap. He opened his mouth to yell a warning; Aphra sprang up and filled the gap with her tongue. He pushed her away, but it was too late.

The red woman sprang at the evacuees, kicking herself into the air, bounding against the wall of the church and carrying herself down into their midst. The Ratcatchers shoved Jeova away. She rabbit-punched their hoods, and even from this distance Silver could hear small bones crumpling inside their faces. The fury brought a long elegant leg swinging up so that her foot – bare and grimy – caught one man below the chin. She tossed him delicately aside, into the closest wall where he flattened.

The second man had time to pull his pistol. Both her hands came chopping down, and the ball discharged into the ground. The same hands twisted, grabbed the bodyguard's legs, and upended him face-first into the mud. There was nothing now between her and Jeova.

Silver dived towards them, but Aphra fought hard, first bringing an ineffective slap down on his chest, then more cunningly wrapping her arms round his waist, so that she caught him as she moved and brought them both tumbling into the street. He dragged himself free, but he was too late. The blur of red slammed Jeova against the wall, her gleaming wand held to his chest.

Nate Silver saw all his friends dying before his eyes. 'No,' he barked. 'Leave him alone! Leave him alone!'

Jeova flicked his wrist and sent the wand spinning out of the woman's hand. It arced down into the street-mud, still glowing feebly. His attacker gaped in surprise at her empty hand, though only in the heartbeat before her intended victim drove one fist into her stomach and another into her face. She went onto her knees, and the slender, helpless fellow swooped on her, seizing the back of her head with one hand, her chin with the other, then pressing his mouth down on her gaping jaw.

Silver couldn't believe what he was seeing. Aphra could; she was struggling to find a purchase on the slippery earth, trampling the back of Silver's legs in her hopeless efforts to rise.

The marriage of Jeova and his assailant lasted a scant few seconds. Black pus – like oil or evil humour – welled around the join of their mouths. Jeova's cheeks billowed and he spat his assassin loose; then he slumped back against the nearest wall, satiation on his curling lips; his eyes serenely closed. Free at last, the woman backed away, gagging and clawing at her throat. She fell into the mud, and Silver saw that her face was smeared with the blasphemous fluid that had spewed from Jeova's guts. It bubbled on her lips, and on her eyes, which he was certain hadn't before been so unreflective, so glazed, and so solidly black. She scrabbled at the smouldering patches on her face, but it made no difference and left no mark.

Aphra Behn dragged herself over to her fallen comrade, saw the same damage, and shrieked like a soldier.

This is Edgehill again. This is my war. This is Hell. Without Aphra's weight on his legs, Silver could rise and walk. He reached Jeova, who smiled at the sound of his approach and didn't open his eyes.

'What did you do to her?' he yelled. 'Who is she?'

It wasn't Jeova's voice that answered him, but something sweeter and suppler. It came from his mouth, but not from his tongue, curling from the lip-corners like steam. *She is my new host. She came here to destroy me, not realising that I had goaded her from the start and was lying in wait.*

'I don't understand.'

She is my escape route. She will become us and carry me home in triumph.

Still, he didn't understand.

'No.'

He turned. Aphra Behn was no longer at her companion's side. There was no softness in her face, none of her fat, it was all muscle and vengeance. 'No!' she screamed. She was at his shoulder. She lunged.

Silver ducked out of her way, but she wasn't aiming for him. A light glinted in her hand as she flew past him. The wand, it was the wand; it shone.

She plunged it deep into Jeova's heart.

⇒ Chapter 22: *Last of the Magicians* ⇐

ABOVE –

A single shot can change the course of a battle, but the shot itself is rarely noticed at the moment it fires. War is a pandæmonium and a cacophony, whose strategic din drowns out the tiny tactical echoes. Only from above does the pattern of the shot reveal itself; its energies and effects spilling out as a ripple that – at this distance – appears ordered and beautiful. How will the great powers react when they hear that first shot and all its consequences blossoming simultaneously to decorate the Spiral Politic?

The elders and archons of Faction Paradox are in no position to react, even if they notice. They are too busy retreating on every front, under the implacable advance of the Great Houses. Once, in their pomp, they would have seen an opportunity here, but defeat-after-defeat has turned their aims inward, towards keeping the Eleven Day Empire untoppled. They have missions scattered throughout the worlds; no doubt there is one that can act in their name, pick up the wounded after all shots are spent, and count the dead. Let them cope with it. Let them report later, when the Wave has broken.

The Remote have been freshly cut loose from the family of Paradox. From world to world, they're rejoicing in the freedom of pure obedience to random impulses, static, and interference. And what's this shot but another signal out of the dead noise of the past? Their distant ancestors – who never knew an electromagnet and could only communicate using fires or flags, inks or tongues – have found an ingenious way of sending them a message through time! If they listen carefully, they'll imagine numbers whispering out of the haze of white noise, and those numbers could mean anything. Charge! Retreat! Keep listening, keep listening.

The Celestis don't hear the shot. They can't. No sound has ever been heard in the halls of Mictlan, nor in its tributary subdomains, Ouroboros, Cinnabar, and Unthank, where nothing is real and nothing is permitted. Still, the Lords Celestial will notice eventually; but to their grey eminences such chaos is spectacle, a faint projection on a wavering surface. It can't touch them. They never existed, so they are safe from all consequences. They will do nothing.

When the Great Houses hear they will *respond, as inexorably as effect follows cause. The long-lived residents of the Homeworld have short memories; they would not recognise the weapon that sounded the shot, they have forgotten it was ever theirs. They have proclaimed themselves the power that preserves the Spiral Politic, the unyielding patterns of nature, and the holy state of things. For them, the shot will not be merely an attack, but a crime against the real. Their terrible gold screwships will turn to weave across the aether towards the Earth, leaving scorched worlds and ashen stars in their wake.*

And their enemy – ?

On the edges of battle, in the corners that the War has yet to reach, other smaller powers have been watching for a moment like this, for a shot that strikes at them directly. The pilots of Civitas Solis have been calculating in fear of this since the day they were granted their charter. They detected the vector of this event long ago, a spike in the probabilities that, unchecked, would worm its way slowly through time into their hearts. Patiently, their pscholars had trawled the deep and subtle numbers for more clues, for the obvious anomaly – An expedition must be commissioned. A bargain must be struck. The hand on the trigger finger must be restrained. Three must descend into prehistory to make it so – But that expedition has fallen silent, the three descendants waking in the all-present with mute and failed memories. Now the pilots turn their great shaggy hoods towards the source, following the numbers that keep them securely unborn, alive, and dead, watching them resolve towards zero.

Civitas Solis, for all its secrecy and its security, is neither secure nor secret. There are always pirates. The numbers are smuggled out in packets, cut, distributed, let loose on a thousand streets below a thousand suns. A certain seam had passed eventually to a woman from another time, another world – not one of us, not of our lineage, an outsider, an exile. She could read the numbers better than most. Buried deeper than the pilots probed, visible only to her, was the signature she had been looking for. She abandoned all that precious data at once, and hurried to a pseudo-market. I need a suit, she said; she knew it would cost her more than pseudo-money, but she had no time to haggle. She had found her enemy. She returned to her latest digs, took out her dusty black uniform, and dressed herself for War.

BELOW –

Aphra Behn turns away from the man she's just skewered. He no longer counts. She only has eyes for her fallen comrade. Silver doesn't look. It feels too private. He gapes instead at the man he calls Jeova, whose whole body is writhing with light, spilling into him through the spike in his chest. It's eating him, it's eating him up from the inside.

Silver thinks for a moment that he must be going mad, and in that same moment he receives ample proof, as the arch to the church fills with bodies. A half-dozen hooded Ratcatchers come prancing through, skipping and pirouetting and tumbling like acrobats. They're dancing to a drumbeat only they can hear, no stately pavane or galliard, but a sensual tribal celebration of limbs and fingers and hips. They're pursued by demons with gleaming unfleshed faces and mirthless smiles. The Faction of Paradoxes drives the dancers ahead of them with raucous whoops and prods at the points of dark and invisible weapons. The Ratcatchers parade into the yard, where they thrash harmlessly for a few seconds more before – one by one – they slump exhausted into the dirt.

Silver whirls round. It's a slow business. Time is slurring round Jeova. The scholar's face contorts. His ghost-hands scrabble at the needle in his heart. It is real, but they are not.

With the Ratcatchers vanquished, the Faction of Paradoxes notices him. There are only three, and Alice isn't with them. The woman – he remembers her from Salomon's House, but not her name – pauses in her twirl; and the larger man drops to his knees and begins a slow, sonorous chant. The woman calls –

Amphigorey, fetch Greenaway. Fetch Mother Sphinx!

For the Grandfather's sake, she's still weak after –

We need her spirit. The universe is about to burst.

Silver looks back to Jeova, and as he looks, the woman – Hateman, of course, how could he forget that name? – joins the chant. They call down all the *loa*. They call down the families and their familiars. They call them down to give them the strength to keep this daughter of theirs from running loose. The smaller man is soon with them. Their words have strength. They keep the sky at bay.

Even so, Silver sees that there is too much power here for even black magic to dam. It will surge over them.

He wonders what it will feel like, when it breaks.

He watches Jeova screaming silently, on the threshold not of life and death, but life and never-living. A hole is opening, a hole torn into the world where Jeova stands, where he has always stood, where he will stand in future-time. Silver sees a crevice splitting through the Earth from now until doomsday, because this man will change the world, and now he has never lived. He leaves a vast gap behind him, as big as God, bigger perhaps. And the world will heal around him as best it can, but who is there to plug a hole that size?

Were they not cut from the same cloth? The voice that speaks in Jeova is, he no longer has any doubt, that of the power that plucked him from the grave. Silver was remade in this man's image, and if Jeova should falter, then he will have to take up the fellow's burden.

Silver steps towards Jeova. There is a little space between them, vegetable-spongy and uncertain beneath his feet. He paces across to meet the unliving man. Each step brings him closer to filling the hole. He sees at last what Nick and Jeova were offering him but did not themselves know, not just the chance to rule, but to leave rules that would last forever. Whole new philosophies will spring from him, new ways of seeing, new laws and new understandings. He will describe the motions of both the tiniest particles imaginable and the greatest, and show how they are the same. He will split white light and make a rainbow, then compress it back into the single radiant colour of God. He will pull back the curtain of the world and expose the clean and perfect working of the machine beneath.

They will challenge him, but they will always quote him, and it will be his methods that define all future ages. His measurements will describe the limitations of the world. He will give mankind a new *physicks*, and he will dedicate it all to his creator. By his achievement and example, man will strive for the stars and commend himself to

Heaven. He will lead a war of liberation against evil and cast down the Devil. He will embrace his human destiny in this new age of miracles and science –

The Silver Age.

There is another movement from the church's arch, a shadow looming so large it might be made from churchstone if it weren't so supple and so jolly. Jolly? Her poise is jolly. Her face is dead, a miraculous skull from the uncanny zoology of distant islands. He remembers the old woman from Salomon's House. She was a lump then, she is a lump now. She rests on her sticks and contemplates the flickering man before her. A shy cat slinks between her legs, trying to bury itself in her skirts.

He sees death.

She touches Silver on the shoulder, and it takes all of his will not to recoil from her touch. She's warm. She has a hot brown hand.

Do what you have to do. You ain't a man. Your Alice, she says you're better than a man.

Then she hobbles to join her children in their half-patient, half-desperate chanting.

Silver takes one last look at the frenzied expiration of his soulmate, Jeova Unus Sanctus, puts his hand on the scalding end of the needle, and lets it burn until it feels seared into his flesh and his bone, an inseparable part of him. This man is his reflection. *No.* Jeova is the real man, *Silver* is the reflection, and now he has the chance to become solid and usurp Jeova's place. The needle flares in his grip.

Then he pulls with all his might.

He prays. He prays! Christ give me the strength to do this! Christ be in my arms and my heart! Christ keep me from this trap that has been set for my soul! If we are one, if his life is mine, then why can I not restore it back to him? Is there not a balance between all things, even souls? Are he and I not opposites and equals, so that I might support him as he stumbles and restore to him the strength to carry his own life? Silver *pulls,* certain that no other hand could do this, and that if he falters then Jeova will be forever lost. His hands are burning, but he refuses to yield his grip. The pain!

He screams, and as he screams, the needle gives and slides smoothly out of Jeova's chest, leaving no mark, only solid unbroken flesh.

ABOVE/BELOW –
There is the hush that follows when a certain shot goes wide.

⇒ Chapter 23: *Newton Sleeps* ⇐

'Right,' Mother Sphinx said, 'which one of you ratfuckers wants to dance?'

And then they danced.

Greenaway didn't know the exact ritual involved, but Mother Sphinx made it look simple. She rapped the point of her sticks on the church floor to a manic beat, and the Servicemen arrayed around her went into spasm. Their arms shook, their legs trembled and jigged, their heads gyrated. None quite matched the step of the others, so the effect was like seeing a raucous dawn chorus made flesh. The soldier who'd pinned Greenaway to the wall fell back from her, skipping on tiptoes, his face alarmed by the crude rhythm possessing his body.

Once Mother Sphinx had escaped, the rest of Faction Paradox joined her, spat one by one out of their shadows into undignified but fleshy heaps on the floor. They stood, at first groggy and uncertain, but the music of Mother Sphinx's laughter rebounded through the church and they drew strength from it. She was singing the family back together. Even Greenaway could feel it, a fine line tugging at her heart. She'd chosen to be part of this; still, she crouched near the shrine door, with Nick Plainsong at her side. Nick alone had been unaffected by the Mother's feverish music, but stood unmoving by the shrine.

'Everyone here fine?' Mother Sphinx declaimed, craning her mask round to describe the room, her blank sockets passing over the shine door and through the rabble of dancing men before latching onto Greenaway's cousins. Three skulls nodded discordantly. Suppression gave a simple affirmative grunt.

'I think I've been sick in my own shadow,' Amphigorey groaned.

'We're... we're okay. You?' Hateman asked, a shrill queasiness in her voice the only hint of what it must have been liked to be trapped in darkness.

'Mother Sphinx is fine,' came the booming reply. 'You all fine. Pretty much everyone here is fine. Even these fellas are fine, they just don't know this is a holy place. This ain't no dancehall. Show them outside.'

At their mother's command, Greenaway's cousins ran at the dancing men, whirling their *sombras que corta* over their heads and driving their captors down the aisle in a frenzy. The Ratcatchers crashed and barged into one another, falling over their comrades in their efforts to escape the Faction's whirling shadows and their Mother's carnival laugh. The cousins drove their captors out of the body of the church and into the night, and once they were gone, Mother Sphinx sagged, her voice deflating back into her body, which looked as fat and as frail as it had ever been.

Greenaway heard herself breathe out. Mother Sphinx heard too. She began a slow shamble across the naked floor and through the field of planted, spoiled *loa*-casts towards her rescuer and her former gaoler. She wheezed once she reached them, resting all her weight on her sticks.

'You two ain't up for dancing?'

'More Faction magic?' Nick asked, in the sour voice of the defeated.

Mother Sphinx pulled off her mask and poked her tiny dark-skinned face into his. 'That magic's older than the Faction, boy. That magic jus' grew. This is the first time I seen you up close. Mother Sphinx had to make herself a choice twenty years ago...' She looked aside, smiling kindly at Greenaway, who had no desire to be looked at but no strength to crawl away. 'Guess she chose right.'

'It looks like I'm immune to your magic, Mother,' Plainsong remarked.

'Guess so,' Mother Sphinx replied, and then she began to thrash him over the head with one of her sticks. He dropped to a crouch under her repeated blows, with his bare hands covering his skull, and his knuckles catching the worst of her violence. She chuckled and wheezed with the effort, and Greenaway almost felt she ought to take the stick from her, as much for her own sake as to spare Nick a bruising.

'Mother Sphinx!' Amphigorey was at the door, yelling. 'Something's going on outside!'

'Kinda busy at the moment.' (Thwack, thwack.)

'It's the mother of all daughters!'

Mother Sphinx nodded, and let the final delicious blow bounce off Nick's scalp, before replacing her mask and making the first of many pained steps towards the exit.

Greenaway heard her own name shouted, but didn't care to follow it, not just yet. She watched as Nick raised his head warily from under the umbrella of his hands, but she did nothing to acknowledge him and he, in turn, didn't even seem aware she was there.

Outside the sky flared scarlet, then purple. Empires were toppling, the rules of Heaven were rewriting themselves, the world was coming to an end. Greenaway got to her feet and brushed the dust and the scattered cobwebs off her petticoats. The shrine itself was providing enough light for her to see, but there was another glint by her foot. She knelt, and found it was Silver's egg, which must have rolled back to her. She picked it up.

Erasmus was nowhere inside her. He had expelled himself along with the eggstuff. She held the reformed egg close to her face, wondering if she could see him there, but the surface was a bland sheen. This had been a mirror once. This had reflected worlds in the making. It showed her nothing of herself.

The sky was white now, visible through the cracks and the gouges in the church walls. Plainsong sat at her feet. His hands went under her skirts, but only to cling to her ankle, for support, for comfort.

What's going on? Erasmus?

~ *A daughter event* ~ *A big one, perhaps the biggest ever, enough to warp history irrevocably* ~

She smiled to hear his voice again, and outside her skull, warming even to these cold words. Can we stop it?

~ *No* ~ said Erasmus.

~ *Nonetheless, it has been stopped* ~

Nate, she thought.

Outside, the sky darkened into the colour of night. Greenaway shook Nick's hands away from her leg and ran to the arch.

Was this America?

How it could be America? – it was London! Yet it felt like America to Aphra Behn, except that it was so cold. It was damp enough. There were parts of America where you only had to step into the open air to become soaked-through by the swamp-wet climate. But those parts were usually baking, they put a coat of sweat and a coat of prickles over every inch of your skin. She had gone buttoned-up everywhere, hating the heat and the damp, hating the demands of costume and civilisation. If she hadn't been such a prim European, one of those dwarfish warty claimants to be masters of those huge continents, she might have stripped down to nothing and gone among the savages and slaves, who – having no choice in the matter – were the *true* Americans, and who were suffering from the white plague that had spread among them. She had seen only a little of their world, and she'd feared it yet dreamt of it ever since. There were sounds and scents that brought back the memories precisely. They were in her head now, and she was transplanted there while remaining in a tiny bleak corner of England. Around her, fully-dressed Englishmen danced until they dropped, like naked tribesmen. A red goddess lay burned and dying at her feet. She had sacrificed a virgin with a sacred knife, as the Aztecs were said to do. The offering had been rejected, the sky had cracked open, and the witch-doctors had emerged from their hiding places to appease the spirits with chants and mouth-music.

If it was not America, then it must be some other new world; anywhere but here.

The hot blood that had guided her to kill the scrawny man had cooled at the very instant she'd stabbed him. She didn't stop to see him die, or even if she'd struck anything more than a glancing blow; it no longer seemed important. She glanced at her hands and found them clean and unreddened. She turned aside – while Silver ran to catch the falling man – and went back to kneel beside Larissa.

She wasn't dead, but she was hurting. Her skin was smouldering where the black acid had spilled, though among these unnatural inky patches were equally uncanny glimmerings, fierce white light that pulsed as it had in the blade of Larissa's stiletto. The black oozed to swallow the light, though never completely, and between them it turned the nymph's body rank and glassy. She saw Aphra through dark new eyes, and stroked gently at her face with half-pale fingers, half-obsidian claws.

'Aphra,' she said. Aphra wept.

'What's happening to you?'

The nymph's charred lips twitched. 'It was waiting for me. It just needs me to help it escape. Don't let it escape.'

Aphra cradled her. 'I killed him,' she explained. 'I killed him with your needle.'

Black fluid gushed from the corners of Larissa's mouth, and Aphra didn't dare reach to wipe it away. 'I'm the quarry now. Don't let me get away. Kill it,' she insisted. 'Kill me.'

'I can't kill you.' Aphra made to stroke her hair, but Larissa's hand snapped out of the mud and caught her by the wrist.

You won't. The voice seethed out of the darkening lines of the nymph's mouth. *I have fulfilled my mission protocols on this world. Time to move on.*

Larissa's grip slackened, her glassy arm slipping back to her side. 'Don't let it get away.'

Aphra looked around, to see if anyone would stop her. No, no one was paying her attention. The Ratcatchers remained collapsed on the ground, some still twitching to the rhythm of their dreams. The witch-doctors were still lost in their chanting; it made a more plaintive noise outside the church than it would have done within its walls, and their praying hands were directed down, into the earth, or in some unseeable direction that she couldn't imagine. Silver was struggling to keep her victim on his feet, to keep him from toppling down into his final rest; as she looked on him, he succeeded in tugging out the needle, and she wondered at how small a wound she had made; it seemed invisible. There was no one who would stop her, except Larissa herself.

Don't let it get away.

The blood still swam stickily inside the contours of the suit, partially obscuring the changes to Larissa's body. It was a smooth costume with no joins that Aphra could see, except at the wrist, the neck and the ankle. That was no good. Ah-ha! There was the hole she had noticed before, the little tear slightly thinner than one of her plump fingers. She hooked one inside. She tore, making it wider.

The fabric split and coated her nail with red liquid.

Aphra closed her eyes, and fitted more fingers into the tear she'd made and forced it wider. Under the line of her costume, Larissa's skin felt hot and glassy; Aphra tried not to touch, tried to put that sensation out of her mind. The hole was almost large enough for her entire hand. She scratched at it. She tore.

Larissa – the creature Larissa was becoming – noticed. *What are you doing?!*

If the suit were destroyed, she had said, I'd be trapped in this world.

'I pledged myself to her,' Aphra said simply. The body beneath her tried to scrabble backwards, but Aphra fell heavily onto its legs to pin it, and ripped harder at the suit-stuff, with both hands. Blood guttered from it – all the blood she had expected from stabbing a man, more. The hole was now bigger than a stomach, and weakened, the suit began to fray in a dozen other places.

The body beneath was no longer a woman's, shaped like a woman but not of human flesh, more like smooth, volcanic glass. Larissa kicked with both legs; the force went through Aphra's body and knocked her away, onto the ground.

When she looked up, Larissa was standing, though clumsily, as if the parasite within her hadn't yet mastered her limbs and muscles. Aphra forced herself up quicker and charged. She wasn't strong, but she had weight, and the additional strength accrued by a body in motion. She slammed into her target and sent them both tumbling, and as she fell Aphra ripped and ripped and ripped.

The Larissa-monster punched her in the face. It still wasn't in command; the blow had only hurt her, where it could easily have snapped her skull or driven the bridge of her nose into her brain.

'You won't trap me here!' Larissa screamed; the worst thing that ever lived screamed, but it had charge of her throat now and spoke in Larissa's voice. The suit was nothing but a string of ribbons on its upper body, and had gashes and weals in a dozen places below.

'An angel,' someone sighed. 'An angel!'

Aphra felt herself flung backwards against the church wall, and then came pain again – all the little agonies she had forgotten in the heat of battle were reignited, in her hips and her spine and her stomach and her head. The worst thing that ever lived leapt. It slammed down on top of Aphra's already beaten body.

Then its hands, still shimmering, still changing, were on Aphra's throat and squeezing the air out of her. Aphra saw her own bloating face in the shiny vestiges of Larissa's eyes. She remembered struggling once before in the strangle-grip of the crucified man, but that had been a long time ago, and not in London but in another world; maybe it was America?

Once the wand – and its annihilating light – was pulled from his chest, Jeova began to breathe frantically and clutched his ribcage, feeling for a hole that was no longer there. His head oscillated more rapidly than before, and Silver realised that the scholar's frantic heartbeats were nodding themselves out through his skull. He was a handsome fellow, in a gaunt sort of way, but all his self-possession had vanished. Was that so surprising? All his self had nearly gone, burned out by the device that still shivered in Silver's hand.

Jeova almost fell, but Silver caught him.

'I saw –' he stammered. 'I saw – I saw –'

'I know what you saw,' Silver told him. He laid the younger man down on the earth.

Around him, the skull-heads of the Faction were bowed in what he wouldn't mistake for prayer. If he'd had his egg, he would have consulted it for the detail, but he could tell this was more than worship. Damage had been done to the world, and it needed to be repaired. Only the Mother of the family responded to Silver's enquiring eye, cocking her head as if amused by the speculation she could see in his breast. The others were lost in their dedications. None of them was Alice. Wait, they had their masks –

No, Alice's mask had been smashed. Nick had done that, not ten minutes before. It felt to Silver that the universe had been born, grown old, and died in that time.

'An angel,' Jeova mouthed, delirious on his filthy bed. 'An angel!' And he pointed; Silver looked round. Aphra Behn fell against the wall of the church as a fury leapt on her, its killing hands on her neck. Her attacker was the woman she had brought here; her hair no longer flame-red but ash-black.

It looked at him as it flew. Its face was a shadow made of glass. Men had sometimes looked that way to Silver, but only after they had died on the field of battle. Sometimes they remained upright, dying at some unlikely point of motion that left them unable to fall. Their jaws would drop open to expel low moans from their gradually-collapsing guts. He saw all this again in the unreflecting bowl of its forehead. It was a ghost that haunted Edgehill, a war-angel.

God had let this thing loose on his world.

'No!' Silver exclaimed. He wasn't sure later why he ran at it; to help Aphra, yes, to pull its hands from her throat, but that was a gentle human urge that had been beyond him at that moment. The force that drove him was pure beast, an instinct, recognising himself in this monster and hungering to destroy it. The war-angel dropped Aphra gasping onto the ground, then stretched out a casual arm-like limb and swatted him away. He landed gently. Soft, familiar arms arrested his fall.

Alice Lynch looked down on him; she was unsmiling, and flinched first.

The war-angel lurched towards them. Its head had once been a woman's, but was now half-marbled and held at a crooked angle as if too heavy for its neck. Behind it, Aphra Behn was retching and clutching her throat. Silver scrabbled backwards, but the angel paid him no attention. It took awkward, unlearned steps towards this Faction Paradox creature, Alice, or Greenaway, or whatever she wanted to call herself. She stood her ground.

I remember you, it seethed from the corners of its mouth.

'You do,' Alice acknowledged. One hand clenched, as if gripping solid air. The other was full. She had the pilot's egg, glowing with a dim, grey light.

'I am Faction Paradox.'

You are Faction Paradox, which abandoned the Homeworld and took so many things with it. You have the means to leave this world.

Alice took a first uncertain step backwards towards the church wall. Silver saw what was coming and almost rose to protect her, but his flesh was too sluggish. The war-angel sheared through the gap between them and pinned Alice against the solid stone, its fingers on her throat. She flailed with her free hand, then screamed and rippled her fingers as if something had burned her palm. Her other hand also splayed, and the egg dropped to the dirt, where it rolled for a moment and lay still.

You should not play with shadow-things. I am a deeper and older shadow than your Grandfather ever cast.

Alice tried to call to her companions – 'Mother Sphinx!' – but Silver cast his head round and found that her comrades were paralysed in the midst of their ritual which was still unwinding the forces of the sky. Mistress Behn was down, as were the Servicemen, and of Nick Plainsong there was no sign. There was no one to help her now except him, and she did not look to him.

The egg was before him, glowing, reassuring, barely a stretch of his arm away. Once again it came back to him, though he'd thought it lost forever. Silver picked up his egg, and recalled the shape of it in his fingers, the purr of its subtle voice, the knowledge it had imparted, everything that Jeova and Nick had denounced as false.

It was a constant. It had been his for all his life – except for that seventeen year prelude, but that had been a different man and a different world.

He held it out towards the war-angel, and towards Alice.

'Help her,' he said.

There was a new note to its voice. ~ *Yes* ~ it said. It flowed from his hand.

The egg became a weaving snake of light. It slithered across the night, opened its narrow jaws, and swallowed both women whole; they vanished into its swelling proportions as it became a globe as large and luminous as it had been at Salomon's House. Silver stood before it, gazing into its opaque depths. He fancied that he could discern shapes out of the glow. Aphra Behn, who was up on her feet again, regarded it warily, her eyes ticking back and forth as though looking for the trick, or at least some reassurance that there was some *reasonable* explanation. And Jeova too was there at their side, on shaky but recovering legs, looking with them into the light.

...and Greenaway finds herself falling again, into the infinite light, as she had at Salomon's House. She has been here before, yet all is different. It has changed because she has changed. She is a cousin now, and more dedicated to the Grandfather than she could have imagined, while her equal devotion to and deception of Nate Silver have tied whole new knots of experience in her character. This time, too, she is not alone. When he left her, Erasmus became a part of the egg; not merely a player, he now surrounds her and guides her.

She is not alone. There is another falling with her, perhaps two.

Erasmus?

~ *Yes* ~

This world responds to my thoughts and fancies?

~ *Yes* ~

Then show me –

She's familiar enough and strong enough to change the world around her, so suddenly she is no longer falling. She's in the garden at Hornsey St. Mary, on the tidy lawn beside the green way where she confronted Father-Mother Olympia and was first shown the mystery of the Faction. She has a new guest now, the Homeworlder, who sits on a bench across the way from her as if waiting for an invitation into her home. The house is gone, of course. She demolished it escaping from this place the first time. What remains is a tiny ocean of chaos and debris in the middle of this precise, unreal, watery world.

The red-haired woman (who was perhaps once black-haired and uglier) has brought a House with her. It's an edifice, a vast tower reaching into the heavens, carried as a great weight in her memories. It's not the only thing she's brought with her –

It sits on her shoulders, with its bulbous bowl of a head peering out from behind her ear. It has been blanched white by the descent into the void. Its limbs are skinnier than Greenaway recalls, but wrapped round and round the woman's body. In places, they appear to be pinned through it, into flesh, into bone, into the gifts of her life.

'Help me,' the Homeworlder pleads.

It is a kind of *loa*, Greenaway sees, but not a healthy one. There is no rapport here, no discourse or symmetry as she has shared with Erasmus. This is a parasite and its prey, and soon the only voice that will speak in this marriage will be that of the brute. She looks closer and sees that its body is riddled with slivers of darkness. This creature is wasting; no wonder it needs to feed on the Homeworlder's soul.

The red-haired, dark-haired woman sees what Greenaway is thinking: 'It's wounded. When the host was stabbed with the needle, this iteration was damaged too.'

'Wounded? Still dangerous?'

'Oh, yes. It's killing me.'

Greenaway uncoils her whip, not a shadow in this world of light, but a solid thing. The creature giggles in its perch on the Homeworlder's shoulders.

You've tried that before, it didn't work.

'It might now.'

It won't. This host is no longer useful and will be consumed. You will be more pliable.

Greenaway whirls her line in an arc. The war-angel preens, poking its featureless head towards her as if sniffing. It unpicks its spikes from the Homeworlder's body, but stays crouched on her shoulders, ready to spring. The woman doesn't move.

Greenaway tells them: 'This world responds to my thoughts and fancies, so I've been told.'

The evil *loa* gurgles and leaps. Greenaway brings her whip hand up to strike.

Erasmus! Now!

And suddenly the pilot-*loa* is apparent everywhere, in every instance and crack of this world, everything that isn't Greenaway, or Homeworlder, or war-angel. He is a swollen pilot-flea again, the sacs of his neck and stomach bulging with ferocious light that radiates outwards in a disorientating burst. The evil *loa* shrills, blasted away by the lightburst, while Greenaway's whip flies past it and coils rounds the Homeworlder's body, tightening there like a fist.

~ *You could leave her trapped here, if you chose to* ~

Erasmus, show me the way out!

And Greenaway finds herself falling again...

Two women's bodies dropped out of the egg's glow and into the mud. Alice fell first, landing purposefully, and rolling clear. Then, less prepared and unmoving, came the red-haired assassin. She had been healed and renewed by her plunge into the egg-light, all the marks of possession cleansed from her skin, though she was soaked in blood – some of it perhaps her own – and her odd costume was reduced to rag and ribbons. Living? Dead? Silver couldn't tell. Aphra, who had been shaking her head in disbelief, now yelled in Silver's ear and shoved him away to throw herself on her companion's body.

The light had flared as the egg expanded, but now it dimmed as rapidly as its source shrank. No longer suspended in mid-air, it dropped to the earth. Silver and Jeova's eyes followed it, solemnly. The street was again lit only by the lamps that had been carried by the dancing Ratcatchers, the glows from nearby windows and adjoining streets, and – just perhaps – the supernatural essences rising from the Thames. Had anyone seen this, Silver wondered? Some passer-by strolling and seeing a stabbing, a brawl on a scrubland that had once been consecrated earth, a mob of drunken men? So they'd shrug and move on, that was London. And if they'd seen seven shades of apocalypse on the air, beast-headed creatures and strange magic, so? It's London.

The egg lay trembling on the ground, and neither Silver nor Jeova moved to take it. As they watched, it began to expand again, to stretch and deform. It rose up from the ground to resemble first a sapling, then a tree with two boughs rapidly sprouting out of its midriff and an unlikely spherical flower blooming at its top. It grew a second root and tottered on it, now becoming a parody of a man. It staggered towards them on freshly-grown legs. Its skin flickered between blacks, dusty greys, and whites, never settling on one shade for more than a moment. In the dome formed a parody of a mouth.

Destroy the enemy, it said, and on hearing this, Jeova swayed on his feet and toppled in a dead faint to the ground. The effort was also too much for the homunculus, and as if in imitation of the Master, it collapsed into a heap that soon ceased to resemble a man at all. It shrivelled back to the size of the egg, then grew smaller.

So, this latest battle appeared to be over. Silver, numbed and hollowed as he had been after all his fights, glanced around at the aftermath. Released from the intensity of their prayers, the followers of Faction Paradox also seemed to have shrunk, until they resembled nothing more than children overdressed in adult clothing and enormous false heads. Two of their number were already slumped exhausted against the wall, casting off their masks to reveal their weary, everyday faces; the third was trying to coax Mother Sphinx into sitting on the ground, but she balanced on her sticks and swatted him away. Aphra Behn was tending or mourning her fallen comrade in the most ostentatious and least practical manner possible. Jeova had no one to attend him but Silver, who knelt to check his health. The scholar had not fallen badly, and his chest swelled lightly; even asleep, his eyeballs flicked rapidly below their soft skins. He was cold, but then he had never seemed a warm man; he would live.

Beside him, the egg had blackened and shrunk to the size of a pebble. Silver picked it up, and found its surface duller and cooler than it had ever been. It had a voice still, but now so very faint, and as he strained to hear it, he was joined by another body. He glanced sideways and saw Alice there. She was crying. He found he had expected that, without knowing. She didn't meet his gaze, but reached out to touch Jeova's forehead.

'Can you hear it?' she asked. 'Your egg?'

He nodded. 'Faintly. Can you?'

'I can hear Erasmus. He was one of your angels.'

'What does he say?' he asked quietly.

'He says' – she took a breath – 'that the power that once possessed this man has been contained inside the egg. He says that you won't be able to use it again, and it will become inert. He says that part of him remains in me, and part of me remains in him, and he says goodbye.'

Silver slipped the remains of the egg into his pocket. 'Perhaps that is for the best,' he observed, flat-voiced.

There were more steps trudging towards them. Looking up, they saw the Ratcatcher-Serjeant and Mother Sphinx approaching, a wary distance between them. She came half-waddling, half-limping on her sticks; she seemed robust, but also old, terribly old. He – the Serviceman, who Nate realised he knew less well than Faction Paradox – moved stiffly, but with a hint of gaiety in his step; he didn't like it, it unsettled his military bearing.

Alice took her hand away from Jeova's head and let him sleep. Silver put a practical hand on her shoulder, then stood to address the serjeant. 'Who do you take orders from?'

'This man here, sir,' came the reply, 'and Mister Nicholas Plainsong.'

'Where is Nick?'

'I saw him haring off in the direction of the bridge, like the devil was after his arse, sir.'

Silver nodded. Nick would right himself in the end; he'd survive. 'They're both indisposed, so who's in charge now?'

'That'd be you, sir.'

For the first time, Silver became conscious of the *sir* in the serjeant's sentences. It was said well, but sounded wrong. 'In that case, this is what I'd like you to do. *These* people' – meaning the members of Faction Paradox – 'are no longer your problem. Providing they don't break any laws, forget about them, do nothing. For tonight at least, leave them alone.'

Mother Sphinx purred, and mouthed a string of pleased-sounding nonsense.

Silver ignored her. '*This* man you will arrange to have taken back to Trinity College, Cambridge, at the earliest opportunity. Make sure he is treated comfortably and well. I've seen men like this before, they sleep easily enough but they have troubled days. And *that* woman over there, Mistress Behn – do whatever she asks of you. I imagine she'll just want to be taken home.'

'Sir,' the serjeant barked, but then something less official, more comradely crept into his voice. 'You've been a soldier, haven't you? You've cleared up after a few spats?'

'Yes,' Silver agreed, 'I was always at my best when the fighting was done. One last thing – when you see Nick Plainsong, tell him that I'm sorry, but my answer is no.'

He let the serjeant go about his business, then turned to Mother Sphinx. 'That goes for Faction Paradox, too. My life is not for sale.' The doyenne of the Faction nodded keenly, and he couldn't detect defeat in her rumbling shoulders, not as clearly as he could on Alice's face.

But then Cousin Greenaway was bound to take rejection more personally than any of the others.

Across the way, Aphra had coaxed the redhead back to a feeble kind of life. Silver went to them. The woman was drained; all the energy and the aggression that she'd put into her violence had been burned out of her. *Good*, he thought. *Good*. She was naked except for her blood-red rags. Silver shed the coat the Service had given him and passed it to Aphra, who draped it over her charge's bare shoulders. The cold air bit through the thin sleeves of his shirt, then fell back, defeated. It might be a bleak night, but he was warm. He was as hot as he'd ever been.

He didn't talk to Aphra, but he leant down and kissed her on the forehead. She winced, a headache. He straightened up and discovered that no one was paying any attention to Nathaniel Silver. This suited his purposes. He turned and walked away, towards the river.

'Nate.'

He looked back. Alice stood behind him, perfectly still. She wasn't pleading. She had gone beyond pleading. She was maskless, except for her true face, which might have been cast from a dead skull.

'Nate,' she said. 'There is love.'

'I know,' he told her. He couldn't imagine what his face must look like, in her eyes.

He turned and then he was gone, into history.

'You got what you wanted.'

'What?'

Aphra, now she could breathe again, now that Larissa was no longer trying to squeeze the life out of her, found herself settling down. The energy had gone out of the night, and all that was left was the opportunity to sit back and watch the wreckage clearing itself away. The churchside was haunted by Servicemen and Faction-folk, who kept themselves in their little huddles. Only Silver had seemed to move easily between them. Aphra didn't want to be disturbed; one of the Ratcatchers had approached her, but she'd waved him away. They concentrated on the jaundiced academic that she'd spiked; he might look like a feeble thing, but tonight had proved him unkillable. *And you too*, she thought, her fingers going to the unflattering bruises on her neck. Oh, they would heal.

And Larissa –

Larissa wasn't dead, though she'd come through her ordeal weakened and strained. She was still radiant, but her light sputtered. She lay like a sleeping cat, with her warm head resting on Aphra's lap. Aphra would devote herself to nursing her back to health. It could take days, weeks, thrilling months dedicated to the care of a deity. Damn, yes, and she could write as well while this woman slept in her bed, and –

Larissa was reading her.

'I'm stuck now,' she explained. 'Without the suit I can't escape this world.'

'You'll find a way,' Aphra promised her, not hopefully.

'I have nowhere else to go. I can think of worse places to be trapped.'

No.

'No,' Aphra said decisively. 'No, you'll find a way.'

She pointed out the coven of witch doctors, who no longer seemed quite so impressive now they were no longer chanting and summoning spirits, but seemed to her like players caught backstage between performances. They were huddled by the church wall, all but one girl, a pretty thing with a distinct patterning on her cheek, that Aphra felt sure she'd seen before.

'These Faction Paradox people? Could they help you?'

'They wouldn't.'

'Maybe they would,' she insisted, in Larissa's ear. 'They look like they could do with some divine intervention. Have you ever seen a more benighted shower? Do you have anything you can offer them?'

'They're afraid of me.'

'Good. Put the fear of God into them!'

'They're at war. They're fighting monsters, and they're losing. I can help them. I know things about their enemies that even their enemies don't know. That's what I can give them.'

'Who are their enemies?'

Larissa didn't answer, but clenched Aphra's hand tight. 'She could have left me, in the void. She didn't.'

'You don't belong in this world,' Aphra whispered. 'It's a bleak world, and you are too bright for it. Besides, I'd soon grow too dull for you. You'd wear me down to nothing. Don't protest, I know all the old stories about gods and mortals. I know it's true.'

Then she said: 'Oh, fuck it!' and kissed Larissa in the mouth for as hard and as long as she could.

Larissa broke free at last, stood slowly and with some effort, and went warily to the church wall, to cast her shadow over Faction Paradox. Aphra walked close behind her, cautiously. The coven bristled at their approach, and the blemished girl put herself in their path.

'I want to strike a deal,' Larissa told them.

'Between the Faction and the Great Houses? That ain't likely,' came the droll voice from within the skull of the fat woman – a fatter thing by far than Aphra, who suddenly felt unusually slender.

'No.' Larissa shook her head. 'Between your group and me. I'm not the Great Houses. I left them long before your war. I don't believe that I'll ever go back.'

Sullen glances passed among the party, which Aphra interpreted as resentment and suspicion. Not quite fear, they were too tired for fear. Larissa was as impassive as she'd even been, but Aphra detected in her a sudden panic that she might be rejected, she might be trapped after all.

'What do you want?' the blemished witch piped up, setting a ripple of visible surprise through her colleagues; even the solid rock of the eldest woman seemed unsettled. The girl turned to reassure them: 'It won't do any harm to talk. Mother?'

'You think you're up to this?' the fat woman growled.

'I'm Faction Paradox. *Yes*,' the girl insisted, and the heavy mask of her mother lowered, as if she were slowly nodding, or fallen asleep, or dead. The girl swung back to face Larissa.

'Greenaway,' she announced, and put out her hand.

Then, before Larissa could speak, Aphra Behn decided that she simply couldn't be doing standing around in the cold listening to divinities and witches discussing formality. It was time to find the serjeant and get back home, to bed, to slip back into her inescapable old life of small triumphs, tiny defeats, the many defects of her body, and the slow erosion of time. She had grown to used to her bleak world; she belonged to it. She slipped away from them, trying her hardest not to look back.

She gave in though. She stole a glance, and saw her nymph and Greenaway shaking hands. Cool or warm? Starting something or closing business? She couldn't tell, she couldn't tell, she walked away.

It took Nathaniel Silver no time at all to reach the banks of the Thames, but once he was there he paused, as he realised that he had no idea where he might go now. The river sludged past him regardless, on the other side of a low wall. He was tempted, for a moment, to throw himself in and see where the current took him. He would not drown. He could not drown, though his body would fill with London's dank water and it would take him years to heal.

He would not throw himself in today, not when he had so many other options, a welter of possible worlds clamouring at him. The political landscape was no longer as plastic as it had been after Cromwell's revolution, so the chances of founding another commune were slim, but why think only of England? There was abundant space and people in the continents of America, or further afield – in those unknown lands of which the egg had whispered. Or he could become a teacher, or find his way into a trade, or turn his pursuit back to pure knowledge and build himself back up without the aid of the infernal or the divine. He could write more pamphlets, or another book! He had been put on Earth to change the world – to drive it to war, but it could be changed in other, better ways. He need not be a weapon. He had seen the futures stretching away from him, some likely, others not, growing the more diffuse the further they extended from the present. Those futures were commanded by the numbers of men and women in the *now*, acting both alone and as a whole. He thought of Alice. She had got away from him.

He would do his best. He would let the numbers fall where they would.

There was a jut pressing against his leg. He slid the infernal needle out of his belt, where he had stowed it after saving Jeova. It no longer glowed, and its point was dull and wouldn't have made a mark on fresh bread. He weighed it in his hand.

No gods and no devils, he decided. *No servants and no masters, no riches and no poverty –*

– and no more generals *–*

– and no laws in the universe but one command: love.

He swung his arm round and tossed the needle high into the air, into the river. He heard but did not see it break the waters.

═ **Chapter 24:** *Glory* ═

Each day a new sun rose on the horizon, and each day it seemed thinner and less bright than before. Each new dawn proved false. Aphra Behn would have preferred a permanent twilight to the little light that came out each morning to mock her. She was dying.

Her curtain had been closed for the past few mornings, as her physician recommended damp and darkness for her condition. Her eyelids only drooped these last months, and even with the window wide open she would have been hard pressed to tell if it was night or day. She would have needed candles close to see her own writing, but she had put her pen down the day before, when the shape of it had become too painful for her hand. Her wrist and forearm had felt ready to snap as she moved it slowly across the page; her fingers contorting round the rigid nib. Her last completed piece was a poem in the form of Pindar, in honour of the new regime. Done for bread, of course, of course, and because she no longer cared. *Come, plant your tulips in my little garden, water our grass with gin and fill England's orchards with oranges, it makes no difference to me.*

She still heard, through the blanked window, the cries of jubilation from the street, though they grew less frequent as the sound and fury diminished and only the nag of uncertainty remained. England's boisterous, drunken mood was giving way to a sore morning's sobriety; let this be an end to it, *please* let this be an end to it. We courted invasion, because we couldn't tolerate on the throne a dull man whose crimes were to be Catholic and fertile. Betrayed by his own people and his own daughter! The true king sweats humiliated in European exile while his country sweats beneath the Dutch yoke and his loyal subjects are reduced to a tiny Tory rump, now named *Jacobite* and *traitor*.

But let that be the end to our nation's earthquake! Let us have a respite! No, no, no, there was already talk of Scottish uprisings in the highlands, and speculation that James would land French troops in Ireland, so a new round of battles would begin afresh on tired soil. Aphra could see it stretching out into the future, just as it stretched back into the years of her infancy. The wars would go on and on and on, war without end. She was glad to be out of it.

All she was aware of now was the pain, and the smell of perfumed shit.

The worst thing about the pain – apart from the sensation itself, eating away at her flesh and marrow – was how it deceived her. With her eyes closed, she could imagine that her arms and legs were twisted and tapering, such was the shape suggested by the whirling agonies of her bones. Then she looked and they were as they had ever been, stumpy and pale but intact. How could she ever have complained about such a wonderful body, that was only now truly betraying her? Her spine felt as loose as string, yet cracked as she moved. Her skin was swaddled in the humid breathless atmosphere of her bedroom, already a coffin.

Her physician, the miracle-worker, was coating that skin with his murky brown concoction, painting it onto her face with a brush. He took pains not to make contact with the bristles himself, as if his touch would contaminate the substance and render it less effective. He had come recommended in society; his cure had its occasional survivors. In between applying dung to her face and back, he would mix alchemical potions then set light to them, filling her airless little room with noxious fumes; he inspected her chamberpot at regular intervals, and tutted curiously whatever the contents; he slipped fingers into her vagina, to gauge the state of her health from her wetness. 'Do that again and I'll brain you,' she'd choked, but she was too weak to live up to her threats.

She wasn't sure what the fellow looked like. She no longer saw people, not in detail. They were clouds; they drifted unfixed and hazy across her horizon, and she relied on memory and gesture. Her only other company was her maid, who looked in from time to time, always peeking tentative through the door as if afraid that this would be the occasion when she would find her mistress dead, always disappointed. She came now, knocking like a little mouse, then thrusting her head through the jamb.

'I'm still alive,' Aphra moaned at her. She heard her own voice, and thought it unconvincing.

'There's a man here to see you,' the maid whispered. 'I think he's a priest.'

Oh fuck, so they had caught up with her at last. 'No!' she bellowed, though the force scored her throat. 'No conversion and no deathbed confession! Tell him I won't go the way of Rowley and Rochester! Tell him I've decided his God isn't fucking real anyway! There, I said it! I said it and I had to wait my whole life to work up the nerve, but it's true!' She glowered at her miracle-worker, who had thrown up his arms in disgust.

The maid looked as if she were about to faint, and Aphra had a change of heart. 'Wait. Send him up. These are tough times for his faith. Besides, it'd take me till doomsday to recite all my sins. I'll keep his God waiting and waiting through my wickedness.'

The maid bobbed. 'I'll fetch him.'

'Thank you, Becky,' Aphra murmured and slumped back on her bed.

'Elizabeth.'

'Sorry?'

'I'm Elizabeth. Rebecca was... before me.'

'Oh yes, yes,' Aphra murmured, letting her eyes close fully and waving the girl away. That hurt. It was hard to raise her wrist, why was it so damn'd hard?

She rested her eyes until the priest came, then she opened them wide as she could manage – because she recognised his nervous bearing, the way he moved as if trying to find a firm purchase on the world – so she could confirm what she saw. She struggled and failed to sit up properly. 'You're no priest,' she accused, though her tone was pleased.

'No,' said Nathaniel Silver, 'but I'm often mistaken for one. It's –'

'– that smug air of holy certainty?'

'I was going to say it must be my clothes – the black.' He looked round awkwardly at the clinging shadows of the dim room, and the pallor of exotic smoke. 'Can we open the window?'

In spite of the physician's frantic gestures, he went to open her curtains, then the glass. Air and light rushed back into Aphra's world. The sun fell across her face and her body. Dwindled though it might be, it felt as good as it had ever done, and for a moment she mislaid her pain. She saw again, she saw clearly.

Why would I ever want to leave this life?

Her physician went into a funk; he put down his pots and brush, and stamped across the room to accuse Silver. The newcomer smiled at him, and the doctor might have thought him simple or humble, but Aphra knew Silver's masks better and she saw no humour in him now.

'The light! The sun disturbs my elixir and robs it of its healing qualities! You have set back her progress and her health will suffer. Fire and air!' his accuser bellowed. 'Fire and air!'

Silver looked, mock-curious, at Aphra, at her shivering shit-painted body. 'This elixir? What does it do?'

'It's a potent mixture of foul substances. It is what we call *vital*, which is to say that the combination of its elements are themselves the healthy state of a decayed organism. The rancour of it appeals to the evil humours that pollute this lady's *corpus* and draws them out through her skin, leaving her organs shriven and purified. Like calls ever to like! That is the first principle of the universe.'

'Really? This new knowledge astounds me. And what's in this elixir of yours?'

The physician was smiling now; he even waggled a warning finger in Silver's face. 'Many things: dung from a goat, blood – of course –'

'Of course.'

'Fluids from the lady's own body, plus other ingredients that must remain secret. I also smoke out her lungs and stomach with fumes, but the elixir in contact with the skin is the most efficacious.'

Silver jiggled his head enthusiastically, but his voice was grim. 'Indeed. You have poisoned her. Get out.'

The physician didn't react immediately, and this was too slow for Silver, who opened his mouth wide and bawled: 'Get out! Get out!' The force of his voice and the fire in his eyes drove the physician from the room, and indeed from the house; Aphra heard his startled footsteps scuttling down the stairs and then the slam of the distant door. Silver scooped up his bags and his apparatus from the floor, and began to hurl them out into the street, one piece at a time. Aphra closed her eyes again and listened to the pleasant sound of faraway glass shattering.

Her bed sagged; she lifted her lids and found Silver had taken the place of the physician beside her. His face – unchanged, she would have sworn, in the years since she'd last seen him – had been emptied of all his righteous fury. What remained might have been compassion or fatigue, or maybe nothing at all, maybe he was a blank wall and she was casting her dying, inner calm across him as shadows. He produced a handkerchief from his breast pocket, and began to wipe the elixir from her skin.

'That was good of you,' she said, pleased to hear that the barb was audible in her creaking whisper.

'He was cheating you. This will do you no good whatsoever.'

'So? I'm dying.'

'Then I'd rather you died with dignity. You're a proud woman, I think.'

'You're not' – she couldn't keep the forlorn hope from her voice – 'here to save me? You have no miracle of your own?'

'No,' Silver apologised. Then his brow furrowed: 'I heard you were dying. I had to come. I felt it was right.'

'I've given instructions to keep well-wishers, gallants, and early mourners from my door. So far my maid has been little troubled. Still, she cries so.'

'I can imagine.'

'Why did you come? Why did you have to come?'

Silver's head, fading back into pink and blonde blur, turned from side to side. 'I...'

'We screwed once, just once. Don't tell me you became enamoured. I've had men like that, boys mainly, following me around with their mouths open, it's a wonder they didn't trip over their tongues...'

'Mistress Behn?'

'Hmm?' Sharper: 'Aphra. No, *Astraea*. I'm returning to my place in the stars.'

'Astraea, you're rambling.'

Her hand inched out across the mattress to make contact with him. He was warm. He put away his handkerchief, and put his hands on hers. Behind him, the door opened and Elizabeth poked her concerned affectless face into the room. 'It's alright,' Astraea told her. 'This is Nathaniel Silver. It's all right.'

Silver also turned to the door: 'I didn't mean to shout so loud.'

That seemed to mollify Elizabeth, that and Astraea's relaxed smile, and the maid retreated. I won't see her again. She looked back to Silver.

'I had to drive him out,' he explained. 'Sometimes men get so lost in their delusions, they don't know the truth until it screams into their ears. And even then...'

She nodded; the nod became a loll, and she fell back into her ample pillows. Silver's hand clenched on hers, and she knew he prematurely thought her dead. She disabused him with a giggle.

'Larissa said I might see you again, but she wasn't certain. You remember Larissa, she tried to kill you once, then you saved her life the second time.'

'Who was she?'

'A goddess, I thought. Except the gods are supposed to be *certain*, and she wasn't, she wasn't at all. I pledged myself to her. She won't come now. I'm glad she won't come. She can remember me the way I was.'

'You don't know who she was, but you pledged yourself to her?'

Astraea shrugged, and even that hurt now. Something broke, quietly and fleshily, inside her ribcage, and she knew it wouldn't be long. 'I loved her.'

Silver said nothing.

'You loved someone too. Last time we met, at the church, I saw you. I saw you talk to her, and then you went off like she'd put a knife in your heart. But it was *you* that left *her*, wasn't it?'

Silver nodded.

'Well,' Astraea said, and coughed, and the cough came out bloody, 'you're not a god. Go and find her. Find her and – whatever the fuck she did to you – fucking forgive her. Because what's your life worth without love? Fuck all, that's what it means, fuck all.'

Silver was nodding again, but hid his deeper thoughts under a soft smile. 'Everyone tells me how fine and witty you are with your pen. No one who'd only read your poetry would imagine you had such a coarse tongue.'

'Yeah, but it's what I do with my pen that'll be remembered. Can you take me to the window? It stinks in here. I want to breathe again. I want to live.'

It was a measure of how sick she'd become that he was effortlessly able to scoop up her body in his arms, that he could carry her without any notable sagging in his step. Her gown flapped round her; it felt like lead on her body, not cotton, it dragged her down. Exhausted, she filled the edge of the sill, staring out not to look down on the street or up into the sky, but simply exulting in the marvel that she could see at all. She could feel the dense splinters pressing into her back, and smell the light odour of Silver's unageing body. She tasted the rank concoction that still clung in patches to her skin, and she felt her hair loosen and tickle across her face in the breeze. She was most conscious of the slur of her heart and the weight of Silver's hands keeping her gently in place at the window.

Aphra Behn raised her head towards her guest, to remember him. She saw him only through a pinkish haze of half-closed eyes, but it was a fine and detailed impression nonetheless. His skin was ablaze in the morning light. She leaned back into the sill – into this wood that had once been a tree, that embraced her in its soft curving bough – then her legs contorted beneath her, and she was dead.

Now I a fourfold vision see
And a fourfold vision is given to me
Tis fourfold in my supreme delight
And three fold in soft Beulahs night
And twofold Always. May God us keep
From Single vision & Newtons sleep

— William Blake

About the Author

Daniel O'Mahony was born in Croydon in 1973. Since then, his life has been quiet. His first contributions to Faction Paradox appeared in *The Book of the War* in 2002. He has also written the novel *Force Majeure* (2007), as well as various *Doctor Who* novels and audios. He lives in Hampshire, England, without any cats.

∞

Acknowledgements

Thanks to Simon Bucher-Jones, Kelly Hale, Mags L. Halliday, and Philip Purser-Hallard for permission to allude to their work for Faction Paradox; to Fiona Moore and Tat Wood for thoughts and comments on the first draft; to Lawrence Miles for creating Faction Paradox in the first place; and to Emily Carter for protecting him from me.

∞

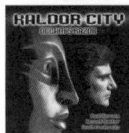

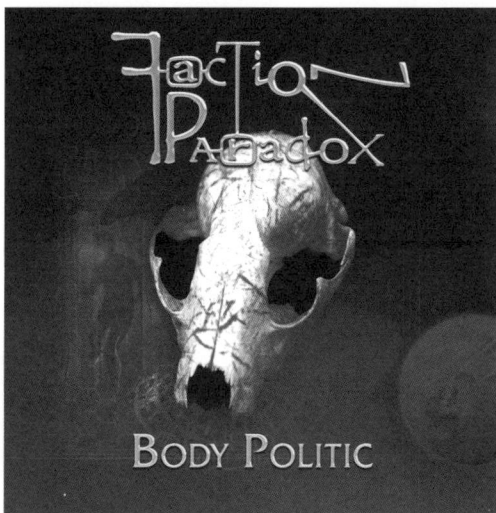